THE STRANGLING ANGEL

THE STRANGLING ANGEL

by

Elizabeth Tyrrell

Dedicated to my dear brother Dave
April 1953 – November 2010

Chapter 1

Delia heard the screams when she was still a good distance from the cottage. She winced in pain from kneeling in the wet grass and leaned toward the sound. The wind whipped long strands of hair into her face and high above, the bent gulls wheeled and dipped in some demented dance at the mercy of the turbulent air currents that blew in off the Atlantic.

She heard the scream again and this time, there was no mistaking her mother's cries, but there was an added desperation to the screams that turned Delia's innards to ice and filled her with fear. She knew her father was blindly intent on inflicting as much pain as he could; focused, systematic, and with a cold determination that always replaced his initial anger and made him infinitely more dangerous.

He would ignore her mother's pleas for mercy and wouldn't stop his punishing cruelty until he was satiated.

She dropped her creel and spilled the herbs and berries it had taken half the day to collect, and ran across the field, oblivious to the stinging nettles and the sharp stones that tore at her bare feet, feeling only the desperate need to reach the cottage before her father did too much damage.

A startled crow rose from the gorse and flapped its wings in her face and she stumbled and tore at the skirts that clung to her legs and held her back from the task she knew she must face— and the punishment she would surely suffer for her interference.

Hunger had weakened her and progress was agonizingly slow. It was as though she waded through a sticky bog and Nature was conspiring to keep her from reaching home, but she was close enough now to hear her father's shouts. His voice was thick and his words slurred from too much drink as the familiar diatribe of venom filled the air. She shivered as she heard his breathless, pig-like grunts as he beat and berated her mother at the same time.

'You've refused me for the last time, my girl,' he roared. 'You're no more use to me than a heap o' stinkin' horse shite.'

Delia recoiled in horror.

'No! Please Dadda! No more!' she cried as she willed herself forward. Every foul name he hurled at her mother was a dagger to her heart and each insult made her cringe.

'You couldn't give my children what they needed,' she heard him roar, 'but you won' say no to me again, you bony-arsed pelt. You mind me woman—and mind me well. You'll open yer legs for me *when* I say so—and *only* when I say so!'

She heard a rhythmic slap of flesh on flesh as she reached the door, in perfect time with his grunting, and fought a growing urge to be sick. The top half of the door was ajar and through the opening her mother was bent, face down, over the table and her father was grinding hard up against her, straddling her in the manner that always turned Delia's stomach. It was the same posture she'd seen the animals in the field adopt whenever they rutted.

She was filled with such intense loathing, she gagged, yet she couldn't tear her eyes from him and gazed morbidly at his hirsute back and pocked flesh.

His grossness disgusted her. His flabby buttocks wobbled with each thrust of his hips and he fought to keep his balance even as he mounted her mother and beat her at the same time— and Delia knew she dare not intervene. He rained down blow after blow in well-rehearsed and perfectly timed movements of lifting and swinging.

She'd seen him use the same stroke many times whenever he chopped firewood; now his leather belt was wrapped round his right fist as he beat his wife about the head with the heavy metal buckle. His free hand gripped her mother's long braid. It snaked through his fat fingers and roped up his arm to his elbow.

Delia closed her eyes and clapped her hands over her ears to block the sickening sounds, and still he raved on, as every sickening thump vibrated in the pit of her stomach and her mother's screams subsided to low guttural moans. It was the transition that galvanized her into action.

Her father wasn't aware of her presence and her eyes scanned the cottage for some means to distract him, knowing he was beyond any calming.

In his present manic state he was determined as a dog in heat with frenzied hold on a bitch; it would take the strength of a bull to pull him away from her mother. Her throat constricted and she felt the panic rise in her chest as her eyes darted wildly around the room—until they spied one of the last remaining items they owned.

The axe lay just inside the doorway; solid and dependable. Its blade gleamed bright against the gray flagstones. It would be sharp. Her father made sure it was always perfectly honed. She'd seen him chop a fir in half with a single stroke of its keen blade.

She groped for it blindly, unable to take her eyes off the hulk of her father's back, and her strength seemed to increase with her rising panic; yet the uneven weight almost toppled her as she lifted with both hands—and swung. Barney Dreenan was so bent on his evil work he never knew what hit him.

Desperation gave her weakened body strength enough to lift the axe, but she could not hope for accuracy. The blow she aimed for his shoulder struck the bulging jugular in his neck and his life blood began to spur from the wound, fast and irrepressible as a swollen spring.

The scarlet stream soaked her mother's braid in a final, macabre coupling as the life ebbed from him and the belt slipped free of his slack fingers. She watched it uncoil, easy as a snake, to mingle with his blood on the stone floor.

As he lost consciousness he slumped forward, and landed heavily on her mother. Then his legs buckled beneath his weight and his body seemed to crumble as he groaned and fell to the floor. Delia heard a distinct crack when his head connected with the hard stone, but he would not let go—even in death.

Her mother's hair was still entangled in his hand, and as he collapsed, she was jerked back and her body landed across his.

She gave a cry of revulsion and Delia dropped the axe at the sight of her mother's face. It was locked in a gruesome expression of agony, and her mouth gaped open in a strangled howl for mercy.

She turned away and baulked as bile rose, hot and bitter in her throat and sprung in a projectile arc, spraying her father's body, and, paralyzed by the horror, she could only stare blankly at the spreading pool of human stew at her feet.

A warning voice began to penetrate her stupor. It until it spurred her to movement, and from somewhere came a superhuman strength as she kneeled and released her mother's braid from his murderous hands and rolled her body free of him.

'Got to get her away from him,' the voice in her head urged. 'Not much time. Get away, before he wakes.'

Her mother was little more than skin and bone, but in her weakened state, Delia found her difficult to move, and it was with the greatest effort she hauled her to the furthest corner and tried to raise her onto the pallet. But her meager strength soon deserted her and it was all she could do to straighten the lifeless limbs and restore some semblance of dignity.

She rested on her heels and contemplated the beloved face she knew more intimately than any other, a face already unrecognizable as the mother who'd sent her out to forage only hours before.

She knelt on all fours, trembling as the combination of shock and starvation took hold. It was a welcome familiar, a sinking from reality and a sensation she'd felt many times lately, as the hunger became more acute. It removed her from the world and temporarily numbed her. It enveloped her in a welcoming fog that softened the cutting edge of her grief, so that she felt removed from all around her and sat through the night with her mother's head cradled in her lap, oblivious to the passing of time and inured from the magnitude of her loss.

Hours later, she was stirred to movement by the needles of pain that shot through her feet, still she moved as though in a deep sleep and began to execute her tasks mechanically; devoid of feeling as she struggled with the knots of her mother's flax belt and the length of string that held the matted braid together.

'Oh! Mammy!' she cried. 'Look at your hair. It'll take me a dog's age to get it clean.'

A black kettle hung from the iron gallow above the fire. For many months, the pot had only been used to heat water or to steep the odd batch of nettle soup. Her mother had hung on to it ferociously and risked many a beating in order to save the kettle. The rest of their belongings had been sold off long since by her father, for his poteen or to finance his gambling.

She dipped her pinny into the water and washed her mother tenderly; scraping gently with her fingernail at the dried blood that lay in the webs of skin between the fingers. Tears fell, unchecked, and she began to ramble as she worked, expecting in her crazed state of mind that her mother would open her eyes and answer her, would give her that familiar smile and utter the comforting words that always lessened her hurt and eased her pain. She sighed and paused to wipe the mess of tears and snot from her mother's face with the sleeve of her blouse.

'There now, Mammy, I'll have you clean in no time at all. You're always telling us it costs nothing to be clean, and there's nothing finer than a good wash to put you to rights again.'

Her grief edged closer to the surface and she felt a sharp stab of pain beneath her ribs as she wiped spatters of gore from her mother's cheeks and recalled the times she'd seen her mother sit weeping in the light of the fire with a dying child in her lap. The door holding back her sorrow strained to open, but she fought it and kept up the distracting chatter while she worked.

'Water is still free, Mammy, and God knows, this country has more than enough water to go round.' The pain seared through Delia again, stronger this time, and she dropped the cloth and doubled over in agony as the full extent of the horror threatened to conquer her last resolve and send her spiralling into madness.

'Oh! Ma, what I wouldn't give for you to open your eyes once more,' she sobbed, cradling her mother's face. 'But you've no more pain now, darlin', no more pain ever again. He's in Hell now, Mammy, where he belongs.'

The face Delia cradled bore little resemblance to her mother. It was devoid of the eyes that had mirrored such a generous, caring soul; eyes that had communicated so much, yet had concealed so much more.

Her brute of a father, 'Barney the Bragger', often boasted to his cronies about how Margaret O'Dogherty, the greatest beauty in all of Donegal had given him the eye at the Muff fair, of how he'd had to fight Matty Geoghan, who'd been setting his cap at her since his balls had dropped.

Geoghan, the cheeky gorsoon who didn't even live in the same townland, that same bucko whose parents had 'loads of everything', according to the gospel of her father. He challenged Matty for the right to dance with Margaret, knowing the one thing poor Matty didn't have was strength enough to beat him in a fist fight. Her father had knocked the lad senseless, and would have killed him if the O'Dowd brothers hadn't stepped in. He was always crafty enough to forget *that* part of the story, but Delia heard the true account years ago from Mammy.

But it *was* true her mother's beauty was legendary and her sweet singing voice the talk of the neighboring communities.

There wasn't a grain of salt in the cottage to sprinkle on the corpse and no pennies to place on her mother's eyes, so she was forced to use two flat pebbles to weigh down the closed lids. Then she covered her mother's head with the last remaining scrap of fabric, the same filthy square they'd used to wipe everything, from dishes and snotty noses to the baby's arse.

Her muscles ached and she was too weary for tears by the time she emptied the last of the water from the kettle to wash herself.

Afterwards, she submerged the blood-soaked pinny in the water and scrubbed fiercely at the dark stains until her knuckles were skinned. She was wracked by a need to wash away all traces of her father, yet she wanted to preserve any tangible reminder of Mammy.

When the apron was draped over the hob she curled beside her mother's body and watched a thin veil of steam rise from the wet garment in the dying light of the fire. She tried to settle her mind to pray, but fatigue dulled her remaining wit and her thoughts were so disjointed she couldn't get beyond 'Our Father'. Instead, she hummed softly a hymn her mother had loved to sing to her and her siblings, until the familiar words left her lips in a scrambled muddle and the weight of exhaustion crushed her.

Beyond the walls of the isolated dwelling, the night sky darkened; silently enveloping the cottage and its tragic trio in a black mantle.

Chapter 2

Delia awakened with an immediate sense of foreboding.

A miserly finger of dawn had begun to pierce the night sky, and as the shaft of light strengthened, it revealed familiar shapes from the shadows. She made out the stout lintel above her head and above that, the vaulted space where pots, pans, lug spades, even the old horsehair saddle, had been crammed, along with the hens and the pig who lodged there during the winter months.

The fire was almost out and she rose to stoke it before the rest of the family awakened, and with thought of her family came the searing pain of loneliness. The grief filled her with fear and desolation and sent her groaning back to the floor where she rocked in renewed spasms of agony, her head bowed to her knees and her arms wrapped tightly around her thin shoulders. She squeezed her eyes tight to obliterate the pain of recollection, and fought to block from her memory the dark form she knew lay ready for burial nearby.

Her hands groped blindly for the wall as she pulled herself up and pinched her nose to block the fetid air until she located the door and felt the rush of early morning air.

It was darker at the back of the dwelling. It faced due west, in accordance with custom and was seldom used for access. The back door was reserved for departing cattle and departing souls, and the cotters were fastidious in their belief. The west door rule was seldom breached, except to release the domestic animals who shared living space with them during the harsh winter.

The onset of Spring ripened the stink from the growing heaps of manure that were piled inside as high as the window sills and there wasn't one among them who didn't heave a sigh of relief at first hint of warmth in the sun, because it meant the manure could finally be shoveled outside. Delia knew it had never smelled as bad as it did now and, disregarding custom she barely made it to the door before nausea overtook her again.

The dung slope was also at the rear of the house, on the downside of a small hillock that afforded the dwelling a little protection from the cutting winds. It hadn't been disturbed in months and was completely grassed over. A clumsily-fashioned manure sled leaned against the slope and she pulled it free of the long strands of grass and backed it into the cottage.

It was a crude contraption; another of her father's pathetic attempts to be useful, and it consisted of two vertical tree branches with three planks nailed horizontally to form a platform. The slipe was worthless, but her father had kept it, intending to barter it in exchange for his passage across the Irish Sea.

Her mother's body was less malleable, and Delia only managed to position the upper torso onto the sled. She looped a length of thin flax rope around her waist and hauled the sled out to the pit her father had dug years before, the same pit that already held her brothers, Vincent and Declan, and her younger sister Niamh—all of them victims of the merciless hunger.

The rough fiber cut into her skin and each painful haul only gained her inches of progress.

'Isn't this the worst of degradation for you, Mammy?' she asked during a pause to gather strength. 'Being pulled to your final resting place on the old manure slipe?' The humiliation angered her and she looked to the sky and shouted to an invisible God.

'Are we to be robbed of every last shred of decency? Is there nobody up there with a scrap of mercy?' In answer came the screeching of the gulls and the incessant moaning of the wind.

Once her mother was in the shallow grave, she wound a simple rosary around her bruised hands and kissed her face one last time. Then she picked up her mother's pipe and ran a finger slowly round the rim of its bowl. It was browned from years of use, and the thin stem was chewed and stained with tobacco juice. She studied the teeth marks and pictured her Mammy resting against the wall of the cottage and her sharp eyes scanning the far horizon as she kept a lookout for her Da.

She placed the pipe in her mother's hands alongside the rosary. It was several hours before she was satisfied with her efforts; until the mound blended sufficiently with the surrounding terrain.

She felt a great sense of shame at not being able to lay her mother out in accordance with custom, but, she countered, she had prepared her with loving reverence and respect, and with as much regard to tradition as her limited circumstances allowed.

The skeletal frame of an old barrel sat almost hidden from view in the tall grass, and she used it for a headstone over the new cairn.

There would be no communal keening for Mammy's soul, but in her heart she knew it didn't matter. Her mother was a saint—hadn't everyone who had known her said so? She was the antithesis of her evil father and it was some comfort to know that Barney Dreenan, murderous bully and most cruel of fathers, was screaming in the fires of Hell and would be for all eternity.

Once her sad duty was complete, she gave vent to her grief and began to rock back and forth across the new grave. Her high-pitched wails pierced the air and sent a flock of small birds scattering toward the sky. Much later, she made her way round to the front of the cottage and rested her back against the rough stone wall. A cleansing rain fell and the drops felt cool on her swollen eyelids and the wind blew away any lingering odor of death from her clothes.

She knew she wouldn't have long to wait. Soon, the scavengers would come with their noses to the ground, as they did every day, sniffing round the cottage, their bony shoulders hunched and wolf-like, with a feral gleam in their eyes. Yet these dogs were more menacing than wolves. They'd once been beautiful hounds; farm dogs and trusted family pets; tame enough to roam freely among young lambs and children. Now, their deepest primal instincts were aroused by an unnatural diet of human flesh and they were driven wild by the unprincipled fight for self-preservation.

Delia was armed and ready with a stout branch when the scattered pack zigzagged across the field. She felt a cold ribbon of fear in the pit of her belly and her bowels turned to water as they drew nearer. Their ears were peeled back and their noses nuzzled the rough ground as they headed for her.

Closer to the cottage, they picked up the seductive scent of blood and in perfect unison, as though on some unheard signal, they broke into a run and bounded toward her. They were close enough now she could see their mad eyes open wide, yet unseeing; blinded by that same manic focus of her father; crazy with lust and hunger. She pressed herself flat against the wall and willed herself not to move, even as her eyes gaped in terror on the yellow fangs and the gelatinous globs of saliva that hung like globs of snot from their muzzles. The whole pack was wild with anticipation of the prey and consummation of the kill.

'God of mercy and compassion—grant me a quick end,' she begged as she made a hurried sign of the cross. There was no time for more prayer. She was the bait and the realization caused her legs to weaken when they were almost upon her. She felt a rush of air and her nostrils caught the acrid cloud of stink before she rolled to one side of the open door as the animals hurled themselves past her, desperate to be first at the quarry.

She thought she must have blacked out because she was on her knees. She heard herself whimper as she struggled back to her feet and as she grabbed for the door she caught a fleeting glimpse of the beasts, but there was no time and she to look inside as she grabbed for the handle and closed the door quickly, and covered her ears to block out the terrible sounds of animal claws that scrabbled on the stone floor, and above it all the high-pitched yelps and growls of the manic wolfhounds as they fought for their portion of flesh.

Then she fled the nightmare, across the field and away from the cottage, toward the seaweed path that led to the ocean.

Chapter 3

The beach was deserted, save for a few gannets who braved the storm-lashed shore. Her senses screamed as she felt herself being sucked into a great vortex of turbulence. Donn, the God of the Dead, who took souls destined for Hell to his dark island before they sank to the depths of the underworld, had joined forces with Arawn to escort her and her father's black soul to eternal damnation.

She knew she must be close to madness and beat wildly at her head with clenched fists in a futile attempt to slow the maelstrom within. Her eyes were almost blinded by salt spray, but she stood on a boulder near the water's edge, stretched her arms wide for balance and turned to face the roiling waves in defiance. 'I will not repent!' she cried.

The wind was fiercest on the shore. It screamed and tore at her and pulled her in every direction, and the needles of spray stung her limbs as she fought to keep her foothold on the slimy rock.

There could be no peace here. Everything was wild and angry; from the leaden sky to the mad screeching of the humped-back birds.

'No more!' she cried. 'Stop it! Do you hear me? Stop it! Stop it! Stop it!' She hurled abuse until her voice deserted her and her throat was raw; until her cries were no more than a hoarse plea; and at last, spent and defeated, she slid to her knees in surrender.

After she was done weeping she raised her head and squinted toward the east, where a blurred sun was trying to break through the dense clouds that hunkered stubbornly over the distant peninsula.

From shoreline to the shrouded mountains lay nothing but water and bog. There were no trees to break up the vista of verdant hills, except to the west, where the land was patched with purple heather and smudges of yellow gorse. It was a rugged beauty that once filled her with joy, but in her present state, she could take no pleasure from the landscape and hadn't in a long while.

How was she to feel any sense of appreciation after the horror she'd experienced? Could anything on God's earth replace the gnawing hunger that clawed constantly at her belly and occupied her every waking thought?

Her mother had been supremely practical, and often remarked, 'We can't eat the landscape; nor are we a herd of cattle that can feed on the green that surrounds us. Sure, there's no succor in any of it. It might as well be barren for all the good it does us.'

Delia heard her people tell of a mighty land far across the ocean. A land big enough to embrace every man, woman and child in Ireland and still have lots of room to spare; where mile upon mile was covered with good healthy corn, as high as a cottage roof—not the 'Peel's brimstone' the English had sent over that was killing the people off as efficiently as the hunger.

Over the water was a place where hard work was justly rewarded; where a family could acquire a plot of land by squatting on it. It was a biblical land of plenty, a traveling teacher had once told them, where the food thrown down to the pigs would make their mouths water and be enough to feed every Irish citizen for a year or more.

The injustice re-ignited her anger and she raised a clenched fist once more to the sky.

'Who is it you're after this time, Arawn? Are you come for me—or is it my wicked father you seek? Come then. I'm not afraid of you. The one I feared most in this world is gone forever—and whether I wanted to kill him or not, I'm glad! Do you hear me? I'm glad! And there are four blessed souls in Heaven who share my delight. Justice has been served this day, regardless of who's administered it, and another accursed blight is removed from this land and I'll not answer to you for the doing of it, so do your worst Arawn, do your worst. I don't care anymore. Do you hear me? I'll be accountable to a more merciful God.'

Her lips were dry and cracked with salt and she tried to clear her eyes of the stinging brine, but it was an impossible task and it made her even angrier.

'God may have turned his back on Ireland, but he has a mother like my own, and she'll not let him burden us with any more suffering than we can handle. So on your way now! Go pick up the hulk of putrid blubber that was once my father and leave me to my sorrow.'

She snatched at the wet strands of hair that blew in her face. 'I've been spared for a purpose and I'll know what that purpose is. God gave me the back to carry the burden and Ireland will not break; nor will she break me. I've had enough of her struggles and I've paid you well for my survival. You have my loved ones, now leave me alone.'

Her voice lost all power as the enormity of her loss swept over her afresh, and when she spoke again it was reduced to a whimper.

'Everything I held dear has been taken from me. All my life I've lived with the lies of a God who was supposed to be benevolent and merciful, my great protector and provider.' She laughed bitterly. 'I'd only to ask with a pure heart and he'd refuse me nothing. Well, now I have no heart, for he took that when he took my Mammy, the last remaining love of my miserable life. I've nothing left of any consequence—nothing!'

Her throat burned and the stinging cuts on her limbs ate into her resolve. Dangerously near breaking point, she longed to lie down at the water's edge and let the ebb tide take her out to sea. She curled up in a tight ball and began to mumble. 'Take me Lord Jesus. This sorrow is more than I can bear. Be merciful and put an end to my suffering.' She knew she had crossed the threshold to insanity when she suddenly remembered Teresa O'Donoghue telling her that drowning was supposed to be one of the better ways to die.

'There's no pain, Delia,' Teresa had told her. 'It's just like falling into a sleep—gradual like, but there's no discomfort or panic. They say God puts on a show of your whole life while you're sinking. There must be some truth in it, for I've never seen a more peaceful-looking corpse than a drowned one. Sure, don't you remember poor Gerry Mullen? God rest his soul.' She released a shuddering breath and thought about Gerry; about how she'd lingered outside his home, afraid to go in and pay her respects to the Mullen family, until Teresa had pushed her through the throng of mourners gathered around the cottage door.

Gerry had slipped whilst gathering seaweed in Trawbreaga Bay and his foot had caught in a tight crevice between two rocks, trapping him until he drowned. No doubt the lad was every bit as hoarse as she after howling for help, Delia thought, and she'd said as much to Teresa at the time.

'He must have screamed for hours before the water covered him Teresa. I'd say he deserved a peaceful death after all that torment. I'll grant you, he broke a cardinal rule—any fool within miles knows you don't harvest seaweed without there being someone with you. But imagine being stuck like that—and him knowing the tides as well he did—feeling the water getting higher with every incoming wave. He must have suffered the worst kind of torture before God took him.'

She'd never believed there was such a thing as a good-looking corpse. 'They're about as bonny as a bucket of snot,' she'd often told her friend at the numerous wakes they'd attended.

But Gerry's mourners had been unanimous. 'Ah, but he looks lovely, Mrs Mullen, more handsome than he ever was in life. Don't you think he looks grand, Nellie?'

And old Nellie Carney, the oldest woman in the clachan, whose opinion was respected above all others because she'd been around long enough to wash many a corpse *and* to attend countless wakes, had been lavish in her praise of the deceased lad.

'I haven't seen a better looking corpse since the Bishop of Derry's wake—and didn't his worthiness have the best of undertakers in all Ireland? His eminence was embalmed and anointed with precious oils, just like Jesus; gussied up for the public viewing.' Nellie Carney would brook no opposition and was impossible to interrupt or contradict once she started her blathering.

'Sure,' she'd opined, 'there must have been thousands of pounds drawn from the collection money to do him up for his final journey. But I can tell you, with me hand on me heart, he didn't look half as good as young Gerry here. I think your Gerry is headed for the sainthood, Mrs Mullen. The sea hasn't marked him at all. He looks fresh as the day he was born—and twice as bonnie.'

Delia wasn't sure about him being bonnie, but Teresa had been right. Gerry Mullen had indeed looked as though he was sleeping; as if, at any moment, his dark gypsy eyes would pop open and scare the beejaysus out of them.

The shrill cries of the seagulls interrupted her reverie and in place of the anger, her pleas were filled with anguish and her words echoed the depth of her sorrow.

'Sweet Jesus, I can't bear it any more. I've no strength left in me. Please don't leave me to suffer this desolation any longer. I want to be with my family, Lord. Show me some mercy and take me up to Heaven and let me be with my loved ones.'

She didn't know how long she lay coiled in the sand, waiting for the sign that never came. It was growing dark when she opened her eyes and the tide was turning. She was in desperate need of rest. She decided if God wasn't going to take her, she must put some distance between herself and the cottage before nightfall.

She shivered as her shawl slipped from her head and fell to her shoulders and as she made a half-hearted attempt to restore it, a sudden renegade gust plucked it from her hand and it sailed over her head and landed with a wet slap on a rock behind her.

She turned away from the sea to retrieve the covering and slowly climbed the small sand dune that led back to the seaweed road, where she could already see a ragged trickle of wraiths plodding wearily toward Buncrana in hope of a free bowl of soup.

Chapter 4

At the top of the rise she avoided the cottage and circled until she found her creel and with it, some of the bounty she'd collected the day before. She buried her face in the fragrant herbs and breathed deeply the aromatic bouquet. 'This time yesterday,' she thought. 'It seems a lifetime ago.' She'd lived through so much since hearing her mother's cries but she side-stepped the train of thought, aware she lacked the emotional strength to dwell on them. 'I must be strong and not think beyond this minute.'

She added some wild parsley and nettle roots to the plants, and tucked them into her pinny pocket. Her mother had been thorough in teaching her and Niamh; Delia was familiar with every plant in the fields, and could identify several varieties of seaweed and the sturdy plants that sprouted against all odds from cracks and crevices in the cliff face.

Before the hunger, she'd had the speed and dexterity of a goat; there'd been many times she'd wanted to join her brothers when they scaled the cliffs for gulls' eggs, but her mother would never hear of it.

'I've lost one brother egg hunting and that's more than enough for this family. You keep your feet on dry land my girl. Leave the egg hunting to your brothers.'

Uncle Joe was killed when a bird attacked him, and caused him to lose his hold on the cliff.

She shivered at the memory and her voice trembled when she looked to the hostile sky. 'Jesusmaryandjoseph! Isn't life hard enough without you sending any more tragedies upon us? Is it to be a long, drawn-out death for me too?'

Delia shook her head in an effort to dismiss the unwanted images that threatened to steal the last fragments of her sanity and when she reached the Buncrana road she kept her head well down and avoided speaking to anyone. But her ears were assaulted by the groans of the sick and dying and the pathetic bleats of helpless children.

She passed fields of stinking potato crops, the slimy black stalks lying abandoned in the shallow drills. Here and there, the outline of crude wooden crosses marked the spot of hastily-dug graves and the horizon was dotted with roofless dwellings. She thought about the happy times she'd spent frolicking in the fields; crouched out of sight among the rows of white potato blossoms that waved in the winds almost year round.

From a distance, they'd reminded her of freshly-laundered sheets hung out across the shrubs to dry. But this was a deceptive blight that gave the people false hope. It wasn't until the spade sliced the ground that the tell-tale stench of rotting potatoes rose from the soil to mingle with the cries of despair from the poor cotter and his family.

After a while, the cold was replaced by a sense of being cocooned in a hazy blanket of she knew not what; only that she didn't want to break the spell. It was a similar contentment of the sort that creeps unawares prior to sleep, as the parting veil of the otherworld reveals ethereal sights and sounds become more and more muffled, until lucid thought is replaced by oblivion.

She began to mouth a prayer to St Brigid. Her lips strived to form words she'd learnt on her mother's lap as a child, words she must have repeated a thousand times since.

St Brigid brought comfort and healing to women. She was

gifted with power to bring life to an infertile soil. But where was St Brigid now? How could the patron saint of fertility turn her back on those same givers of life and their precious babes? Why had she not prevented this terrible blight on the soil of Ireland?

Delia waited for a sign, and in answer came the chorus of pitiful wails from the starving column ahead of her. The ditches were littered with evidence of those who'd succumbed. Reduced to rotten carrion, they were denied all dignity in their final hours of suffering, and most of them perished without the comfort of a priest to see them through to the afterlife.

Ireland was forsaken by God and all his saints, including St Patrick, and by the hard-hearted English and their miserable Queen. Even the priests had turned on the people. Delia had heard stories of how they'd been seen helping the bailiffs with the evictions. God had sent down a plague on Mother Ireland alright, and only he knew when this living hell would end.

She was disturbed from her reverie by a sudden shout. It was a lusty call that claimed her attention by its unusual energy. It was full bellied, unlike the weak, subdued whimpers she was lately accustomed to hearing.

A cart sped past. The wheels spat out muddy water and chips of stone from the deep ruts in the road. She felt the heat of the beast and caught a whiff of the horse's sweat and saw the panicked look in its eyes as the driver pushed it to its limits.

'Go on, you lazy bastard! Move your fat arse—or it'll be more than the sting of me tongue you'll be feeling.'

The rider lashed out with a long whip and Delia was close enough to feel the faint rush of air from the whip's tail as it was brought down hard on the horse's rump.

Her subconscious registered the cargo of sacks and she turned to watch, pitying the animal for having to pull such a weight, when she heard a sudden excited cry.

'Blackberries, Mammy! Look Mammy! Look!'

As the carriage receded there was a sudden flash of movement as a young boy ran across the road—straight into the path of the horse and cart.

It was so quick and unexpected nobody moved; everything was suspended for what seemed an age, until the noise of the cart was almost a distant rumble—and then a chilling scream pierced the stunned silence.

The child's mother sank to her knees beside the boy whose body lay in a contorted heap. His head appeared large in proportion to his skinny neck and emaciated torso, and he was prematurely bald, except for a few sparse, matted stumps that reminded Delia of clumps of dried hay left in the fields after harvesting.

The wheels of the cart had sliced through the child's distended abdomen and his innards lay scattered on the road.

She stared down with detachment. He reminded her of a young lamb she'd seen at the booley house a couple of summers before. It had been killed by a fox and she and her brother had stared in morbid fascination at the pearly sinews and entrails that stretched from the open wound, laid bare for scavenging predators.

A few of the men shouted and waved angry fists at the disappearing cart. The driver knew he'd hit the boy, but why would he stop? He knew the travelers were half dead and none had strength enough to chase him. Even if they did, there would be no restitution. These were the starving Irish—a different breed; a transient, temporary breed; to those who were well fed, they were, all of them, utterly useless and entirely expendable.

Delia joined the circle of women gathered round the weeping mother and they clucked about, making sympathetic noises and whispering words of comfort as they took turns to hold her. Then they began to lead her away from the crushed body of her son.

The men were rolling the body toward the ditch with their feet, but the mother sensed the movement behind her and turned.

'No!' she screamed, as she strained to break free. 'Not the ditch. Don't put my boy in the ditch to be devoured like an animal.'

Weak though they were, the men could not ignore the mother's anguished pleas and they nodded to each other in silent assent and broke off to gather rocks from the fields.

By nightfall, they'd buried the boy beneath the canopy of a fuschia hedge still heavy with blossoms. The shrub bowed beneath the weight of the flowers and the raindrops that hung like tears from the delicate petals. And after the mourners dispersed to seek a place to rest, the woman's keening could be heard on the still night air for a long time.

It used to take Delia and her father little more than half a day to reach Buncrana, but that had been when they were healthy and strong and fortified by a good breakfast.

They'd always had a horse and some type of cart so she could ride part of the way, and some willing soul would always give you a cup of milk or a slab of bread on the journey if you troubled to ask.

'This is worse than a slow walk into Hades,' she thought. Every torturous step was laden with dread and each footfall demanded all the resolve she could muster. 'Why in God's name,' she wondered, 'didn't I stay on the beach and give myself up to whatever it was that was hell bent on squeezing the last bit of life from me?'

Her hands were filthy, and when she looked down she saw a maze of cuts on her feet and legs: slashes of red against the dirt. Some of the sores on her legs had festered, and her hands were also covered in scratches. She looked at them in disgust. She'd always hated them. They were ugly hands; big, square and mannish.

'Like ham shanks,' her Da used to say. 'They're worse than useless when it comes to weavin' or playin' the fiddle, but a farmer would love them. They're good for working the land.'

She'd envied Niamh, who had inherited mother's graceful fingers. The brute had called them piano fingers. 'A fat lot o' good they are in this house. Isn't it enough your mother has useless hands, without Niamh being cursed with them?' he'd frequently complain. 'They'd break if you so much as blew on them.'

Niamh was unfazed by her father's criticism; she knew she was more skilled than anyone when it came to tickling the trout.

Her sister had the gentle touch and the soothing voice, enough to hypnotize the fish. Yes, Niamh could calm them, no matter what.

Her attention wasn't on the road and she almost toppled when her foot slipped into one of the deep ruts. It shook her out of her daydream as she struggled to regain her balance. It was growing dark, yet she sensed it was not yet evening. There were no light patches in the sky to gauge the position of the sun, but it felt like late afternoon.

She left the road and walked the fields behind the hedges of furze, looking for a good place to rest until morning. She settled in a likely spot and pulled her shawl tight about her shoulders as she hunkered down for another long night. The birds had stopped singing and the wind had dropped; behind the hedge, the noise of the walkers diminished as they dispersed to seek shelter. She was far from feeling peaceful, yet thinking of her sister had provided unexpected comfort.

She plucked a blade of grass and chewed on it as she thought of Niamh. Her sister was barely thirteen when she succumbed. She'd been the first to go. Plagued with stomach problems from birth, her death was hastened by a sparse diet and Peel's brimstone, and when she left them it was a manifestation of the family's unspoken fears and they were left to wonder who would be next.

Declan passed away soon after. He was the spitfire brother and often showed traces of her Da's temper. But Declan had the speed of a hare and was the family hunter during her father's frequent absences, and he regularly brought home rabbits and fat pigeons. It almost killed Delia's mother to see the transition in Declan as his vital energy deserted him. When Vincent died, it was inevitable the pace of her mother's decline would escalate.

Vincent had been her baby and only eight years old. He was an angel-faced, introspective child.

'Keep an eye on him,' her mother cautioned. 'He has the face of a cherub and must be a torment to the wicked fairies. The Farleeuh won't rest until they have him in their clutches.'

Vincent spoke little and seldom complained. As young as he was, he could be profound, and he often showed a degree of wisdom well beyond his years.

Mammy had earmarked him for the priesthood, but sweet Vincent died as he had lived—quiet and uncomplaining, in Mammy's chair beside the fire.

Delia recalled an early memory of her three siblings. She pictured them clearly, looking up at her with their fingers and lips stained with berry juice and an empty basket swinging from Niamh's delicate hands.

'Foley's dog attacked us,' they'd fibbed, when she'd asked where the berries had gone. 'We had to run for our lives and we dropped the basket in our haste to be away.' She could still see Declan and Vinnie nodding in agreement, with the evidence smeared all over their upturned faces, as Niamh tried to convince her.

She felt a rush of hot tears and tried not to dwell on them.

'You've another three angels to add to your growing supply.' She said bitterly. 'How many more families will you destroy before you've had enough?'

She no longer expected answers and all she could see was a sky filled with black clouds that hovered above the fields and obscured the peaks of the distant hills.

Chapter 5

By the third day she'd reached her limits of endurance and focused only on staying on her feet and placing one foot in front of the other. To lie down was to die.

She had no direct contact with the rest of the rag tag army and she gave no thought to those unfortunates who dropped to the ground ahead of her, but only stepped aside as they fell and kept on walking.

The air was constantly peppered with the cries of little ones too young to understand the pain of hunger. Children who felt, by some primitive osmosis, the fear of their parents; little ones who'd seen police and bailiffs throw their belongings into the dung heap and chop down the doors of their homes; even burning the thatch to prevent those evicted from seeking shelter.

What was a mother to say to her children when they asked 'Why'? How were they to make sense of the ranting of desperate fathers? Would they ever understand the selfishness of the greedy landlords, who evicted loyal tenants from land they'd tilled for generations? And how were they to take solace from the heart-rending beauty when they were living witnesses to horror and suffering on such a scale?

Delia had been taught that each generation learns lessons from the elders, and that the most meaningful are learned at the lap of a parent. But parents were dying and leaving young survivors with the premature bitterness of an injustice that couldn't be denied, for weren't they a living part of it all?

She was dizzy from staring at the ground and raised her head to scan each side of the road and to find her bearings. She lagged behind a dozen people who were a good half mile behind the main group.

The rain had eased to a fine spray mist and now that she was some distance from the ocean, the air felt a little warmer. Now and then she caught sight of a body in the ditch, an abandoned collection of lifeless limbs. She mourned for the good, hard-working people who were dropping like windfalls; left to rot in ditches or sod hovels.

'They're reduced to fodder for the soil of Ireland,' she thought bitterly, 'and what's worse, they're suffering the final indignity of dying in their own excrement and with all manner of parasites hovering nearby.'

Two large crows picked their way over a corpse that lay width-ways across the ditch. As she drew level, she saw that one of the birds was pecking at the face, while the other suddenly stopped and stared at her, as if waiting for her to pass. She averted her eyes, but too late; her brain had registered the vile scene and she turned away and retched violently, clutching her stomach as the spasms of pain increased and her ribs ached with each convulsion. A cold sweat broke out on the back of her neck and she felt an involuntary flush of warmth between her thighs and groaned in shame as she lost control of her bladder.

For two interminable nights she'd slept behind hedges, helpless as a fledgling sparrow—filled with fear in the suffocating blackness, hearing unfamiliar sounds and without so much as a pinprick of light from moon or stars for company. She knew she'd have been safer in the ditches—most of the travelers settled into them while there was sufficient light to examine the ground before they lay down for the night.

Ditches were safer than the open road or the fields. The

raised banks offered some protection and support for an aching back. But it was impossible to stay dry in a ditch and there was always a greater chance of waking in the company of a rotting corpse, or worse—of being gnawed by rats or attacked by one of her people.

Her uncharitable thoughts shamed her and she wondered if she was becoming hardened. Was it possible to be rendered heartless by such vileness? When the boy had been killed, she'd made appropriate noises with the other women, had shushed and cooed with the rest, but she had sensed a certain detachment in herself. Her movements were rehearsed and automatic and she couldn't muster any feelings of compassion or pity for those around her. It was as though an impenetrable shell had formed; her private shield of armor. In company with the rest, she was coveting every last thing she had, including her feelings.

The trickle of people ahead of her began to sing. Delia wasn't sure if it was for the boy, or if it had sprung from some last faint trace of hope that sputtered weakly among them. It was a melancholy choir and they sang without passion. Their dispirited voices were no match for the normally rousing hymn to the patron saint and their offering was sung at a dirge-like pace.

'Hail glorious St Patrick, dear saint of our Isle. On us, thy poor children, bestow a sweet smile—'

The chanting continued, and whenever it threatened to trickle to a stop someone would start with a line of another hymn. The supplications were kept up for most of the day, until the voices dwindled as fatigue defeated the last of the plaintive voices.

Delia was desperately thirsty after hours of walking. She was used to coping with the hunger and had managed to find bits and pieces of edible fungi and a few wild berries along the way. She'd even spotted an apple tree near a ruined farmhouse, and discovered one or two windfalls hidden in the grass. She'd crouched behind the tree trunk with her hoard and stuffed the apples down her, seeds and all, and suffering griping pains for hours after.

When she reached the familiar crossroads and the milestone that indicated Buncrana was still a further six miles distance, she turned off the road and followed an overgrown path that led to a small boreen hidden below the level of the road. She and her father had quenched their thirst at the swift-flowing water many times on their way to the market towns.

She fell upon the brackish water and scooped up handfuls greedily. It was a sheltered spot, and once her thirst was satisfied, she immersed her feet in the water and lay back to rest. She was in another world.

She breathed deeply and counted the drops of moisture that fell on her arms from the overhanging shrubs and lingered until her feet were numbed from the icy water. It was with great reluctance that she finally stood up to leave, knowing she dare not follow the creek to its source; it meandered over fields and under roads in such a haphazard way that she'd never reach Buncrana alive if she were to follow its course.

'Sure, Ireland is full of water,' she thought, as she climbed up the bank to rejoin the road, 'but most of it is contaminated— like the soil.' Everything was rotten since the pratties had failed. Year after year, the insidious rot spread further as the soil became sodden with the effluence of failed crops and the increasing filth and disease of thousands of starving people.

The water revived her a little, and it wasn't long before she reached Buncrana.

The approach road widened to twice its width on the edge of town. The army of people swelled as they joined the main column entering the town from different directions. She recognized the old disused mill and beyond, a prosperous-looking property she'd always admired.

O'Donnelly's castle loomed in the distance. The original had been built in 1710 and jointly owned by the O'Donnell and O'Dougherty families for centuries, until the old tyrant Lord Chichester had captured Cahir O'Dougherty and claimed the castle for his own. After the acquisition, the arrogant English, always believing possession to be nine-tenths of the law, had awarded the castle, the surrounding land, and best part of County Donegal to the baron, or to 'Our Lord' Chichester, as he was cynically known among the rural people.

Buncrana was a town besieged. Delia could see half a dozen burly-looking men guarding the entrance to the new mill and uniformed police milled among the crowd. The line shuffled along at a snail's pace and she was almost level with the large brick-built meeting hall and church, and was about to slip in to escape the sharp eyes of the police, when she saw the sign nailed to the door: '*Church and schoolhouse closed until fever passes*'.

'Typhoid fever. Yet another burden,' she murmured, as she blended back into the crowd. At least it would be easy to find the soup depots; all she need do was follow the thick crush of people.

Hunger had sharpened the travelers' sense of smell and they followed the tantalizing aroma of onions with all the skill and precision of the hounds. As she shuffled along Delia pleaded constantly to all the saints in Heaven to keep her on her feet until it was her turn.

She studied the jostling crush of people around her. They were mostly women and children and her heart suddenly ached with grief at sight of the little ones' sad faces, hollow eyes and skeletal limbs. Their journey must have been much more harrowing than hers. '*How unbearable for a mother*', she thought, '*to be burdened with the responsibility of keeping a child alive in these desperate times.*' The lips of the women moved in prayer and she joined the invocations.

'Pray for us, O'Blessed St Martin. St Columb, keep us safe

from harm. Holy Mother, look down upon us with pity and ease the suffering of these poor children. God of mercy and compassion, look upon us with kindness and spare the weakest among us. Not my will Lord, but Thy will be done.'

But their supplications fell on deaf ears and the pleading was in vain. Heaven and its saints had denied them, and long before Delia reached the servers, the large vats had been scraped clean and those ahead of her were being turned away. An elderly man near the front began to sob loudly as he pleaded with the Quaker volunteers.

'Give me a lick of the ladle, missus. Please missus, that's all I want—just a lick of the ladle to keep me goin'.' There were a few disgruntled murmurs from those around him, but most of the people seemed resigned. What was the use? It would gain them nothing to rant and complain and none of them had strength or energy enough to raise a cry, let alone a fist.

They began to disperse reluctantly. Some seemed to evaporate like wisps of smoke into the deep shadows between buildings, while others skulked with drooping shoulders down the narrow side streets. A few, like Delia, hung about the square, listless and undecided.

She sat on the curbstone and hugged her precious creel to her chest, too tired to cry and too utterly defeated to even think about her next move.

Her fingers groped in her pocket for the remains of the mixed herbs and she removed a sprig of wild parsley and put it into her mouth under pretense of a cough. The taste of it sent her salivary glands wild and her mouth watered for more, and it was all she could do to fight the urge to eat the rest of her precious supply, but she knew she must ration, and fought the temptation.

Her eyelids felt gritty and the small voice urging her back on her feet to seek shelter faded to the ghost of a whisper as her chin drooped on her chest and her eyes closed in a troubled sleep.

Chapter 6

She dreamt it was late spring and she and her family were in the fields with the rest of the cotters. Every man, woman and child worked alongside each other to clear the fields of stones before seeding began.

It was unseasonably warm and through the heat haze the distant mountains rippled like a mirage. Laborers huddled in small groups, sharing food and drink, while children played games of hide and seek among the rows of oats, their cries of excitement adding music to the heady scent of the yielding countryside. The air was thick with the smell of freshly-turned earth and busy insects hovered in small clouds.

Her mother beckoned her, and as Delia drew close, she saw that the location had changed and Mammy was about to begin spring sowing. A bed sheet was wrapped around her shoulders, shawl-fashion, and she had tucked the left front under her elbow to form a crude sling for the precious seeds. The men used the more traditional 'seed pipes', designed along the same principle as the musical bagpipes they played at céilidhs. The bladder of the seed pipes were tucked under the arm and each squeeze expelled a precise amount of seeds.

Delia dipped both hands into the sack and scooped up handfuls until she'd filled her mother's sling, and then she followed her into a fallow field.

Beneath her bare feet the land thrummed with energy and

promise. The soil had warmed to the peak of fertility and all around were signs of abundant life. Early sowing was Delia's favorite. As soon as the ritual was complete the entire clachan turned their surplus energy to scrubbing the farms and cottages. Freshly white-washed homes sparkled like diamonds among the lush hills, as though they'd been scattered from the sky to fall in glistening clusters among green velvet folds.

Delia's mother took the first handful of seeds in her right hand and threw them across the rump of a plough horse that stood grazing nearby. She'd brought a measure of ash from the family hearth and she mixed it with the seeds as a good luck token for a healthy crop. Then she began to walk in easy rhythm among the drills, scattering from east to west and never missing a spot. It was considered the worst of bad luck and a portent of death to find a bare spot in a field of growing crops.

The community worked hard to complete spring sowing by May Day, and any farmer not having sown by that time was known thereafter as a laggard, or a 'cuckoo farmer', and was shamed publicly for his tardiness at every opportunity.

The location and season changed again, and she found herself in a pratty field with no sign of her mother. It was a cold, blustery day in late autumn and in the dream, Delia was every bit as miserable as the weather. Everyone seemed out of sorts, and even mild tempered Niamh was complaining that Declan wasn't doing his share.

Delia hated working in the pratty fields. It was hard, back-breaking work and the children spent tedious hours removing stones from the lazy beds, or else they were made to carry heavy baskets of seed potatoes, which they threw, four at a time, into a hole filled with manure and soil. They were expected to keep pace with the dibber in front *and* the old nark of a gugger behind, who waited impatiently to close the soil over the newly dropped seed spuds.

In an effort to maintain a steady rhythm of work, traditional planting songs were chanted:

'Four little tatties to a tatty hole
Drop one for the mole and another for the crow
And two for the planters who help the tatties grow.'

Her people were happiest when they worked the land together. Fields became hearth and home for the duration and they shared every scrap of food and labor until every parcel of land was readied and the great bonfires could be lit.

Then people sang and danced until their voices were hoarse and their feet blistered; only then would they rest around the fire with their faces flushed from exertion and happiness. Adults hugged children close as they listened to old Nat Dooley, the storyteller. Dooley would keep them entranced for hours, until their eyes closed in sleep and their slumber was filled with images of the good fairies and the mischievous woodkerns who danced through their dreams.

Other times, Nat would scare them half to death with tales of the mythical creatures in the vast forests that once covered the best part of Ireland, before the English chopped down all the trees.

And when the fire was reduced to grey ash and weariness overcame them, fathers would scoop up sleeping babes, and dutiful daughters would offer aging parents a helping hand; while strong youths, reluctant to call it a night, would gather spades and forgotten tools before following the contented trail of cotters making their way home through the fields. The faint essence of wood smoke clung to their garments, and stray wisps of chaff drifted free of their clothes and hair for many days after.

They were linked in common contentment; reliant upon each other and all of them safe in the knowledge that help was always at hand. Their ways were unique and time-proven, *and they worked for them.*

Delia's mother had been able to recall a time when the clachan had no use for money. It was seldom needed and even now, coins were only used for a game of ha'penny toss or the occasional trip into market towns.

When an animal was slaughtered or a harvest divided, the blacksmith and the priest were given their due portion. After all, the laborers reasoned, was it not the smithy who kept the plough horses shod and the lug spades good and honed? And didn't the priest have a direct line to the Almighty? Who better to put in a good word for a bumper harvest? There wasn't one among them who didn't contribute for the good of the whole, and all were held equal in each others' eyes.

Her dream shifted again and this time her mother pulled her away from the great bonfire. She led her into a different field, and in the warm glow of the fire, tall stems of wheat shone like golden rods and their plaited ears swayed in the night air, gently distressed by the brush of her shoulders as she passed among them. She felt tiny and dwarfed by the tall, densely-planted rows.

Her mother gestured to the plants in wordless invitation. But when Delia reached out for a golden rod it became soggy and turned black and slimy in her fingers, and the entire plant quickly turned into a blood-soaked braid. Once more she was enveloped by the sickening stench of death and decay as she opened her mouth to scream, but her cries were unheard as the black stalks reached out to curl through her hair and slither down to her neck in a strangling grip.

She sprang into wakefulness and winced in pain as her head snapped back. She looked around wildly, trying to make sense of her surroundings; too close to the nightmare and still within the clutches of the horrific dream and wondered if she really *did* hear the sound of horses' hooves and the grating rasp of metal-rimmed wheels on the cobbles. The horse that killed the boy had been the first she'd seen in a long while and the familiar sounds thrust her back to another somnolent memory of her siblings riding barebacked on Barley the pony; whooping with delight as they gripped its flank with sun-kissed legs and hung on for dear life with their hands gripping Barley's mane...

And then the paralyzing image of her mother's braid wrapped around a monster's murderous hand came sharply into her head and jolted her into wakefulness.

A carriage approached at quite a pace and when it turned into the Diamond, the front nearside wheel separated and it fell into the road with a great clatter and spun crazily on its hub. The unbalanced conveyance lurched and the horses sensed the insecure load and fought to gain hold on the slippery cobblestones.

It began to lean at a crazy angle and the driver struggled to keep a grip on the reins when one of the doors suddenly flew open and a small child was thrown, almost at Delia's feet.

She heard a sickening thud as the body connected with the ground and in an instant was beside the still form. Removing her shawl, she placed it beneath the girl's head and scanned her face anxiously.

She was a beautiful child. Her eyelids were fringed with thick dark lashes that fluttered feebly on her cheeks like the first tentative spread of a butterfly's wings. Delia was shocked at how like Niamh the little one was. She stared, unable to tear her eyes from the girl's face, until she was suddenly grabbed roughly by the arm and pulled away.

She was landed hard on the cobblestones and recovered in time to see her basket disappear beneath a woman's cloak. She lunged at the woman's skirts and after a brief tug-of-war managed to retrieve the creel. The altercation had attracted some attention from the crowd and she backed away and hovered, unwilling to leave without her shawl. A well-dressed woman pushed people aside and knelt beside the girl. She began to rock to and fro with the little one's head held tightly to her bosom.

'Please missus,' Delia heard herself say. 'Don't do that. If she has a head injury you'll be making it worse.'

The woman stopped rocking and raised an anxious face toward Delia, taking in her shabby appearance at a glance. She looked around wildly, as if waiting for someone remotely qualified to come bursting through the gathering throng of spectators.

'Is that your shawl?' she asked, nodding toward the rolled garment.

'It is,' replied Delia, holding out her hand. The lady was reluctant to give it back, or else she didn't want to touch it.

She looked around again in silent plea at the audience of paupers but nobody came forward to offer help and the groom was still busy calming the horses. The lady appeared to be traveling alone and she reluctantly turned to Delia again.

Her gaze was directed somewhere over Delia's shoulder and she appeared to address the entire assembly.

'Will you help my daughter? Can you tell me if she has any broken bones at least?'

Delia moved forward slowly, conscious of every pair of eyes upon her. She was hesitant to touch the child and afraid of the attention, and she clutched her basket even tighter. She doubted she could be of any use. What little she knew she'd learnt from looking after her madcap siblings, who'd had many a nasty fall between them. But perhaps she could at least ascertain if the girl was concussed or not.

When she bent and touched the child, her whole body was unexpectedly flushed with a tremendous wave of all the loving emotions she'd felt while tending her young brothers and sister.

A hard lump formed in her throat and she fought to compose herself and to calm the flood of tenderness that washed over her in waves. Her body trembled from want and she felt a rising flood of tears that, once started, would surely never stop. *'Time enough for grieving later,'* she told herself sternly, *'when I'm alone'*. She dare not give in to it now for fear of attracting attention.

The little girl never moved or made a sound and her eyes remained tightly closed.

Delia squatted on her heels and squinted up at the lady. 'I'm almost certain none of her bones are broken, ma'am,' she said. 'The colour is coming back into her cheeks and I'm sure she'll be fine when she wakes, but I'd keep her quiet and still until a doctor sees her. She has a lump on her head the size of a duck egg, and with your permission I'd like to apply a herbal poultice until help arrives.'

Water and a clean handkerchief were produced from a nearby inn and Delia unfolded the snow-white square carefully, acutely aware of how filthy her hands looked against the pristine linen.

She was low on herbs, but she wet the cloth and folded a sprinkling of Valerian root and Calendula into the fabric before she placed it beneath the child's head. Her anxious mother waved smelling salts under the girl's nose and, almost immediately, the little one began to fidget and turn her head from side to side.

Delia tried to keep the impatience out of her voice, but the woman was proving quite useless.

'I'm in need of a strip of cloth to keep the poultice in place, ma'am,' Delia said, in an effort to distract her. 'Do you have anything long enough to wrap round her head?'

The request proved enough of a diversion and a basket was retrieved from the open carriage that still leaned at a precarious angle toward the curb.

She produced a couple of napkins and made a futile attempt at tearing the finely-sewn cloth, but she couldn't manage it and as she looked around her, she saw the futility of asking the spectators. They were all as grubby and emaciated as Delia;

none possessed strength enough to tear a piece of paper, but for very different reasons.

A sudden disturbance erupted and Delia watched a well-spoken gentleman wrestle his way through the crowd. His rich baritone voice boomed across the square.

'Make passage for the doctor!' He struggled to elbow aside the closely-packed observers until he was within sight of the child. 'Will – you – let – me – through and stop your gawking. Give the child room to breathe, you bunch of heathens. Let me pass, I say!'

He poked away at those reluctant to give up their ringside view of the proceedings and when he finally emerged through the last of the onlookers, he bent and unlocked his valise, removing a folded kerchief, which he placed beneath his right knee to protect his breeches from the cobbles.

The doctor was extremely well-built, in keeping with his vocal strength and Delia noted his black frockcoat and trousers were so shiny at the knees she wondered why he took such pains to protect them.

Whoever did his ironing was not properly trained, she decided. He gave her a blank look and she saw his florid complexion was much like her Da's—as were his bulbous eyes. They lacked any trace of concern or compassion: two qualities she would have expected a trained healer to possess. She watched him scan his new patient and decided she wouldn't seek his help if she were on her last legs and dying—and then she realized that, in common with most of the crowd around her, she *was* dying.

He doffed his hat briefly at the child's mother before he peeled back the poultice and lifted the fragrant square to his nose. After he placed it on the cobbles he proceeded to perform the same cautious examination Delia had done moments before. When he finished, he replaced the poultice and began to question the young patient, who was now starting to show some signs of recovery.

There was a further commotion when the smithy arrived and he and the groom set about replacing the carriage wheel. Delia wanted to slip away while everyone was preoccupied, but she couldn't leave without her shawl.

The noise and the large crowd soon attracted a constable and at sight of his uniform, she felt the first chill of fear since her nightmare at the cottage. She stared at the cobbles and prayed the ground would open and swallow her up, while she watched from the corner of her eye for any chance to escape and get back on the road where she could lose herself among the other travelers.

She wished she had Ethne's power to become invisible. Ethne was the Celtic goddess who was rescued by the monks after she lost the power of her protective cloak and became visible to mortals. *'If I had such a cloak,'* Delia thought, *'I'd walk into the nearest inn this minute and help myself to the entire contents of the larder. I'd stuff myself like a pig 'til I was sick.'*

The doctor stood and turned his attention to the child's mother and Delia noticed he addressed her in a much friendlier tone.

'She's coming to, ma'am, and I'm sure she'll be fine.

A slight concussion but no bones broken. Keep her quiet for a few days and have your physician look her over when you reach your destination. You may keep the poultice applied for the time being, it will do no harm; indeed, it will help reduce the swelling.'

The doctor suddenly remembered Delia and spoke to her. 'What was in that poultice you applied, lass?'

She opened her mouth to answer, but the little girl uttered a cry and the doctor kneeled again as his attention was diverted to his patient.

'Hello, young lady,' he smiled. 'What's your name?'

'Her name is Magdalen,' the child's mother piped up, and

the doctor scowled and shook his head.

'Madam, please allow her to answer for herself. I must ascertain her level of lucidity.' He muttered something under his breath and smiled down at the child. 'Now then—how old are you, Magdalen?'

The girl had the most riveting blue eyes Delia had ever seen, but they were filled with alarm as she glanced around anxiously at the sea of dirty faces until they settled on the face of her mother and her troubled expression relaxed a little.

'I'm almost six,' she whispered.

'You've had a nasty fall and banged your head,' the doctor said, pulling the child's lower eyelids with his thumbs. 'I daresay you'll be covered in bruises by morning, but you're a strong lass and a very brave one. And before you continue your journey, I think you owe this young woman a word of thanks. She did very well by you before my arrival, and a good thing for yourself and your mother she happened to be near.'

Delia shrank back. She wanted nothing more than to be on her way, far from the curious eyes, the inevitable questions and the attention she was attracting. But the woman stood and took a step toward her.

'I'm very grateful and would like to pay you in some way for your trouble. Would you mind traveling with me for the remainder of my journey?' She glanced around and lowered her voice a little. 'I'm useless on my own, and I've had such a fright I can hardly stand, let alone look to my daughter. If she should need me while I'm in such a state of flux—'

The woman put a gloved hand to her forehead and began to sway. The doctor stood quickly and supported her on his shoulder before bringing out his own smelling salts.

'I'm sure this young colleen is in no hurry,' he said, waving the bottle of ammonia under the lady's nose. 'She will be glad to accompany you; but, first things first. Let's get the child into the carriage before these ghouls scare her half to death.'

The woman had the grace to look ashamed at the doctor's insensitivity and she stood nervously to one side as he and the elderly groom settled Magdalen among blankets on the padded seats of the carriage.

Delia felt almost sorry for her as she became aware of the woman's vulnerability. She shone like a precious gem among the shabby crowd, hemmed in as she was, and in grave danger of being set upon for her finery. She was obviously the wife of a landowner or, worse, a member of the gentry. '*And she's about as welcome in this town as the pox doctor,*' Delia mused.

She hoped there might be a bowl of soup at the end of the journey, and knew the doctor had been right in one assumption: it didn't matter much where she ended up.

She bent down for the shawl and tucked it into the creel, anticipating a comfortable ride to the lady's home.

'I'd be glad to travel part of the journey with you, ma'am,' she said, bobbing a quick curtsey.

'Good,' said the lady, gathering her skirts and making her way to the coach. 'You may travel up top with my groom.'

She turned to the doctor, who held her elbow as she placed a fashionably-shod foot on the step of the carriage.

'Doctor, would you mind calling on us at Keenagh Hall? I'm sure you know where it is and, of course, you'll be amply paid for your services.'

The doctor's countenance changed markedly for the better.

'With pleasure, ma'am,' he said, bowing low and tipping his cap. 'Doctor Henry Nowland, at your service. I shall be out to see young Magdalen in a day or two. Until then, I wish you a safe journey and God speed.'

Delia was hauled roughly onto the carriage by the reluctant groom, and with a cry to the horses and a swift crack of the whip, they were on their way.

Chapter 7

Once clear of Buncrana, the carriage rolled along at a good clip. Delia wasn't used to being so high off the ground, or traveling at such speed, and she gripped the sides of the dickey box tightly and tried to keep her bottom in contact with the smooth leather seat.

The groom hadn't so much as glanced at her since they left the town, but he couldn't ignore her presence as she slid closer to him with each bend in the road.

It was hard not to touch him, and each time she did, he cursed and let forth a continuous litany of complaints in Gaelic, against God, his mistress, his workload, and the Devil himself.

When they reached the tiny hamlet of Dumfree, the carriage wheels echoed through the deserted square and they were unhindered by any traffic, human or otherwise. The village showed signs of neglect. There were no tell-tale ribbons of peat smoke curling from the chimneys and no sounds of children splashing in the boreen that ran beneath the dilapidated bridge. Even the birds were silent in the face of such complete desolation.

Delia scanned the dwellings as they passed and looked for some sign of movement or evidence of occupation. She strained her ears for the familiar cries of little ones being put down for the night, or for the clatter of supper plates, but nothing penetrated the eerie quiet, save for the rumble of the carriage wheels and the steady clip-clop of the horse's hooves. Only the eerie moaning of the wind disturbed the quiet.

Their very presence was a rude intrusion in the ominous silence and a shiver ran through her as she made the sign of the cross and pulled her shawl tight about her head and shoulders, afraid to look any longer.

Carndonagh, by contrast, was a much larger town and not yet abandoned and as they made their way slowly through the town center she saw the familiar evidence of a soup kitchen queue.

The groom had great difficulty negotiating the prostrate forms in the road. He guided the horses around shapeless bundles that could have been discarded clothes, but could just as easily be a man, woman, or child.

There was a sudden swell of noise and movement when the large cauldrons of soup came into view, spurred by an added sense of desperation that tipped the scales for those on the cusp of madness or even murder, as the strongest fought their way to the front and shoved aside the weaker ones. Delia and the groom looked on in horror as mothers, babes and the frailest among them were knocked down to disappear in the throng. They behaved like animals fighting to the death as they kicked and spat and gouged to gain a few precious feet closer to the food.

Her heart wept to witness the disintegration of her people; to see the gentleness and compassion of an ancient race subverted and replaced by such dark bestiality.

The stronger among them were better fed. Most likely they'd recently landed in Buncrana from the mainland, she thought, with their bellies still full of sustenance. Yet, the stronger ones had started the stampede that she and the groom were now reluctantly witnessing.

The gorge rose within her and she turned away, with her head and heart a whirlpool of emotions. She was shamed by her feelings of envy toward those who'd been fed, and filled with loathing for the monsters who'd jumped the queue.

What kind of demon had overpowered them enough that they would kill each other for a bowl of soup? Who but a devil would take advantage of those weaker than themselves and unashamedly shove women and children out of their way, as if the pain and suffering of others meant nothing to them?

She caught the groom's eye and he saw the distress in her face. He coughed and averted his gaze as he lashed out at the horses and he vented his anger on the animals until they'd cleared the center of the town and had left behind the latest outpost of Hades.

She must have dozed briefly. Her sleepy head lolled against his shoulder as she lost consciousness, but she was shocked out of her slumber by a sudden painful dig in the ribs.

'You try that again, my girl, and next time I'll let you fall. It's no skin off my nose if you never make it to the house. You stay over on your own side. I've enough weight on my shoulders without you adding to it.'

For the rest of the journey she had to pinch herself hard in an effort to stay awake. She was in no doubt the groom meant what he said—she was no more than extra cargo to him.

It was almost dark when they reached the house and turned into a long, gravel drive. The horses came to a halt at the foot of an enormous set of stone steps and the weary animals whinnied and tossed their heads in unison in a last defiant gesture, as the groom pulled hard on the reins and dismounted.

A liveried man ran down the steps and helped the lady from the carriage before taking the child in his arms and without a backward glance they hurried into the house and disappeared behind two great oak doors.

Delia searched for a way down, but the groom stopped her with a flick of his whip.

'You stay where you are, scruff. It's the back of the house for the likes of us.' He brought the horses to a final stop in a high-walled courtyard. Once on firm ground, he offered the handle of the whip up to her. 'Here! Grab this and jump, and don't look at me like that—it's not as far as it looks.'

Delia didn't trust him and she was terrified her brittle bones would snap upon landing; but her choices were limited—find a way down, or spend the night on the dickey board. One thing was certain; he was not going to touch her if he could help it.

She ignored the whip and found her own way down. When she reached solid ground, she glared at him and secretly wished the wrath of the gods on his balding head. He caught her malevolent look and was about to address her again, when a door opened a crack and a disembodied voice echoed across the hollow courtyard.

'Jesusmaryandjoseph! What's he brought with him this time? Catherine! Fetch a crucifix. Quick now! Do you hear me? Matty Friel is after bringing one of the Devil's minions to our doorstep.'

The door slammed shut and the groom looked Delia up and down, secretly marveling at the cook's accuracy. The girl *did* look like one of the Devil's messengers. By God, it took a lot to unravel Mrs Cleary, but the sight of this 'thing' he'd brought home had plainly scared the wits out of the cook *and* the kitchen maid.

Matty Friel was about to say something to her, but he changed his mind. Instead, he shoved his hands deep into the pockets of his moleskins and leaned back on his heels, studying her closely.

'Don't be counting on any thanks from the mistress of this house, girl; she can be forgetting her own daughter's existence when she's a mind to, so I can't see her giving *you* a second thought. If Mrs Cleary hasn't had word from upstairs by now, you might as well start walking.'

Delia felt a burning indignation rise in her. '*By Christ, I could put you in your place,*' she thought, '*and very quickly too,*' but for now she hadn't strength enough for even a mild protest.

'I'll just rest here another minute,' she told him, squatting on a boot scraper. 'And by the way, my name is Delia, and not, 'girl',' she said, pointing a finger at him. 'And *you*, mister, are only a hair's breadth away from being in my position yourself, so don't be lording it over me, or ordering me around either. I was invited here. Remember?'

When the groom opened his mouth to give her another earful the door opened a crack again and a hand poked through, holding a slab of bread the size of a doorstep.

This hand also had a voice. 'There's a water tap near the stables and the cook says you're to wash your hands and face— and then come back here.'

Delia snatched at the bread and began shoving it into her mouth. She caught the startled look of the groom and was momentarily filled with shame, but even before the 'voice' had finished speaking, half of the bread was gone.

She devoured the rest with her eyes tight shut; not pausing to chew, or to savor, as the long-forgotten, homely scent of fresh-baked soda bread filled her nostrils and sent her salivary glands into raptures. The dark, nutty taste of the crust and the richness of the creamy butter flooded her mouth and slipped down into the yawning chasm of her empty stomach.

She ached for a second slice and licked at her dirty fingers greedily until every trace of the butter was gone and only the memory of the delicious bread lingered on the back of her tongue. She licked her lips again and again in search of a last remnant of flavor.

Matty Friel watched her in silence and was humbled. He looked at her filthy feet and clothing, and the way she had tight hold of her shawl, while her free hand shoved bread into her mouth as though Mrs Cleary herself was about to appear and take it from her.

'Come now,' he said gruffly. 'I'll show you where the tap

is—but mind your mouth. I meant what I said before. You may not hear from the mistress, but if Mrs Cleary has given you the nod to wash yourself you might get a gander at her kitchen—if your luck's in, that is.'

'Did you say *luck* mister?' she asked him sarcastically. 'My *luck* is it? Have you lost your eyesight or something? Can you not see I'm covered in luck? Sure, I've so much luck, I'm bogged down with it.'

She'd had quite enough of the man's rudeness and he'd rubbed her up the wrong way once too often since they'd left Buncrana. 'Aren't I the very picture of health and wellbeing?' she asked him brazenly, holding open her shawl. 'My cup's overflowing with luck. I've so much of it you can have some for yourself—and you'd be welcome to it.'

The groom removed his hands from his pockets and took a step toward her. 'By Jaysus! There's nothing wrong with your mouth, though, is there? I'll say this for you. You've got some spirit in you. Come on with you now and let's introduce you to some soap and water.'

When Delia didn't follow him, he paused and looked back to where she stood, exactly as he had left her; legs akimbo and hands on her hips. She stared at him in open defiance.

'My – *name* – is – Bedelia – Margaret – Dreenan,' she told him, enunciating each syllable slowly and precisely. 'I had a mother and a father, and I'm legally baptized into the Holy Roman Catholic church.' So saying, she brushed past the startled groom and headed for the tap that was visible above the horse trough outside the stable door.

Matty could only watch dumbfounded as she drank her fill of the cold water before she started on her hands.

Later, when she was finally admitted to Mrs Cleary's 'Holy of Holies', she genuinely *was* at a loss for words. The kitchen had the proportions of a church, with its high ceiling and large windows that stretched the full height of the walls. A stout, wooden table almost filled the length of the room, and down one side were half a dozen chairs. Mrs Cleary positioned herself at the head of the table and looked Delia up and down carefully.

'Let's see your hands before you come anywhere near this table, and if I see any tidemarks like the one on your neck, you'll be eating the rest of your meal in the yard with the dogs.'

Delia had made the most of the sliver of soap Matty had given her at the trough, and she'd worked up a fine lather from hand to elbow. She'd had to repeat the exercise several times, but not being able to see her face, she had only given it a cursory wipe. The cook kept a careful distance between them when Delia held out her hands for inspection.

'By God, but you've a man's hands! Would you look at the size of them!' She looked down at Delia's feet. 'What size are your feet?'

'Size?' Delia asked. 'For shoes, do you mean? I wouldn't know; I've only ever had grass or sand between me and the soles of my feet. I never had shoes in my life.'

Mrs Cleary sniffed and studied Delia's feet again. If she was surprised at the girl's hands, she experienced an even bigger shock when she paid closer attention to her feet.

'Dear God in Heaven, I thought you were wearin' black shoes. That's never your feet, is it? It'll take a month of Sundays to scour them, but scour them we must. You can't go traipsing over the mistress's carpets with them feet.'

'Well now, missus,' Delia told her, as she tried to repress a smile. 'I can't go traipsing over the mistress's carpets *without* them—unless you'd like me to walk on my hands, that is.'

Mrs Cleary glared at her and then spun round to reprimand the kitchen maid, who was stuffing the corner of her apron into her mouth in an unsuccessful effort to stifle her laughter.

'Well now, Catherine Nolan, let's see if I can do something to wipe that smile off your face. Go upstairs and bring me down a pair of your stockings. Be quick about it, and when you've done that, get the auld bucket from outside and fill it with warm water for this girl's feet. Hurry now, before the mistress sends for her.'

With Catherine Nolan duly dispatched, Mrs Cleary pulled one of the chairs well clear of the table and motioned Delia to sit.

'As if I haven't enough to contend with,' she grumbled. 'Now I'm expected to clean up lousy tinkers. Where did the mistress find you, anyway? How in God's name did you come by her attention?'

Delia told the woman about the events in Buncrana and, during the telling, the cook's face displayed a whole range of undisguised emotions.

'By God, but you've the luck of the pox doctor himself,' Mrs Cleary cried.

'Glory be! You people are fond of taking the Lord's name in vain,' Delia said defensively. 'I'd say it was your mistress who has the luck, for if I hadn't helped the child her mother would've seen her into Heaven for sure.'

'Whisht now! Watch what you say, and don't speak unless you're spoken to or I'll—'

Catherine's reappearance stopped Mrs Cleary in mid-sentence and an older gentleman entered silently behind the kitchen maid to inform the cook that Delia was to be taken upstairs.

'As soon as the family are done with supper,' he told them with some authority.

Chapter 8

She couldn't hold back the expression of bliss that transformed her face when her feet submerged in the hot water.

She closed her eyes and felt the welcoming warmth seep slowly up her frozen calves toward her knees. This time yesterday, she'd been cold and starving; yet here she was, sheltered in a warm kitchen and with the prospect of a meal ahead of her.

She decided there and then. If the lady offered her some additional reward, she would ask for more food.

She bent to scrub at the dirt ingrained in her feet, but a thorough cleaning was impossible. As hard as she tried to remove the grime, her toenails stood out pink against the blackened skin.

By the time the cook instructed her to dry off and put on the stockings Catherine had left over the back of the chair, she was feeling weak and dizzy from being bent almost double over the bowl. But now, the appendages that Mrs Cleary had mistaken for black shoes were recognizable as feet.

Delia found putting them inside long stockings was a new torture. Catherine had given her two lengths of string to hold them up, but when she stood to follow the cook they slipped down her skinny thighs and gathered in a wrinkled heap at her ankles. She hated the feel of them and was unused to having any form of restrictive clothing.

Mrs Cleary was becoming more rattled by the minute until she lifted her own skirts, removed her elastic garters and tossed them to Delia.

'Here,' she said irritably. 'Put these on, and be quick about it.'

She rolled a couple of dried peas along the table and Catherine showed her how to twist them into the stocking tops, ligature style, until they were secure enough.

'Make a hem,' she said patiently, watching Delia's pathetic efforts, 'by rolling the tops between your fingers; then tuck the pea inside and twist it round and round until the stocking tightens enough; then tuck the pea under the hem to keep it in place.'

Mrs Cleary's legs were much fatter than Delia's and there was a lot of surplus elastic to tighten, but, she persevered and with Catherine's guidance, she managed it first time. But there was no sitting still: she hated the feel of them and she plucked and pulled at them constantly.

Her fixation with the stockings was interrupted by a flurry of activity around her. Catherine and the cook were preparing the family's evening meal and she was forced to watch in mute horror as they threw discarded peelings and bruised fruit into a slop bucket.

She'd been instructed not to move a muscle and could only watch in agony the creation of a deliciously aromatic dinner. *'This is the worst kind of mental cruelty after what I've suffered,'* she thought.

Later, after the family upstairs had eaten, and Catherine had begun to tackle the mountain of dishes, Mrs Cleary removed her apron and motioned Delia to follow her. They seemed to traverse endless shadowy passages and climb dozens of stairs, and they had to stop twice to adjust Delia's stockings, which refused to stay up for any length of time, even though they were wound so tight she thought they would cut off her blood supply.

At last, they emerged from the gloom into a brightly lit hall. A massive fireplace dominated the square entrance and a roaring fire blazed in the cavernous hearth. *'And with nary a soul in sight to enjoy its warmth and cheer,'* thought Delia, as Mrs Cleary tapped on one of the numerous doors leading off the hall to announce them both.

After the relative cool of the corridors, the room felt stifling. The mistress sat beside yet another generous fireplace and close by, Delia could see the outline of the child who lay swaddled in blankets on a nearby chaise. The lady motioned them forward and they made their way slowly across the large room.

Delia was so engrossed in staring at the opulence around her that she missed the first whispered exchanges between the mistress and the cook.

Never in her life had she seen such grandeur. Mr Kane, her hedge school teacher, had told wonderful tales of Kings and Queens who lived over the water, in houses with so many rooms it'd take best part of a year to explore them. But as good as her imagination was, she had never envisioned anything this grand.

'This room's the size of a field,' she thought as she caught her reflection in the gleaming brass of the fire irons. One wall was completely dominated by an enormous dresser that was loaded with silver serving dishes and candlesticks bigger than Delia had ever seen, even in the church processions.

There were numerous chairs and couches placed around the room, all upholstered in a rich red velvet, and the tall windows were drawn against the night sky with heavy drapes made of the same plush fabric.

Her toes curled inside the stockings Catherine had grudgingly given her. It was all so overwhelming.

She wasn't yet used to being warm, let alone having to make sense of all this richness.

An unfamiliar smell invaded her nostrils and as it grew

stronger she tried to concentrate on identifying it. *'A bit sweet,'* she thought, as she tried to switch her focus back to the women.

But she seemed to be receding somehow and felt powerless to stop the process. She was shrinking, and so was the room. Her throat constricted as her panic grew and she licked beads of moisture from her upper lip. *'I must be dying, Am I dying? Is this how it is at the end? No more than a gradual fading of senses? But it's not fair,'* she thought. *'I can't die now, not when I'm about to be given a new chance at life.'*

She heard a loud rushing noise and a deafening 'swoosh!' roared through her ears. She *was* going to die. God had tormented her with a little taste of Heaven before snatching it back and sending down his messengers for her.

She attempted to open her eyes one last time, but the effort was too much, and her final thoughts were filled with the irony of two strangers being the last earthly images she would ever see.

The women loomed over her and spoke. She could see their lips moving but there was no sound, and she was only vaguely aware of the curious expressions on their faces, before she finally surrendered and sank to the floor in one fluid motion.

When she came to, she was still lying on the floor and Mrs Cleary was wiping her face with a cold cloth. She caught the odor of donkey piss in her nostrils and tried to turn away but the woman was leaning over her so close their noses almost touched.

'The salts are working, ma'am. I think she's coming round.'

Over the cook's shoulder Delia could see the lady of the house. Her face was creased in worry and she wrung her hands in agitation. When she spoke it was without a trace of local accent.

'Give the poor child a drink, Mrs Cleary. Has she had anything to eat since we arrived back from Buncrana?'

Mrs Cleary squeezed Delia's arm so tight she thought she would faint again from the pain. She opened her mouth to howl but at sight of the cook's panic-stricken face she stopped. As the cook made to answer her mistress, her eyes never left Delia's and her grip tightened even more when she spoke.

'Yes indeed, ma'am. I gave her some soup and she's had bread and milk. Sure she was in a swoon when Matty brought her through the door, but I'm afraid the food may have been too rich for her poor starved stomach. We'll need to build her up slowly like, until her belly has a chance to stretch.'

Once she was satisfied Delia wouldn't expose her lies, the cook released her grip and brushed a stray curl from Delia's clammy forehead, feigning concern enough to fool the mistress again.

'Are you feelin' better, darlin?' the crafty woman asked her. 'Ah, you poor creature. Will I get Matty to carry you back to the kitchen? And after all you've suffered—'tis no wonder you're weak.'

Delia met the cook's gaze and, without missing a beat, told a whopping lie of her own, leaving Mrs Cleary with no doubt as to her degree of skill in that department.

'My legs feel awful strange, Mrs Cleary. I don't think they would support me just this minute. Might I lie beside the fire in the hall, just 'til I feel stronger like? I promise I'll be out of your way by morning, but I couldn't stand now if you were to lead me to a feather bed and invite me to live in it for the rest of my days.'

To illustrate the point, she made a feeble attempt to shift for herself, feigning more weakness than she really felt. Her spirit was returning, and she sensed a small glow of energy deep in her stomach.

It was one tiny affirmation that she still lived and breathed. But though the scrap of bread may have been enough to bring her back from the brink of starvation, and even re-kindle her love of life, she knew she wasn't out of the woods yet. It would require all her wits to hang on to this fragile thread.

As the cook helped her to her feet, she cried out suddenly and clutched at the woman, who was trying to keep some distance between herself and the louse-ridden girl. '*A mere chit,*' the cook thought, one who, right this minute, seemed to have the strength of a bull. As hard as Mrs Cleary tried to pull away, Delia resisted.

Her ladyship mistook the meaning of the scuffle between them and approached to help the struggling women. Mrs Cleary, by this time in a state of near panic lest her mistress should become infested, put up her free hand to stop her.

'It's quite alright, ma'am,' she gasped. 'I can manage her.'

Lady Keenagh placed a restraining hand on the cook's free arm. 'She is not to sleep in the entrance hall, Mrs Cleary.'

She turned to Delia and spoke to her directly. 'I owe you a great debt child, and the least I can do is give you shelter until you are strong enough to travel. Mrs Cleary,' she said, over her shoulder, 'I'm sure we can find some night attire for—what *is* your name, child?' She asked, and Delia could have kissed her.

'My name is Delia Dreenan, ma'am. I don't want to be a trouble to you, but I—' She closed her eyes and swayed again, as she reached out blindly for the cook, who was now staring with a mixture of incredulity and awe at the quality of acting she was witnessing. Delia buckled at the knees again and the cook had no choice but to catch her as she sank to the carpet, this time with all of her senses quite intact.

Matthew was summoned and between them, they half dragged, half carried her back to the kitchen, where she was dumped unceremoniously into the same chair, well away from the kitchen table.

The flustered cook ordered Matthew to remove his cap and jacket and leave them outside. Then her own cap was thrown out also, and she took Matthew by the elbow and moved him closer to the fire, the better to see him as she bent back his collar and searched under the cuffs of his sleeves for vermin.

As she rooted through his sparse hair she spoke without looking at Delia, though it was clear the comments were intended for her.

'That was quite a performance you put on, you crafty little beson. You've gained yourself a few days, nothing more, so don't be gloatin'. When I'm finished with the de-lousing, Matty can fix you a straw mattress by the fire, but you're not to wander about this kitchen until I've cleaned you properly. Your clothes will have to be burned. How in God's name am I to get you clean without us all becoming lousy? My wages don't cover half the things I do as it is, and now I'm expected to clean bog tramps.'

Once Matty and Catherine had passed inspection the cook had Catherine examine her own head. She slapped impatiently at the girl's hands and complained loudly whenever the comb became tangled in her thick hair. Delia was forced to sit and watch quietly, but her face burned with shame and embarrassment. She could hardly argue with the woman. She was quite aware of her filthy state and wanted nothing more than to rid herself of the dirt and stench; to eradicate all traces of the last few days.

She didn't think she had lice and was about to suggest a reliable home remedy, but then she thought better of it, seeing how expertly the woman had examined Matthew, who'd escaped from the kitchen so quietly that they were all surprised when he reappeared, struggling under the weight of a straw palliasse and a couple of horse blankets.

Catherine was sent to the scullery for the tin bath, and by the time she'd run back and forth a half dozen times more for towels and a couple of nightdresses, she wasn't feeling very benevolent toward Delia either, and her sour looks were enough to curdle the milk.

A surly Matthew was dismissed, muttering under his breath as he was given strict instructions not to come near the kitchen until morning. Once the scuttle was filled and the fire banked with fresh bricks of peat, the women set to work.

Delia stripped down to the buff and threw her dress and pinafore into a corner as ordered. She was glad to have them off her back and quite happy to burn them, but not the shawl. The shawl was different. She would not part with it. It had been Mammy's shawl, hand-knitted long before Delia was even born, while her mother had been a young girl.

The green wool was crafted into an intricate pattern of shells, fashioned with yarn as soft as gossamer; each stitch as perfect as the day it was first knitted. It was a durable shawl of generous proportions and had proved an ample wrap for both mother and babe. It had also been an extra source of warmth for Delia and her siblings on cold winter nights, when the merciless Atlantic winds whistled beneath the cottage door and eddied in icy puffs around their bare ankles.

No, the shawl had become a second skin and a means of comfort to her; her one last tangible link to her mother. She would leave this place, as comfortable as it was, before she would give up her shawl.

'I'll hang it outside and wash it myself in the morning,' she said. 'It's my last possession in the whole world, and I won't part with it.'

Mrs Cleary was out of all patience and she suddenly whirled on Delia. She slapped a wet towel down hard on the table and leaned toward her until their faces almost touched, so close that Delia could see every pore and every purple vein in the cook's plump cheeks, could even make out the glistening beads of perspiration that broke out on her forehead.

'You'll do nothing of the sort, you brazen little upstart. There's no saving that shawl, so there'll be no need to take it anywhere. It'll likely walk out of here of its own accord with the legions of lice that are doubtless marching through it.'

'Your mistress was glad of it.' Delia crossed her arms and

prepared for battle. She had faced bigger threats than this woman and was determined to stand her ground.

'And just what do you mean by that?' the cook demanded.

'I used it for a pillow when the child fell out of the carriage,' Delia said, stepping smartly into the tub and hopefully out of the woman's reach.

Cook's face turned crimson.

'Merciful God, don't be telling me that! The child will be walking alive by mornin' and the mistress herself most like. Can ya see the trouble you've brought, and you only here this last couple of hours? T'was a sad day for this house when the mistress ran foul of you.'

Mrs Cleary had been trying hard not to stare at the naked girl. Truth be told, most of her anger was not directed at Delia at all, but, like Matty, she was angry at the injustice of the girl's circumstances.

She now saw with her own eyes evidence of the horrific stories she'd heard about the hunger victims, but nothing could prepare her for the sight of this poor girl. She'd washed down many consumptives in her time and prepared many of them for burial. Feeble, wasted bodies they'd been, with ribs so sharp they stuck through the skin for want of a bit of flesh on them; but they'd all been dead, This girl was the first she'd seen of the walking dead.

She wanted to vent her anger on the unfeeling monsters who could allow such a travesty, who could sit down to a feast fit for a king night after night and sleep the sleep of innocents afterwards, and never give these starving people a minute's thought. *'If there's any justice at all, the bastards will die screamin,'* she thought to herself as she turned away, wringing the towel in her hands while she imagined it to be a ligature around one of the landowner's fat necks.

Delia was safely submerged to her shoulders in the warm bath and her mind was happily occupied with the unexpected sensations of pleasure and relaxation as the heat penetrated her skin and softened the aching tissue beneath.

She could feel the warmth of the fire down one side of her face and she gazed dreamily at the dancing flames. Catherine was on the settle nearby, also staring into the fire's depths. The maid's eyelids drooped on the verge of closing as the hypnotic movement of the flames lulled her into a stupor. Mrs Cleary was speaking to her, but Catherine was paying no heed: she was somewhere else and far, far away.

'Do you hear me, Catherine Nolan? Put on your shift and get that uniform into a pillowcase. You can throw it outside with Matty's stuff.'

Catherine sat up sharply at the thought of stripping off in front of strangers, even if they were the same sex.

'But Mrs C!' she wailed. 'How am I to get to my room with only a thin shift between me and decency?'

The cook was in no mood to negotiate. 'Ah, there's nobody uses the back stairs except yourself. Now get going, before I give this one here your bed for the night.'

After Catherine left, the cook bustled about the kitchen, muttering under her breath as she prepared a breakfast tray before she settled into her fireside chair with a cup of hot tea.

The bath water was beginning to cool but Delia didn't care. She studied the wrinkled tips of her fingers as though she was seeing them for the first time. She'd forgotten how pink she was beneath all the dirt and it was heavenly to feel clean again. The soapsuds were turning scummy as they congealed in the cooling water and they left a grey demarcation line across her shoulders and chest.

As she washed it away she stole a glance at the cook, who appeared to have fallen asleep. Delia listened to the woman's steady breathing as it kept time with the lazy tick of the clock. The only other sound in the room was the occasional sputter of a spirited flame from the dying embers of the fire.

She stepped out of the bath reluctantly and rubbed herself down with the rough towel, purring with pleasure as the soft flannel nightgown slipped over her head and enveloped her in a fragrant cloud of lavender. Her skin tingled when the fabric slid across her thighs and her body convulsed in a shiver, even though she wasn't in the least bit cold. She pressed her palms over her breasts to quell the ripples that rose in waves from below her belly and she looked over at Mrs Cleary in a mild panic, feeling guilty without knowing why.

Her hair still needed to be washed and she bent over the tub and dipped the long strands as low as she could into the tepid water. After three washes, the cake of soap she'd been given was no more than a sliver, yet still her hair did not feel clean.

It would need a few more washes, she decided, before it reached an acceptable level of cleanliness. But she *was* free of lice and had been almost as surprised as Mrs Cleary at the discovery.

The cook hadn't moved for a while and Delia had no wish to disturb her. She lay down on the mattress and pulled the blankets around her, breathing in the familiar scent of horse and hay. Her hands made a pyramid beneath the blanket as she began her evening prayers; yet formal prayers were inappropriate and she began to talk very quietly to herself, visualizing a new God, a different, kinder God.

'God of mercy and compassion, cleave my suffering soul to thee. Bless everyone in this house and keep these kind people strong and in good health. Let me not be a burden to any of them. Enfold my darling brothers and my sister Niamh in your loving embrace and number them among your angels, Lord. Take all pain and fear from my dear Mammy's heart and reunite her with her weans, and Lord, give comfort to all your suffering people in Ireland this long ni…'

That was as far as she got before sleep overtook her; before her breathing joined the night chorus of contented sounds in the warm kitchen, where Mrs Cleary sat, motionless, with her empty cup resting in the folds of her apron; and where the firelight caught the silent tears that slipped from her half closed eyes and slid silently down her cheeks.

Chapter 9

The sound of cutlery being banged about and the tantalizing aroma of breakfast cooking woke her, and it took her a few moments to assimilate her strange surroundings.

She lay close to the hearth where a lively fire already blazed. Two pairs of unshod feet were visible beneath the table; a stout pair with stockings rolled down to the ankles that belonged to the cook, and a second, skinnier set of legs that could only be Catherine's. The women were already busy with morning chores.

Straw from the palliasse tickled her nose and both women turned to look at her when she gave a loud sneeze.

'About time you stirred,' said the cook. 'There's some bread and a cup o' milk on the settle there. Get them down you quick, and then out you go and help Matty in the stables. When I get a minute to myself I'll take a comb to that head of yours.'

As Delia reached eagerly for the food, she noticed a grey dress and a pair of leather boots lying beside the repast. The cook, who missed nothing, followed her gaze.

'I've had word from her ladyship,' she told her, nodding toward the items on the bench. 'You're to have those clothes.' Delia gaped at her in wonder. 'Close your mouth when you've food in it!' the cook scolded. 'Catherine will alter a pinny for you later, when she's done with her chores.'

The reminder of the extra work the chit was causing seemed

to irritate the cook afresh, and her tone became more hostile. 'God, you're as slow as a wet Sunday! Hurry up now and shake yourself. You've slept best part of the morning away and Matty is in sore need of an extra pair of hands.'

The bread and milk were still warm and Delia offered up a silent prayer of thanks as she ate. She made an effort to chew slowly, and she savored every morsel of the aromatic slab of bread. In between bites, she studied the deep indentations her teeth made in the thickly spread butter and she swished the frothy milk round and round her mouth and licked away the foam that clung to her upper lip.

When the bread was gone, she tipped her head back and stuck out her tongue to catch the last few drops of the milk and circled the plate with her forefinger until every stray crumb was captured and the plate was quite clean.

Mrs Cleary felt the indignation rise as she watched her and shouted at the girl somewhat harshly, without quite knowing why.

'Enough now—you'll have the pattern off the plate if you rub it much more,' she said. 'Outside with you; there'll be more food later, after you've earned it. Tell Matty you're to be back here once the stables are mucked out.'

Matty set her to raking out the stalls. It was familiar work and she was soon deep in thought as she mulled over her sudden change of circumstances.

For one thing, she was still here and nobody was saying anything about her leaving. The claws of hunger were abating; she'd been offered food, shelter, and a warm tweed dress, and her feet were shod, though she would rather they weren't. She'd never worn shoes in her life and, while she was grateful her feet were warm and dry, she couldn't bear the unfamiliar constriction of leather and laces.

She *wasn't* wearing the stockings. They were rolled inside her shawl and she'd left the garters and dried peas on the settle for the cook to find. She raked fiercely as she pushed uncharitable thoughts of the woman to the back of her mind.

'Father, forgive my ingratitude,' she whispered. 'For these, and all Thy gifts, make me truly thankful—and heap blessings upon these good people.' When she finished, she went outside to help Matty separate the manure from the mound of stale hay piled in the yard.

They worked in easy silence and Delia was glad of it. She needed to think; needed space to absorb her unexpected reversal of fortunes. God was in a more charitable mood. On a sudden whim, he'd snapped his fingers and altered every aspect of her life in the space of a single day.

It was *her* turn to be plucked from the never-ending struggle and grief beyond the walls of this grand house; her turn to be given a taste of a sweeter existence. '*All the more cruel,*' she reflected wryly. '*When I'm turned out to fend for myself once more, it'll be so much worse for having tasted such luxury as this.*'

Matty brought fresh hay for her to spread through the stable, and she filled the nosebags with the mash he'd made and watched him lead the first of the animals away from the trough.

'This is Hazel,' he said, patting the animal's nose.

'Do you know how to brush her down?'

'Indeed, I do,' Delia replied haughtily. She took the brush from him and swung it in a wide arc down the crest of the mare's neck to its shoulder. The horse shifted slightly and snickered as it sensed a stranger's touch.

Delia nuzzled the mare and murmured softly into her ear and by the time she was ready to brush the horse's rump, Hazel was content to let her lift the dock of her nut-brown tail and give it a firm and thorough grooming.

She led her into a clean stall and hooked a feedbag over the mare's head and waited until Hazel was munching contentedly.

Matty was impressed. '*She knows how, God love her,*' he thought to himself. '*She has the technique alright, but not yet strength enough to groom herself, let alone a large horse.'*

They were gathering up tools when Catherine appeared in the doorway. Her features were indistinguishable against the rapidly lightening sky beyond the gloom of the stable.

'Mrs C says it's time for breakfast,' she said, and disappeared as quickly as she had come, back to the kitchen.

Delia had never seen such a feast. She couldn't wait to get started, but she was forced to sit on her hands and endure a delay as each of them obeyed Mrs Cleary's order to recite a line of prayer before she would allow them to lift a spoon.

'God bless the pig that pays the cotter's rent.
God bless the horse that tills the field.
God bless the cow that gives us milk.
Grant us Lord, sufficient yield.'

Delia crossed herself quickly and her mouth was full even before the last notes of the 'Amen' had faded.

The others seemed equally as hungry and they lifted their spoons together and bent eagerly to the food. Four deep soup plates of steaming oatmeal lay at hand, and a large server was piled high with thick slices of toast.

She reached for the porridge and watched a yellow finger of melted butter drip down the sides of the toasted soda bread and settle in a golden puddle on the plate. Her fingers itched to dip into the yellow pool and her mouth began to water, just as it had when she and Matty had detected the appetizing aroma of bacon as they crossed the yard.

She'd found courage to speak to Matty on their way back to the kitchen. She was confused and shy, and still a little fearful in his presence, and she'd spoken without looking at him, still conscious of the intensity of his dislike.

She was good at sizing people up, but Matty was proving a challenge. She thought he was softening toward her, though it wouldn't do to make any presumption. Besides, she might not be here long enough to have to fathom any of them.

'I think you might be right, Matty,' she'd said to him. 'I am a lucky girl indeed.'

He'd turned his head away from her and cleared his throat loudly and the gob of phlegm he spat landed in the corner of the yard with expert accuracy.

'Ah, you've come round to my way of thinkin', have you?' He spoke sharply, but she could see out of the corner of her eye the beginnings of a smile that he tried to hide by wiping his mouth on the sleeve of his jacket, and when they reached the kitchen door he'd stepped to one side and held it open for her.

The gesture confused her. It was as alien to her as the stockings *and* the stiff boots that were aggravating the cuts on her feet, and she wasn't sure if she was supposed to wait or not.

'Are you going to stand there gawping 'til the porridge is cold?' he'd said. 'Get inside with you, before Catherine eats your portion.'

Halfway through breakfast, Delia was unexpectedly overtaken by fatigue. She startled the others by dropping her spoon as waves of tiredness washed over her.

She felt much as she had the day before, just before she'd fainted clean away. She gripped the edge of the table with both hands and willed herself to stay upright, afraid to descend into that dark abyss again. That first faint had been a frightening experience and she recalled with dread the loss of control as she'd sunk into the unknown, and the anxiety she'd felt when she emerged from the strange limbo in case she'd disgraced herself by peeing on the lush carpet.

She felt that same sense of helplessness now. She was sliding and powerless to stop the fall. A strange smell invaded her nostrils and she was vaguely aware of a faint 'clink' as the spoon dropped to the stone floor—and then strong arms pulled her upright and dragged her toward the fire.

There was an unbearable heat as her eyes tried to focus on the blurred image of hungry flames licking at the dark outline of a peat brick.

Suddenly, the big man was leaning over her, the same man she'd seen in Buncrana. She was confused. Why was the big man's ear on her chest? He was much too close and it frightened her. What did he want with her? She was suffocating and tried to push him away; to fight him off. But he was so big and powerful and she screamed out in terror.

'Help me Mammy! Don't let him touch me. He wants to take me away. Mammy! Where are you? *Please* come, please, please Mammy! Don't leave me alone with this strange man—'

The searing body heat that she was sure would consume her was replaced by ice-cold bands of water that flowed over her face and down the neck of her shroud.

That was it! She was wearing a snow-white shroud and the man was trying to drown her!

With fists clenched, she reached out and pushed with all her might, but stronger, bigger hands grabbed her thin wrists, and fat fingers tightly gripped hers; fingers that belonged to familiar, grossly-formed hands that conquered hers with ease and pinned her arms to the sandy bottom as her lungs burst and she fought to raise her head above the water. Her feeble strength was no match for him.. Her arms turned to jelly and she had no more strength or willpower to fight him off.

Then she saw Gerry Mullen. His bloated body floated across her vision and his face stared down at her from just below the surface of the water. Dark eyes stared, wide and expressionless and his seaweed hair flowed in long, green tendrils behind him, while trailing ribbons of blood flowed from the stump of his leg, and stained the water red.

She opened her mouth to scream and the water filled her until her body felt unbearably heavy. It slackened as she fell away, down, down, into a long tube of blinding white.

The falling sensation left her, yet she couldn't open her eyes. The insides of her eyelids were the same frieze of blinding white, so intense it hurt more to have them closed. She put an arm across her forehead to shield them and opened her eyes a crack.

She lay in a voluminous canopied bed. Beyond the expanse of white counterpane, she discerned the shadowy form of a gentleman outlined against the blinding glare of a window. He was well dressed and wore a hat, and he carried some sort of stick, but beyond that, the rest of him was a blur.

She opened her eyes wider and tried to focus, squinting against the brightness until they hurt so much she had to close them again.

The sea water had made her thirsty and she knew she must find the hidden stream off the boreen. She longed to taste the sweet cold liquid and to submerge her fiery limbs in the stream's cool depths.

Although her body burned , she knew she couldn't be in Hell. Hell was black. Yet she wasn't in Heaven either; she had no sense of happiness or contentment. She felt only a constant and extreme heat, so intense it melted her eyeballs and welded her lids shut and forced her, against her will, into another cameo of nightmares.

She was swept along in the feverish otherworld for three days, although she didn't discover until later how long she'd been ill. The doctor noted the swelling in Delia's limbs and told Lady Keenagh that the girl had been on the verge of famine dropsy and would have slipped into the last fatal stage of starvation if she hadn't been rescued.

He reproached himself for not having looked at her more closely in Buncrana. '*Thank God it wasn't the typhoid and she wasn't contagious,*' Dr Nowland thought.

He shuddered when he dwelt on the folly of offering the girl's services to her ladyship. If she'd been infected with typhus the whole household would likely have come down with the disease and he would have no reputation worth saving. He'd seen plenty of typhoid cases, hundreds of them these last few months, and he'd been witness to the widespread panic among rich and poor alike whenever there was mere mention of the word, 'fever'.

Dread of disease permeated every segment of his people and grossly exaggerated tales were being spread through the country faster than the fever itself, to the point where, anybody with a stench about them was suspected of having the typhus. Friends and close knit families were becoming estranged as they pushed aside their natural instincts to be neighborly. Instead, they isolated themselves to avoid any contact with each other for fear of contagion.

But the biggest tragedy of all was that slowly, and just as insidiously as the disease itself, the indestructible fabric of the Irish people had begun to tear and disintegrate, until, before long, close associations and old friendships dissolved, eroded like the potatoes that had started the holocaust, and a people's love and trust were destroyed forever by a universal sickness known as fear.

Chapter 10

Delia was confined to bed for almost two weeks. She was settled into Catherine's room and the kitchen maid and the cook were forced to shared a bed as long as Delia remained feverish.

Once the fever left her and the healing powers of undisturbed sleep restored her strength, she had time to familiarize herself with her new surroundings. She was still extremely weak, but slowly, her energy increased and she found herself with lots of time to simply sit and stare. The sick room was small and sparsely furnished but more comfortable than she would have thought for a kitchen maid's quarters.

The bed was the first real bed she'd ever slept in, and Delia delighted in the luxurious comfort of the flock mattress and warm blankets. The room was also draft-free, due in part to the solid wood panels that lined the walls from floor to ceiling; the same oak panels she'd imagined were closing in on her during the worst of her fever. A wardrobe; dresser; bedside table and small bookcase displaying some of Catherine's personal items, completed the furnishings.

One morning, she left the safety of her bed for the first time to use the chamber pot. The bedroom window overlooked an orderly vegetable garden far below and at sight of the neat rows of vegetables, she felt the first stirrings of hunger since her illness.

She leaned against a dresser and admired the grains in the

oak and the smooth surface of the wood. A well-thumbed bible and a simple rosary lay on the bedside table. Fingering the beads evoked an image of her dead mother and she replaced them quickly and shivered at the memory.

A large wardrobe contained just two garments: an outdoor cloak and a spare uniform.

'*Not much to show for being employed by the rich,*' she mused, but then it occurred to her the rest of Catherine's clothes would have been moved to Mrs Cleary's room for the duration.

Her legs were turning to water and she felt cold, and as she turned to close the wardrobe door she caught sight of herself in the mirror. The reflection was both strange and unexpected and she gasped, momentarily shocked by the grotesque image that stared back at her. She could not believe it was her own likeness. Her skin was almost transparent. It stretched tight across her cheekbones, and she ran her fingers over the rivers of blue veins that were clearly visible on her forehead and temple. But it was her eyes that shocked her most of all.

They were sunken orbs of ebony and they were ringed with deep shadows. 'I wouldn't like to meet you on a dark night.' She told her reflection. 'I'd mistake you for an exhumed corpse.'

It was the first time she'd seen herself full-length and she stared, fascinated, yet strangely detached from her image.

It was very different from the distorted self she was accustomed to seeing reflected in a pool of water, and she studied her features and the shape of her body curiously, and with a cold criticism of what she perceived to be physical faults. When she lifted her nightdress, she felt a stab of pity at sight of her skeletal frame, and was dismayed at how wasted her limbs had become.

There wasn't a single redeeming feature in her sorry reflection, yet she didn't care so much about her appearance—it was all new to her. She knew she hadn't looked much different from the other travelers she'd passed on the journey into Buncrana.

What saddened her more than anything was the change in her *hair*. Her features were nondescript and she accepted it, but she *was* proud of her hair and had been complimented often over the years.

Now, she looked like some demented creature of the wild. Her scalp itched all over, and when she began to scratch, it was so sensitive, every touch sent shivering ripples coursing through her.

She studied her hands, to see if they had changed. They felt like giant sea sponges, without strength or form; yet here they were, gross appendages of skin and bone; still they felt much bigger than they looked—the same way her eyes looked in her wizened face.

Her entire body felt out of kilter and she wondered if she were still feverish; if this vision was some illusion brought on by her fever. She sighed deeply and thought she was too weary to care one way or the other. She was trying to crawl back into bed when Catherine came into the room and caught her.

'What are you doing out of bed? You could have had a fall, or even worse, caught a chill.' Catherine took hold of Delia's feet and swung them onto the bed non-too gently. 'Your feet are freezing cold,' she scolded, 'Have you taken leave of your senses altogether? Stay put now, while I fetch a warming pan.'

The maid stoked the fire and slipped a hot brick into the warming pan before she stuck it under the bedclothes. Delia groped for it beneath the sheets until she felt the welcoming heat penetrate her toes, and when she spoke her voice sounded small and weak to her ears.

'Thank you, Catherine. You won't tell Mrs Cleary I've been out of bed, will you?'

Catherine fussed with the sheets and wouldn't reassure Delia until she was quite satisfied there wasn't an inch of skin exposed, except her head, and she would have covered that too, had Delia not put out a hand to stop her. The girl recoiled at her touch and drew back her hand quickly, but she was sensitive enough not to wipe it on her apron and Delia ignored the gesture.

'This is your room isn't it, Catherine? I'm *really* sorry. I know I must have caused you mountains of extra work, but I'll make it up to you as soon as I'm allowed out of bed. I swear to you on my moth—'

Her mother's memory was too close to the surface, and with a piercing stab of grief, she remembered she was no longer alive and quickly amended her oath. 'May God strike me down dead if I break my promise.'

Catherine looked long and hard at her, then reached out shyly and took one of Delia's hands in her own. She kept her eyes averted, but she gave a half smile and Delia felt the maid give her hand a slight squeeze before she turned and left the room, closing the door softly behind her.

She was pampered for another week before being allowed out of bed to use the commode, and just when she was beginning to feel unable to tolerate the heavy burden of guilt at being waited on hand and foot, the cook agreed she could spend some time downstairs in the kitchen.

Catherine helped her down the back staircase each afternoon and settled her beside the fire, where she endured further agonies of guilt as she rested with her tea and watched the women bustle about, hot and bothered, performing the endless multitude of tasks that consumed all their waking hours.

It was towards the middle of December when she sat near the large windows and caught sight of Matty and the stable lad piling holly boughs and long trails of ivy against the far wall of the courtyard.

The busy hum of the kitchen escalated as everyone busied themselves with extra preparations for the Christmas holidays, and the air in the kitchen was heady with the exotic aromas of spices and dried fruits. Delia thought the large dresser must surely collapse beneath the weight of the serving dishes, the cutlery and the exquisite linens that were brought out especially for the festive season.

As the days passed, she spent longer periods downstairs and was eventually allowed to help a little. Mrs Cleary gave her some of the lighter tasks; jobs she could do sitting, like folding linens or polishing some of the smaller pieces of silver.

One morning, she sat enjoying the warmth of the fire, contentedly weaving a garland of winter-greens Matty had brought in earlier. He had entered the kitchen with his arms piled so high he could barely see over the top of the boughs. The cook chided him for leaving a muddy trail of boot marks across her clean floor, but he ignored her and dropped his cargo near Delia's feet.

'Mind your hands on the holly leaves now,' he cautioned. 'Those thorns are sharp as a hedge pig's quills.'

Matty's manner was much less gruff of late and she was glad he was softening. She'd sensed a degree of acceptance from the women too, since her illness.

She smiled up at him and went back to her weaving. She was focused so intently on the task; she didn't hear the kitchen door open and was unaware of the child's presence until one of the holly thorns caught under her fingernail.

She gave a startled cry and dropped the garland, tasting the metallic tang of her own blood as she sucked on her finger.

She looked up to see if Mrs Cleary or Catherine had heard, and was startled to find herself confronted by the unforgettable cobalt-blue eyes of the child she'd last seen lying prostrate on the cobbles in Buncrana.

There was such sweet concern in the little girl's face that it touched Delia's heart and she barely had time to swallow back the tears that rushed unexpectedly to her eyes.

'Are you alright? Is your finger bleeding?' the little one asked, her wide eyes never leaving Delia's face. Delia cried more easily since her illness and was almost overwhelmed again at being the recipient of such kindness. She hastened to reassure the child.

'Bless you, darlin'. I'm quite alright. It was my own stupid fault. Matty warned me often enough about the thorns.'

The girl took Delia's hand and kissed the tip of her injured finger and Delia thought her heart would burst at the unexpected show of affection. She coughed to dispel the tears and dabbed at her eyes with a corner of her apron.

'Your name is Magdalen, is it not?'

'How do you know my name?' the child asked, as she picked up the dropped garland and placed it gingerly in Delia's lap.

'Ah, but I have magical powers,' Delia said, leaning toward her, 'given to me by the great goddess Blodeuedd.

Do you know about Blodeuedd?'

The lovely eyes grew large as saucers and the little one stared, open-mouthed.

Delia seized the moment and prepared to tell Magdalen the tale of Blodeuedd but, as busy as Mrs Cleary seemed, she had half an ear to the proceedings and came over at once to intervene.

'Aye, that's all fine and dandy, but Blodeuedd gave *me* some powers too,' she said as she approached. Her arms were covered to the elbows in flour and she wiped them absent-mindedly on her apron and swept back a lock of hair from the child's upturned face.

'Does your mother know you're down here? I don't need either of us getting into trouble right now. I've enough to contend with, for I've an invalid on me hands,' she nodded toward Delia, and then to Catherine, who was busy at the sink, '*and* a dim-witted maid, who doesn't seem to know one end of a fork from the other most days, and there's a growin' mountain of work yet to be done.'

Catherine ignored her and Magdalen, unfazed, took one of

the cook's floury hands in her own and told her firmly.

'Mother says I'm to do what I can to help without getting in the way. She says I can stay until lunch.'

'Well now, is that right? Sure, half a loaf is better than none I suppose. Do you think you could help Delia finish the garlands? And do you think you could be smarter than she is, and not get your fingers pricked on the holly thorns?'

Without giving the child a chance to reply, Mrs Clearly settled her down in her own chair opposite Delia and gave her some of the greenery. 'Watch awhile now, until you get the hang of it. But stay on your own side of the fireplace, for none of us is sure yet that Delia doesn't have a catchin' disease, and you don't want to get sick before St Nick comes now, do you?'

Magdalen sat quietly, and watched intently as Delia sorted carefully through the remaining boughs before selecting her pieces and weaving them together. She remained silent, having decided to let the child set the pace of any conversation between them. She wasn't sure what Magdalen remembered of the accident in Buncrana, or if the recollection would prove traumatic.

'What's *your* name?' asked the girl, her eyes fixed on Delia's busy fingers. Delia looked up from her work and found she could almost smile in the face of such blatant innocence. She felt the beginnings of a warm glow inside her for the first time in years.

'Did you not hear Mrs Cleary call me by name just now?' Delia teased. 'My name is Delia Dreenan, and before you ask, I'm eighteen, and I was born right here in Donegal and... Oh, wait! I suppose you're wanting to know if I have any brothers or sisters? Well, the answer is "No",' Delia lied. 'I'm an only child.'

Magdalen's eyes and mouth had opened even wider, believing Delia really *did* have the power to read her mind, for hadn't they been the answers to the very questions she'd been on the verge of asking?

'So am I,' she said. 'But I wish I had a brother or sister. I have my dollies and I love them, sure enough, but they're no company when I'm lonely, or when I'm missing Pappa. My dollies can't talk back to me can they?'

It was Delia's turn to stare in amazement. 'How old did you say you were?' she asked, greatly surprised at the child's intelligence and mature way of thinking.

'*You* can tell *me*, if you really do have special powers.' Magdalen's head was bent close to the garland as she spoke, but Delia could just make out a pink tip of a tongue sticking out of her mouth as she concentrated hard on her first attempts at braiding the boughs.

She thought back to the pale, lifeless form that had landed at her feet in Buncrana and recalled the doctor asking the child's age as she regained consciousness.

'You're not quite six,' Delia said with uncertainty. 'But you will be very soon.' It was a calculated guess; the child could have had her sixth birthday while Delia had been ill, but she knew she'd guessed right when Magdalen's head shot up and those incredible eyes looked at her in amazement again.

Catherine interrupted them with milk for Magdalen and hot sweet tea for Delia and they shared a plate of warm oatcakes in companionable silence. Both of them worked, in between bites, until they had used up all the greenery Matty had brought.

'Shall I tell you about Blodeuedd now, the goddess who gave me the powers?' Delia asked her.

The child put her empty cup on the floor and climbed back into Mrs Cleary's chair, and Delia watched in amusement as she wiggled from side to side, until her bottom touched the back of the settle and her legs stretched out straight in front of her. She rocked until she freed the folds of her smock and smoothed out the creases; then she folded her hands in her lap and became quite still, looking at Delia expectantly.

'I was resting in a field one sunny morning,' began Delia,

'and I started to come over all sleepy with the warmth of the sun on my face and the sweet songs of the birds serenading me. I thought I'd fallen asleep altogether, but now I know that it was Blodeuedd—she'd sprinkled magic dust in my eyes, so I wouldn't be able to see her properly, me being a mere mortal and all.'

'But who *is* Blodeuedd—and what is her magic?' asked Magdalen.

'Didn't I tell you that already?' Delia asked her in mock surprise before continuing. 'Blodeuedd was born of the flower world. She was the fairest of all the goddesses, made from stout oak broom and fragrant meadowsweet. The gods don't like us to see them, unless they're in the form of a mortal, but you probably know that already. Anyway, Blodeuedd was given the worldly form of a snowy owl, for not only did she have the wit and the beauty, but she was also very wise.

'So she tells me, in a voice sweeter than wild honey, that I was the first mortal she'd come across that day and, as such, I was entitled to a wish of my very own.

'I didn't have a lot of time to think and there was so much I wanted, but I suddenly thought how fine it would be if I could read the mind of my teacher and all the other wise people around me.' Delia bent to pick up the poker and jabbed at the fire. 'This happened some years ago, you understand, when I was not much older than yourself.'

She glanced across to Magdalen, who sat spellbound; she hadn't so much as blinked.

'I thought that if I could read the teacher's mind then I'd be the brightest girl in the clachan,' Delia continued. 'So I told Blodeuedd what I wanted, and she told me to close my eyes tight, for she was going to take on mortal form, the better for me to see her. But when I opened my eyes she'd gone, and what do you think? There was a snow-white owl perched on a clump of whin nearby and it flew across and landed on my head. It stayed there for a minute and then it, too, disappeared. And just in case you're wondering, *you* are the first person I've ever told. You know, don't you, that each time you tell a mortal soul about your magical powers, those powers become weaker with the telling, until after you've bragged about the magic so many times, there's none of it left, and one day you're left looking like the village idiot, with your powers completely gone and you clackin' your jaws faster than knuckles on a bhodrun; bragging to all and sundry, not knowing your gifts are gone.'

Catherine came to collect the cups. Her face was an inscrutable map, but it was plain from the silence in the kitchen that both she and Mrs C had been listening to every word.

'Is St Nick going to bring you any gifts?' asked Delia, bending to sweep fallen berries and loose leaves into the hearth. She was immediately sorry she'd asked when Magdalen replied.

'See if you can guess what I asked him for; use your special powers. *I* will think about the things I want, and *you* can tell me what they are. Close your eyes now and think hard.'

Delia had to think hard *and* fast. It was going to require some craftiness to keep ahead of this child.

'Ah, now I should explain something to you, Magdalen,' she said quickly. 'I can only read in your mind what has already happened, and then only some of the time. I can't read things that *might* happen in the future. Imagine how much fun we'd miss if we knew what St Nick was bringing us ahead of Christmas, or if we could see our birthdays before they even happened? Don't you think the best part is the waiting?'

Delia's eyes were still tightly closed as she said this, but the child never answered and seemed satisfied for the moment. Out of the corner of one eye, Delia watched her as she stood and brushed crumbs from her smock and, after making sure Catherine and Mrs C weren't watching, she sidled up to Delia and stretched tall to whisper in her ear.

'Father says I'm old enough to learn to ride, and in the spring

Matty is to give me lessons, so I think I might get my very own pony.' Her whispers floated on warm puffs of air into the shell of Delia's ear. 'I have to go now, but if Mamma allows it I'll come back tomorrow.'

These last words were said in the same breathless lisp, and she brushed her lips against Delia's cheek, light and gentle as a feather; so gentle, Delia wasn't aware the child had gone until she opened her eyes and heard the muffled closing of the kitchen door behind her.

She discovered Magdalen was a regular visitor to the kitchen and had been almost from the day she'd started to walk. She was loved to distraction by the staff, and during the remainder of Delia's convalescence they enjoyed long walks together, during which Magdalen showed her various paths and shortcuts through the estate.

The extensive grounds were an endless source of wonder to Delia and she was glad to discover them through the eyes of a child, albeit one as smart as a new whip. It gave her license to give full vent to her delight at each new discovery, without need of restraint or self-consciousness.

Her biggest surprise had been the vegetable garden, the one she'd seen from her sick room, with its neat rows of cabbages, sprouts and mangel wurzels, and she explored in wonder, the large glass house that protected endless rows of young seedlings and exotic plants, as well as a comprehensive selection of herbs.

Magdalen mirrored Delia's own delight for she, too, loved nothing more than to be away from the restrictions of the house and its over-attentive adults.

Pleasant hours were spent naming flowers and plants and Matty, who was very territorial when it came to his gardens, became used to their frequent appearances and even allowed them to help with the constant weeding.

Chapter 11

Delia was summoned upstairs two days before Christmas, to the same large room where she'd experienced her first fainting spell. It was a crisp, glorious day and a light snowfall dusted the large expanse of lawn. It gleamed in the morning sun and cast a welcome brightness into every corner of the room. Her eyes were drawn to the east-facing windows that were already suffused with the coral blush of the rising sun.

On the broad terrace, McVey exercised two wolfhounds. The long-legged dogs ran in wide circles and sent up wisps of steam from their coats as they chased each other, exhilarated by the cold morning air. McVey stamped his feet and walked in smaller circles, his hands tucked beneath his armpits in an effort to warm them.

A polite greeting brought Delia's attention back to the room and she jumped, aware she hadn't been paying attention, and for a third time, she found herself under the scrutiny of Lady Keenagh.

Her ladyship stood near the tall windows, wearing a dress the exact color of her daughter's eyes and she gave Delia a welcoming smile and waited until she'd made her way across the large expanse of carpet before extending her hand.

'Good morning, Delia. How are you feeling today?'

Delia took a deep breath and tried to her rapid heartbeat. It thumped so strongly she felt sure the vibrations must be visible beneath her blouse. '*How unlucky,*' she thought, '*to be dismissed at such a time.*'

She knew her dismissal would come; she'd been amply paid for her kindness and the child's family owed her no further debt. Indeed, she had prepared for this moment; yet she'd have liked to have stayed a few days longer, just until after the holidays. She wasn't sure she was emotionally strong enough to face the pain of spending Christmas alone on the streets. She summoned her courage and looked the lady straight in the eyes.

'Good morning to you, ma'am, and thank you, I'm feeling a lot stronger.'

Lady Keenagh didn't overly scrutinize her and Delia was grateful. The mistress seemed sensitive to her nervousness and got down to business immediately.

'Are you quite recovered from your illness? I know something of your suffering from Mrs Cleary and Matthew. Our country is enduring an immense tragedy Miss Dreenan, and I am sorry to hear of your part in it.' She indicated a nearby chair. 'Would you like to sit?'

Delia did some mental juggling during the brief moment it took her to be seated. She knew she must have cried out during her fever, but she could only guess at the content or clarity of her ramblings. Far better to assume these people knew nothing, she decided. Let them believe that anything she may have said had been uttered in delirium, while she'd been quite out of her mind.

Now, she must choose her words most carefully; she must somehow evoke in this woman sufficient compassion for her plight to allow her to stay at the Hall a few days more.

She looked at the landscape and watched a solitary blackbird search for worms on the snow-covered lawn. Its glossy head swiveled and bobbed erratically as it pecked at the hard ground. McVey and the dogs had gone, leaving behind faint traces of footprints and skid marks on the flagstones.

Way above, a goshawk patrolled lazily in widening circles until it suddenly swept down and out of sight as its keen eyes spied a movement in the gorse below. She nodded toward the blackbird and began to speak, slowly and very quietly, her voice almost a whisper.

'Well now, would you look at that? It's a struggle for the lowliest of God's creatures. Do you see the blackbird on the lawn there? He's following a pattern all too familiar to me. Outside the boundary walls, not too far from the secure gates of this house, thousands of our good people are doing exactly what that bird is doing, and they're having about as much success finding food. Indeed, they'd be glad of even a worm.

'The road between here and Buncrana is littered with human crows—ugly skeletal forms, barely fit to be called human.' She crossed her arms and shivered at memory of the starving. 'They peck away at the ground, just like that bird. They suck on stones and rip the flesh of their mouths on stinging nettles and gorse. Why, they'll even tear up grass if they've strength enough, as they forage for anything to put in their empty bellies. Some are so desperate they commit unspeakable acts to ease the consuming hunger that claws constantly at their bellies.'

Her ladyship heard the mounting anger in Delia's voice and shifted uncomfortably. It couldn't be true—the girl had to be indulging in gross exaggeration. Perhaps she was not fully recovered from her fevers and was still a little delusional. Lady Keenagh knew that rural folk were renowned for embellishing the truth, but looking at the girl now, and witnessing the raw anguish in her eyes, Lady Keenagh was inclined to believe things were much worse than her husband had led her to believe. He left the confines of the Hall more often than any of them. He rode out frequently, and when he wasn't abroad, he visited his banker in Londonderry once a month.

He spared his wife the more harrowing accounts of the ongoing tragedy and would only opine, if she pressed him, that conditions were 'better' or 'worse'. She had no reliable means of information.

Lord Keenagh was not eccentric, but he *was* fanatical about his newspapers and forbade anyone, except McVey, to touch them.

It was his practice to fling them into the fire as soon as he finished reading. He once told his wife, jokingly, that since it had been in his private closet with him, the newspaper was fit for nobody's hands but his own. Sometimes, when they were short of chitins below stairs, Catherine would salvage it and bring it to the kitchen to use for fire starters.

Lady Keenagh knew the girl was right about one thing. She and her family were protected from the worst of it; safe inside the grounds of the great house, and without cause to leave since the riots in Buncrana. Her husband insisted she and their daughter were not to venture forth without his personal supervision.

Catherine tapped on the door and entered with a tea tray. She scurried across the room with her eyes downcast, even as she arranged the cups, and left in the same manner, without seeing anything but the floor beneath her feet and the tray in her hands.

Delia watched her in sympathy, remembering how her mother had always chided her and Niamh for walking with their heads down.

'You'll miss so much of life,' she'd tell them. 'Always hold your head high and look forward; 'that way, you'll be one step ahead of life's surprises.' Delia glanced around the room and thought how horrified her mother would be by such opulence and excess.

She declined tea, afraid she would drop the delicate cup being offered and waited until Lady Keenagh had finished fussing.

'I was eleven when the first of the rotten harvests visited our people. The tang of the Atlantic was overcome by a stinking red cloud that crept in silently from the ocean on the westerly wind. It shrouded every field and farmhouse, every cottage and clachan for miles around. None of us had ever seen anything like it and we were afraid. Our elders said Fear Liath was angry with the people for being wasteful with previous harvests. Everything that moved was brought inside that day. Animals were gathered, windows were covered and doors bolted against Fear Liath's evil cloud of corruption.

She rubbed her eyes with her apron. 'When we dared to look out next morning, the cloud had disappeared and the day was full of innocence, bright and sunny, just like this one. But an air of unrest pervaded the people, as though the cloud had somehow found purchase through unseen cracks in the walls of their homes and down chimney stacks until it permeated our skins, as we all breathed in the fetid air, ignorant of its deadly power.'

Lady Keenagh stood to refill her cup and interrupted.

'I remember hearing of the big cloud,' she told Delia. 'I also remember thinking the coastal dwellers must have been terrified; nothing like it had ever been seen before.'

'You're quite right, ma'am. It wasn't until the men returned from the mainland to harvest the pratties did the cries of fear begin to ring out across the fields, as one after the other, the cotter's spades upturned the foul-smelling tubers.

'After that, the people's fears magnified. They knew for sure the red cloud had brought the blight, and along with it, want, destitution and death.'

Delia turned away from the window and moved closer to the fire. She felt cold, in spite of the excessive heat in the room. She sat on the edge of a chair and clutched at the arms with both hands, and Lady Keenagh noticed the girl's knuckles were white from the determined effort to maintain her composure.

Her Ladyship never spoke, but followed and settled on a nearby chaise. Delia looked into the fire for a long moment before she gave a shudder and waded deeper into her distressful recollections.

'My heart's been broken from the sights I've seen, and I've been sick to my stomach many times from the constant filth and stench of it all. May God forgive me, but it got so bad I was sorry I didn't think to eat my own bile; it would have been a lot more palatable than some of the things I've been forced to swallow. The dramas unfolding on the roads and in the fields of our beleaguered country are bigger and more evil than even the Devil could invent.'

She covered her face with her hands and when she resumed her words were muffled. Lady Keenagh was forced to lean forward and crane her neck in an effort to hear them, but Delia withdrew her hands with a heavy sigh of resignation and clasped them together tightly in her lap.

'I cannot speak of it any more, your ladyship,' she said, with a shake of her head, ' except to say, after my Mammy and Da succumbed, I walked away and I kept on walking. I don't know why I was spared. I've asked God many times. But as I walked among the suffering, I imagined myself to be an observer who strolled through the pages of a storybook. I was witness to a tragedy and powerless; not part of it, but an onlooker. Perhaps that helped me through it, I can't say. But as God's my judge, and in the presence of him and his Blessed Mother who gave him life, I swear I will not go into that quagmire again.' She raised a tear-stained face and made a fist. 'And if I have to commit mortal sin in the taking of my own life, I will do it. I will sell my soul to the devil—if he will promise to keep my belly full in payment.'

She heard Lady Keenagh's sharp intake of breath and saw her blanch at hearing her sacrilegious vow. Her ladyship stood quickly and Delia noticed she clutched a soggy handkerchief, which she pulled at with great agitation, and the lady's eyes were moist with unshed tears when she addressed her.

'Dear girl,' she said, looking at Delia in some distress. 'I can only make a poor attempt at imagining your suffering, and I know it will take some time for your heart to heal, but nobody here will ever force you to talk about it again. Only, heed my caution child, for talk about it you must one day.

'It'll be a cleansing for your soul and will help remove any traces of hatred and bitterness from your heart. I cannot help you heal in mind and spirit, only God in his own time can do that; but I *can* promise you a warm shelter and a full belly.'

She made a feeble attempt to smile as she reassured her. 'And you don't have to sell your soul for our hospitality either. My daughter has come to love you, and you've proved more than willing to work for your keep, so you're not to look upon this offer as charity. I *invite* you to stay, at least until his lordship returns from America. Would you like that?'

Delia was very glad to be sitting. All sensation in her legs seemed to drain and she was overcome by a powerful surge of relief and gratitude. She had an urge to kiss Lady Keenagh, but she still retained a sense of place and knew enough to obey the strict rules of class.

But she was bold enough to take one of her ladyship's hands as she thanked her.

'I can never repay your kindness ma'am, but I will provide good honest work, and I'll do my best to earn every crust of my keep. May God heap blessings upon yourself and your loved ones, and may his Archangel Gabriel keep you safe from harm.'

'Amen to that,' said Lady Keenagh, as she tucked the damp handkerchief deftly into the waistband of her dress. 'I will talk to Mrs Cleary in the next few days and decide your duties. In the meantime, you may continue to share a room with Catherine, and I hope you'll be willing to take Magdalen for walks, whenever the weather permits.'

Chapter 12

The weather did not permit. Immediately after Christmas, the county was paralyzed in the grip of two months of the coldest temperatures in living memory. As the sub-zero conditions prevailed, Delia was never so grateful to have a roof over her head, but she fretted constantly for the unfortunates who she knew still struggled to survive beyond the boundaries of the great house.

There were only a few days when it was possible to take even a short walk but they braved the freeze one morning and the minute they stepped out of doors, the moisture froze in their nostrils and their breath flew ahead of them in small clouds of steam as they walked briskly round the perimeter of the house and ran the last few yards to the kitchen to escape the bitter cold.

Washday had to be be observed, regardless of the weather, and they flew in and found the cook had draped damp laundry over every available chair. The fire was almost obscured behind a wall of wet garments and a wide column of steam misted the windows and rose toward the high ceiling. Mrs Cleary's hair was plastered in wet tendrils to her face and the front of her apron was soaked. She threw up her hands as soon as the girls appeared, red faced and breathless, in the doorway.

'Shut that door, before we all freeze to death!' she scolded. 'How am I to get things dry in this weather? I can't hang them outside. Matty is after bringing in the sheets and they were stiff as boards. I had to dry them all over again, after they thawed.'

The girls hurried toward the hearth, peeling off gloves and scarves and dropping their coats to the floor in their haste to get close to the flames.

It was during such a spell of inclement weather that Delia began teaching Magdalen basket weaving. As soon as a hot drink thawed them they settled at one end of the big table amidst piles of wet bog grass Matty kept trimmed and soaked for them out in the stable.

Sometimes Delia told stories to keep Magdalen absorbed, but there really wasn't any need. The girl loved working with her hands and it was always Delia who had to end the sessions amid loud protests from the child.

And it wasn't only the child who regretted their sessions coming to an end. Catherine and Mrs Cleary also loved to listen and hours of tedious work were made lighter by the entertainment provided by Delia and her young apprentice.

In the steamy kitchen, Delia and Magdalen bent over an unfinished basket. Delia's expert hand guided Magdalen's hesitant fingers through the last crucial sequence of weaving and tying off, and as they cleared the mess, Delia began to sing softly to herself and Mrs Cleary stopped her work at the sink to listen.

There was nothing remarkable in the girl's voice, she thought; but it was pleasant enough, and she carried a tune well. What interested Mrs Cleary most was the lyrics. She recognized the melody as a well-beloved and ancient one, but the words and the theme of Delia's version were different:

'I once walked these fields of fine clover,
My heart and my eyes filled with joy.
Now the joy and contentment are over,
Since I lost my sweet Donegal boys.

They were sent as two stars from the Heavens,
To bring laughter and love to our home,
But their cots are now bare and empty,
 And my beautiful angels are gone.'

Delia was unaware she had an audience, and was about to begin another verse when Mrs C coughed loudly several times and Delia, surprised by the intrusion, glanced over in time to see the cook wipe her eyes with the back of her hand. She cleared her throat again and sniffed loudly, before plunging her hands back into the sink.

'Where did you learn that?' she asked Delia, as she scrubbed fiercely at a plate that hardly warranted such violent scouring. 'I know the tune well enough, but I've never heard those words before.'

Delia knew she'd peeled back a protective layer of her heart; she'd opened a sacred place she wasn't yet ready to share with anyone. She was surprised she'd sung *anything:* the melody had escaped her lips unwittingly and she felt guilty at revealing her sadness through song.

She'd exposed her private grief to strangers and betrayed her mother, brothers and sister; had somehow sullied their sacred memory.

'I don't remember where I heard it,' she lied. 'It may have been at one of the fairs, at Muff or Derry.'

'Ah, it's lovely,' said the cook. 'I love a heart-scalding song. Give us another verse or two.'

'That's all I remember,' Delia said sharply, tying off the damp bog grass. She hated lies and detested herself for her deceit, but she had given too much away already and was terrified these people would start to probe and poke until they made a small hole in her armor.

She was afraid her past would escape through any fissure in the dam she'd built inside her, that one day it would come gushing out in a raging torrent of painful emotions.

'It's Magdalen's turn to entertain now,' she said, in an attempt to deflect attention. 'Have you a favourite song or verse for us, Acushla?'

Delia couldn't be sure, but there was something inscrutably different about the way the child looked at her, as though she was trying to make up her mind about something.

'I'm going to sing Annie Laurie,' Magdalen said in a deliberate tone, still looking directly into Delia's eyes, 'or as much of it as I care to recall.'

'And *where* did you learn Annie Laurie?' the cook wanted to know. 'That's a song from the Scots, is it not?'

'Mamma has a book of poetry and song by a Scottish gentleman and she's teaching me to play Annie Laurie on the piano.'

'Well now, won't that be somethin' to hear when you're ready to perform. Let's have it then: sing your Annie Laurie, or as much of it as you care to,' Mrs Cleary mimicked.

'Maxwelton's brae's are bonnie, where early fa's the dew, and t'was there that Annie Laurie gave me her promise true…'

The pure dulcet tones rang through the lofty kitchen as Magdalen sang the sad tale. She'd chosen a spot in front of the fire for her stage and the moving curtain of steam provided a backdrop. She stood stiffly to attention, proud as a soldier on parade,with her head held high and her arms at her sides.

Each verse was sung flawlessly and she acknowledged their applause like a true performer as she bowed to her small audience of three.

They were busy turning the damp clothes when McVey, the old gentleman Delia had seen on the terrace, entered the room and stopped just inside the door. The cook made her way round the big table toward him and they huddled together, talking in hushed tones, until the cook looked up and caught Delia's eye and motioned her to join them. Her shrewd eyes scanned Delia from top to bottom as she spoke.

'It seems the doctor's paid her ladyship a surprise visit and he wants to give you the once over before he leaves.'

A silent McVey took her the same route as before, to the hallway on the main floor, where the doctor stood talking to Lady Keenagh.

They both stopped when Delia and the old butler appeared and, before McVey had been dismissed, the doctor addressed her.

'How are you doing, young miss? I must say, from where I'm standing you look a good deal better than the feverish waif I attended not so long ago. Mrs Cleary must be looking after you well.'

'Yes sir.' Delia answered. 'I'm overcome by the generosity and kindness of everyone in the Hall, and I thank you again; I'm feeling better by the day.'

'That's grand,' said Doctor Nowland. 'I'm glad to hear it. Have you any aches or pains, any dizziness or sudden weakness?'

'No sir, as I said, I'm quite my old self.'

The doctor smiled at her and turned to Lady Keenagh, peeling on his gloves as he spoke.

'Well, perhaps not quite your *old* self,' he chuckled. 'Your *old* self was at death's door, and I for one am very glad you didn't decide to knock and enter *that* particular portal.'

He fixed his attention on Lady Keenagh. 'I can't tell you how gratifying it is, your ladyship, to come across complete recovery in these bleak times. So much of my work is dealing with death these days and I don't mind telling you I'm heartsick with it all, for there seems no end to it. The cases are multiplying fast and the hospitals and workhouses are bursting at the seams with the sick and the dying. I hear the coroners have been ordered to suspend official enquiries; there are so many undocumented deaths, and not staff enough to investigate or record them. And more and more churches are closing their doors because the clergy have been stricken with typhoid and cholera.'

'How tragic,' said her ladyship with genuine distress, 'for those left behind, to see loved ones die and not be able to give them a decent Christian burial. Will this blight never end?'

Delia didn't hear any more. Her mind was already going over the implications of what the doctor had said about the coroners. Did it mean she could return home? If the doctor's information was accurate, her father's death would not be questioned. If he hadn't been found by now, after almost four months, surely there would be nothing left to find, except his torn clothing … and a blood-stained axe.

But, she tried to reason, it would be discolored and rusted by now and the dogs would likely have licked it clean after… She'd gone too far and felt the gorge rise quickly from deep in her stomach. She clamped a hand over her mouth, unable to suppress the violent spasms of retching. With her free hand, she grabbed the corner of her apron and tried to cover her mouth, but she had left it too late and she vomited on the polished tiles of the entrance hall.

'Oh my dear!' cried Lady Keenagh. 'How could we be so insensitive? Here, sit down and I'll open the door so you can get some air. Doctor Nowland, do you have your smelling salts with you?'

'This woman thinks smelling salts are a panacea for every ailment,' thought the doctor. He prudently ignored Lady Keenagh and sat beside Delia.

It was not smelling salts the child needed, he decided, but body salts. There was no substance to her and she still displayed traces of dehydration. He noted the parchment look of her skin and how the flesh had not completely filled out over her cheeks. He examined her mouth and placed a cool hand briefly to her forehead.

'No fever, thank God,' he declared. 'I may have been a bit

premature in thinking you well, my girl.'

'No sir,' Delia protested weakly. 'Really, I feel fine. It's only that I got myself into a state before I came upstairs. I've an overactive imagination and I frightened myself with thoughts of being dismissed.'

She tried to stand, but Lady Keenagh placed her hands on Delia's shoulders and bent low until their faces were level. She moved a hand to the girl's knee, suddenly shocked and filled with compassion when her fingers detected the sharp protrusion of bone beneath Delia's skirt.

'Listen to me now.' She told her. 'You're not to worry about that. There's nobody in this house, including the good doctor here, who will ever turn you out, so you mustn't fret or torment yourself with fears that are unfounded. You'll never recover completely if you do. Consider this your home for as long as you want to stay.'

Delia's mouth was foul with the bitter taste of bile and her ribs ached from retching. She turned her face toward the cold air that streamed through the front door.

How she hated deceiving these kind people, but what choice did she have? She knew she wasn't strong enough to strike out on her own, especially after what the doctor had said. From the sound of it, things were no better beyond the boundaries of the Hall. And what kind of God would judge her for choosing safety and a regular meal over an impossible struggle for survival?

She didn't speak again, but only nodded mutely in assent when asked if she'd like McVey to help her back to the safety of the kitchen.

Lady Keenagh may have done much to assuage Delia's fear of being turned out of the house, but she was as powerless as Delia herself to prevent the onset of nightmares.

Recurring scenes of suffering and death came without warning to invade her precious sleep, always catching her unawares and at her most vulnerable.

They reappeared later through the dark door of night: silent and poisonous. She awakened in a lather of cold sweat as fear transformed her innards and gripped them in a tightening vice of dread and panic, as she waited, afraid to open her eyes for fear of seeing the ghoulish images verified.

She held her crucifix tight to her chest and tried to concentrate on Catherine's steady breathing as she frantically whispered prayers, needing the reassurance of a familiar voice.

'Lord, I know you must be displeased with me, and I beg forgiveness for my lies, but I can't be sorry for what I did to my Da, and I can't promise I ever will be, and that's the honest truth. So if you can't accept it, you can show me by turning me out of here and I'll understand your message well enough. I'll accept my punishment until you see fit to redeem me, but in my defense, Lord, I rid this country of something evil. And although my poor Mammy is beyond his cruelty, I know he'd have found another weaker than himself to persecute, and he'd have used me for his perverse wants, so I've spared myself and the next poor woman from his wicked clutches. I shan't call him names Lord, for you know better than I, he was not one of your creations, but spawned by Beelzebub himself.'

She shivered violently at the recollection of her father and moved closer to Catherine, hungry for the warmth and presence of another.

There was no moonlight to penetrate the dark; no delineation visible between window and wall and when she dared to open her eyes and look she couldn't make out anything, but seemed to be afloat in an impenetrable cloud of blackness around her.

Chapter 13

Lord Keenagh returned from the Americas after almost two years absence. Her ladyship had received word of his impending arrival two weeks before his ship was due to dock in Belfast; from there he would visit his bankers in Londonderry.

The Hall was a frenzy of activity, much as it had been during the two previous Christmas holidays Delia had spent there. The only other time she'd ever seen Matty in such a tizzy had been earlier that year, when Hazel produced a sturdy colt with the exact markings of the stallion they had chosen to sire the mare.

Magdalen named the young horse Earl because, she told them, she'd been reading about the Flight of the Earls when Matty had brought news of the colt's birth. She was ecstatic and assumed ownership and care of the animal immediately. She insisted on being involved in every aspect of his grooming and Matty had nothing but praise for her efforts. The child never shied away from even the dirtiest of jobs, except to hold her nose and remark on the copious amounts of manure the young horse produced every day.

Between the new responsibilities, the girls still managed their daily walks. They explored new paths to stave off boredom and always found something new in nature to admire. Delia suggested a walk around the perimeter of the estate one day, and they followed the high stone wall to the Keeper's Lodge at the main south entrance.

It was a glorious September morning, one of the last hot days of summer. The meadows were dotted with generous clumps of daisies and the rowans were at the peak of their beauty. Their branches were dense with foliage and hung with grape-like clusters of red and yellow berries.

A faint perfume of maturing fruit scented the warm breeze and though it was not yet noon, it was already balmy enough to warrant the removal of their pinafores and bonnets.

Immediately they were out of sight of the house they took off their boots and stockings and laced them together. Everything else was stuffed into the deep crown of the bonnets they slung over their tanned forearms. They swung the hats carelessly as they strolled along, each of them inspired by the loveliness of the day to sing an impromptu verse or to recite odd lines of poetry.

They dawdled so much the sun was almost directly above them before the main entrance finally came into view and as soon as they turned the last corner they caught sight of Dermod, the lodge keeper, waving to them in the distance.

Delia was hungry and feared the old man would keep them chatting; but as they drew nearer, she saw that he was agitated. He shouted something neither of them could interpret and when he drew level with then, his breath came in such ragged bursts he was unable to speak coherently. Delia barely understood the tail end of the old man's announcement.

'Da's here, about this half hour past...' he gasped, and he leaned forward with both hands on his thighs. His head was bent almost to his knees as he fought to regulate his breath after rushing to meet them.

'What's wrong Dermod? Is it the foal?' Magdalen asked anxiously.

Dermod slowly straightened. He took time to unroll his shirtsleeves and wipe the sweat from his brow before answering. He inhaled deeply through his mouth and blew the air out noisily between pursed lips.

'No, miss Magdalen. Bless your heart. It's not the foal, but your *father*. He's after driving through these gates some half hour past and he'll—'

Magdalen heard no more. She was already flying down the driveway so fast Delia had no hope of catching her. She could only watch her recede and pray the child had heard her plea to put on her boots before her father saw her.

When she approached the house she saw the two figures huddled together at the top of the steps. Father and daughter had their heads bent close and each was totally engrossed in the other and Delia's heart melted to see His lordship's protective arm around his daughter's shoulders.

They didn't see her and she paused to watch them for a moment, feeling a deep poignancy and longing for something she'd never had. She felt like a thief: intrusive, as if she'd penetrated something precious and become an uninvited witness to their intimacy.

She sighed and walked slowly round to the back of the house, filled with a feeling she couldn't at first identify, until she recognized it as something she'd experienced before, and she hated herself for it. It was envy, pure and simple. Born of a deep yearning and a sense of loss for a father's love she'd never had, and could never hope to have.

She didn't meet Lord Keenagh formally until two days later, when Magdalen came into the kitchen pulling her father behind her.

The women stopped what they were doing at once and bobbed a curtsey to his lorship, who was forced to apply himself to dodging the kitchen obstacles his excited daughter tried to ignore. Delia heard the commotion from the pantry where she was wiping down the shelves. Once Magdalen spotted her, she let go of her father's hand and made the introductions.

'Father, this is my new friend Delia who has been very sick, so you are to be extra nice to her and not frighten her.'

His lordship laughed and gave his daughter's braid a playful tug.

'Yes, ma'am,' he said in mock compliance, bowing low. 'I am glad to have you in my household, Delia,' he told her with a smile. 'My wife has informed me of your recent circumstances, and of your kindness toward herself and Magdalen. I thank you and commend you for showing such concern, when you yourself must have been suffering a great deal.'

Delia bowed her head and then looked up again into eyes identical to Magdalen's. They were the only remarkable feature in an otherwise nondescript but friendly face. He wasn't a handsome man, though none of his features were displeasing, and he had no visible deformities. He *was* one of the tallest men she'd ever seen, and he wore a riding habit, minus the whip, that Magdalen now used as a drumstick. Her erratic rapping on the wooden table echoed through the unusually quiet kitchen.

Lord Keenagh glanced fondly at his daughter and smiled.

'She seems to have grown a great deal taller in my absence, and from what her mother tells me it could well be due to the frequent daily exercise you are both fond of taking.'

'I've grown very close to her, sir, for she's a loveable child. Her energy knows no bounds, but she's been a great comfort to me.' She saw his quizzical look and explained. 'I'm prone to fits of melancholy from time to time.'

'I'm glad to hear she's a solace to you,' said his lordship. 'Thank you again Delia, and I hope you'll find some measure of contentment while you're here.' He turned on his heel and addressed his daughter, who had now gathered a collection of cups, plates and glassware on the large table as part of her makeshift drum set.

'Come, my precious, and let the women get on.'

But Magdalen had already become used to having her father home and was secure enough to be parted from him. She stayed in the kitchen to help Delia re-stack the pantry shelves, and chattered non-stop about her father the great adventurer, who had, she claimed, travelled all over Ireland and across the Irish Sea to Scotland, England and France and other faraway places she couldn't yet pronounce.

Delia resisted the urge to straighten the jars Magdalen had stacked randomly on the lower shelves and bent to kiss her instead.

'We'll ask your parents if we can use the globe in the library one day soon. McVey can get the big atlas down for us and I'll show you all the places your father has visited.'

Magdalen wasted no time and approached her father in short order for permission and his lordship granted them use of the library for a couple of hours each day, after their walks. Delia felt strangely comfortable surrounded by the walls of books in the amply stocked library. She'd never owned a book, nor was she likely to, she thought, but she *was* familiar with the bible and there'd always been a good stout edition in her home, until her father filched it for his ale money, along with everything else he could lay his thieving hands on.

Books had been the sole ownership of her teacher, the Great John Kane, and he had been generous in allowing Delia and some of the other children access to such books as he possessed. The students' interest had been sparked by the illustrations which had prompted many lively discussions and added credence to the text.

'How Mr Kane would have loved this room,' she thought, as she scanned the shelves that first morning. But it was also Delia's Utopia and she ran her hands over the rich leather spines and her fingers traced the deep indentations of the gilt-embossed titles. She lifted an older volume to her face and caught the unmistakable fustiness of ancient hide, and she delighted to hear the crackle of parched paper as she carefully turned the yellowed pages.

'What a treasure trove this is!' She said to Magdalen. 'There was nothing like this in my Hedge school. We were lucky to have four walls and a roof, never mind books for the learning.'

She browsed a section that seemed dedicated to young scholars and pounced eagerly upon a book she knew and loved.

'Well! If it isn't Freeny the Robber! Isn't that typical of him, being where he's not supposed to be?' She sat on a window ledge and flicked through the pages. 'I remember the stories of Freeny well. My teacher had no time for him and would never allow the telling of his antics among us kids. Sure, there must be a hundred books here, and I had to bump into Freeny. The old finagler could squeeze his way in through a crack in the wall.'

Magdalen was at the piano, thumbing through her Annie Laurie music, and she answered absent-mindedly.

'There's a lot more than a hundred books. Father knows the exact number. There's a great to-do whenever a gap appears on the shelves. Pappa can tell at a glance if one is missing.' She stopped suddenly and turned to Delia. 'Where's Hedge School?' she asked, already losing interest in her music.

'Not *where* but *what*,' Delia replied. 'Come here to me and I'll tell you all about my school.'

They settled on the window seat and tucked a shawl around their legs to protect against the cool of the glass. It was still early and the sun had not yet warmed the panes, nor melted the light layer of hoar frost that capped the hedges outside. Delia felt the familiar strong surge of love as she made Magdalen comfortable.

The child couldn't know how painful it was at times for Delia to be so close to her. At moments like this, with her little head resting on Delia's arm, or whenever she looked at her with those eyes filled with the degree of complete trust and honesty only a child can offer, the same way her siblings had done, whenever she'd told them stories, these moments brought back bittersweet memories and a yearning for the sheer contentment of old times.

She wasn't aware her eyes had filled with unshed tears until the child asked her why she was crying.

'Bless you darlin'! I'm not crying. I was gazing into the brightness outside for too long and it's made my eyes water.'

They fussed until they were both settled and Delia began, but not before chiding Magdalen. 'Now—you've to sit still and not fidget, else I'll tell the cook you have worms in your belly and she'll make you eat a worm cake, and you won't like *that* one bit.' She flipped a plait over Magdalen's shoulder and began her history lesson.

'In 1690, long before you or I were even thought of, the English lawmakers banned education for all Catholics in Ireland...'

'Why?' the child asked innocently.

'*You* didn't wait long to interrupt now, did you?' Delia scolded. 'I'm not sure why. But I think it was their King and Queen decided, after rumour reached their ears about our cleverness. Sure, weren't we able to outwit all the fancy dandies that came over from the mainland to persecute and bamboozle us?'

'The English were afraid we'd get too smart altogether, so they forbade us the learning. But they soon discovered how sharp-witted we are. Our people were determined to show the English and the rest of the known world the strength of our spirit; so before long, teachers came out of hiding and taught under cover of any shelter available to them. I was lucky. In my townland there was a wealthy lady who gave our teacher free use of her barn. She even provided slates and chalks and the odd bundle of clothes for us ragged urchins. Most of the cotters' poor children got the learning hiding under hedges or in deep hollows, without shelter from wind or rain. There was no telling where the learning would be given from one day to the next. Hedge School teachers were always dodging the authorities, especially in my grandmammy's day.

'My teacher was Great John Kane, the cleverest man in all

of Inishowen. He was training for the priesthood at Maynooth, but lucky for me he changed his mind and decided teaching was his true calling. He was passionate about the learning and passed his enthusiasm to his pupils. On a good day, there were only six of us in that barn, and there were long periods when Great John Kane never got paid so much as half a spud, but whenever we could, we'd bring a brick or two of peat or a couple of eggs for his fee.'

She paused and smiled at sight of a contented Magdalen chewing at the end of one of her braids, happy as a solitary cow in a field full of clover.

'Mr Kane persevered without regular wages because we were such a bright bunch; we had the cuteness about us.'

Delia had forgotten her young charge as she became embroiled in memories of her childhood.

'He was champion at telling the tales. He even taught us girls some Latin and the boys a little Greek. Before long, word of his cleverness spread and many a time he was challenged by usurpers—bright young boreens and traveling teachers, some of them with heads bursting from all the learning they'd had at the fancy colleges in Dublin and Belfast. But none could outwit Great John Kane. He was highly respected among gentry and clergy alike. A lovely man he was, gifted and generous, as was his father before him. It was his father taught my Grandmammy, God rest her soul.'

She shifted Magdalen's elbow from beneath her ribs and continued while she still had the child's attention.

'I remember Mammy told me a story once, about a Mr Wakefield from England, who visited grandmammy's school. He told the local dignitaries he was astounded at the amount of knowledge, and the quality of the learning in the people. But there'd been schools in grandmammy's parish since long before her time, and you can't snuff out the desire for learning in anyone, not once the flame is lit.'

The child began to squirm and Delia decided to cut her story short. Magdalen had unbraided her hair and was twisting the long strands around and around her index finger.

The movement disturbed Delia and she couldn't think why; or why she spoke so sharply to her.

'Come on, Fidgety Fingers, let's go and see if Mrs Cleary will let us have a treat before lunch. I'm thirsty and in great need of a cup of tea after all my blathering.'

'But I want you to tell me about Freeny the Robber!' Magdalen cried, as she tugged at the ends of the shawl Delia was trying to fold.

'Is that any way to ask?' Delia scolded. 'Wouldn't your mother and father be mightily put out if I was to tell them you've lost your manners?'

'Please, please, please, and more please.' The child begged with her hands joined in supplication and her face contorted in such a tortured expression, Delia's unease dissolved, and she burst out laughing.

'Calm down now, and sit beside me.' She waited until Magdalen stopped fussing with the folds of her skirts. 'Are you quite finished now, Miss Fidget? At this rate, it'll be dark before we get started. I'll save Freeny for another time and tell you about Timmy the Tinker instead.'

She put a finger to Magdalen's lips to silence further protest, and related her version of Timmy the Tinker.

Chapter 14

Magdalen hadn't moved for a while and Delia thought she'd fallen asleep. She shifted slightly and began to slowly free her arm which was trapped beneath the child's head, but Magdalen suddenly sat up, wide awake.

'I missed the end of the story!' she wailed. 'What happened to the tinker?'

Delia laughed and cuffed her chin playfully. 'Timmy did alright for himself, and I *will* tell you more of his adventures, but that's enough for one day. I said I'd tell you one story, and one is all you're getting.'

Browsing through the library collection and telling the tinker's story released a flood of childhood memories in Delia. It was as though the years had been trapped between the pages of the books and as she turned a page, images of her teacher at the entrance to the barn where he'd always greeted each child by name, came floating back.

She'd been one of his favourite pupils, and she in turn had loved him. He seldom raised his voice and never used a hazel rod on his charges. The worst punishment he inflicted was to make them stand for an hour on a hay bale with their backs to the class, and, more often than not, he would lift the offender down before the hour had passed.

In winter months, the pupils piled the bales into makeshift windbreaks and huddled behind them, protected from the brunt of the wind that found purchase between the broken slats and the ill-fitting doors, and during a freeze, when their fingers stiffened so much they couldn't hold a piece of chalk between them, or when rumour reached them the authorities were on the prowl, they would climb high into the hayloft and hide beneath a rough blanket of straw until the coast was clear.

The last memories were so clear she felt an itch and a prickle behind her knees and unconsciously bent down to scratch them.

Great John Kane fostered her love of hedgerow plants and birds. He took his charges on long nature walks and showed them the invisible life that teemed beneath the rocks and in the shallow pools on the beach. She had dreaded being dismissed for the day because it meant she would have to turn for home and the uncertainty of what might greet her whenever her father was back from the mainland.

The teacher had been astute enough to notice the bruising and cuts on Delia and one or two of the other pupils. He knew they were not the result of a fall or a childhood scrap. He'd even been bold enough to challenge Barney Dreenan once or twice when Delia's beatings had been severe, but although he was respected by the clachan he was powerless to interfere, and his intervention only made it worse for the children. He was forced to accept the disturbing evidence before him and constantly battled with his conscience. It was the main reason he could not bring himself to punish the children while they were in his care.

Magdalen tugged impatiently at her arm. 'Are we having another story—or going for tea?' she asked.

'I'm sorry, sweet one. I was miles away, thinking about my old school. I'll tell you what, we'll do both. Let's go and get a drink and I'll tell you some tales in the kitchen, that way Catherine and Mrs C will have benefit too.' She closed the book and replaced it on the shelf. 'Will I give you a piggy-back to the kitchen?' she asked. A delighted Magdalen hoisted her skirts in answer and wrapped her arms around Delia's neck as they walked and 'galloped', in unladylike fashion along the hallway toward the kitchen stairs.

After lunch, it rained so heavily it drummed loudly against the windows and they watched from the warmth of the kitchen as water gushed from the downspout in a fierce torrent and ricocheted off the cobbles.

'Just the weather for a story,' Delia remarked, as she turned away from the miserable scene outside. 'There isn't a break in the clouds and I'm betting this is on for the day.'

Magdalen had lunched with the three women and was now practicing another recently-acquired skill of knitting. It was the women's habit to knit mittens, scarves and hats for the poor people of the parish. But, since Magdalen had not quite mastered the basic stitch, she was given a length of flax string and shown how to knit a simple dish cloth. She grunted and growled with impatience and suddenly flung her work away from her and crossed her arms defiantly.

'What's brought this on?' the cook asked, as she bent to retrieve the knitting. 'Are you after droppin' another stitch?'

Magdalen pouted and stuck out her chin. 'I'll never get the hang of it. I've been on the same row for a week and you've all done so much.'

'Aren't I tired tellin' you,' Mrs Cleary said patiently, 'the best way to learn is by watching. Sit still and watch, and you'll be knittin' Donegal shawls in no time.'

'But you all knit so *fast*,' Magdalen complained. 'I can't see what you're doing. Your fingers are flying.'

Delia listened with sympathy, remembering the times she'd pleaded with her Mammy to slow down so she could learn the basic stitch. She put her work to one side and reached out for Magdalen.

'Come. Sit on my lap and we'll go through it together,' she

said. 'Hold on to the needles and I will guide your hands.' She covered the child's hands with her own and slowly made a stitch.

'The right needle goes through the loop on the left needle. That's it. Now, wrap the flax over the lower needle and keep the thread taut with your right hand. This is the tricky part, so let me guide your right hand. Slowly now, pull the lower needle toward you and catch the bottom of the stitch you're working on. That's it! You've almost got it. Pull it up onto the right needle and slip the left loop off and away.'

Magdalen's stitches were tight and the coarse flax thread had no slide against the rough wooden needles, making it difficult to maintain the correct tension, but they persevered to the end of a row.

After a few repetitions, the child resumed her efforts and the women took it in turn to slow down whenever she needed to watch closely, and for a while the only sound in the kitchen was the click of knitting needles.

Once Magdalen relaxed, she remembered Delia's promise of another story and this time, Delia saw there was no getting out of it and she shared more childhood memories of school.

'Did I tell you my teacher was also a champion seanachai?' she asked her. 'Lord, but he was a grand one for the stories. He was no Timmy the Tinker for sure.'

'Do we have any lady teachers in Ireland?' Magdalen suddenly asked.

'We certainly do,' Delia answered. She took the child's knitting from her and picked up a few slipped stitches before giving it back.

'It's still much too tight, bye the bye,' she added, cupping the child's chin in her hand. 'Are you not keeping company with three of the best lady teachers, right now?'

It took Magdalen a moment to understand. 'I don't mean *you*! I'm talking about *real* teachers." She said. 'Do we have any women with "great" before their names, like your John Kane?'

'Sadly, we do not,' Delia told her. 'But anyone with a grain of sense knows mothers are the best teachers in the world; sure, their lessons are invaluable—and what's more, they don't charge a farthing for them. Now—do you want to hear about my school or not?'

'I would like to hear about the adventures of Maeve the warrior queen, and Cuchulainn and Conall and big Red Hugh...'

'Now you know it's not our part to speak of such things,' replied Delia, before quoting an old saying of her mother's.

'A woman's work is to take the wool and all the night to weave, while the duty of the men is to tell the tales of the braeve.'

'Is that enough to settle it with you?' she asked, and Magdalen nodded acceptance.

Young as she was, she knew the ancient tales of heroism were the sole domain of the men. Besides, many of the stories took days to relate and heroic tales could only be told after dark, since the the people believed the devil only appeared at night, and he wouldn't dare enter a house where tales of bravery were being recounted.

The tillers of the soil were also the seanachais or storytellers, and each of them was closely monitored during a recitation. Errors were not tolerated among the men, but contested immediately; for this reason, father and son, brothers and close kin could not witness a storytelling together, in order to preclude any risk of discord within a family.

In this time-proven way of committing their ancestors to memory, they kept their Irish history intact; indisputable, and alive through the centuries.

They led a hard life in a wild, inhospitable land, yet her people were a gentle, easygoing race, faithful to the Gaelic tongue and fiercely protective of each other. Most had no ambition to explore beyond their own towns or clachans.

It sufficed them to travel the boundless world of the imagination; to enter in dreams the mythical adventures of the larger-than-life characters that dominated the ancient tribes.

They were united in a common thirst for knowledge. They hungered for education, and both male and female scholars doggedly mastered the intricacies of Latin and Greek, and learnt by heart the lengthy verses of Oissin, Ireland's greatest poet. The stories of St Patrick, one of Oissin's most ardent admirers, were among their most beloved.

There were no petty jealousies; no definitions of poverty or class; how could there be, among a people who shared everything they had and were equal in every possible way? Their only differences were physical, and strong blood ties ran deep and pure, perpetuated in large part by a terrain that served to isolate them but also bonded them.

They cohabited in harmony with each other and with the land they tilled, and even the shortest separation was a cause of great distress among them. When they weren't at honest work, they delighted in each other's company as they ate, sang, danced and played together.

Explorers and learned travelers occasionally infiltrated the communities and wrote in amazement about the gentle people who possessed incredible powers of retention, perfected from the need to commit everything to memory. It was not uncommon to find men, women and even young children fluent enough to recite hundreds of lines of verse with total accuracy, in the ancient tongues of Gaelic, Greek and Latin.

'Do you know that every time you tell a story you get a blessing from God?' Delia asked Magdalen. Her eyes met the cook's and she winked slyly at her but Mrs Cleary chirped in before the child could reply.

'Now *that's* new to my ears. I've never heard that said before. But it's no good to me, for I can't keep anything straight in this head o' mine.'

'Don't disturb your good self, Mrs C,' Delia told her. 'The work of your hands is the best form of prayer and a supreme offering to God. And aren't you at it morning, noon and night? Sure he must be heaping blessings on you by the hour.'

'Ah, now it's one thing to have the learnin',' the cook replied. 'But being cute with it is quite another matter—and you're cute with it, Delia Dreenan. I bet you could charm the birds out of the trees with your blarney.'

They knitted quietly for another hour or two, until Matty came in from the rain, ragged as a drowned rat.

'Dia agus Muir libh,' he intoned. 'May God and Mary be with us all.' The women returned his greeting and Catherine dropped her knitting at sight of him and fetched a towel for his hair.

'I'm after blatherin' with Joey O' Doherty at the crossroads,' he mumbled, his face hidden by the folds of the towel as he rubbed his hair vigorously.

'He tells me there's to be an official countin' of the people in a week; most likely it'll start on the feast of Beltane.'

'Sweet mother o mercy!' Mrs Cleary cried. 'They couldn't have picked a worse time. May Beltane is madness. The men'll be running in all directions to scatter the seeds and the women'll be fair distracted from hidin' the butter!' She put down her knitting and pointed one of the needles at them. 'And I don't have to remind any of you that *nothing* is to leave this house, not even a whisper from your mouths, on the feast of Beltane.'

Matthew removed his dripping jacket and gave it a vigorous shake at the kitchen door before he put it back on again and headed upstairs.

'I'd best tell McVey, and he can pass the news to his lordship as he sees fit.'

Delia gleaned more in the next couple of days as tidbits filtered through from upstairs. She didn't have any memory of the '41 Census but thought it unlikely her family had ever been enumerated. Like most cottages, theirs would have been deserted during the daylight hours, particularly during the busy months of spring. She didn't want to be home for this one either, and spent anxious hours worrying about escaping the questions the census officials would ask.

She'd never told anyone at the Hall her townland of birth, but that would be the first piece of information the census clerk would want to know—unless she was away from the house. But how was she to escape for the day without arousing suspicion?

The matter was taken out of her hands. April 30th, the eve of Beltane, occurred on a Wednesday and coincided with Catherine's day off, leaving little chance for Delia to be anywhere other than the kitchen. There were many rituals to be performed and she was busy from first light, when she scattered the thresholds of the Hall with flowers as an invocation to St Brigid to bless the house with a plentiful harvest.

Matty and the laborers had gathered Hawthorn branches and a large bunch was placed in the center of the kitchen table, the gold and white balls symbolically representing butter and milk. Outside, the men had already prepared a bonfire, one of many that would be visible all over Ireland once darkness descended.

Someone would bring in a burning stick from the bonfire, as a further symbol of purity and good luck for the house. Then one of the laborers would be given the honour of performing the ancient ritual of taking a smoldering brick from the bonfire and carrying it round the perimeter three times before flinging it into a newly sown field, a further plea to St Brigid to keep the soil warm enough to root the seeds.

Catherine had picked bunches of Yarrow before she left and they were hung about the bedrooms of the house to ward off illness.

But it was Matty who had the most important task of all. He took the milk churns from the dairy and washed them thoroughly in three different streams, which meant a ride to the well in Culdaff, a second wash in the Keenagh River and a third in the stream that ran through a neighboring estate.

May was the month of Mary and time for the re-birth of nature. Everything had to be pristine and the gods satisfied if they were to have healthy crops in the autumn.

At first light Mrs Cleary gathered the first batch of freshly churned butter and went forth to hide it and Delia was left to deposit the rest in a crudely made, but very effective, cool box, buried in the ground and concealed beneath a couple of cobblestones outside the kitchen door.

The dark hole was big enough for several slabs of butter. It was a time-proven and efficient method of keeping it fresh. Delia's back ached from churning half the night and her knees felt numb from contact with the hard cobbles. She sat back and rubbed them hard, momentarily distracted by a pair of Brimstone butterflies that made their way haltingly across the yard.

They fluttered a couple of inches above the ground in a secret ritual; the male close behind the female, until they paused on a small carpet of white petals that trembled in the cold wind of a spring still reluctant to come.

She shivered and remembered the mountain of tasks that awaited her. As she turned to go back in the house, she almost collided with Matty, who was going in ahead of her carrying a large bundle of whin. She stood behind him and watched obediently as he wound flax string tightly round the spiky shrub, until it resembled a broom head. This he thrust up and down the chimney, paying little heed to the generous fire that burned in the grate.

He chanted aloud, as he worked hard to rid the aperture of any pishogue that could be lurking, ready to steal the butter.

'Bless all of us here O' Queen of the May, and send any mischievous Woodkerns away.'

When he was satisfied the chimney was clear, he threw the whin among the flames saying, 'This hearth is purified and free of bad spirits.'

When it came to the precious butter, whin was the best protection. Delia joined Matty and cook around the fire and they held hands as they chanted the final prayer for Beltane.

'May God bless this dwelling, fireside and walls, and all the hearts that beat within. Amen.'

The remainder of the feast day was stringently observed and not even a whisper escaped the doors of the Hall. There was no time for mischief. Beltane heralded the busiest period and everyone was kept occupied with extra chores.

Chapter 15

His Lordship received the census forms from Derry and interviewed each of the staff in turn. By the time Delia was summoned, she'd been rehearsing her answers for ten days and was surprised how easily the falsehoods tripped off her tongue.

She told his lordship she thought her birthplace to be the remote island of Tullaghobegley, but that she couldn't be sure, since her deceased parents had never been in agreement about where she'd been born.

She didn't deceive him any more than she had to, and was truthful about her siblings, but she changed the forenames of her parents, as well as her mother's maiden name.

When asked about their deaths, she told him their father had deposited them at the gates of Buncrana workhouse and instructed them to wait for his return. Her abandoned family had died one after the other, and she didn't know the time and place of her father's death, since he had been out foraging when he'd succumbed; indeed, she couldn't be absolutely sure he *was* deceased. He had simply not returned.

His lordship sensed her pain at recollection of her family and did not press her for details. He put down his quill and spoke gently to her.

'My latest understanding is the situation is beginning to ease and food supplies are becoming available, although many counties are still in desperate straits. Survivors are fleeing the country and ships continue to leave the ports of Derry and Queenstown daily, filled with poor souls eager to try their luck in America or Canada.'

Lord Keenagh pulled a large kerchief from his waistcoat pocket and wiped his hands, studying them closely as he continued to speak.

'There are one or two unscrupulous landlords whose sole aim seems to be the acquisition of maximum profit, from tenants who are hard pressed to find even a ha'penny for a crust of bread. It is said they will not cease until their lands are cleared of the cottiers and replaced with more profitable and less spirited grazing cattle.' He cleared his throat awkwardly and gave a derisive laugh. 'I suppose we must be grateful they are small in number, but they are a bad example of the Irish landowner Delia, and I fear their reputation sullies the rest of us.'

When she related this later, to Matty and the cook, Matty was able to update them further.

'His lordship is misinformed,' he told them. 'Buncrana is no better than when we last rode through it, and I hear the evictions are still being served during the winter months, to avoid the landlords having to compensate the evicted tenants for any crops left lying in the soil.'

Matty was clearly very angry and his voice was filled with bitterness. 'It's murder!' he cried. 'Cold blooded murder! To turn out a poor family with no food in their bellies and no clothes on their backs in the cruel months of winter is to murder them in the most heartless fashion. The poor bastards are doomed to suffer a lingering death. Who'll be accountable for all this? That's what I'd like to know.'

His anger was infectious and the women became incensed, and Delia struggled to keep hers under control when she answered him.

'No moneyed persons will ever be held responsible, I can tell you that much. Our people are broken in body and spirit, easy prey for the English vultures who begrudge them their last breath. Do you know that insensitive Queen of theirs paid a visit to Queenstown last summer? They had such a lavish party, the Lord Lieutenant of Ireland was left with a bill for two thousand pounds. Can you make any sense of it at all? While she and her minions stuffed themselves with sweetmeats in the Town Hall, her subjects were groaning on the quayside not yards away, begging for a stale crust or a cup of water.'

Matty suddenly punched a fist hard into the palm of his hand. 'I hear now that the Quakers have pulled out,' he said. 'And the rates have increased one hundred fold, from thirteen shillings to thirteen pounds. Even the auld hag's favorite newspaper is calling for some compassion for our people. It defies all reason, all sense of decency. It's got me flummoxed, I don't mind tellin' you. The English bleeders wouldn't give us so much as the skin off the milk.'

The growing intensity of Delia's rage frightened her. She grabbed her coat and stepped out into the yard to calm down. Through the tall wooden gates she could see vivid splashes of wild primroses and bluebells sprouting among the blades of grass. The air was sweet and wholesome after the rain, but the beauty distressed her after hearing Matty's news. *'Endless beauty: hand in hand with unimaginable horror,'* she thought sadly. *'Two unlikely bedfellows; is it any wonder I'm torn to pieces; it's too big a burden for me.'* She was tired. Tired of the constant reminders and worn out with guilt and sorrow. She sat in the yard and wept bitterly for her family and for the ongoing suffering of her people.

Through the blur of her tears she saw, on the brow of a distant hill, a clump of Rowans. 'Flying Rowans,' Matty called them. He'd explained the young trees were not deliberately planted, but had sprung up from seeds dropped by the birds. The

Rowan tree was shrouded in mystery and, over time, its wood had been used for anything that smacked of the supernatural, from water diviners, and lightning rods to magician's wands.

Sprigs of it still hung about the stables and cattle pens; trusted simples against disease, and Rowan berries were harvested for treatment of many ailments. To stand beneath the branches of a Rowan was to be protected from all harm. *'A pity the birds didn't drop enough seeds to create forests of Rowans. Sufficient to protect the whole population,'* thought Delia sadly.

The jovial mood of the day was lost and she turned abruptly back to the house, feeling helpless and deflated; at odds with the beauty beyond the gates, and she wondered for the thousandth time if she'd ever see a period of peace and plenty in Ireland.

It was months before she could shake off her depression enough to appreciate anything. She woke one morning feeling vaguely out of sorts. Apart from a nagging ache in her lower back she could find no reason for her malaise, but she felt the onset of a headache and decided a breath of air was what she needed.

Autumn was now upon them and it was quite dark when she stepped outside, but the temperature was mild and she unbuttoned her jacket and removed her hair ribbon, shaking the thick tresses free as she scanned the sky and sucked in deep gulps of bracing air.

Her headache was soothed by a tremendous flood of gratitude for her changed circumstances, and for the magnificence of nature that gradually revealed its glory in the emerging light of a new day.

'This is my bliss,' she thought to herself. *'All this majesty — this breathtaking loveliness, is my bliss. It swells my heart. I breathe, and am blessed with the precious gift of life. My cup is overflowing Lord and I am grateful, but please, don't give me more than my fair share*

while others are suffering. The weight of guilt is too much for me.'

She strolled down a gravel path toward the formal gardens and the man-made lake beyond. She hadn't been this way for a long time. She thought the manicured landscape too perfect in this area of the grounds and found the precision and orderly layout of the gardens somehow detracted from the natural beauty.

On the far bank of the oval lake, two trees loomed above the rest, dominating the view. They were ugly specimens and they towered above the other shrubs and plants; incongruous against the dark, glossy leaves of the Holly and Rhododendron bushes and the rich copper leaves of the Red Maples. The entire far bank appeared to rise from behind a screen of tall bull rushes, a vista of perfectly blended hues and textures along the water's edge.

A pair of white swans glided elegantly across her field of vision like two ethereal ghosts emerging from the layer of early morning mist that lingered above the surface of the lake. Their majesties barely disturbed the mirror surface of the water, yet a russet leaf in their wakes spun like a miniature coracle.

It was breathtaking, but she wondered if the deliberate design had replaced a former natural scene, superior in beauty.

She was about to turn for home when a series of sharp pains in her lower belly brought her to her knees.

She bent in shock and waited for the spasm to pass and went through a mental list of what she'd eaten the night before, to find a reason for the sickening pains that were rising again as she folded herself double in a new wave of agony.

She gritted her teeth and waited for the pain to ease, but as she did, her belly tensed in anticipation of the next spasm and she became aware of a wet stickiness beneath her skirts, a loss that had become a vague memory. After an absence of years, her monthly bleeds were back with a vengeance.

The pains gripped her every few minutes and each time she

had to stop and bend forward with her hands pressed hard against the location of the agony. She cursed each crippling wave and it took her an hour to re-trace the path of her short walk until at last she staggered into the kitchen clutching her abdomen and groaning loudly.

Mrs Cleary and Catherine needed no explanation and she was seated beside the fire with a cup of chamomile tea and a warming pan to her belly, whilst Catherine fetched some cotton strips.

'Mother of God—must I always be cursed with something?' she cried, as she waited for the herb tea and the warmth to bring some relief.

Mrs Cleary tutted loudly and scowled at her. 'Whisht girl. 'Tis a blessing on you, and not a curse at all. Isn't it proof of your healing? God's way of lettin' you know you've the gift of childbearing in you?'

'You've a strange way of looking at things, Mrs C,' Delia gasped between spasms. 'But I daresay you're right. Except, if this is a sample of the agony of childbirth, I think I'll keep my legs firmly crossed until my childbearing years are safe behind me. I wonder if God gave his own Blessed Mother such punishing agony every month.'

Mrs Cleary's routine had been interrupted and she was in no mood to comfort or reassure. 'Ah, behave yourself. God doesn't send you any more than you're able to bear. What you're goin' through is nuthin' compared to the agony of Jesus in the Garden o' Gethsemane. So get that tea down you, and when you're done you can start on the darnin'. I'll spare you from any standing chores for the day. Catherine is away off now and Matty is after taking her ladyship and the little one into Malin, so you should have a few hours peace while they're gone.'

She was very glad of the unexpected quiet and it transpired that she and the cook had the kitchen to themselves for best part of the day. Delia darned her way steadily through a deep basket of worn socks while the cook did her scheduled work, as well as Catherine's, until she was finally able to sit down for a tea break in mid afternoon.

'Jaysus,' she sighed, as she heaved herself into her chair. 'My string's gettin' too short for this load. My auld bones are achin' for want of a rest.' She cradled the teacup in both hands and looked Delia over carefully. 'Are your pains any easier? My God, but you're as white as a sheet, girl! Would this be the normal course of things for you?'

Delia was feeling much better and hastened to convince the cook. 'I'm grand, Mrs C. To tell the truth, I'd forgotten all about the bleeds. Mine have been stopped these many months past.'

The cook studied her thoughtfully and never took her eyes off her as she deftly cut off a chunk from a solid cake of tobacco and pushed it tightly into the bowl of her pipe, padding it down with her thumb. Delia had seldom seen her indulge, except for the rare occasions like today, when there was nobody around to disturb her enjoyment. Mrs Cleary sat back and puffed away contentedly on the thin stem of the pipe as she eased her feet out of her shoes.

'I never had the chance to ask if you're quite settled here,' she began, 'but I think I know the answer. For its plain to see on the faces of young Magdalen and Catherine Nolan that you're a welcome addition to this house. I've been glad of your help many a time myself, and I know Matty Friel won't hear a word said against you.'

'And all this time I've been here, I've never really thanked *you* properly, Mrs C,' Delia replied. 'It's to my eternal shame, since I've much to be grateful for and many people to thank for saving my life. And you're right, I should be down on my knees thanking God that I'm able to feel anything at all. From now on, I'll take any suffering he sees fit to send me without complaint, as a penance for my own selfishness.'

'I'm sure you've had more than your share o' Purgatory already,' said the cook. 'Do you want to tell me what you were doing before Buncrana?'

Delia replied quickly, perhaps too quickly. Mrs Cleary stopped pulling at her pipe and scrutinized her closely.

'I don't, Mrs Cleary, and that's the truth of it. My heart bleeds afresh whenever I think of my loved ones lying in an unmarked grave, without so much as a stone, as if they counted for nothing on this earth. And here am I, sitting here complaining about a little bellyache. I'm filled with shame. I'll tell you the bare facts but no more; if I go too far into it I'll be away with the fairies, as sure as God is my judge.'

She busied herself and struggled to swing the heavy fire kettle off to the side so she could poke new life into the smoldering peat, and not until she'd coaxed flames from the dying bricks did she begin to speak of the horrors once more, pausing to compose herself whenever she felt the onset of tears.

'My family died from the hunger—my younger sister and two baby brothers and my darl... my parents. I'm careworn with asking God why he chose to spare me, but I've no answer, except if it was to punish me for someone else's evil doings then I've well paid the price. I've looked into the jaws of Hell, Mrs C, and I've felt the Devil's foul breath on me more than once.'

Mrs Cleary crossed herself quickly and tapped out the pipe on the hearth, knocking it sharply against the stone three times. She blew into the bowl to dislodge the last of the tobacco ash and tapped three times more.

'The Father, the Son and the Holy Ghost,' she intoned in time with the second set of tapping. 'Protect us, Lord, from the Devil and his dark angels.'

She leaned up to replace the pipe on the mantel. 'It's still awful bad for the country, Delia. I hear things from the delivery men, and Matty has told me of unmentionable suffering he's seen on his trips beyond the hall. Disease is outstrippin' the starvation and the doctors themselves are droppin' like flies. Now we've instructions from upstairs not to allow deliveries inside the gates. The butcher has to leave the meat at the lodge and collect his payment from Dermod. What's to become of us? Will this nightmare never end?'

'I've no answer for you,' Delia said wearily. 'Another war or a major revolt may be the only solution for Ireland, but there's little chance of that, with the general populous being so weak. There's hardly one among them could raise so much as a fist, let alone an *army.'*

'I'm awful glad that my own Ma and Da are not here to witness the desperate suffering,' said Mrs Cleary. She sighed. 'I'll make us another cup of tea and then I'll read your tea leaves, if you like.'

The light was fading as Delia put aside the mending and began to light the cruisies and candles scattered around the room. There was a delicious-smelling stew on the hearth for both family and staff, so little preparation was needed for the evening meal.

The cook had baked some bread and there was fresh fruit and cheese for upstairs. Her ladyship and Magdalen would have lunched in Malin and wouldn't require the usual four or five courses at dinner, and Lord Keenagh was not fond of too much food in the evenings, believing it impaired his sleep and encouraged bad dreams and indigestion.

Delia drained her cup and inverted it onto the saucer, turning it first to the right and then to the left. She then passed it to Mrs Cleary, who lifted it eagerly and leaned toward the firelight, the better to see the clump of dark tea leaves at the bottom of the cup. Delia decided she didn't need to hear any more prophecies of bad luck and was about to tell the cook, but she hesitated a moment too long.

'My stars, but you've a lot goin' on here,' Mrs Cleary exclaimed, peering into the cup. Delia leaned forward, curious to see for herself, but the cook stopped her.

'A minute now, 'til I sort the chaff from the wheat.' She cradled the cup in both hands and squinted into its depths. 'I see a great body of water here, a mighty sea, and there's two white horses riding the waves and a barking dog on the deck of a ship—I don't like that. The horses are lucky enough, but the dog is a sign of vexation. Someone close to you is going to be angry and there'll be ripples for a long time when this particular dam bursts...'

She was warming up nicely and Delia was about to remind her that she didn't have anybody close to her, since her family were all gone, when the kitchen door opened and Matty stormed in with a face like thunder.

'Delia Dreenan!' he shouted, wagging his finger at her. ''Tis shocked I am, shocked and sharoose. You've let me down and no mistake, and you've got me into a firkin o' boilin' water altogether.'

She was about to ask him why, when she remembered she'd promised to see to Earl in his absence. She was supposed to groom and feed him and she'd forgotten.

'Oh Matty—please forgive me. I've been sitting on my arse all the day and have no excuse to save me except for a poor memory.'

Mrs Cleary took Matty by the shoulders and pushed him into a chair, and he sat there mumbling, until she brought him a bowl of the steaming stew and a generous chunk of bread.

'Now Matty Friel,' she began sternly, 'you listen to me. The girl hasn't been herself today. Look at her—she's as white as a winding sheet, and I think I'm partly to blame for keeping her occupied. My tongue's been going like the clappers all the day and the poor lass had no choice but to sit and listen to my blatherin'.'

Matty began to soften, helped by the delicious stew and Mrs C's explanation.

'I suppose the horse won't come to much harm,' he said grudgingly, 'but it's a poor man who has no woman to rely on. There's three of you here, and not one of you able to see to the animal between you.'

Mrs Cleary passed him a cup of tea and scowled back at him.

'Give your tongue a rest, Matty Friel. Why, anyone would think it a daily event the way you're carryin' on. Finish your tea and have a puff o' your pipe, while me and Delia go check on Earl.'

They didn't quite make it to the stables. As they crossed the courtyard, McVey rushed out from the door leading to his quarters and asked Matty's whereabouts.

Chapter 16

McVey was the quintessential butler, and Delia had never seen him lose his composure before, but he was clearly agitated as he passed on his news.

'Miss Magdalen is poorly and her ladyship requires a doctor immediately.'

Both women turned and ran after McVey to the kitchen entrance.

'And *where* is his nibs, may I ask?' enquired the cook, when she caught up with him. 'Is he not at home?'

McVey gave her a venomous look and stared down his long nose when he replied. 'His *lordship* is not expected home before midnight.'

She turned to Delia and spoke quietly. 'I don't like this one bit, but it's going to require some checkin'. Her Highness upstairs can be a little hysterical on occasion. I'd best go up to her and get the lie o' the land myself.' She pulled at the knots of her apron string. 'Bad cess to that man for never being here when his daughter needs him,' she added, as she headed for the staircase.

By the time she returned, Matty was already dressed for the ride into Buncrana to fetch Doctor Nowland and Mrs Cleary wasted no time and gathered items even as she fired orders at him.

'She has a bad fever, Matty, so put the foot to the treadle

and be as quick as you can. If you pass by his lordship, tell him he's not to spare the horse either.' She turned to Delia again. 'I'm going to need lots of bricks for the bedroom fireplace and a couple o' good-sized pans. I've a bad feelin' I've seen this before, when my own acushla was little. I think the Strangling Angel has come for young Magdalen.'

Upstairs in the sickroom, her ladyship hovered while Delia and the cook busied themselves. Mrs Cleary prepared the bed and Delia built a generous fire and put one of the large pans filled with water directly on the flames to boil. She made several trips up and down to fill ewers, bowls and large saucepans, and soon they had an ample supply of water and Magdalen was tucked comfortably in the bed.

Her long hair felt damp and she was slack and listless in Delia's arms when she put her between the warm sheets. Now she lay wheezing, her small face flushed an unnatural red and her eyes bright as jet beads. The women made a tent over her by anchoring the corners of a large sheet at the foot of the bed and holding it over their heads to form a canopy as they bent either side of the young patient and balanced between them a large bowl of hot water to which Delia added some camphor oil.

She'd hung a small cotton bag of camphor crystals around Magdalen's neck and the astringent aroma filled the steam tent and wafted through the sickroom.

It broke their hearts to hear the child's hacking cough, and to watch helplessly as she struggled to take a breath between spasms. With each coughing spell her face grew redder and her lips turned blue as she fought to inhale sufficient air. Delia emerged from the steam bath to refresh the water and felt a brief pang of pity at sight of her mother, who could do nothing except walk from window to bed, wringing her hands in distress.

'It all came on so quickly,' she said, to nobody in particular. 'I didn't know she was out of doors until Mrs Moore's daughter brought her to me, soaked to the skin. She had chased the family's dog after it escaped the house and was out searching in that dreadful rain without coat or bonnet.'

Delia thought it best if her ladyship had some distraction, so she asked if she would take her position beneath the steam tent whilst Delia ran downstairs to the kitchen for some goose grease.

Dashing back with the grease, she took the stairs two at a time and could hear Magdalen's bark from the far end of the landing.

The coughing spells were now almost continuous and it was clear that something had to be done to ease the child's breathing. Delia put the grease aside and pulled back the sheets.

'Mrs Cleary, I'm going to sit her up a little and see if I can get some of that phlegm off her chest.'

The child was soaked when Delia put her arm around her shoulders. She took a warm towel from the fireguard and wrapped it around Magdalen's head, while Mrs Cleary replaced the damp pillow.

'Magdalen, my darling,' she said in a tone that belied her mounting panic. 'I know you can't speak, but listen to your Delia now. I want you to open your mouth wide and breathe out of it as hard as you can, so every bit of air is gone. Forget you have a nose, acushla, and just use your mouth.'

Magdalen bravely pinched her nostrils shut and did as she was told and immediately the cough became more acute and her tiny shoulders heaved with the effort to take in every scrap of air between loud barks. Delia thumped between her shoulder blades with the flat of her hand, amidst protest from her ladyship, and looks of doubt from the cook. But if Delia heard them she chose to ignore them.

'That's it, darlin', that's my clever girl. Now, again if you can, mouth wide and huff as hard as you like. Say "ha", and again my sweet, a big loud "ha" through your mouth.'

The second spasm caused her to retch and without warning, Magdalen expectorated a glob of thick yellow mucous and fell back against the pillow, exhausted.

Delia rubbed her chest with the goose grease and added more camphor oil to a replenished bowl of heated water.

Her head was wrapped in warm towels until her hair was dry and, after a couple of hours, she slipped into a fitful sleep. Her breathing still sounded laboured and the cough erupted at frequent intervals, but she seemed to sleep through most of the bouts. Delia had her propped on several pillows, explaining to the two women that it would be easier for Magdalen to breathe and to expel any mucous if she was semi-prone and not lying flat.

His lordship and Doctor Nowland arrived within minutes of each other in the early hours of the morning. By then, the women were exhausted and took the opportunity to return to the kitchen for some tea while the doctor conducted his examination.

Catherine had returned to the Hall at some point and had fallen asleep in one of the fireside chairs. Mrs Cleary poked her and vented some of her tiredness on the unsuspecting maid.

'Get your lazy arse out of that chair, Catherine Nolan, and set a tea tray for three,' she shouted to a thoroughly flummoxed Catherine. 'And while you're at it, make a mound of toast. The doctor will be glad of some and I'm betting it won't go to waste. It's going to be a long night, so don't be entertaining any ideas of going to bed, for you'll be needed along with the rest of us.'

A very miserable Catherine took the tray upstairs, and Delia and the cook made the most of the opportunity to put their feet up while they sipped their tea.

When the maid reappeared, she reported the doctor had finished his examination and was conferring with Lord and Lady Keenagh. Delia and Mrs Clearly made it back upstairs just in time to see the doctor leave. He doffed his cap at the two women as he passed and left without saying a word.

Magdalen seemed to be sleeping easier and his lordship took them to one side and spoke in low tones.

'Doctor Nowland suspects it may be diphtheria, but he cannot be sure at this stage. He will return tomorrow. In the meantime, we must try to keep her fever under control and give her as much fluid as the poor lamb can take. I will sit with her, if you would be so kind as to assist her ladyship with her night toilet, Mrs Cleary?'

Delia felt sick at hearing the diagnosis. If it was the strangling angel, the child was doomed. There was nothing she or anyone else could do, except she was determined to stay with her until the end. 'I beg pardon, your lordship,' she said. 'I don't mean to speak out of turn, but Mrs Cleary and I can sit with Magdalen. May I respectfully suggest, sir, that both you and her ladyship must get your full rest. We'll work together to ensure we get sufficient sleep and that the routine of the household is not disrupted any more than is necessary.' She turned to the cook. 'That's if *you* are in agreement, Mrs Cleary?'

The cook looked exhausted and was much too tired to feel affronted at the girl placing herself above her, and she nodded. His lordship straightened his jabot and picked up his jacket to leave.

'It seems I'm always thanking you, Delia, but once again you have proved invaluable to my wife and I. Please see that I'm called the minute there's any change in Magdalen's condition.'

He thanked the cook, then he bent low and kissed his daughter on the lips, glancing back at her one last time before closing the bedroom door behind him.

Delia spoke quietly. 'I'm not a doctor, Mrs Cleary, but I'm hoping Nowland is wrong shipped this time. I'm betting it's a bad case of bronchial congestion and, if I'm right, we should see a change for the better by morning.'

'Oh Jaysus, how I wish it were the case,' Mrs Cleary said wearily. 'There's not many have escaped the strangling angel's evil clutches. Didn't I lose one of my own to him? I turned from my babby for a minute and he was snatched from me in the blink of an eye.' Her tired eyes misted and she sniffed and wiped at them with the corner of her apron. 'A day—that's all it took to change my wee one from a healthy child to a corpse. The Strangling One has no mercy Delia. He took away my Jimmy and three more bairns from our clachan on the same day. If the child is marked, there's not much we can do about it. The strangling one will not be denied.'

Delia hugged her tightly. 'We can pray to the Archangel Gabriel and ask him to protect her. She's a strong bairn Mrs C.' She tried to sound convincing, but in truth she was very afraid and she spent an exhausting night of prayer between Magdalen's violent and prolonged spells of coughing.

She massaged her chest and expectorated again with the same result and they kept the steam levels so high in the room both women were soaked by morning.

Magdalen settled down into a more peaceful sleep just before dawn. The two women gazed out the window and watched with heavy eyes, but lighter hearts, as the sky revealed a good omen. It had turned orange and they were blessed with a welcoming sunrise after the deluge of rain.

The cook disappeared to prepare the family's breakfast and Delia tidied the sickroom, but really there wasn't a lot to do, so she sat at the bottom of the bed and watched the frill on Magdalen's nightgown rise and fall in time with her breathing. She looked even more angelic with the rosy flush on her cheeks, but her breathing was shallow and her limbs and forehead were unnaturally hot, and Delia thought her chest rose and fell much too quickly.

She racked her tired brain for suitable herbs. Was it Tansy for sore throats and fevers, or Yarrow?

She was too weary to think straight. '*No, neither of those,*' she suddenly remembered. It was Milkweed! She could use Milkweed, Thyme or Lavender. She resolved to visit the herb garden as soon as Mrs Cleary came to relieve her.

'*Thank God for a good supply of herbs,*' she thought later, when Matty brought them to the kitchen.

She made an infusion, adding a little ginger and allowing the mixture to steep while she ate a hurried breakfast. Her eyes drooped as she chewed on a piece of toast, but the tea revived her and she was back in the sickroom within the hour. Magdalen was awake but not at all her usual bubble of energy. She was very weak and couldn't even manage a smile when Delia bent to kiss her.

She ran her fingers lightly through the child's hair and straightened it a little.

'Remember when you had that nasty fall from the carriage, my darlin', and I put some medicine on your head to make it better? Well, I've brought something to make that nasty cough go away. Do you think you can open your mouth again for me, acushla?'

Magdalen shook her head, made a deep croaking sound that could have been a 'No' and turned her head firmly away.

'It's alright darling one. I'm not going to make you cough. But I want you to try and swallow this herbal mixture. I'll not lie and tell you it tastes nice either, because it doesn't. But I know how brave you are, and how you'd much rather be walking through the fields with me than lying in this bed, now wouldn't you? Aren't I right? Do you think you can manage a tiny spoonful for me?'

But no matter how much Delia coaxed, Magdalen steadfastly refused. She glanced at Mrs Cleary, who tried in turn to persuade the child, to no avail, until Delia had the idea of mixing it with some honey and, at last, Magdalen swallowed a half teaspoon of the mix, and promptly coughed most of it back.

'I did warn you it might taste strange, but things that are good for us don't always taste nice.'

'Throat hurts,' Magdalen croaked. ' I can't swallow.'

Mrs Cleary looked at Delia with renewed fear in her eyes, convinced that the child now showed some classic symptoms of the dreaded strangling disease.

Delia handed the herb mix to the cook, who was careful to place it well away from the bed, and returned to persuade the child to let her look at her throat.

'I promise I'll keep my hands behind my back and not touch you. I only want to look. But you must open as wide as you can for me, and turn your head toward the window so I can see the back of your throat.'

She caught a glimpse of redness which could have been the result of the coughing, and her neck was a little swollen, but she was unable to tell if there was any obstruction. Magdalen wouldn't allow her a proper look.

She heard Mrs Cleary sniffling and hastened to reassure her. 'Rest easy, Mrs C. I don't think it's the strangling angel. There's no sign of the skin in her throat peeling and her breath is sweet as it should be.'

Mrs Cleary burst into a noisy fit of crying. She'd been saying the rosary near the window and now she shoved the beads into the deep pocket of her apron and hid her face from view.

Delia put her arms around her and whispered soothingly.

'Hush now—or you'll put the fear of God into the child. Why don't you go downstairs and have a, you-know-what and a cup of tea. His lordship will be here to relieve me shortly, so you can pour me a cup as well.'

Delia knew the cook's outburst was largely due to extreme fatigue. Mrs Cleary was not excused from the many other tasks she was expected to get through in a day, and she may have been hard on Catherine; but in truth, she needed to be. Most of the time, the girl was neither use nor ornament.

She turned her attention back to Magdalen, who was still tossing her head from side to side. Delia mistook the movement for obstinacy and she held up her empty hands in clear view.

'It's alright acushla, I'm not going to give you any more medicine without your say so. Look, my hands are empty.'

But Magdalen continued to toss her head and delia saw a glazed look in her eyes, and another, more sinister look she'd seen in the eyes of the starving children and she was afraid.

She drew closer to pull Magdalen into a sitting position but before she could hold her, the child began to convulse and her eyes widened in unspoken fear. Delia suppressed the urge to cry out; she called over her shoulder for Mrs Cleary to fetch the master and mistress and stared into Magdalens terrorstricken eyes, hardly able to believe the speed of the transition.

'I'm here my darling one. Don't be afraid. I'll not leave you and Mammy is on her way.'

As quickly as the convulsions began they stopped and time hung in the air as Delia held her breath and listened with all her being for the child to breathe or to cry out—but all was still. She pleaded with God even as she felt the heat of Magdalen's body dissipate and the child grow limp and heavy in her arms. Her tears soaked Magdalen's hair and her shoulders heaved in uncontrollable weeping.

'No God,' she sobbed. 'Not my Magdalen. She's an only child Lord. Give her back; spare us this agony oh merciful God. Don't take this child from us.'

She could not summon the courage to look upon the child, knowing that to look would be to accept the truth that lay in her arms. Still she knew Magdalen was gone and a part of her was in awe at the speed and ease of the child's passing.

'As quick as the snuffing of a candle flame,' she thought. Magdalen was here; Magdalen was gone.

She lay her head gently against the pillow and straightened out the child's damp curls. Magdalen's face was a blur through her tears, but Delia felt the peace and knew there would be no sign of suffering.

'*Babes bow to your will without a fight*,' she thought bitterly. '*They're easy pickings for you aren't they Lord?*'

She heard Mrs Cleary's wailing and the sound of hurried footsteps along the passage, and then there was a stifled cry behind her, and a dull thump, as Her Ladyship collapsed in a swoon.

Without a care for convention, she kneeled beside the bed and buried her face in the folds of Magdalen's nightgown and sobbed unashamedly.

The pall of death hung over Keenagh Hall long after Magdalen's funeral. The household was united in not wishing to see her buried, but they witnessed her being lowered into the ground, yet it was impossible to accept she had gone from them, and her absence, though undeniable, was somehow incomplete.

Delia felt her presence keenly. Magdalen's spirit was everywhere and her energy seemed to vibrate through the rooms. Even during her solitary walks she had a strong sense of the child's presence.

Rumours filtered below stairs from McVey and Matty, that Lord and Lady Keenagh were about to embark on a long journey abroad. The staff were secure for the time being, but His Lordship could not promise they would keep their jobs on his return. Lady Keenagh could not remain at the Hall and he hoped the time away might cause her to have a change of heart.

Delia felt her position was more tenuous. She had lost her companion; her sole reason for staying at the Hall and she wasn't sure she could bear the constant reminders either. She'd enjoyed comfort and safety and never considered her and Magdalen would ever be separated, but when she pondered her situation she had to accept she'd been naive.

Magdalen had been of an age where she would have been

shipped off to school and Delia's position would have been redundant. She began to seriously consider the possibility of a change for herself.

It was time to move on. America had always been an option and His Lordship had vowed to help her if it was what she wanted, but she wasn't sure she could face the pain and upheaval and resolved to put off any decision until His Lordship returned from abroad.

Chapter 17

Spring arrived and the first hint of warmth from the sun set everyone into cleaning mode, as cupboards, drawers and long-locked chests were flung open and swept free of cobwebs.

She scrubbed the smoke stains from the kitchen walls before Matty white washed them, and she scoured every utensil, under the critical eye of Mrs Cleary. Loud sneezes echoed through the hallways for weeks as staff disturbed the clouds of dust.

She had missed her walks for several days but she managed to slip out one morning, and she began the perimeter walk she and Magdalen had come to love best. It was a pleasant day and she was glad of the peace and solitude after the chaos of the Hall. Every shrub and every tree seemed to be in bud; fat, swollen, and eager to burst forth in flower and leaf. She paused to watch small hedgerow birds dart to and fro with materials for their nests.

A climbing rose bush gripped the sandstone wall, its stems gnarled and thickened with age. A few of last season's rosehips clung stubbornly to the tangled shrub. Unappetizing even for the birds, the shrivelled berries were at odds with the abundance of fresh green shoots and new life that surrounded them.

She sat on a low bench and looked above her through the overhang of tangled branches. A spider's web caught her eye. It was suspended between two boughs, its complex lines silhouetted against the sky. She studied it and thought about the intricacy of its design. Then a sudden rustle of movement in the hedge startled her, as a sparrow landed and then flew off again.

The motion caused the web to tremble, and the glistening droplets of dew shook and shimmered like crystal beads, caught in the piercing light of a sunbeam. She sat in admiration of the skill of the spider, one of God's lowliest and most despised creatures.

How could such a small thing craft such complicated beauty? A spider was so easily obliterated beneath the pad of a human finger or a foot, yet is possessed sufficient skill to produce a finished web more delicate than a dragonfly's wing, but strong and deadly enough to trap one forever in its gossamer threads?

Her skirts were damp from sitting on the dew-soaked bench, but she lingered and sucked in more of the sweet air and breathed deeply the fresh scent of grass with its faint undertones of leaf mold and wood rot. There was a deep silence in this corner of the grounds and she absorbed the stillness. There was no movement on the horizon and even the birds had fallen silent and for a few precious moments there was nothing to disturb the utter quiet.

She rose carefully, reluctant to break the sanctity of the moment, and resumed her walk, following the high wall that separated her from the road leading toward the lower meadow. '*Only the width of a brick separates me from Hell,*' she thought sadly.

'*If I were on the other side of this wall, I would be walking over the remains of my countrymen. Ireland is, and Ireland will forever be, one giant graveyard. To tread its fields is to step on hallowed ground.*'

Future generations would walk over the starved martyrs and unknowingly grind hidden bones beneath their feet. With every plowing, they would crush, unaware, the remains of their own ancestors. They would reap the bounty of the country's soil and never know the full measure or cost of the fertilizer that leeched into the ground beneath their feet.

'No wonder it's silent as the grave,' she pondered. 'That's what the countryside has become; it's what makes this silence so oppressive. I feel the spirits of the thousands who've perished.'

It was time to think about leaving not just the Hall, but Ireland. She was as happy as it was possible to be without Magdalen, but she'd sensed a tiny seed of discontent in herself of late; an urging to venture forth and make her own way once more, and in order to do that, she would have to leave Ireland's shores and the painful memories it held, far behind.

The weeks sped by in a predictable blur of increased activities, during which time Delia informed the household of her decision.

She told Lord Keenagh she would like to leave as soon as travel arrangements could be made.

But oh, how many times she longed to have the power to stop the clock and hold back the rapidly approaching hour of her departure.

When it finally came, Delia, cook and Catherine clung to each other and wept buckets of tears and until Matty broke them apart and led Delia to the carriage. She thought her heart would break at sight of their distress and she waved and watched them grow smaller until the carriage turned onto the road and they were lost from view.

Then she burst into fresh weeping and gave vent to the depth of sorrow she hadn't felt since Magdalen's passing.

Chapter 18

Delia was astounded by the changes in Buncrana. She had become familiar with the area surrounding the Diamond during earlier visits with her father and they had developed a routine that seldom altered. While her father bartered for a pony during the May fair, or sold the beast off again at the late October gathering, she would stroll among the stalls proffering the goods she'd brought.

Sometimes it was a basket of exquisite lace doilies, tatted by her mother; or sturdy baskets she and Niamh had helped Mammy weave during the winter months. Occasionally, it was a length of woollen tweed or a knitted shawl she traded.

She had strict instructions from her mother to trade rather than sell, and *if* she ever had coins, Mammy cautioned her, she was to hide them in the hem of her skirt, keeping back one or two for her Da, whose routine it was to search her once they were on the outskirts of the town and before they reached Dooley's tavern. Once he found the hiding place in the hem of her skirt, and a few other, more intimate ones besides she was forced to hide the coins in her mouth and endure the agony of keeping her lips pressed together and trying not to gag on the excess of vile-tasting saliva, until her Da was safely in Dooley's.

Today, the town was bustling and Delia was able to enjoy the sights.

Buncrana was a beautifully appointed town, situated on the eastern shores of Lough Swilly and nestled in the sheltering arms of the Ennishowen Mountains. From the busy quayside she could look west and see, just offshore, a brightly painted red and white lighthouse.

To the south was a large outcrop of rocks her father had called 'Silly Rocks'. Buncrana castle loomed over the Diamond, protected by a sturdy bridge that spanned the Crannagh River, one of the two well-stocked rivers that flowed through the town.

It was considered a safe port for sea vessels and had prospered from years of healthy trade. The stalls groaned beneath the weight of freshly caught sole and plaice and some of the biggest oysters Delia had ever seen on Malin beach, or during her time at the Hall.

There was a salmon farm and several mills south of the rivers. The mills she was familiar with, her father having often delivered sacks of oats or flax to be ground and collected on their return journey.

Local blather claimed that, during spring, salmon the size of sharks leapt in large shoals upriver and threw themselves onto the banks as an offering to the nearest angler, thus saving them the trouble of casting rods or nets.

Clearly, it was more prosperous, and the town was crowded with a variety of visitors enjoying the first promise of warmer weather.

It was a far cry from the scene that had greeted Delia only a few years earlier when the air had been fetid and filled with the mournful wailing of starving women and children, and the main streets had been littered with the dead and dying.

The inn was still there, just as she remembered it. The sign that hung above the entrance had been freshly painted and the low thatched building was now buttressed either side by solid stone-built houses that boasted the added luxury of gleaming glass windows and tall chimneys. Shop windows glistened in the sunshine and gardens were ablaze with purple Iris and an array of bright spring flowers.

Matty halted the carriage in front of the inn. This time, he was very solicitous and he helped her down before he retrieved her bag. 'Here you are, my darling, Dee-Dee. Give old Matty a hug and a last kiss, and mind you write to us.' She studied his craggy face one last time and tried to brand into her memory every beloved feature. His hands shook as he adjusted her shawl and he fussed unnecessarily with her bag. When he spoke she heard the anguish in his voice.

'You've the gift of a fine storyteller in you Delia, so you can keep us happy with tales of Americcy and all your 'ventures.'

Delia swallowed hard and tried in vain to remain composed, for both their sakes. She'd come to love this man so much; Matty was her surrogate father. But no, to compare him so was to do him a grave injustice. He was more like her gentle mother and had gifted her with his quiet wisdom and compassion.

She would never forget the hours they'd spent happily working the soil; weeding and pruning the vast gardens at the Hall, or sweeping leaves and gathering moldy windfalls from the fruit trees on the estate. Matty had a knack of making her feel like a precious and much-loved daughter, at a time when she had despaired of ever knowing a father's love.

During her worst bouts of melancholy it was always Matty she'd sought first. Her 'melanconkers' he called them. He could pretend otherwise, but deep down, he was calm and unflappable; always at one with the easy rhythm of the land he loved to nurture, and he had a knack of filling her with peace when she was most rattled.

She bit her lip hard and took a deep shuddering breath.

'A bit different from the last time we were here, Matty. As I recall, you kept me at whip's length and wouldn't give me a sideways glance. Now you'd think it was St Brigid herself you were saying goodbye to.'

Matty was clearly distraught and did nothing to stem the flow of tears that ran down his face.

'Ah… Delia, darlin', you were no more than a bony waif then, and so dirty I couldn't see what I had sittin' beside me. But you've blossomed into a beauty, and no mistake; as lovely inside as you are out. It's a lucky man that's marked for you, a lucky man indeed.' He wiped his face on the sleeve of his jacket in an effort to compose himself, but then he lost his composure completely.

'Me poor heart's broke, acushla. How will I live now, without sight of your smiling face to greet me on cold wet mornings? And not even wee Magdy to comfort me when I get back. Ah… but I'm thinkin' I'll not make it that far, for I can feel the hole in me heart gettin' bigger by the minute. It'll be a blessing to me if God should see fit to take me before I've gone too many miles from you.'

Delia couldn't bear his distress a moment longer. 'Oh Matty, please don't say such things. My heart is scalded with pain as it is. Goodbye darling man. I promise you'll get a letter from me as soon as my foot touches American soil. Give Mrs C and Catherine a last kiss from me.'

He stepped back from her then and attempted a smile and a joke. 'Not even for you, Delia Dreenan. If it was a choice between kissing them two hags and a horse's arse—the horse would win every time.'

She loved him for trying to make her smile and wrapped her arms around him, squeezing his thin shoulders to her as her resolve weakened, and they both gave full vent to their weeping, impervious to the waiting coach and the curious passengers.

They were forced apart by the impatient shouts of the coachman as he shouted into the open door of the inn after the stragglers.

'Bring out yer dead, or keep them another day, as you please.

We're leavin' in five—with or without yizz.'

Matty still had tight hold of her hand and Delia knew she would have to break the last contact. She gently pushed him from her and kissed his forehead and without a backward glance, she climbed into the carriage and fixed her gaze on the brightly-polished toes of the boots opposite her. She didn't look up until the noise of Buncrana's market square had faded, and she was sure there were no more tears behind her swollen eyes.

Chapter 19

Thanks to dry roads and good stout horses, the coach made good time between Buncrana and Derry. They stopped briefly at the crossroads in Burnfoot, long enough to pick up mail and to refuse a couple of pedestrians seeking a free ride to Londonderry.

Their progress slowed the last few miles into the city and Delia began to take some interest in her surroundings. She'd never travelled this road, nor seen a city so large, and she found the noise level deafening after the quiet of the country lanes. When the coach stopped inside the city walls, it was some time before she collected herself enough to look around for the ongoing transport to Belfast, caught up as she was in the hustle and bustle of the townspeople.

Her ticket gave no further instructions, but upon enquiry she was directed to an information office, where one of the harassed clerks pointed out her next embarkation point.

'Look for a coach sporting a yellow stripe. It should have Belfast written on it, or else you can look for the number five. Here,' he said, grabbing a pencil. 'I'll write it down for you.'

Delia was still sensitive from her recent farewell, and she was in no mood to be nice to anyone.

'There's no need to waste your paper,' she said curtly. 'I can read well enough, thank you.'

The clerk scowled at her and uttered a Gaelic curse before

turning back to his work. She sat on a low wall outside and ate the bread and cheese Mrs Cleary had wrapped for her, and gazed distractedly across the water. Beyond the strip of land on the opposite bank, lay the lough and, for a few pennies, she could have a boatman row her to Moville. From there, she could easily find her way back home…

Home: somehow the word didn't sit comfortably anymore. Where *was* home? Was she thinking of retracing her steps back to the Hall, or was her subconscious tempting her to turn northeast toward Carndonagh, back to the crude resting place of her family? It occurred to her that she hadn't thought about them for days, and seldom had disturbing dreams of them anymore.

But she was still healing. Those last images of her parents had power enough to immobilize her with fear and she knew they would never leave her, but she tried especially hard not to linger on thoughts of her father. She hated him, would always hate him, but the hatred no longer consumed her as it once had. Life could be sweet, hadn't she had proof of it these last few years? And now she was on the verge of a new and exciting 'venture', as Matty called it.

Her insides churned in anticipation and she felt a mounting impatience to get to America; a growing eagerness for a fresh start with a clean slate.

She'd been happy at Keenagh Hall, but there'd always been a nagging fear of the unexpected knock at the door, an uneasy feeling whenever a carriage approached, and a constant dread of meeting someone who would know her dark secret. But now she was beginning to sense real freedom and a release from having to choose her words carefully.

A young fisherman's wife leaned against the breakwall close by, nursing a grizzling babe. He wouldn't settle to the breast and the mother jiggled the crying infant on her knees and sang a wordless jig.

'Oh diddly de de die de die, diddly die de doh,' she trilled, in a futile attempt to pacify the infant, who howled all the louder for being bumped about so vigorously.

The mother was totally oblivious to Delia, who envied the deep intimacy between the woman and her child. It brought back memories of Magdalen and her father, but she also saw herself as a young girl, when she'd bounced her siblings in much the same way.

The woman gave up jogging and wrapped the infant snugly in her shawl. She smothered its face with kisses and cooed softly, and then she produced from beneath her wrap a large cork and moistened it with her tongue before placing it to the baby's lips.

The crying stopped abruptly as the baby began to suck fiercely at the makeshift teat and the young mother walked in small circles, rocking the infant and wetting the makeshift soother at intervals, holding it firmly as the baby sucked contentedly.

Delia imagined herself as a mother and wondered if she would ever know such joy and fulfillment as this young woman showed. Or was she forever destined to play mother to other women's children? If Mrs C was right about her bleeds, she should have no difficulty conceiving a child.

She had a good idea of *how* a woman's belly became implanted with a baby, and she knew a man was necessary. The method had been demonstrated to her often enough by her father, she recalled bitterly. The filthy brute hadn't always waited for cover of darkness either.

She shuddered as she pictured the part she would have to play if she was to ever have a family of her own, and raged against being submissive to anyone, yet she would have to submit one day, if she wanted to hold her own baby in her arms. She looked again at the young mother and decided it was worth any measure of discomfort. Yet Mammy hadn't made a child every year, in spite of her Da's continuous demands.

The difficulty would be in finding a man to father one. She decided she would be as choosy as if she were selecting a thoroughbred horse, and would insist on a trial run before committing herself to any man, with or without the approval of the church.

She had dawdled too long. At the top of the slope, near the castle gates, the passengers were starting to board the Belfast coach that would take her even further away from all that she loved.

Her heart was being torn in opposite directions with each mile that separated her further from home, and these scenes of contentment and well-being only aggravated the struggle within her as she weighed the agonizing decision to stay or go.

In this strange town she was an unknown entity; of less significance to those around her than a leaf blown by the winds; inconsequential and indistinguishable. Nobody would give a second's thought or a care to her origins. The train of thought depressed her again and she felt strangely disembodied and older than her years as she began her trek up the hill to the waiting coach. When it pulled out of Buncrana, her eyes devoured the beauty of the passing scenery, and soon they neared the east coast and she caught sight of the water that would separate her from Ireland forever.

The *Ariana* was anchored in Belfast quay and the coach dropped them as close to the ship as possible. It was full dark when they arrived at the quay and most of her fellow travelers headed straight for the vessel.

Delia didn't feel the least bit hungry, nor was she in any fit mood to join the festivities already taking place among various groups huddled on the deck. The ship's rails were packed with passengers determined not to miss a last look at their beloved country. She could hear the sound of women softly weeping under cover of night and the whispered words of comfort from the men.

It was tortuous and she was very glad it was dark, even though it denied her a last glimpse of the coast. She stared into the black canvas of night and tried to make sense of the poorly illuminated buildings on the quayside whilst striving to ignore the heart-wrenching farewells around her.

As soon as she could, she slipped away from the thick of passengers and found a space near the port bow, where she crossed herself in readiness for evening prayer.

As she breathed in the salty air and tried to quiet the tumult of emotions that intruded on her meditation, a snippet from a book of poetry she'd once read popped into her head.

'The air is full of farewells to the dying and mournings for the dead…'

Random snippets followed and she abandoned all attempts at formal prayer and addressed her mother directly, believing her to be among the angels and, therefore, able to intercede on her behalf.

'Dearest Mammy, please don't be angry at me for deserting you and my darling family. You are forever in my heart and nobody will ever fill your place. May your sweet soul be held eternally in God's gentle keeping. I have to leave, Mammy; to stay in Ireland is to be forever tortured. No matter where I go, I'm haunted by memories and the loneliness won't lift from me. But I take comfort in knowing your departed spirit will forever be in Donegal, and always, always, in the deepest recesses of my being. Look after Magdalen and ask the Angel Gabriel to watch over me. And if my own time should come while I'm at sea, may God grant me a place with you in Heaven. God bless Ireland and her people, and grant my loved ones eternal rest. Amen.'

She ended with a short Act of Contrition and as she turned

her back on her homeland for the last time, one fitting line of farewell pushed to the forefront of her memory. This poet she remembered because he'd been her mother's favorite, and she sent the beauty of Gray's words echoing across the dark void between land and sea.

'Nor cast one longing, lingering look behind.'

She never felt such crushing pain or desolation as she did at that moment. Her shoulders drooped from fatigue and a with crippling sense of defeat, she walked away from the rail and made her way across the deck.

A kindly crewmember escorted her below to a cramped two-berth cabin and gave her a key, instructing her to return it before disembarking next day.

She was grateful to find the tiny cabin empty, and for a second, hoped she might have the berth to herself. However, a carpet bag and a shabby-looking hat had been deposited on the lower bed, so she stowed her own belongings at the foot of the upper bunk and, after climbing into the narrow space, cried herself into an exhausted sleep.

She didn't feel the *Ariana* slip her last link with Ireland, nor did she witness the lights of Belfast fade to pinpricks as the vessel began the voyage across an unusually calm Irish Sea toward Liverpool.

Part Two

Chapter 20

She slept undisturbed and woke with a start when the vessel bumped against the quay. Her head instinctively turned toward the window of her bedroom at the Hall, but instead of a morning chorus of birdsong she heard the rumble of heavy chains.

Somewhere out of the dark came the barking voices of men, and she curled her nose in disgust at the odious mix of stale porter and putrid flatulence that filled the tiny cabin.

There wasn't room to stretch in the coffin-sized bunk and she touched the ceiling above her head without even straightening her arms. Every bone ached and she craved fresh air and the open space of the deck after being cramped in the narrow space for so long.

She crawled along the pallet on all fours to gather her belongings and stuffed her boots into her valise before lowering herself quietly to the floor, careful not to disturb the occupant of the lower berth. But she needn't have worried. Her fellow cabin mate was in a dead sleep and continued her loud snoring as Delia pulled on her coat and retrieved her bonnet.

As she tied the ribbon, her hand brushed the bulge of the drawstring purse Madgalen had given her the first Christmas she'd spent at Keenagh Hall. It nestled in the deep crevice between her breasts, undetectable beneath the generous ruffle of her blouse.

She checked the pockets of her coat, reassured to feel the bulk of the travel voucher and the loose coins, and left the stuffy cabin, carefully picking her way through the sleeping passengers and baggage that blocked the narrow corridor leading to the upper staircase.

She was surprised to find the passenger's lavatory vacant and was able to perform a decent toilet, given the thin trickle of cold water that coughed reluctantly from a single rusted tap. After checking her reflection and shoving her unruly curls beneath her bonnet she made her way to the upper deck.

The vessel was shrouded in a thick, sound-muffling fog and out of the grey curtain ahead, the dark shadows of passengers gradually emerged. They passed without seeming to notice her, bleary eyed from lack of sleep and too much poteen.

There was a strong smell of damp wool and she saw their heads were soaked after hours spent in the damp air. She felt ashamed to have thought her bed anything less than comfortable; she had at least been warm and dry.

As she sidestepped her fellow passengers, she tried to remember the layout of the deck from the night before. She was forced to rely on senses to guide her to the gangplank but soon she heard crew members responding to orders and she could hear the distant splashes as the heavy ropes slapped the water, and from somewhere close by an assortment of sharp commands pierced the fog.

'Make fast! Foreward! Move it, yer lazy bleeders. Move it— before I wrap me hook around your necks!'

Another man shouted, this time from the *Ariana*, to the stevedores on the quay.

'Make less noise, yer miserable bleeders. I'm tryin' to get some shut eye.'

The men on the quay were evidently familiar with the verbal assaults and were sharp and immediate with their replies.

'Shut yer ugly gob, Mickey Dooley. Anyone would think

you were the only sailor aboard.'

A third disembodied voice, this one with an unmistakable Irish accent, chipped in.

'Hoy! Mickey! They don't call you Rip Van Winkle for nuthin'. We all know you've slept through best part of the voyage. We've sailed with ya before, remember? So get your stinkin' rump out of that hammock and give us a hand.'

She was distracted from the theatricals by a young crewmember who made slow progress through the throng of passengers waiting impatiently to disembark. It was the same man who'd escorted her the previous night.

'Form an orderly queue if you please, and no shoving. Nobody's going anywhere until the skipper gives the nod. Passengers with cabin keys, have them at the ready please.' He had issued this last rhyming order in a sing-song voice which brought a smile to Delia's lips.

The skipper was in no great hurry and it was a good hour later before her feet touched English soil, and the flagstones of Liverpool's George's Dock.

The fog had begun to dissipate in a fresh breeze that blew off the River Mersey. It revealed a broad quayside packed with precarious-looking towers of lumpy sacks and bulging bales of raw cotton. Every remaining space between was filled with wooden barrels, carts, horses and all manner of livestock. The early morning quiet was quickly overwhelmed by an increasing cacophony of sounds and she distinguished several alien tongues amongst the more familiar lilt of the Irish brogue. She had been to many busy fairs in Ireland, but this was on an grander scale than anything she'd ever seen.

She wasn't aware she'd stopped at the foot of the gangplank until she was roughly jostled from behind. Once on solid ground, the noise level increased even more and she was mesmerized by the vendors who cried out to the potential customers leaving the ship.

'Luvly oranges here—all the the way from Spain! Juicy an' sweet—only three a penny.'

'Chestnuts—hot and fresh roasted! Ha'penny a bag!'

She blushed to her toes when a ruddy-looking man stood in front of her. 'Here y'are luvly, feel these. Don't be shy girl. I'm only talking about me buns. Raisin' buns—baked this mornin' and still warm!'

Before he left her, a young girl carrying a very large basket held out a cup with no handle and shoved it rudely under Delia's nose.

'Here miss, smell the brine on these winkles, harvested this mornin' on the first tide. Ha'penny a bag to you, Miss, but you can have a farthing's worth if you like.'

Porters of every shape, size and color jostled with each other and harassed the confused passengers. Some tugged at luggage handles and unashamedly bartered to undercut each other's prices in the hustle to gain a share of the custom.

Delia stood transfixed by the absolute contrast to the fog-shrouded silence of the ghost ship she'd stood on moments before. It was as though she'd been transported into the pages of one of Lord Keenagh's geography books about the tropics and all the wondrous things she'd read about and tried to imagine were gathered here in this spot.

Her senses were overpowered by the tang of fruits and spices, and the less pleasing emissions from the cotton and other raw materials, and the orchestra of new sounds was music to her ears.

Somebody pushed her from behind again and she began to walk away from the gangplank and into the busy crowd where she was carried along by the swell of people.

There was an unbroken line of handcarts, three deep in places, selling an assortment of goods, and a cheeky organ grinder shoved his cap at her while the monkey on his shoulder nibbled at a nut.

The produce on some of the carts was displayed like works of art, arranged to show off the bright vegetables and exotic fruits to best advantage. But it was the potatoes that caught Delia's attention. Every other cart was stacked with pyramids of several varieties of potatoes.

She thought she knew her spuds, but there were specimens she'd never seen before.

She stopped a third time without thinking and was shocked when a woman tried to squeeze past her with a large cloth bundle balanced on her head.

'Move over, girl, before you get mowed down,' she said rudely. 'If you're not buyin', don't stop them that are tryin'.'

Delia moved out of the way and tried hard to remain aware of pedestrian traffic. She bought a drink from a tea boy who looked to be no more than ten or eleven years old. He reminded her of a milk maid. He balanced a wooden yolk across his shoulders and metal cups hung from the contraption. In addition to the weight, he carried a heavy flagon of steaming tea and as willing customers mingled around him he warned them they were not to wander off with his mugs.

She sat on her valise and nursed her cup; abstractedly watching a young man purchase tea. He looked around him for a place to drink the scalding liquid in safety, away from the dense flow of pedestrians who were shoving along in a never-ending stream; absorbed in their own affairs; seemingly oblivious to others.

The young man came toward her and doffed his cap.

'S'cuse me, miss, but you look familiar. Have you just sailed in from Belfast?'

Delia lowered her cup and tried to quell her nerves. She wasn't used to men and was still tongue-tied and awkward around them. With the exception of Matty and his lordship, she hadn't had much experience, but she always trusted her instincts and now they were telling her this man was not to be feared.

He sensed her unease and tried to explain himself better. 'I was on deck duty aboard the *Ariana* and I fancy you were among the passengers.'

'Yes,' Delia said shyly, keeping her eyes lowered. 'You're quite correct.'

He sat close to her, asking permission even as he parked himself on a nearby bale.

'Have you any objection to my sitting here? I've been standing all night and my legs are jiggered.' He sat quietly for a moment drinking his tea, and she noticed he swallowed great gulps of the scalding liquid without any sign of discomfort. He caught her staring and smiled.

'My Mam says I have an asbestos lining in my mouth. I've asbestos fingers too. I can pick up hot things without burning them, which comes in handy if a cob o' coal falls out of the fire, or if the candles need snuffin.' He held out his free hand. 'My name's Daniel. Can I know yours?'

'Delia,' she replied. 'Delia Dreenan. Are you a sailor?'

'Yeah,' he said, chuckling to himself. 'But don't let that put you off. We're not all tarred with the same brush you know, if you'll pardon the pun.'

'I wasn't making any judgment,' said Delia, who detected a familiarity in his accent. 'What part of Ireland are you from?'

'Donegal,' he told her. 'Moville lad; born and bred. What about yourself?'

Without thinking, she replied. 'Same county, but it's Keenagh I'm coming from.'

'Don't think I know it,' he said. 'But we never strayed far from Moville in our family, except for the rare trip into Derry.'

Delia finished her tea and handed the empty mug to the tea lad, who hovered nearby. She took her gloves from her pocket and bent for her bag, ready to resume her search for the shipping agent's office.

'It's been nice talking to you, Mr—?'

'Daniel Harkin at your service miss, and very glad to be so,' he replied. 'Would you be in need of directions from here? I know Liverpool like the back of my hand.'

Delia patted her jacket pocket for the travel voucher Matty had put there the day before. She remembered with a pang of affection the great trouble he'd taken to fold it so that it fit snugly in her pocket and was in no danger of falling out.

'That piece of paper is worth its weight in gold,' he'd warned her. 'So guard it carefully, and mind you're not pulling things out of that pocket all the time. Here, put your flotsum in the other pocket.'

She smiled as she remembered how proud he'd been for calculating the ticket would be safer in the pocket on her gammy side, which was her left. But her smile quickly faded and her face drained of color when she discovered the ticket was gone and her left pocket was quite empty.

'Oh Merciful God, no!' she cried, tearing off her gloves and searching again. 'Don't do this to me Lord, please.'

Daniel picked up her valise at once to protect it from the nimble-fingered thieves who'd no doubt stolen her ticket. The girl was so agitated she wouldn't notice if they were to return and lift the hat from her head.

'You haven't lost your ticket, Delia,' he said. 'Your pockets have been picked. This dockside is crawling with vagabonds and thieves—more skilled than any you'll find in Ireland. They've no scruples at all. Sure, they'd rob the last breath from a dying man and not lose a minute's sleep over it. Where were you going after your tea?'

'I was looking for the shipping agent's office,' she cried. 'The voucher was to be redeemed for my berth on a ship to New York. Dear Lord, what am I going to do now?'

'Well, you can calm yourself for a start. We can find the ship and see if the captain has your name on the manifest. What's the name of the vessel?'

Delia remembered with renewed dismay she didn't have a specific vessel assigned to her. 'The voucher was good for the first available sailing,' she explained. 'I was instructed to give it to one of the agents who'd provide me with details of my voyage. It was all arranged and paid for months ago by my employer.'

Daniel pulled at his chin and adjusted his cap before speaking.

'Ah lass, it's no use my getting your hopes up. You're in a right pickle and no mistake. I don't know what to suggest. There are a dozen ships sailing from this port on every tide. Don't you know it's the busiest in the world? Without proper documents you don't have a hope. The dock area streets are filled to bursting with Irish people who've been robbed of their last belongings and forced to squat in worse conditions than those they left behind.'

He saw the increasing panic in her face and without thinking he blurted, 'I don't live far from here myself. If you're willing to come home with me, I'll ask my Ma if she has any ideas. I can't promise anything, for we're overcrowded and poor as church mice ourselves, but you'll be safe with me, until you have time to decide your next step.'

Delia decided his offer was the lesser of two evils. But did this man really live with his family, she wondered, as he led her away? If not, whatever he had in mind for her couldn't be any worse than the danger she'd face wandering the Liverpool streets alone.

She nodded her assent and hung on to the hem of his jacket as they jostled their way through the crowd and out through the massive gates of the docks that had held so much magic for her when she'd landed a short time before. Now she felt as vulnerable as she had during the Great Hunger and the quayside and everyone on it seemed hostile and threatening.

It was only a five-minute walk to the home of Daniel Harkin.

He lived in one of the small terraced houses in Stone Street, within sight of the high sandstone walls of Clarence dock.

It was a dismal-looking road, with a long row of identical terraced dwellings on one side and an imposing brick warehouse on the other that blocked out most of the available light. It was on a steep incline and from the bottom she could see a row of brick arches at the summit that spanned the full width. It was a bridge of sorts, unlike anything Delia had ever seen. Beneath some of the arches she could see makeshift stables and a couple of cart horses stood fettered to nearby railings.

Daniel caught her looking at them and explained.

'They're railway arches, and if you stay long enough to have a cup of tea you'll likely hear one of the iron monsters rumbling by and find most of your tea in your lap after it's passed through. Ma reckons they'll shake these houses from their foundations before long.'

Delia had seen early illustrations of trains in the library at the Hall and had read newspaper reports of the rapid growth of railways in the larger industrial cities on the mainland. If the bustling commerce on the quaysides at Belfast and Liverpool were any indicators, she could expect to see and hear a lot more trains and traffic.

Daniel's mother was sitting on the front step of number eighty-four when they turned into the street.

She wore the traditional long black skirt and shawl, similar to the druggets worn by most of Delia's kinfolk, and her hair was drawn back severely from her face in a tight bun. Her face was careworn and Delia estimated her age to be close to fifty. Mrs Harkin made no move to get up when they came in sight, but only squinted up at them, using her arm to shield her eyes from the sun.

'Mam, this young woman is Delia Dreenan. She's just off the Belfast boat, on her way to America, except the pickpockets had other plans for her and now she's stranded here until she can contact her relatives back home. I didn't know how to steer her, Ma, so I brought her home hoping you might.'

'Ah, Daniel lad, if I had a penny for every countryman that's been robbed in this city I'd be a rich woman.' She turned her head to peer at Delia. 'I'm sorry for you love, for I'm sure you've been through Ireland's Purgatory. If you've any money at all there's lodging for young ladies in Shaw Street. Daniel will walk you there.'

She turned to her son. 'Ask around for Rosie Heilbron's place. I can't remember the number of the house, but anyone on Shaw Street will point it out.'

Delia thanked Mrs Harkin and followed Daniel up the hill and under the railway arches. They walked through identical-looking streets all named after naval heroes and great explorers, and she felt they were climbing steadily, away from the river, passing through a maze of identical streets of terraced houses and dismal courts. At last they stopped to cross a wide road that was cramped on both sides with more shops and inns she had ever seen.

Daniel laughed when she commented on the numbers of inns.

'Inn is far too polite a word for them,' he told her. 'They're alehouses, and there's one on every corner of every street. This is Scotland Road, occupied almost exclusively by Irish and Italian settlers. But I can't think why it was named so. Piss Drunk Alley would be a more fitting name for it, if you're asking my opinion.'

Delia had never seen so many people, even on the quay, and they waited a long time for an opportunity to cross the wide road in safety. They dodged steaming mounds of horse manure and ducked to avoid people who lugged heavy hand carts or balanced large baskets and bundles on their heads.

Shaw Street seemed palatial in contrast and, as they turned into the wide tree-lined street, they almost collided with a group of Africans who were milling outside one of the large

Georgian houses that stretched in an elegant row down one side. A couple of the men sat on the steps reading newspapers, while others stood in tight circles throwing dice and smoking the familiar clay pipes.

Daniel knew one of them and he stopped to shake the man's hand.

'Samuel! How are you? I haven't seen you on any trips lately. Have you been sick or something?'

Samuel touched the peak of his cap in greeting and answered Daniel in a voice as deep and thick as the dark treacle tone of his skin.

'I been down the docks every sunrise for a week, but nobody's takin' on any negros. Them riots in the Piazza Goree made folk skittish o' my kind. The gaffers are jittery as moths round a candle in case there's more trouble.'

'I'm sorry for you, Samuel. If I get the chance I'll put in a good word for you. Do you happen to know Rosie Heilbron's house? I'm seeking shelter for my cousin, Delia, here. She's just after docking from the old country.'

Samuel pointed out the house and they proceeded further down the row of elegant homes.

Daniel explained as they walked that this part of the city was once occupied by wealthy merchants and local dignitaries. However, this end of Shaw Street had fallen out of fashion with the wealthy, who were now vacating the city in large numbers in favor of the seaside towns further up the coast.

They passed several boarding houses and a military barracks that had been cleverly disguised to blend with the adjacent homes. Through an archway floated the familiar pungent smell of horse and she caught sight of a partly uniformed soldier grooming his animal as they passed. Opposite was a large tract of open parkland. It was elevated high above the city and its grassy mounds were broken by massive sandstone boulders.

'Known locally as "Shawry Canyon",' Daniel told her.

It was already late afternoon and the lamplighter was making an early start. She could see the faint reflection of yellow pools of light as he made his way along the darkening pavement ahead of them. They reached the house and read the information on a large brass plaque that gleamed, incongruous, against the faded peeling paint of the shabby door: 'Heilbron Shelter for Young Ladies. Strict Curfew 10pm.'

As they waited for somebody to answer their knock, Delia asked Daniel. 'Why did you tell that man I was your cousin? Surely there was no need to lie?'

'There was every need,' Daniel answered sharply. 'In this town, you don't let your left hand know what your right is doing. Better for them to think you're related to me; that way, they might think twice before doing you harm. It's easy to see you're as green as the hills you've left behind. When this door opens, you'd better leave the talking to me.'

She was stung by the sudden hostility in his tone, but she didn't get the chance to rebuke him. The flaking door was opened a crack and a stout woman asked their business.

'We're looking for Rosie Heilbron if you please, missus,' Daniel said.

'There's no Rosie here,' the woman retorted. 'I'm *Rose* Heilbron, and if it's any of your business, I *don't* please. What is it you want?'

'Safe lodgings for my cousin, here; she's in need of shelter until she sails for America.'

'Well, she'll get none here, for I'm full 'til the end of the week.'

Neither of them got to actually *see* Rosie Heilbron. The half-open door was then closed quickly and firmly in their faces.

Daniel gave a derisive snort and kicked at the door. 'It's been a pleasure talking to you, missus,' he shouted through the letterbox, before taking Delia's arm and leading her away.

'Are there any other reputable lodgings in the area?' She asked him. 'I must find a room for the night before it gets dark.

I can't go wandering unfamiliar streets.'

'Now don't you start fretting,' said Daniel. 'You're coming back to the house with me.'

The return journey took a good deal longer. Daniel seemed to know every other person they met and, between the frequent stops to socialize and the numerous enquiries as to boarding houses, it was tea time before they turned into Stone Street.

She was filled with dread at the thought of facing Daniel's mother a second time, since she the woman hadn't shown much warmth when they'd first been introduced. However, when they arrived at the house and entered the tiny back kitchen, Katy Harkin reacted with surprise more than annoyance.

Daniel explained what had happened and she looked at Delia for a long time, seemingly weighing up the girl's situation.

'You can stay here for the night lass, but you'll have to sleep on the floor. We're three to a bed as it is, and my girls have to get up for work in the morning; they need their sleep.'

'Sure, I've slept on worse, Mrs Harkin,' Delia assured her. 'I'm grateful for a safe roof over my head. Can I pay you for your kindness?'

'Mother o' God no! Aren't we both sisters of Ireland after all? We have to look out for each other, especially in a strange country. Daniel, make the girl a cup o' tea—and toast her a slab o' bread before she goes down for the night.'

Delia sat by the range and drank her tea while Daniel crouched in front of the fire beside her and speared a thick slice of bread onto the poker, holding it close to the flames to brown. In between checking the bread, he chatted to the women, recounting his meeting with Sam and the various characters he'd met on Scotland Road.

'There are some awful shenanigans at the docks,' replied his mother. 'Your father told me how ruthless some of the boss men can be. They're either drunk with power or drunk with ale— either way, it's making them belligerent and biased toward their own kind. Makes me ashamed to admit I'm Irish at times.' Mrs Harkin was at the sink, scrubbing away at a bowl full of dark socks. At sight of her, Delia was suddenly transported back to the kitchen across the Irish Sea, where Mrs C was doubtless bent over her sink in like manner.

She felt the familiar flush of warmth while watching this woman. The two kitchens were at opposite ends of a spectrum, yet both had a welcoming fire and Delia soon felt relaxed and more than ready for bed after a long day of travel and uncertainty.

She must have dozed off, and woke abruptly when Daniel leaned on her chair to rise, abandoning the toast as Mrs Harkin led Delia upstairs to her daughters' bedroom.

'You won't be disturbed, lass. Our Kathleen and Susan are working late shift at the bag warehouse and they won't be home 'til ten. And God knows what time his lordship will fall in—some nights this house is as busy as Casey's Court with all the comings and goings. I'm only sorry I can't offer you a bed. Have you a shift to wear?'

Katy Harkin bade her 'Goodnight' and left the room without waiting for an answer. Delia made no attempt to stifle a yawn as she opened her valise, feeling strangely comforted by the sounds of Daniel and his mother chatting in the kitchen below.

Her nightgown was cold against her skin and she hugged it to her body, trying to take the chill off it before pulling it over her head. She lay down on the oilcloth-covered floor with her valise for a pillow and thought about how her fortunes had changed again; of how her plans and hopes had been snatched away in a minute by a pickpocket's slight of hand. She shivered and pulled the coarse blanket tighter and said a short prayer of thanks for Daniel and his mother.

'God be within and without them; God be beside them always. Amen. Oh! And please God—put some work Samuel's way soon,' she added, before she fell asleep.

Chapter 21

The room was filled with pre-dawn shadows and she stepped over items of the girls' clothing as she groped along the dark landing to the stairs. She was desperately in need of a lavatory and wondered if the family even had one. If they did it had to be outside. Mrs Harkin had pointed out the only other room upstairs the night before as the one she shared with Daniel's Da.

She crept down to the kitchen, glad of the dim light the fire provided and stepped out into the yard. She was startled on her return from the privy, to see Daniel standing in the doorway waiting for her.

'Are you alright, Delia? I'm just off to work. Da's gone already and the girls don't start until later. Ma's usually up by now, so she'll not be far behind you. The tea's brewed, so help yourself, and I'll only be gone an hour or so. I'm only signing on this morning, so I shouldn't be too long, and when I get back, we'll go searching for some decent lodgings for you.'

After he left, she enjoyed a few precious moments of solitude, the first she'd had since leaving Belfast, and she basked in the sanctity of silence and pondered over her situation as she gazed into the glowing caverns of the fire. Being robbed was a painful violation, but her circumstances weren't totally desperate. She had money, and in a city of this size and importance, she should have no difficulty finding decent lodgings.

She would have to write to Lord Keenagh and confess her

carelessness, but if there was any decent paying work to be had, she could pay him back before too long and continue her journey to the New World.

Someone stirred above and she rose to pour an extra cup of tea. She remained standing until she was sure she hadn't taken Mrs Harkin's favorite chair, but when Daniel's mother appeared she greeted Delia with a quick wave of a hand and hurried through the back kitchen on her way to the lavatory, stopping on the way back to re-fill the coal bucket.

Delia watched through the small window as Katy huffed and puffed her way up the yard. She held the coal bucket with both hands, used her backside to close the door behind her and grunted loudly as she dropped the scuttle onto the hearth. 'Phew!' She gasped. 'I couldn't do that twice in one day.' She pursed her lips and blew hard, rubbing the small of her back as she did so and held out a hand for the cup.

'Is that tea for me? God bless your heart. Did you sleep alright up there?'

Daniel's mother had Mrs Cleary's habit of asking multiple questions without waiting for any answer. They had no sooner settled themselves by the fire when one of Daniel's sisters rushed through the kitchen, also in urgent need of the lavatory. She held her hands over her bursting bladder as she tried to dash down the yard with her legs crossed. Delia couldn't help but laugh at the sight.

'That's our Kat,' Mrs Harkin said with an air of resignation. 'Short for Kathleen—and by the way, you're to call me Katy while you're here. Our Suzy has the good fortune to be the only Suzy on either side of the family, so she gets her proper title. You'll not get a glimpse of her this side of noon hour. "Snoozy Suzy," her father calls her. The other one couldn't sleep in if she wanted to, and the same one could piss for all of Ireland.'

Delia almost choked on her tea but Katy qualified the statement without a hint of a pause.

'She pisses like a horse, our Kat does. Her father says we should've rented her out to a tannery years ago. Sure, we'd have made a bleedin' fortune by now.'

Delia dabbed at the tea stain on the front of her blouse and found herself warming to Katy, and she thought she liked both girls before she'd formally met them. She learned that Daniel was indeed the first born and, at twenty-three, was only two years older than she.

All of them were as warm and as open as her adoptive Irish family at the Hall, and when Daniel returned he found the four women seated around the kitchen table, chatting amiably as they finished a late breakfast of fried egg sandwiches.

Delia felt as if she'd known them all her life and Daniel might have been a fly on the wall for all the notice they took of him, until he butted in and reminded them of the time. There was a mad scramble at the table as the two sisters jostled to get past each other and out to work.

'Are you as thick as you look, Daniel Harkin?' shouted Suzy, grabbing her coat from the back of the door. 'Why did you wait 'til now to shake us?'

Daniel threw up his hands in exasperation and shouted down the lobby after the departing girls.

'Who do you take me for, the knock up man?' He turned to his mother. 'Them two could out gab a politician in a filibuster, and *I'm* the one accused of making them late.'

He spoke as though annoyed, but Delia could see the hidden smile that crossed his eyes, and it spread to the rest of his face when he turned to her.

'I can't think why you're so happy, Delia. Are you ready to do battle with the Liverpool streets again?' he asked, holding the door open.

They spent the afternoon walking from one lodging to another without much success. The few boarding houses that had vacancies all had some drawback. Either the location was

171

too seedy or the cost of lodging more than she could afford. Part of Delia's dilemma was her total lack of experience. She had no yardstick for determining what was fair in terms of boarding. Liverpool was so expensive and she was thankful to have Daniel's knowledge of the city and the protection of his street wisdom.

She'd been sheltered during her five years at Keenagh Hall, time enough to soften the edges of her survival instincts and dull her once sharp wits.

When she and Daniel left the house that morning, Katy Harkin invited her back for tea, reminding Delia that she'd have to return for her things anyway. But they were no further ahead when they trudged wearily up Stone Street, just in time to hear the loud whistle from the warehouse and to be caught up in the throng of workers who poured from the exits and quickly flooded the darkening street.

She hovered on the step, reluctant to go inside and fought back tears of frustration. Daniel had been kindness itself, but she knew he was missing valuable hours of work escorting her round the city and the family could ill afford to lose his wages. She sighed and resigned herself to the fact that tomorrow she must make her own way.

Katy Harkin stopped plating the boiled bacon and cabbage when they walked in. She saw the despondency in Delia's face immediately.

'I take it you've had no luck, then?'

Delia felt the tears build up again and spoke before Daniel had a chance to explain.

'I feel terrible about all this. I can't keep availing myself of your kindness and good nature, Mrs Harkin. Daniel must be losing precious work time and I know the burden of having an extra mouth to feed has tipped the scales for many a poor family. If I'm to stay then you must let me pay my portion.'

'Now listen here,' Daniel's mother said. 'How many plates

do you see on this table?' She paused with the serving spoon wedged into her hip and Delia could see that she had portioned out food enough for six. She was lost for an answer but, in any case, Katy Harkin didn't give her a chance.

'Didn't I ask you back for tea when you left this morning? And did I not tell you that we Irish have to look out for each other? Do you think we're goin' to be any the poorer for you havin' some bacon and cabbage with us? Now sit yourself down and drink your tea. After we've eaten, we'll put our heads together and see if we can't sort something out.'

She inverted plates onto the girls' suppers and placed them in the warming oven to the side of the fire. 'I hope to God they don't dry out before the girls get home. There's talk of them getting out early tonight on account of the troubles in town, but our Kat says it depends on the shift gaffer. One of them is an auld snide of a man, who's so mean he wouldn't give ya' so much as three cheers if you swam from here to Dublin and back.'

All three were on the end of their meal when Mr Harkin surprised them by showing up, just as they were wiping dry bread around their plates to absorb the last of the cabbage juice.

He greeted them in Gaelic and sat straight down without washing his hands. He sniffed the air and rubbed his palms together in anticipation. Katy placed his meal in front of him and deftly removed the saucepan lid that covered his plate and released a fragrant burst of steam into the air.

'You're early.' She said, returning his kiss. 'How in God's name did you manage to pass by the alehouse without stepping inside, Joey Harkin?' She put a hand to his forehead and he brushed it aside.

'I'm just checkin' to make sure you're not sickening for somethin',' she joked.

'I was more hungry than thirsty if you must know, woman, and anxious to meet this handsome colleen here.' He turned to

Delia and spoke to her for the first time. 'Dandy Dan here told me about your troubles, Delia. Have you found somewhere decent to doss down yet?'

She and Daniel took turns to relate the day's events and Delia ended by apologizing to Mr Harkin for the upheaval her arrival had surely caused.

'Not at all,' he told her. 'I remember the many kindnesses shown to me when I first touched English soil. I hear you're from Donegal? In that case, you'll know how keenly our people feel the sting of separation. It's a mark of our closeness and a measure of the love we have for one another. One more mouth won't make a ha'penny worth of difference in this house lass, so sleep easy in your bed. You're a welcome sight an' all.'

He stopped suddenly, as if he'd just remembered something and turned his attention to his wife who was busy at the sink. 'Has a man to die o' thirst before you'll get him his tea, woman?'

'It's comin' up, Joey, have a little patience.' Katy Harkin lifted the big brown teapot off the range and brought it to the table. She was careful to fill her husband's cup before topping up everyone else's, but when she finished she banged the teapot down in front of him to get his attention. 'Delia here can't sleep easy in her bed because she doesn't have one. Now—what are you goin' to do about *that*?'

As soon as the dishes were cleared away, they re-grouped at the table and between them agreed Delia must stay. Daniel would sleep with his father for the time being and Katy would share the girls' bed, while Delia could use the downstairs couch in the front parlor that was normally used by Daniel.

'We don't use the front parlor much,' Katy explained. 'You'll find it quite sparse, but the couch is comfy and you'll be warm enough with a couple of hot bricks and some extra coats over you. I'll ask some of the market women about safe lodgings for you when I see them in the morning. We don't need newspapers in this town as long as there are barrow women, for there's very little that slips by their notice.'

Delia went to her temporary bed that night with a full belly and a full heart and her prayers were offered up exclusively for her newly-adopted family in Stone Street.

Chapter 22

She quickly slipped into the routine of the little house in Stone Street. She awoke as soon as the men stirred for work and made sure the tea was brewed and the fire well stoked before the women rose. Joey Harkin always left at first light for his stevedore job at the docks but Daniel's hours were fairly regular, since he worked the ferries that sailed from Liverpool to Dublin three times a week, and he had one day off after every third crossing.

The girls got along well with each other and were no longer afraid of sleeping in, now that Delia was there to wake them in good time for work.

She kept the house clean during the day and scoured the 'Situations Vacant' column and the 'Lodgings for Rent' in the *Liverpool Mercury* and the *Daily Post* whenever she had a spare half hour.

Most days Katy Harkin headed for the fruit market after picking up her cart from the top of the street, where she stored it with one of the stable owners. She boasted of having the busiest spot in Great Howard Street and her patch was only a short walk from the house. She normally didn't return until late afternoon, unless she managed to sell her wares to the hungry workers who poured out of the numerous warehouses and distilleries in the area during lunch hour.

As soon as the girls left for their noon shift, Delia took tea and bread and butter to Katy's patch, and sometimes she gave Delia a list of things they might need for the evening meal.

There was never any talk of payment for her lodging, but Delia was happy knowing she would be able to return their generosity once she found a job and permanent rooms, and she secretly vowed to find a way to leave some monetary remuneration at the house, knowing they would never take it from her openly.

She'd been with the Harkin family about three weeks when Suzy and Kat told her one morning there'd been an accident at the bag warehouse the night before and one of the girls had been injured when her arm got caught in a stitching machine.

'It was horrible,' Suzy told her. 'The poor girl's screams could be heard above the noise of the machines and yet the gaffers never broke stride. They wouldn't even turn the machine off, but pulled the nearest sweeper off the job to stand in for the maimed woman. They say she'll lose an arm for sure.'

'Life is cheap in the factories,' Kat said. 'Don't ever take a factory job if you can help it, Delia. A lot of these accidents are caused because the girls are so tired. The hours are too long— we're standing too long—and we've waited too long for decent pay and conditions. And it's murder when you're having your monthlies.'

'Kat's right. I've watched some of those poor girls drain of colour and pass out right before my eyes,' Suzy chipped in. 'They bleed so heavily from standing all the day. They should be home in bed instead of risking life and limb in that miserable warehouse.'

'It would be more accurate to call it a *workhouse*,' fumed Kat. 'Some of the gaffers should be hung, especially the females. You'd think they'd have more compassion, wouldn't you? But they don't. They're harder than the men. Did you hear, Suzy, about that pig's melt of a woman, Mary Sheilds—the one that supervises the cutting room? She was set upon after leaving

The Grosvenor pub the other night, and left for dead. I'd like to shake the hand of the one that nearly killed her—God forgive me, I would indeed.'

'I have to agree with you, Kat. I've seen crimes inside that warehouse that would warrant a lengthy prison term. You mind what she's tellin' you, Delia, and find a better situation for yourself. You've the bearing and breeding of a better class and you'd not last long in the warehouses or factories around here.'

'I was hoping for a governess or companion position in America,' said Delia. 'I've never been work-shy, but I think you're right about the factories, Kat. I wouldn't mind a shop assistant's job or a post that involves children. I love them and seem to relate well to little ones.'

As usual, Fate had other plans, and Delia found herself taking charge of Katy Harkin's barrow, after Daniel's mother slipped on some slimy orange skins at the fruit market and landed heavily on her hip, fracturing the joint as well as antagonizing an old back problem. Months of enforced bed rest followed, and any plans Delia had were put on indefinite hold.

The rest of the family called it Divine Providence that Delia had come to them when she was needed most, and there was a certain comfort in knowing she was helping them ward off the bailiffs. Every penny in the Harkin household was spoken for and there was no room for accidents or sickness.

She found she enjoyed the work, if the weather was dry. It offered variety and it gave her opportunity to meet new people. She learned to appreciate the irascible Liverpool wit and the playful nature of the brash Liverpudlians, most of who seemed to be natives of Ireland or Wales.

She overheard the Gaelic tongue frequently around the markets and although it was mostly confined to traditional greetings or short blessings, she thrilled to hear it.

Daniel helped her on his days off, pushing the heavily-laden cart full of fruit and vegetables along Cazneau Street and down

Burlington Street to Katy's patch. He'd slip home and bring back a can of tea and a bacon sandwich. It gave him a chance to check on his mother and make sure the girls were up and out.

She loved having Daniel's help. He knew so many people in the area and they had no trouble selling the stock when he was around.

'You could sell a newspaper to a blind man, Daniel Harkin,' she told him one afternoon as they made their way back to the stables with the empty cart.

Her pocket was heavy with coins and they were both filled with the contentment that comes from an honest day's work.

'You've missed your calling,' she told him. 'Do you prefer to be on the ships?'

'Not at all,' he replied. 'I'll go wherever work is to be found. I'm not particular, except I agree with my sisters—but don't ever tell them that, about not working in large factories, I mean to say, I couldn't do it. I don't take well to others telling me what to do. It's different on the ships—we learn our duties and we're left alone to carry them out. And I love being on the water. Someday, I'll be my own boss though.'

He stuffed both hands in his pockets and scuffed his feet as they made their way down the street toward the house. He began to hop over the cracks in the flagstones, darting this way and that in an impromptu aerial dance, with his hands still tucked firmly into his pockets.

'You've quite the nimble feet there, Daniel Harkin. That's a fine jig you're dancing. Did you learn that in the old country?'

He stopped and waited for her to draw level with him. 'I've never thought to ask you that same question, Delia. Do *you* like to dance? There's a céilidh every Tuesday night at Holy Cross. Would you fancy coming with me one night, just for the dancing like? It starts at half six and we'd be home by nine. What do you say? Or would you like me to ask Ma's permission to take you?'

'I would prefer that you ask your Mother, but I think it

would do us both a power of good to kick our heels up for an hour or two. But we mustn't leave Katy alone for too long, so let's see how your Father feels about it.'

'Done and dusted!' Daniel said, grinning from ear to ear. He looked as smug as a cat in a creamery and for some reason she found it necessary to temper his pleasure a little.

'We're going dancing, Daniel, nothing more. Two hours you said, and it won't even be that long if you step on my toes.'

He danced around her. 'There's no danger of that, Delia. I've been jigging since I could walk. You are looking,' he continued, glancing down at his boots, 'at enchanted feet. I may have been at the back of the queue when God was handing out faces, but I definitely got the first pickings of the feet.'

'You also missed out on a portion of modesty I notice, you cheeky gorsoon,' Delia replied and Daniel caught the sarcasm in her remark.

'I might as well blow my own trumpet,' he told her, 'for who else will blow it for me?'

'We'll see how good a dancer you are soon enough,' she told him. He seemed chastened for the moment and they fell silent until they were back in the house.

When the girls found out they were going to the Holy Cross céilidh, they were green with envy. Both girls were on the unsociable 'two til ten' shift at the warehouse and it precluded them making any plans for evenings.

They complained that the late shift ruined their nights *and* their days. Both girls worked alternating shifts of two weeks duration and found much to complain about with both schedules.

When they were on 'earlies', as they called it, Delia would meet them at the warehouse gates when they finished at two and they would walk along the dock road and into the heart of the city. They'd purchase meat pies from one of the carters and, if the weather was fine, they'd sit on a bench at the Pier Head and watch the sailing ships glide through the Mersey toward the open sea. They devised a game of speculation and each of them took turns at guessing the destination of the vessels.

Delia kept them entertained with stories from her time at the Hall, and sometimes, she would bemoan the chance she had missed, sharing with Kat and Suzy the dreams of the life she'd envisioned in America.

'You'll get there one day, Delia luv,' they would tell her, 'if and when God intends it for you.'

During the outings with the girls, she learnt more about their family's circumstances. The Harkins had left Moville in the summer of 1848. Theirs was a story with an all too familiar ring. They were long time tenants on land scheduled for clearance and were forced, along with the rest of their clachan, to sell their remaining possessions in lieu of rent. Their landlord had been cruel in the extreme and word of his inhumanity soon spread throughout Donegal.

Vermin, he'd called his tenants, and he was determined to purge his lands of every last one of them. It was said his constant evictions kept the polis and gaughers in employment for years.

Joe Harkin had been given leave by the landowner to attend the Greencastle Fair in August of 1848, in order to sell the family pig. The proceeds were to be handed over to offset his rent arrears. He was escorted by Johnson, the landlord's agent, and a constable, who was to relieve Joe of the money once the sale was complete.

But Joe Harkin had given his family precise instructions the night before. They were to follow at a safe distance and wait at the turnstile on the approach road into Greencastle. Daniel, being the eldest, had shadowed the three men on the journey and, once they arrived at the fair, it had been easy for him to blend in with the crowd of men who hung around in hope of securing seasonal work on the busier farms or on the English mainland.

He stayed close and, as instructed, he seized the first opportunity to relieve his father of the pig. Joe let the sow go without too much of a struggle, knowing it was his son doing the 'stealing'. Johnson knew Harkin was of no further use to him once the sow was gone, and Daniel's father was set free with the threat of immediate eviction ringing in his ears.

Reunited; the family walked south-west to Carrowkeel, where they traded the pig for the boat fare to Derry. They had sufficient money left to pay for transport to the east coast and relatives sheltered them in Dundalk until they were able to work their passage to England.

They were safe on the mainland before Johnson discovered their abandoned dwelling and long before the cruel whip of retribution could harm them. They'd squatted in the Stone Street house for weeks, laying low whenever the rent collector made his rounds. By the time they were discovered, all four had found employment and the landlord was only too glad to let them stay. It saved him the bother of having to find new tenants for the run-down house.

A strong camaraderie persisted among the Liverpool Irish in the dockland area, just as it had in their homeland. They bonded together against all perceived outsiders, including the unfortunate rent man.

'I wouldn't have his job for a big clock,' Katy was fond of saying. 'He's about as welcome as the undertaker in these parts.'

'It's a miracle to me he gets back to his office in one piece on collection days.'

She was growing irritable from prolonged bed rest and, when Daniel told her of his intention to take Delia dancing, he expected some resistance, but she surprised him by being pleased.

'She's a lovely girl, Daniel,' she told him; 'but a word o' warnin' to you, son. She's made of finer linen than we're used to and there's a lack of the rural about her at times. I'd advise you to tread carefully, lad.'

'For God's sake, Mother! I'm taking her to Holy Cross to dance with me—not to marry me!' He was surprised at his own vehemence, and so was his mother. She'd never known him to lie to her, but she had to wonder why he became so defensive. Both mother and son were united in wondering if he was becoming more attached to Delia than he cared to admit.

Daniel knew he felt differently toward her than he did his sisters. While he loved them, and they could warm his heart, his sisters didn't have the power to cause the tingling in his lower belly, and his manhood didn't stiffen at sight of them; not the way it did when he imagined kissing Delia.

She was a goddess in his eyes. Yet he never felt beneath her and she never adopted superior ways with any of his family. But there was no question her habits were refined and she had more of the learning than the rest of them put together.

He didn't dwell on his changing feelings any further, until she came downstairs the night of the dance. She stood in the hallway, wearing a soft grey skirt with a matching blouse. Her hair was drawn back from her face and held with a bow of grosgrain ribbon in a deeper shade of grey, and her dark hair, still damp from washing, hung to her shoulders in thick chestnut-colored curls.

He'd only seen her in druggets, aside from their first meeting on the quay, and he was dumbstruck at sight of her and could only stand in mute admiration and stare.

He *did* feel a physical reaction, and he was very glad there was nobody in the hall to witness it. He could hear his mother, however, shouting down from her room, and her unseen presence shook him from his stupor.

'Isn't she gorgeous, Daniel?' Katy called. 'Come up here to me now and let's see if you're a match for her.'

He detected a faint whiff of roses as he squeezed past her on the stairs and had another warning of the power of her beauty when he hardened from the slight brush of her skirts as they passed. He kept his head lowered and his hands over his crotch, not daring to look at her lest he should draw attention to the tell-tale bulge.

In spite of the effort he'd made sponging his jacket and trousers, he felt shabby beside her. His clothes were shiny from wear, which was more than could be said for his boots; no matter how vigorously he polished them they refused to shine.

They were quiet on the walk to the church hall. Daniel worried about Delia. He was afraid she might feel self-conscious among the women but his fears were unfounded. The hall was packed with smartly-dressed females, but not one of them could hold a candle to her. All eyes were on her the minute they entered, and a few of his mates from the docks called out to him.

'Where did you pluck the rose Dan O' Harkin?' asked one cheeky gorsoon. He was a good friend and he sauntered across and brazenly admired Delia. 'You're a dark horse, Dan me boy. Where have you been hidin' this luvly flower? Picked her fresh from the auld country, I shouldn't wonder. You didn't find *her* in Lime Street now, did you?'

Daniel replied good-naturedly and steered Delia onto the dance floor, before anyone else beat him to it.

They danced without a break and the lively jigs left them breathless and prevented any real conversation between them. But even the odd touch of her, or the brush of her hair against his arms, sent his head spinning and his trousers tightening, again and again.

He was glad nobody tried to break them apart, yet disappointed they weren't able to make themselves heard above the loud music and the heavy thumping of boots on the wooden dance floor. It wasn't until they were walking home that Daniel had a chance to tell her how lovely she looked.

She had linked her arm through his, but removed it quickly and began to fuss with her hair.

184

'Bless me! I'm a mess. I'm hot and sticky and I—' Daniel caught her hand and held it firmly in his own before she could protest further.

'You look lovely, Delia, even lovelier than before we left home. Your cheeks are flushed like a summer rose and you must know how becoming it is to a man. Sure, you must have driven the buckos mad in that place tonight. I'm glad none of them tried to dance with you, because I tell you, I'd have landed in the Bridewell lock- up if they had.'

She laughed and squeezed his hand, only for a second and ever so lightly, but it was as good as a kiss to Daniel. He smiled to himself under cover of dark and wished the house in Stone Street was still miles away.

Katy heard them as soon as they opened the front door and they had no choice but to go straight upstairs and give her a full account of the evening. She wanted to know every little detail, and while Delia described the dresses and recalled the list of reels and jigs the fiddlers had played, Daniel added some meat to the tale, telling his mother about those courting couples whose parents were known to her.

Delia made tea and they sat around the bed entertaining Katy until they heard the girls come in just after ten. All three were surprised at how much time had lapsed. It turned out to be a very late night for them all, since the account had to be repeated for Kat and Suzy, and for Mr Harkin, who returned just as they were tucking into a second round of tea and toast. The women were screaming with laughter between mouthfuls as Daniel performed some remarkably accurate imitations of some of the men.

'Oh now Da, don't be an auld grouch,' Kat said, catching sight of Joe's sour expression. 'Our Daniel and Delia here have given us such a lively account of the dance. It was almost as good as being there with them, and they've been a good tonic for Ma.'

'These two would make a great double act down at the Shakespeare theatre,' Katy said as Joe bent to kiss her. 'But away with you now to your beds. It's high time we were all asleep. Make sure you bank the fire up, Daniel, before you come up for the night.'

As the household settled down for the night, Daniel knocked sharply on the parlor door and shouted 'Goodnight' to Delia.

She wished him likewise and lay staring dreamily at the shafts of light from the street lamp outside, and it was a long time before she felt ready for sleep. She re-lived every magical moment. Daniel had not been boasting—he *was* a fine dancer and she couldn't have asked for a more amiable partner and it had felt so good to kick up her heels.

Her thoughts turned to Ireland, and to Magdalen, who, by this time, would be fast asleep in her new school. She would have loved every minute of this evening. She determined to write and tell her at the first opportunity.

Her thoughts drifted to her mother's stories of her early courtship. She was no more than a child when Barney Dreenan lured her from her family at the fair. He had thrown her down in the grass as soon as they were out of sight and that first assault had set the pattern for their marriage. There was to be no gentle courting or coaxing for young Margaret McLaughlan; no lover's tokens or compliments either; only the shame of being used as dispassionately and as frequently as a mongrel bitch to satisfy her father's animal urges. Barney Dreenan took his wife day or night, and without regard to his children lying beside them on the same pallet.

Delia shuddered with disgust at recollection of the grunts and slaps she'd heard during his assaults on her mother, and the painful digs he'd given her when she dared to complain. If he didn't have enough drink in him, the humping would go on for hours—and if he had too much, the frustration of his own drunken impotence would increase until some nights none of them were spared his fat fists and vile groping.

Her unhappy thoughts had destroyed her mood and she was forced to admit her Da still had power to get the better of her. *'The devil has a long reach,'* she thought. He had intruded on her precious dreams and it set her to wondering if Joe Harkin or Daniel could be capable of such cruelty. The possibility disturbed her, and it was a long time before she was calm enough for sleep.

Daniel was gone when she came down next morning.

She left his sisters sleeping and took tea up to Katy before she prepared the porridge, and thoughts of her father were pushed to the back of her memory as she did her chores and basked in the warmth the Harkin family had shown her.

Chapter 23

She and Daniel didn't have an opportunity to dance again for a long time. Katy mended sufficiently to accompany Delia with the hand cart, but her contribution was restricted to taking the money from the customers. She couldn't stand for long periods and precious room on the cart was taken up by the kitchen chair they had to bring along with them.

Delia now felt justified in calling herself a barrow woman. She loved the work and had already met some fascinating characters. She'd learned some valuable tricks and knew enough to be among the first buyers at the fruit market. The wholesalers soon learnt that although she was fresh off the boat, she was not easily fobbed off with damaged fruit. Katy had taught her well and she insisted on closely examining every box of produce before she purchased.

Daniel's mother had a broad variety of customers and they trusted her to provide them with the freshest and the best, and Delia had no wish to jeopardize the faith and loyalty Katy's customers had shown her.

The busiest period was always after lunch, when the streets filled with people changing shifts and making their way home with thoughts of the evening meal in their heads.

It was during one of these spells, when the cart was surrounded by potential customers and Katy's chair was hidden from view by the crush of bodies waiting to be served, that Delia met Lavinia Corcoran. The woman was taking particular care in choosing pears and she handled them so much that Delia was afraid Katy would see her. If she did, she would waste no time in asking the woman to keep her hands off the merchandise. She looked up and caught Delia staring.

She held up a pear in each hand and smiled hesitantly, and Delia asked if she could help.

'I wonder—which of these varieties is more suited to poaching?' she asked her, but Katy had seen, and before Delia could answer, Mrs Harkin interjected rudely.

'Are you in the habit of washing fruit before you eat it, madam?' The woman turned to her, startled both at the question *and* the sharpness of Katy's tone.

'Yes of course. Why do you ask?'

'Because,' Katy continued, slowly and deliberately, 'most of my customers don't wash their fruit *or* their hands, which is why we don't encourage them to handle the merchandise. The fruit on this cart is the best in Liverpool, because we insist on high quality and high standards, so if you are in any doubt about buying them pears, please put them down and don't handle them, unless you have intentions of taking them home with you.'

The woman was flabbergasted. 'I do apologize. Please wrap these for me and add another four of the same,' she said to Delia, who was feeling a little sorry for the woman. As posh as she was, she'd seemed to visibly shrink in the face of Katy's rudeness.

Delia took the money and handed the pears over. 'These are Bartletts, ma'am, and just ripe enough for poaching. I'm sure your family will enjoy them.'

The woman thanked her and Delia watched her walk a short distance and stop at another cart further down the street. She kept an eye on her as she served a couple more of Katy's customers, and noticed that the woman had quite a number of bags by the time she'd finished. She saw her get into an open carriage that was soon swallowed up in the busy traffic.

'I think we may have lost a few shilling there,' she murmured quietly, yet somehow, Katy heard her above the hullabaloo.

'She'll be back. I've seen her before and I know her type well. The likes of her don't have to penny pinch, but she's renowned for trying to bargain with the carters. She won't pay the asking price if she can help it—that's how her kind get rich.'

Katy's unique wisdom was spot on as always, and the woman appeared again a few days later. It was raining heavily and most of the wares had been covered with sacking. Only the sturdier root vegetables were visible to customers.

They'd been slack most of the morning, but road traffic was constantly passing, and both Delia and Katy were soaked from the carriage wheels that sent cascades of dirty rainwater over their feet. Their shawls were heavy with rain and no longer any protection from the steady downpour.

Delia felt cold and miserable and prayed Katy might call it a day soon. She longed for a cup of tea and a warm fire, but in all consciousness she couldn't suggest an early finish and felt ashamed; knowing Katy must be every bit as uncomfortable as herself.

A heavy dray wagon rolled past at quite a clip and sent up a wall of water that soaked them both afresh. Katy shook a fist at the driver and shouted curses after him.

'Bad cess to yer—and to yer family an' all!' she called. 'I hope your horses lose their shoes and the ale goes bad on yer.' She shook her heavy skirts in an effort to dislodge some of the rainwater. As an afterthought, she raised both fists again and roared even louder at the ignorant drayman. 'An' may yer always be found wantin'. Ignorant bleeder!'

She was attracting a fair bit of attention with this tirade—not from the carters, who'd heard it all before, but from customers, most of them amused by her reaction. But they were unaware they smiled at their peril, for she caught one of them laughing and turned her razor-sharp wit on the hapless man.

'What are *you* smilin' about?' she asked him. 'Do you want to swap places with us? Let's see if you can keep that smile on your face doing *this* job, mister. Now! Are you buying—or are you just here for the entertainment?'

Delia averted her eyes from the unfortunate man and picked up a bag ready to take his order, but he walked away. As she looked up for the next customer, she saw it was the woman who'd bought the pears a few days earlier and before she could offer a greeting, Katy tapped her on the arm.

'I'm slipping into the Grapes for a warm. I'll not be gone long and you can go in after me.'

'I'll manage fine, Katy. You stay in there as long as you want.' She removed her heavy pocket, weighed down with coins from the day's takings, and gave it to Katy, who gave her some change before heading into the nearby alehouse. Delia turned to the woman and gave her a smile.

'How were the pears?' she asked her. The woman looked at her blankly for a moment before answering.

'Oh yes, the pears,' she said, remembering. 'They were excellent. Our dinner guests were very complimentary. What can you recommend today?'

Delia lifted the damp sacking to reveal the more delicate fruits. 'The plums are sweet and juicy and the cooking apples are just in. I stewed some last night and they were delicious— although you do need a fair bit of sugar with them.'

'I have brought a list,' said the woman, offering Delia a slip of paper. 'I wonder if I might leave it with you? It's rather a lot for me to carry. Mr Corcoran and I are entertaining again this evening and I need fruits and vegetables enough for eight guests. Is there anybody who might deliver them to my home, do you think?'

Delia was at a loss. She'd never been asked to deliver before and didn't know how Katy would react. On the other hand, it was likely to be a good-sized order and she was loath to let the business slip away.

'Would you mind if I asked Mrs Harkin before I give you an answer? She is sheltering not far from here and I don't want to say yes without first consulting her. She owns the cart, you see. I'm helping her out.'

The woman agreed and, as she darted into the Grapes, Delia asked Jack Donovan, who managed the adjacent barrow, to keep an eye on things until her return.

She found Katy at a table closest to the fire. She looked up startled as Delia approached, surprised to see her inside the ale house. She looked very settled, with a large glass of porter in front of her and her feet resting on the fender, as close to the burning coals as she dared.

Daniel came in behind her. He had brought some food for their lunches and had found them both missing and a strange woman in doubtful charge of their livelihood. Mrs Corcoran had explained the absence of the two women.

'It's alright, Delia,' he said. 'I've told her I'll take her order to her before we put the cart away for the night.' He turned to his mother. 'It's a few shillings Mam, and well worth the trouble. Here, have a look at the order.'

Although he'd said this to his mother, he offered Delia the slip of paper. Katy couldn't read or write but, like most of her peers, she could curse fluently in two languages and knew a wide variety of songs in English and Gaelic.

Delia followed Daniel out into the rain and began to assemble Mrs Corcoran's extensive list. She was careful to select the best they had and after she finished, she sheltered the produce well under the cart to protect it from the worst of the rain.

Later, as she and Daniel pushed the cart back to the stables, Daniel told her Mrs Corcoran lived in Crosby, a distance of about five miles from their patch.

'Don't tell Mam,' he said. 'It'll only set her off again, but I see a great opportunity here, and if we can get a few more orders as healthy as Mrs Corcoran's it'll be grand for business.'

'May I come with you, Daniel?' Delia asked, and Daniel tried not to show his delight at the prospect of having Delia to himself again.

Later that evening, he borrowed a decent pony and trap from the stables at the top of the street, in exchange for grooming the horse on his return.

During the journey, Delia had ample opportunity to look around a part of Liverpool hitherto unknown to her. They turned into Great Howard Street and trotted in a northerly direction along the dock road, passing Katy's patch and the large imposing entrance gates of the Clarence and Stanley Docks, where she could see, above the high walls, a complex jumble of masts from the fleets of moored ships.

They passed a large sawmill and, as they left the city behind, they drew level with an enormous building site where she spied a solitary watchman bending over a brazier. He rubbed his hands together vigorously as a stream of bricklayers and young apprentices poured onto the road, shouting their farewells to him and to each other as they dispersed into the maze of streets. 'This new construction is the result of the railway expansion,' Daniel explained. 'It's been constant since we arrived in the city and it won't be finished a moment too soon. The roads are becoming more congested as more and more goods are being loaded from the ships, and new docks are being built one after the other. On the way back I'll take you a different road so you can see the canal. It is every bit as choked as the roads. There's a continuous flotilla of barges carrying everything from coal to chalk dust, all of it needed to feed the industrial towns sprouting further inland.'

The road curved eastward and the river was lost from view by back-to-back houses as they slowed to a trot and turned into the south end of Crosby Road. This area wasn't half as busy and, apart from the occasional inn and a few scattered shops, it had a distinct rural feel about it.

The Crosby homes were on an even grander scale than the Shaw Street ones and she stared in fascination at the size and variety of structural designs, admiring the skill and workmanship of the decorative yellow and copper toned brickwork.

She caught a whiff of the Mersey and spied a brief glimpse of the water as it glistened in the reflection of yellow gaslight and twinkling signals from the many ships.

They found the Corcoran home before total darkness descended and brought the horse to a stop. Daniel hooked a bag over the animal's nose and tied the reins to a lamppost while they carried Mrs Corcoran's order back to Crosby Road and into the forecourt of number twenty-two.

'We'd better use the back entrance,' Daniel suggested. 'We don't want to spoil the logbook now, do we?'

A nervous-looking maid answered their knock and invited them to step in while she fetched the housekeeper, who appeared in short order, looking every bit as ruffled as the maid.

'Is there any chance you could come back tomorrow for your money?' she asked, looking appealingly at them both. 'Mrs Corcoran hasn't left any payment and I hate to disturb her. She's dressing for dinner.'

'Is she now?' Daniel said sharply. 'Then she's very lucky. Some of us don't have the luxury of anticipating an evening meal most nights of the week. We've travelled a long way, missus, and we're not leaving without being paid. We can't afford to give credit to our own kind, never mind those more privileged among us.'

'How much are you owed?' the harassed housekeeper asked. 'I'll look around and see if between us we can't make the money up.'

She turned to the young girl. 'Sally, do you have any money until I can prevail upon the mistress?'

Sally didn't have a single penny, and they scuttled around the room like a pair of mice, searching beneath various ornaments and jugs and feeling in coat pockets. But they only managed a few pennies between them.

'You'll have to take the order back,' the woman finally said, seeing they were at an impasse. But the young girl felt Daniel's growing anger and tugged at the housekeeper's sleeve.

'Mary, go up and ask for the money or we'll never get the dinner ready on time.'

Daniel did nothing to disguise his annoyance and Delia saw unmistakable shades of his mother.

'Yes Mary. Do as the girl says and drag your fat arse upstairs, so we can be paid and on our way.'

He threw the bags down decisively on a nearby table. 'I'm not taking this order back. For one thing, I won't be able to sell it for the same price tomorrow because it'll be wilted and we don't sell wilted produce. Secondly, if I take it back I lose twice over because there's the expense of the horse that brought us here, plus time lost in travel.'

They were all relieved when Mrs Corcoran entered the kitchen, dressed in an elaborate gown of copper silk. A ridiculous-looking bow of black velvet and two dark feathers hung over her face and the feathers waved back and forth in rhythm with her speech.

'Blown about by the hot air coming from her painted mouth,' Daniel would later say, when he told his mother.

'Oh, I'm so glad I caught you both,' she said breathlessly. 'Please accept my apologies.' She turned to the housekeeper, who had adjusted her stern countenance and was now acting as though she hadn't been troubled in the least by her employer's oversight.

'I left the payment in the front hall, thinking they might

knock at the front of the house this first time. I'm sorry, Hannah. I should have told you.' She handed Daniel an envelope and smiled at Delia.

'I think you'll find it correct and please don't be put off bringing any further orders. I promise you won't be inconvenienced again.'

As soon as the back door closed on them Daniel checked the contents of the envelope.

'I don't know where that woman's head is, but I think she's away with the wee folk. She's given me a whole shilling too much. But she'll have to wait for it, same as I did, for I'm not going back into that house again.'

A few days later, when the lady showed up at the cart, Delia immediately pointed out the error in payment and was delighted when Lavinia Corcoran confirmed the amount to be correct. The surplus, she explained, was compensation for their troubles.

During supper that night, Daniel was forced to change his opinion about the lady and Katy chastened him into accepting future orders from the Corcorans of Crosby Road.

Chapter 24

The Crosby delivery soon turned into a weekly trip and both Daniel and Delia looked forward to the journey. Mindful of the lucrative business and the generosity of her only 'high falutin' customer, Katy Harkin allowed them to finish a little earlier on delivery days so they could be on their way and back home before dark. The stable was paid a regular fee for the loan of the horse and although it was never discussed, Delia had no doubt Lavinia Corcoran tipped Daniel generously.

She accepted it was none of her business; it was enough for her to be allowed to accompany him. It gave them ample time to get to know each other more intimately and, before long, Delia found herself wondering if it was love she felt for Daniel.

It was no use asking the girls, for they claimed to be smitten so often. Yet Delia felt it was appearances that turned the girls' heads rather than emotion and she was left to search her own heart for answers. She only knew that the strange effect he was beginning to have on her was something she'd never experienced before and that in Daniel's company she was utterly content and felt differently toward him than she had for her siblings and Joe Harkin, who had now replaced Matty as her surrogate father.

She was serious by nature—her early life had made her so—but she was quick to laugh when Daniel was telling the jokes and his frequent imitations of the people they met always creased her with laughter. Many times she had to plead with him to stop, because he knew when she was helpless and would only exaggerate his behavior until her sides ached from laughing and tears of merriment ran down her cheeks. Lying in her bed she knew for certain she would welcome Daniel's child.

He was equally as besotted with Delia. When he was apart from her the light seemed to dim a little for him, and his family knew long before the couple themselves acknowledged it: their friendship had developed into something deeper and more precious to them both.

They attended Holy Cross dances whenever they could and after a while, the digs from friends' elbows and the frequent jibes from Daniel's workmates became harder to ignore. Until one night, as they made their way home, Daniel stopped under a streetlamp before they turned into Stone Street and spoke to Delia. It was one of the rare times she'd seen him looking so serious and it alarmed her.

'Don't look so frightened, Delia Dreenan. I never want to see fear in your lovely eyes again, especially when they're turned on me. But you must know by now. My feelings for you have deepened beyond the sisterly.'

He saw the relief in her expression and it warmed him and gave him confidence enough to continue.

'I think you plucked the heart from my chest the first day I saw you on the deck of the *Ariana*. But it was more pity I felt for you then; you looked so scared and lost and alone. Ma said, that first time you met her, that you were made of finer linen and there's no point in me trying to be what I'm not, besides, you know me well enough by now.'

He towered above her and looked down into her eyes with such intensity she felt he must see into the deepest part of her soul. The thought made her shiver, and he took the folds of her shawl and draped it over her head, holding on to it as he pulled her gently closer.

'I'm a worker who never seems to get beyond subsistence, so I can't offer you anything much, except my promise to work my fingers to the bone for you and to protect you as long as there's life in me.' He gave a nervous cough and took her face in his hands until she was looking into his eyes. 'Delia Dreenan, in the presence of God and all the saints, I swear I love you. And right this minute I'm praying, as I never have in my life, that you might come to love me too.'

Delia savored every word without speaking. He *loved* her. He was the first decent human being to *love* her. The tears came as she tried to smile, to reassure Daniel, who looked panic-stricken in the face of her unexpected weeping, but she was totally overwhelmed. Never in her life had she heard anyone say they loved her, not even her poor mother.

She knew, of course, that she *had* been loved. There could be no doubt in her mind of the stark contrast between love and hate, or indifference, the latter of which she'd had in spades from her Da.

But to hear Daniel's declaration, so openly given, and to feel his warmth, to be wrapped in his strong arms and to bear witness to the love and concern that shone from his eyes—it was too much. She was overpowered by a mix of emotions that churned up from deep within, provoked by the wonder of feeling cherished for the first time in her life.

She rubbed at her eyes with her pinny and wept into its folds. When she tried to speak her words were a muffled jumble of broken sentences interspersed with loud sobs. She knew he must be panicked by her reaction and could see the confusion and uncertainty in his eyes, but she could do nothing to stop the flow of tears. It felt so good to release them.

Her chest expanded, the tightness receded, and her whole world seemed lighter.

She took his hand in hers and brought it to her lips, kissing the tips of his fingers as she poured out her feelings to him.

'Oh, Daniel, I don't deserve such good fortune and that's the truth. Your family have given me such love and shown me such kindness. I will never be able to repay them. But you hold me in too much esteem and I am not deserving of such adulation. You know nothing about me, and 'tis folly to pretend I'm something more than a cotter's daughter who happened to be given a chance in a gentleman's home. Dearest Daniel—my best friend in the whole world. Do you not wonder why I don't go to church with you all?'

She couldn't bear to see the joy and hope fade from his eyes and she lowered her head and studied the calluses on the palm of his hand. He was a good man, and a hard grafter—but he was much too good for her. How could she marry *any* man? She could never justify dragging a lover into her dark past?

But somebody loved her—and it felt so good. She took one slow, shuddering breath and continued.

'I cannot soil God's house, for I have all but turned my back on him, Daniel. I live in mortal sin and, what's worse, it doesn't bother my conscience one bit. If your parents knew they would kick me out and not spare me a second thought. I'm not even worthy of your friendship, Daniel, let alone your love.'

Daniel's own eyes were misting with unshed tears. He could not bear the possibility she might refuse him. He pulled her into the shadowy doorway of a vacant house and tried to tilt her face but she wouldn't look at him and he thought his heart would split in two at seeing her so distressed.

Delia couldn't make out his features in the dark entrance, but she heard the awful sorrow in his voice and felt his warm tears touch the back of her hand when he held her close.

'I will make you another promise, acushla,' he said. 'I will never ask you about your life in the old country. Our people are going through terrible hardship over there and you and I are among the lucky ones. We have a chance to put it behind us, my precious love, to make a new start, and maybe in some small way to make amends for the atrocities, by loving our fellow Irish and showing them kindness whenever we can, and praying that our union will create a new generation of our people.'

He wrapped his strong arms around her and squeezed her so tightly her feet came off the ground.

She clung to him in desperation, never wanting the strength of his embrace to leave her. She wanted the protection of his arms and was hungry for the sense of safety this wonderful man gave her.

He kissed her forehead and brushed a stray lock of hair from her face, resisting the urge to kiss her lips until he knew where he stood with her. His voice was strong and calm and Delia was soothed by his words.

'Our business now is to foster love and charity. I see it as a form of repayment for my own family's redemption from the years of hunger and the depravation we suffered. We must show the English what true and honorable love is. Can you not look at it in the same way, Delia? Can you not give a fellow countryman a chance to purge his miserable soul and to love and cherish a good woman? Please Delia. Let me spend my days making you happy. I know it's all I want.'

She pulled him back toward the light of the streetlamp and brushed his wet cheek tenderly with the back of her hand.

'Daniel, you can never come close to knowing me as I really am. If you still want to take your chances with me, I, in turn, will promise to be true and to love you always. But you must know this: I have a dark past that I have not shared with a living soul. I come to you wearing a black shadow that will follow me to my grave. I can never shake it off.'

'Then I promise, for as long as I draw breath, your shadows will never get any darker, my darling; not as long as I'm here to love you. I beg you Delia—give me permission to speak to my family.'

He didn't waste any time and Delia was still drifting in a cloud of conflicting emotions when they entered the kitchen a moment later. She knew they must have looked a sight after their wailing and weeping.

Katy and Joe were sitting either side of the fire and if either of them noticed any change in the couple, they never gave a sign. Joe was reading items out loud from the *Penny Post*, while Katy sat with Joe's snuff box on her lap, taking the occasional pinch as he read the juicier stories aloud from the newspaper.

'Did you have a good time tonight?' Katy asked them, before they'd even removed coat and shawl. 'You're a bit later than usual. I hope you haven't introduced our Delia to the drink, Daniel.'

Daniel laughed and bent to kiss his mother. 'I'd never do that, Mam. What man with a ha'porth of sense would want a lush for a wife?'

Joe looked up from his reading and then both he and Katy simultaneously stood and stared, open-mouthed, before Joe dropped the paper and gave them both a hug. Delia's sharp nose detected a faint trace of onions and tobacco as Katy hugged her tightly, and both women blubbered helplessly as she congratulated them both.

'I couldn't be more pleased. Aren't I the luckiest woman in Liverpool—to have another lovely daughter to add to the two I'm already blessed with? Wait 'til our Kat and Suzy hear about this! It'll be jars out all night.'

Joe was sent out at once for a jug of porter, with a good natured warning from Katy to keep his mouth shut, and Delia had her first taste of spirits when the family offered up several toasts to the happy couple.

When the girls arrived home, they found the four of them red-faced from a potent mix of happiness and ale and were pleased there was enough left over for them to raise their glasses to the health and joy of their brother and future sister-in-law.

Daniel's proposal seemed to set off a chain of fortunate events for them both, as though their happy delirium infected everything around them in a positive way. They were to be married quickly and without ceremony and with a minimum of guests, no more than immediate family. The girls would naturally be bridesmaids, and Daniel asked a fellow seafarer friend, Jackie Maguire, to be his best man.

The only obstacle was the church banns. Permission from Daniel's parents was one thing, but to find a priest who would marry them was quite another. Yet, it proved easier than they anticipated.

Holy Cross church was within their parish and the dance hall was the source of their happiest memories; those factors made it a natural selection for the wedding ceremony. They arranged an interview with Father Sullivan, who required certain family details, but the priest saw nothing unusual in Delia being unable to furnish written proof of her religion or her parentage.

During the interview, Delia gave her surname without any reservation, as well as the townland of her birth and the church in Culdaff where she'd been baptized.

There was only one moment of slight hesitation when the priest asked if her parents were still living, but Delia only told him what she'd told Lord Keenagh. Her entire family had been victims of the great hunger, and Father Sullivan, weary of hearing horrific tales from his parishioners, did not press her further for details.

There could be no immediate prospect of them renting their own home and it was understood by everyone they would stay at Stone Street until they could find an affordable rental.

The sleeping arrangements could not be changed, however, and in the end the couch in the front parlor was pushed against the wall and a second-hand mattress purchased from Paddy's Market served as their first marital bed.

The wedding banns were announced from the pulpit at Holy Cross on three consecutive Sundays and for the first time in years Delia attended church in order to hear them. She paid no attention to the mass and once the church notices were read and the sermon concluded, she waited in dread for the worshippers to file to the altar for Holy Communion.

Being in a state of mortal sin, she dare not receive the sacrament until she'd been to Confession and had the priest's absolution, so she took the only course open to her—when the congregation began filing to the altar to receive the sacred host, she feigned one of her fainting spells and a concerned Daniel half dragged, half carried her out of the church and sat her down on the wide steps.

He looked so frightened and fussed over her with such tenderness she felt herself flush with shame at deceiving him.

'I'm alright, Daniel my love,' she hastened to reassure him. 'But you must see that I can't take communion. I haven't been inside a church for years and I can't even bring myself to pray yet. My soul is still filled with bitter gall. Do you see the kind of woman you're marrying, Daniel? How can I give you any assurance that I won't always feel this way? That I'm not completely out of my head?'

She turned her face away to hide her torment and his words flowed over her like precious balm. 'I know the difference between love and hate Delia, because every time I look into your eyes my heart swells with gratitude for the love I see radiating from them.'

She could hear a restless stirring behind her as the congregation rose for the final blessing. 'Still, there is hate and anger too. I'm angry at God and, as much as I know it's not right, the resentment won't leave me. The price I paid for his love is too high. God expects too much of me Daniel, and I won't go down on my knees and worship him with a false heart.'

'You mustn't fret my sweet one. God is nothing if not wise, and He knows you'll be back when you're good and ready. He's lost lambs before you know.'

Delia gave a cynical laugh as Daniel helped her to her feet. 'Aye, he has that, but the same God has allowed the innocent slaughter of thousands of them, too.'

It pained Daniel to hear her talk this way, although he admired her honesty. But he wondered how terrible her life had been in Ireland. He had never pressed Delia or any of his countrymen to tell of their experiences. He'd read enough accounts and seen some of it with his own eyes before his family had left Ireland's shores and he understood completely their need to keep it buried. The subsequent announcements were witnessed by his sisters and, to their credit, none of the family reproached her or questioned her about not attending Mass.

Delia had two dresses she'd brought from Ireland that were still in good repair, having only worn them for the dances and the odd Sunday walks with Daniel. She chose her favorite blue; it flattered her most and was believed to be a lucky color for new brides.

The close-fitting bodice was cut in a deep V and overlaid with sheer creamy muslin that stretched from a softly-rolled collar in curling folds down the front of the bodice to the waist. The delicate fabric was embroidered with a picot edging of lace and the tiny buttons were covered in ivory silk.

The market women made her a posy of flowers and they were mindful of custom and included a traditional sprig of furze, the symbol of wealth and fertility. She wore a smaller spray on her bonnet and Kat gave her a length of blue ribbon for her hair, while Suzy loaned her the only thing she had of any value, her well-thumbed rosary.

On the day of the wedding, the procession chattered excitedly as they jostled along the narrow lobby to the front door. Daniel's mother stopped and handed Delia a horse's shoe she'd carried at her own wedding. Delia hugged it to her breast and hugged Katy tightly, overcome at the kindness shown her, and grateful again for being taken under the protective wing of the Harkin family.

The rest of the wedding day went by in a blur for Delia. They drove to the church on a cart festooned with paper flowers. Even the horse was smartened for the event. His collar was beribboned and bright with flowers. Delia sat up top with Daniel, while the rest of the wedding party arranged themselves as best they could on the back of the cart.

The route to Holy Cross took them so close to the Mersey that whenever they left the shelter of the densely-packed buildings the unpredictable wind blew off the river and threatened to send the women's bonnets soaring out to sea. The sun came out in short bursts from behind clouds that scudded fast across the sky. Daniel and Delia elbowed each other when they overheard Katy curse the weather with exaggerated annoyance.

'The sun has a right twist 'o the colic for sure,' she cried. 'What a day! At this rate, we'll be blown to the church in double quick time—if we don't end up in the river first.'

'Happy the bride who feels the wind and sun, for every day of marriage will be a happy one. The wind's a good omen.' Suzy told her.

Jackie Maguire waited patiently on the church steps and, aside from a few worshippers in private prayer at the smaller side altars, the large church was empty. Jackie went into the vestry to let Father Sullivan know of their arrival and, less than twenty minutes later, Delia Dreenan had pledged her troth to Daniel and emerged from Holy Cross forever changed in name, as a blissfully happy Mrs Delia Harkin.

Back at the house, the neighbors had set out a bridal tea and throughout the day and well into the night, the tiny kitchen was filled with well-wishers.

Nobody came empty-handed so there was never a danger

of running out of food or drink, and not until a red dawn was breaking over Stone Street was Daniel able to bolt the front door and lie for the first time with his new bride.

Chapter 25

The furze the women tucked into her bridal posy proved its potency as a charm, and not three months had passed before Delia began beating the girls in the race to the privy each morning. She dry-retched noisily all the way and fell short of her target most times. Then she would have the odious task of cleaning her own vomit, a job which made her nauseous all over again.

Katy knew immediately, even before the possibility had crossed Delia's mind, and she shocked her daughter-in-law with her suspicions one morning as Delia sat back in Joe's chair by the fire, damp with perspiration and utterly spent from being so violently sick.

'Well now, isn't that grand? Me son has proven himself a man. Fancy that! Me and Joe are going to be grandparents, for I'm certain God will bless our family with a new babby this side of Christmas!'

Delia was still wallowing in her discomfort and it took her a moment to grasp Katy's meaning. She sat up straight and placed her hands over her belly.

'Oh Katy, I'm so dense at times. It never occurred to me, but you may be right. I haven't seen any blood since my wedding day.'

'That's almost two months ago, Delia love. By my reckoning, you should come to term in December. But let's hope the child doesn't show up early. That would really set the tongues waggin' around here.'

It was all Delia could do to keep her happy news to herself once the girls arrived home from work, but it was only right that Daniel should know first and since he wasn't yet home she and Katy had agreed the good news must wait until they were all settled after supper.

As soon as he'd finished his meal, Daniel went out to the front step for a smoke and Delia nodded knowingly to Katy before she joined him.

He smiled down at her and offered his pipe teasingly, knowing she'd never been tempted and would pull a face at the thought of smoking it.

'It's a lovely night, Delia. Would you look at that sky? You should see a clear sky from the bow of a ship my love. Out there, in the middle of the ocean, you feel you can touch the stars. Do you fancy a walk before bed?'

She fetched her shawl and they walked up toward the viaduct and across Love Lane to the stile that led to the canal.

The banks were deserted and they had the narrow towpath to themselves. Several barges were moored either side of the narrow strip of water, the shadowy hulks of the cargoes lying silver-tipped in the moonlight. It was very quiet and a little scary and Delia was glad to have the protective arm of her new husband.

She found she was whispering; reluctant to disturb the stillness.

'It's so quiet, Daniel. Not a sound from man, bird or beast. It would be easy to believe we are the only two people on earth this night.'

His voice echoed in answer as they walked under one of the stone bridges, even though he also whispered.

'When I'm in your presence, we *are* the only two people on earth. Ah, you and me under a blanket of stars. If we had nothing else I could be content with this moment, my lovely,' he said. 'For I have all a man needs when you are beside me. Give me a kiss, my darlin' Delia, and tell me again you're my own precious wife, for I still can't believe it.'

She slowed her pace before they emerged from the concealment of the bridge and placed her hands beneath his jacket. She loved to feel the warmth of his back and the firm bulk of his muscles when she hugged him. She pressed her cheek to his shirt and inhaled the lingering fragrance of his pipe tobacco, and smiled in the concealing dark, gloating in the knowledge her husband's precious seed lay burrowed deep within her belly.

'Believe it, my darling man. I am yours, Daniel Harkin, and proud to be so. God has blessed me more than I deserve, and I think we must have pleased him a little by our union.'

She slid her hands down to his waist and circled them round to the front of his trousers, hearing him gasp at the shock of his own involuntary response at the boldness of her touch. It was the first time *she* had made any advances since their wedding.

She had barely brushed him, yet there was a quick hardening beneath her fingers and her own body responded with a tingling in that most sacred place between her thighs.

Her news was forgotten in the rising pleasure she felt, as strong waves of heat began to wash over her.

He kissed her neck and licked her earlobes and she clung to him and pressed her body hard against his in response. There was no resistance or delay. She could think of nothing but her longing to be totally fused with him; to feel again the ecstasy of him deep inside her and the rush of his seed filling her belly.

She was awed by a touch that had power enough to transform her so completely and at the same time, a little scared of the magnitude of her own appetite, of how insatiably greedy she was for his loving. The world could disappear for all she cared; just as long as she and Daniel were free to love each other unhindered.

She moaned and relaxed into the curve of him, feeling limp as she melted in the warmth of their bodies. He was murmuring sweet promises into her ear and she clung to him as he dropped his hands to her hips and pulled her closer. 'Christ! I've a mind to take you right here, Delia. I can't wait until we get home.'

He lifted her skirt and she leaned back against the arch and lowered her arms in surrender, ready to give herself up to him, until she felt a quick burst of warm fluid down her thighs that woke her rudely and completely from her rapture. In an instant her demeanor changed and her passion was replaced by a cold fear. She pushed him away and placed her hands protectively across her abdomen. It was impossible to see his face clearly in the deep shadows beneath the bridge, but she felt his confusion at her unexpected rejection and when he spoke she wanted to weep for him—and for their loss.

'What's wrong, my darlin'? Have I offended you by my haste?'

Delia pulled him by his coat sleeve out of the shadows and along the bank into a better light until she could make out his features.

'Daniel, I was about to tell you—Katy thinks I'm with child and I'm sure she's right. I've been awful sick in the mornings and she tells me that's a sure sign. I've also—' She hesitated, unsure how much to tell him; still a little shy of mentioning the more private functions of her body, even to him.

She cringed with shame at the scope of her wild imagination and of its power to drive her to such wantonness, and now her wickedness had damaged their unborn child. *How was she to tell him?* But Daniel was so smitten with her disclosure he didn't give her a chance to explain further.

He picked her up and swung her round and round on the

narrow path until she beat at his chest and cried out for him to stop, afraid they would both end up in the water.

'Daniel, wait! We must get home fast. I feel—that is, I'm suddenly wet. Oh Daniel! I think we are losing our baby.'

Daniel couldn't make sense of it. She babbled all the way home and fairly ran down the street ahead of him. But she was consumed by a fear she'd brought this loss upon them and she wanted to get back to the house quickly. Back to Katy, who would surely know what to do.

Katy saw her distress immediately and helped her onto the bed in the parlor, sending Daniel to make some sweet tea.

Once she'd calmed her down and made her comfortable, Katy took a look beneath her daughter-in-law's petticoat.

'There's no sign of any loss here, lass. Tell me—what exactly did you feel? Was there any sharp pain in your belly?'

'No.' Delia tried hard to quell her panic. She made a mental scan of her body for any unusual signs of discomfort or pain, but there was nothing. Her body was free of pain and her limbs felt as relaxed as they had when she and Daniel—she blushed at the thought.

'Oh Katy, I felt wet, as though I was relieving myself, and I thought it must be the baby leaving my body too soon.'

Katy looked at her closely and shouted for Daniel not to bring the tea until she called him. She asked Delia to tell her something of the circumstances leading up to her loss.

'It may be that your bladder is under pressure from the child,' she suggested. 'Were you coughing or exerting yourself in any way when it happened?'

Delia blushed again to a deep shade of red as she cast her mind back to the events under the bridge. She didn't want to confide in her mother-in-law but she had to know her child was safe.

'Daniel and I were having a kiss beside the canal,' she confessed, fussing with her dress to avoid looking at Katy, 'and

I suddenly felt moist. But it wasn't the same as having a pee Katy, it was different. I was… I thought it must be something to do with the baby.'

To Delia's consternation, Katy Harkin burst out laughing so loudly it brought Daniel rushing into the room just in time to see his wife looking totally flummoxed while his mother obviously thought the situation a cause for hilarity.

'Oh Bejaysus!' Katy cried, clutching her ribs, 'I thought I'd heard it all, but I was wrong shipped again.' She grabbed Daniel's arm on her way out. 'Your babby is safe, Daniel lad, and you've nothing to worry about—unless you consider your wife's innocence a hindrance to you.'

She was still laughing and muttering to herself as she left to wet the tea, and after she'd fetched a cup for each of them, they could hear her chuckling as she made her way back to the kitchen. They sat on the mattress, quietly sipping their tea, until Daniel took the cup gently from his wife's hands and laid her back on the pillow.

'Are you feeling better now, Delia? Are you secure in your mind that our child is safe?'

'Yes, Daniel, I am, but you're not to laugh at me. I know I've caused a deal of bother, but I don't think it's at all funny.'

'Mam doesn't mean any harm, love, she loves the bones of you, and I'm glad you're recovered. 'To think I am to be a daddy; I can't believe my luck, Delia.'

He looked at her closely, to see if this new knowledge had changed her in any way. She was even more beautiful, but now there was an added lustre to her eyes and something else; something inscrutable, almost enigmatic in her expression. This new and unborn being had changed the order of things between them already. He felt he had been supplanted, yet it didn't matter. His child had first claim to her from this moment on. Mother and child were bound tighter than was possible for two earthly beings. Delia loved him. He knew that; but he also knew she was not exclusively his and that now he must share her. It was a bittersweet feeling and he felt something akin to jealousy and a boyish need for reassurance from his wife. The child within *him* was rising to the surface and he had the urge to creep into her lap, to feel her arms around him and lay his head on her breasts. Her body was his until their child was born. He needed to hear her say he was *her* Delia, would *always* be her Delia.

He resolved to reassert his position. He must love her the way only he could. She drove him mad with the urge. Each time he made love to her was like the first time all over again, and he knew himself to be the luckiest man on earth to have been gifted such sweet innocence.

'Delia, put down your cup and let me love you.' He took the cup from her as he spoke and gently pushed her back against the pillows. 'We can carry on where we left off under the bridge and I guarantee you'll feel even better than you did half an hour ago. Would you like that?'

She smiled up at him, her eyes already bright with anticipation. 'I would. But I can't speak for our child.' She patted her stomach. 'Do you think our son might object at all?'

'I think not, especially if he has some of my passion in him. It can only do him good to feel our mutual adoration, and I do adore you, Mrs Harkin, every last morsel of you. Now where was I?'

His voice had grown husky and she had learned already that it was a sign his passion was reaching its peak. He kissed her with unusual urgency, long and hard until her lips were burning from the pressure of his kisses and then he stopped abruptly and gripped her by the shoulders. 'Do you love me Delia? Do you really and truly love me?' There was a slight desperation in his voice that scared and confused her and she hastened to answer him.

'With my whole heart Daniel; with my whole body—and

to the depths of my soul. I love you with every ounce of my being. You are my life blood. Without you I cease to be; I would not *want* to be, if you were to go from me. I give myself to you gladly dearest husband.'

She had said this with her eyes locked into his, and when he released her, she clasped one of his hands and renewed her sacred vow again. '*In sickness and in health; forsaking all others, I shall love only you, my darling man, as long as I shall live.*'

He held her to him and tried to dismiss the shame he felt at having doubted her. She had a heart filled with enough love for both him and his son, and he made his own silent vow to protect and cherish them both. Delia rested her head on his chest and listened to his heartbeat, content to feel his presence and with her own heart bursting with renewed gratitude.

Chapter 26

When Delia was six months into her pregnancy her limbs began to swell and Katy insisted she should stay at home. But long periods of inactivity drove her mad with guilt and to ease her conscience she began to take in washing for a couple of the shop owners around Scotland Road.

Lavinia Corcoran got wind of the new laundress and Delia soon numbered her among her customers. But it didn't feel right to charge her and she laundered the weekly bundle at a reduced rate.

Daniel adopted a routine of picking up and dropping off clothes whenever he delivered produce to Crosby, and before long, Delia had four extra customers in the town, thanks to Mrs Corcoran's recommendations.

Lavinia proved to be extremely generous. She'd taken a liking to Delia and Daniel and found them to be honest and reliable—two qualities she looked for when hiring staff.

Toward the end of Delia's pregnancy her energy deserted her and even the smallest task left her exhausted, to the point where she even avoided the walks she enjoyed so much. Daniel came home as often as he could, stealing an hour from his barrow duties and a little longer if the Irish Sea was too rough for shipping. He always brought her a treat of some kind and one day he burst in, shouting her name from the lobby as she tried to rise from the chair; positive she'd heard a note of panic in his cries. He flung the kitchen door open and waved papers at her.

'Look what I've got you, Dee my darling!' he shouted, his face creased in a wide grin. 'One of the lads found an overnight bag in the toilets onboard ship. It was full of shaving tackle and hair brushes. Jackie was quick to claim the razor and the lads are already calling him Sweeney Todd.'

He rummaged in his rucksack and brought out a couple of pens. 'Paddy Nolan took the nightshirt, and he's hereafter known as Wee Willie Winkie—*and I*,' he said, pausing with a flourish of the hand and a theatrical bow; 'thought my lovely wholesome wife might like these best of all.' He bowed again and offered her two contraband pens and some sheets of fine writing paper.

Delia took them reluctantly and rolled the wooden pens slowly between her fingers as she thought about what Daniel had done. They were of a common wood type, with simple unadorned stems and copper nibs, but they were new. The wood was pristine and the nibs had clearly never been dipped in ink.

The paper, however, was *not* cheap. It was good quality velum, thick and opaque, and when she held it up to the light from the window she could see an official watermark.

'Daniel, we can't keep these.' She told him. 'They're stolen goods and we'll bring bad luck on the house if we keep them.'

'I thought about that,' he said, as he helped her back into the chair and reached over to the fireplace for the teapot. 'But Jackie made every attempt to find the owner. He scrutinized every disembarking passenger that didn't have a bag. Me and Paddy even waited at the bottom of the gangplank and watched them all coming off the boat. There wasn't a likely-looking owner among the lot of them. The passenger could have thrown himself overboard for all I know.' He caught her cynical look and became more defensive. 'It's been done many times before.

There wasn't a thing in that bag with the man's name on it and we tried our best to find the owner, Delia love—we all did.'

'But why didn't you give the bag to the skipper?' she asked.

'Out of the question!' he replied sharply. 'Mitchell's a Protestant, and a bloody tight one at that. He's also the biggest robber on the docks. I'd have been strung up by my own workmates for even suggesting it.'

She waved the ill-gotten bounty in front of his face. 'But Daniel, I can't use this paper. I was robbed myself once, remember? My conscience would plague me if I was to write one word on these sheets.'

'For Christ's sake!' He suddenly shouted. He banged the teapot on the table with such force the lid flew off and skimmed her arm.

'There's no need to swear Daniel,' she said calmly as she tried to bend for the lid. 'Oh yes there is,' she heard him say, 'there's every need. You've got far bigger things than a cheap pen and a few lousy sheets o' paper on your conscience as it is—or so you're always tellin' me, so I don't know why your conscience is bothering you so much *now*.'

The angrier Daniel got, the calmer Delia became.

'Do you have to let the whole street know you've been thieving?' she asked, brushing past him to close the door.

'And did I not ask you to stop blaspheming Daniel?' When she faced him, he had his hands on his hips and looked ready to defend his right to swear—*and* to keep the stolen goods.

'I could have told you the bloody things were given to me, and you'd have been none the wiser,' he said.

'Oh, but I would, Daniel Harkin. I may have married a thief, but I married an honest one. You've never lied to me; you're face is too transparent for you to get away with lies.'

His alluding to her past crushed her. He'd promised never to bring it up and she was deeply wounded by his betrayal. He knew she was hurt and he softened a little and tried to reason with her. 'Aw, Delia,' he pleaded. 'Where's the harm in us keeping a few paltry sheets of paper that some well-to-do-gobshite left behind? But the look she gave him left him in no doubt. He felt the sting of her disapproval and his resentment rose again. The last couple of months had been a strain on both of them. He had cosseted her as much as he could, but could she not see he was suffering too, waiting for the child to be born? He was out of all patience with her and he grabbed his cap from the table and mumbled as he headed for the door.

'I must be the only fool at the docks to marry a self-righteous nun.'

She heard the remark and called after him. 'I hope you're going to confession Mr Harkin. I want you to know I'll be right behind you. I'll not have our child born with the burden of our wrongdoings.' She thought he'd gone, but he came slowly back down the lobby and pushed open the door and when he looked at her there was a cold look in his eyes she'd never seen before, and didn't ever want to see again.

'He who casts the first stone Delia...' His eyes remained locked in hers as he spoke. 'Father Carney won't give me penance for my measly misdemeanors—but you've much bigger things plaguing your conscience. Think on THAT, Mother Superior, next time you're kneeling in the confessional!'

After he stormed out she sat staring at the kitchen door for a long time. It was their first argument—the first time they'd disagreed about anything, and all over a couple of cheap pens and a few sheets of writing paper. The baby was upset as she was and her belly heaved, and she felt the hard outline of a tiny fist.

She wanted to weep for the pettiness of it all, and almost threw the paper into the fire, but the thought of needless waste held her back. She would have to use them: to hand stolen goods to someone else would be to worsen the offence in God's eyes. But, if she had to use them, she would put them to honorable use. She'd only written to Lord and Lady Keenagh once since her arrival in England and Matty and Mrs Cleary were overdue a letter from her. She would use the paper to inform them of her marriage and to share the news of the baby.

Daniel may be right about one thing; she was fretting unduly over the paper; keeping it couldn't make her soul any blacker than it already was. Perhaps it was put into their hands for a purpose after all.

She sighed deeply and struggled to rise from the chair. She was used to doing everything at top speed, but these days every little task seemed to require such effort. The baby heaved again and she massaged her belly in slow easy circles. 'When are you going to come out and welcome the sun, my darling one? Don't you know how much your father and I long to have you in our arms?

She took a teaspoon and a cup from the hook at the side of the fireplace and scraped some soot from the chimney until she had enough to make a thin black paste to serve for ink. Then she poured herself some tea and sat at the kitchen table to begin her letters, the first and most important of these to Daniel.

Darling Daniel,
Forgive me. My heart aches because I am the cause of your anger. I have disturbed the harmony of our home and given you pain and, in the doing, I have broken a promise to never hurt you. Put me out of my misery, darling man, and say you forgive your thoughtless wife.

She laid the note aside to dry and began a letter to Matty and Mrs C.

My darlings, Matty and Mrs C,
So much has happened in the last year I scarcely know where to begin, but I only have this one sheet of paper

so I must be prudent. I am now Mrs Delia Harkin, proud
and happy wife of Daniel, the finest man in Liverpool. We
are living with his parents until we can save enough for
rooms. I have some money left, but Daniel will not hear
of using it, so it sits in the lovely purse Magdalen gave
me, and I propose using it for my unborn child, should
God see fit to deliver me safely.

Our little house is crowded at times, but always full of
laughter and love, just as I remember dear Mrs Cleary's
kitchen. Everybody has employment except for me. I
am kept at home with a lively babby in my belly, one
who's so impatient to be bounding over the furniture,
he's practicing before he sees the light of day! Our child
is expected late December and if we are blessed with a
boy, I shall call him Joseph Matthew and, if a daughter,
Margaret Magdalen after my own dear mother and my
precious Magdalen.

I pray for you all every day. There isn't a moment you
are not in my thoughts and in my heart. God keep you
all safe until we see each other again. If you would give
my news to Lord and Lady Keenagh and tell them of
my happiness. May your hearth be ever warm and your
hearts held gently in the loving hands of the Lord,until
he should see fit to reunite us, and may peace and good
health be a constant among you.

Yours ever, Delia.

She sat back and read what she had written. The makeshift
ink had made the task difficult and the letters meandered across
the page in spidery scrawls and varying degrees of density. An
unsightly row of blots trailed across the foot of the page, 'Like
the slimy path of a snail,' she thought. But she knew Matty
and Mrs Cleary wouldn't have to struggle to read what she
had written because none of the staff could read or write. They

would give her letter to the priest or the incumbent teacher, or even to his lordship to relay to them.

She had toyed with the idea of addressing her letter directly to Lord or Lady Keenagh, but there was a chance they might overlook sharing her news with the staff below stairs. In any case, it was hardly proper for her to write to the gentry.

When she'd written to his lordship informing him of her loss of the ticket it had been different. In that instance, he had every right to be informed of her carelessness. She still smarted with embarrassment whenever she thought of it.

But this was news of a more personal nature. A tear dropped onto the sheet and smudged the last line and she was forced to re-write her closing sentiments. She'd finished, and was waving the letter back and forth to dry when Katy burst through the door, bringing with her a cold blast of air.

'By God but it's freezing out there. My feet have turned into blocks of ice and I've no feeling in my fingers. How are you feeling, lass?' she asked as she shoved her hands under her armpits.

'I'm glad you came in when you did, Katy. I was coming over all melancholy, thinking about how much I miss little Magdalen.'

'Ah, but you've too much time on your hands. That's not a good thing for a cloud watcher such as yourself. Listen to me now, for I'm never far wrong. 'Tis *you* makin' you suffer. Once the babby is born you won't have time to mope.'

Katy removed her shawl and took a small brown parcel from her pinny pocket. 'I brought two slices o' brawn for our dinner. Make a couple o' sandwiches while I wet the tea.' She saw Delia's wistful expression and quickly chided her. 'I have to get back to the cart, so put the warp in the gears and get a move on! At the rate you're goin' it'll be dark before I get any sustenance.'

After Katy left, Delia took some coins from the purse she

kept hidden beneath the flock mattress and wrapped herself tightly in her shawl before heading out into the cold afternoon.

Her argument with Daniel had deeply affected her; still, she was unable to account for such low spirits. But Katy was right about one thing—it didn't help to sit and brood.

She determined to make up for her behavior and headed up the street toward the shops on Scotland Road. It was quite a walk and uphill most of the way; but in Scotland Road, she would have a better selection, and she told herself to stop moping and make reparation by buying something special for the family's evening meal.

Chapter 27

There were numerous butcher shops along Scotland Road, and they displayed their wares with as much care and ingenuity as the carters. Meat was a relatively recent addition to Delia's diet. Even during her time at the Hall, meat had been a rarity among the staff and her intake had been restricted to the occasional leftovers from above stairs.

She stopped by several butchers before she selected, a dozen fat pork sausages, two each for the women and three apiece for Joe and Daniel.

She selected cooking apples at the greengrocers, knowing she'd be in trouble all over again, once Katy knew she'd bought them from a rival. But she was weary and wanted to buy everything she needed with minimum effort and as soon as she was done, she began the downhill walk home.

Back at the house, she banked the fire and topped up the kettle and busied herself with the meal, and by the time they straggled in, cold and driven mad by the aroma of fried sausage and onions that greeted them, the kitchen was hot and steamy and the table set with a generous plate of fresh chunks of soda bread and the rare luxury of a quarter pound of creamy Irish butter.

Daniel arrived ahead of the rest. He stood framed in the kitchen doorway and stared at the table, sniffing the air like a hungry hound.

'My God Delia, what's that I smell? Is it sausages you're frying?'

'It is, Daniel. Let me take your jacket now and sit yourself down while I fetch your tea. There's a *Penny Post* for you to read on your Da's chair, so keep out of my way until everything's ready. And keep your hands off the bread, at least until you've washed them.'

Daniel bent to pick up the newspaper and Delia's note fell out of the pages where she'd placed it deliberately. At sight of the rich vellum he glanced at her questioningly and then sat and read it slowly and out loud. Her heart went out to him when she saw how his fingers traced the letters of the partly obliterated words. When he reached the last of them, he looked up at her and held out both his arms.

'Come here to me, acushla.'

She felt suddenly shy around him and fussed about. She stabbed at the sausages and turned the teapot handle away from the flames.

'Leave that, Delia,' he said softly. 'Come here to me now.'

He spoke softly, but with authority in his voice and she stopped what she was doing and walked into his outstretched arms.

He rested his chin on her swollen belly and looked up into her troubled eyes with an expression full of concern.

'You've been out in this desperate weather, haven't you? You know I don't like you walking out while it's so cold and the pavement so icy. What if you were to fall, with our little one so close to being born?'

'Oh Daniel, I was feeling so morose. I couldn't stand the torment of having hurt you, and you weren't here for me to tell you how sorry I am. And then your Ma came home and I set her off too. I've been a proper minx this day. I'm telling you, I can't stand myself of late, I really can't.'

The tears came then, with a burst of passion that shocked

even Delia, who couldn't stop weeping until Daniel gently lifted her tear-streaked face to his and kissed every part of it, absorbing her tears with his lips. He thumbed away the salty trails that ran down her cheeks to the edge of her trembling mouth.

'Don't take on so, my sweet. It's not good for our child. I was as much at fault for not making allowance for your condition. Let's make up this minute, or else I may be in danger of never getting to taste them lovely sausages you've prepared. But you must promise me you'll not go out in this foul weather unless one of us accompanies you.'

She sniffed and nodded and gulped down the last of her sobs before she answered him. The sight of her eyes; red and swollen from weeping, drove him mad and he crushed her body to him as best he could and buried his face in her hair. It was perfumed with the aroma of the foods she'd prepared, but beneath that he detected the familiar lavender water she always used to rinse her curls, and he murmured softly to her until he was satisfied she was comforted.

They heard the bell from the warehouse across the street and Daniel held her away from him and cupped her chin in his hands as he spoke.

'That's the Wilkinson bell, Delia. Know what that means?'

She looked at him in confusion, her head still mired in the last traces of turmoil but Daniel spoke again without waiting for her answer. 'What it means, my darlin' wife, is this: you and I have a good half hour before the rest of the Harkin clan invade. Can I show you how much I love you, Delia Dreenan, before I tuck into them sausages? Because I don't know which is drivin' me madder with lust—the hunger in my groins for you, or the hunger in my belly for the sausages. Either way, I'll not be denied.'

He felt their child move as he held her and he pulled her closer, silently in awe of the force of the movements as the baby tried to shift, restless in the close confinement of his wife's womb.

Not until the baby had stilled did they place the pan and kettle to one side of the fire to keep warm; then they linked arms and made their way to the front parlor.

Chapter 28

Joseph Daniel Harkin left the safety of his mother's womb on Christmas morning and entered the world to the joyful sound of bells that rang out from the half dozen Catholic churches in the vicinity of Stone Street.

Katy and the girls provided excellent nursing and Delia was comforted by their presence. She was particularly glad of Katy's experience of childbirth. During the transition, when the pains turned to an unbearable urge to push, her mother-in-law reassured her that things were going according to God's plan. There was one brief moment of panic when Delia thought another baby was forcing its way out, but it was one last strong contraction to expel the afterbirth.

It was an uncomplicated delivery and Joseph needed no encouragement to breathe, but cried lustily and sucked his fingers as soon as he emerged.

'Put him to the breast when you've had your tea,' Katy told her, as the girls washed her down and made her comfortable.

Later, in the local pub, Katy bragged that *nobody* was more suited to motherhood than her daughter-in-law. 'She's fertile and fearless,' she laughingly told the women, 'and she'll likely give us a fine brood o' grandchilders. How could she fail, with my handsome buckeen of a lad to keep her warm in bed at night?'

Once the glow of the baby's birth dimmed a little and they'd grown used to having the dresser drawer that doubled for the child's cradle parked on the kitchen table all hours of the day and night, the lack of space began to irritate them all.

Delia felt it was time to press Daniel into rooms of their own, before they exhausted the goodwill of the Harkin family. They shared their concerns with Joe and Katy one night over a jug of porter.

'You must have read my mind because I've been giving it some thought myself,' Katy said. 'There's an empty shop on Marybone with living quarters above. I'm thinking my string's getting too short for me to be standing out with the barrow in all weathers. Between us, we should be able to make a go of the shop.'

'How does that help us, Ma?' Daniel wanted to know. 'Wouldn't we be swapping one rabbit hole for another?'

Katy picked up the baby, who'd begun to grizzle, and looked at her son with scorn.

'Sometimes I have to wonder what God gave me for a son, Daniel Harkin. Has fathering this child made you soft in the head as well as the heart? You gormless heap! You and Delia could live above the shop and keep an eye on it for me and your Da. You'd be doing us a favor—and keeping the robbers at bay at the same time.'

His father spoke up and shook them all into silence. Joe Harkin was a man of few words and he never chided his wife in front of others.

'Now then Katy, there's no need to call my lad names. Hasn't he proved himself man enough by siring a strapping son in short order? And didn't he choose the best girl in the city to mother our grandson?'

Katy snorted back at him. 'Well Joe, I'm surprised I have to tell you of all people, but your son has the best part of him between his legs! He has more brains below his belt than above his collar!'

Joe and the rest burst out laughing at this last remark.

'You leave my private parts out of this, Mam,' Daniel teased, 'and remember this: I'm my father's son. When you insult me, you insult your husband too.'

Katy was enjoying herself too much to stop her banter. 'Hey! she cried, elbowing Daniel in the ribs. 'I've no complaints when it comes to *my* bed fella. To my mind, you'll prove yourself only after you've given Delia a couple of daughters to look after you both in your old age. Until then, keep honing your skills until you get it right.'

This ended the playful sparring and they settled into a comfortable silence. Joe returned to his *Penny Post*, Katy disappeared upstairs and Daniel sat beside Delia and watched his son feed.

His wife was just as lovely in profile and he found the sight of her with the infant clasped to her breast erotic in the extreme. He had a longing to hand the child to his father and to take her into their room.

There was something in the way she and the infant were remote from everything around them that aroused jealousy in him. It was a depth of intimacy he and Delia had not reached and he was ashamed to feel the physical evidence of wanting to claim her rise beneath his folded hands.

He heard a wet 'plop!' and caught a sudden sweet smell of breast milk when she pulled the baby away from the glistening nipple. The breast hung free as she began to rub the baby's back to wind him. It shimmied in rhythm with her movements and Daniel felt he would go mad from the force of wanting her. Her breasts had been for his pleasure alone, until this little usurper had come along and stolen His wife's heart, along with his own. The little prince had his every need filled by his mother without hesitation or delay.

He shifted uncomfortably in his chair and acknowledged a new and baser desire growing in him. He knew it was forbidden, but God Almighty! He was mad for her and envied his own son for having constant access to her.

The baby latched on to her second breast easily, and she looked up and caught Daniel's eye, and he felt suddenly dirty from guilt at being discovered.

She saw the raw lust in his eyes, yet she smiled knowingly at him and, after checking to see that Joe Senior was still absorbed in his newspaper, she gave Daniel an almost imperceptible nod toward the parlor.

He understood at once and they stood together. Daniel lifted the makeshift crib off the table and used it to hide his tell-tale bulge from his father. But Joe never looked up as they bade him goodnight, and they heard Katy's blessing from upstairs before they closed the door of their room.

Little Joseph burped loudly when Daniel placed him in his cot and was asleep before the shawl was tucked around him.

The little fella was filling out nicely, Daniel thought with pride, as he gazed down at him. The baby's face was flushed from contact with his mother's warm flesh and his pink lips were full and pouted and still wet from feeding.

Daniel was torn between wanting to watch this new miracle in his life and needing to ravage the child's mother, who lay propped on one elbow on the mattress watching him intently.

He kneeled down beside the bed and rested his head close to her shoulder.

'Did I ever thank you for giving me that beautiful boy?' he asked her.

She lay in a faint cloud of lavender and baby scent and he fought his impatience to have her. When he could trust himself to look at her again, he was choked by the passion that flooded him. She was lying back, lazily coiling the long tendrils of hair that spread in a profusion of chestnut silk over the pillow and around her bared shoulders.

He groaned and buried his face in her hair, too shy to have

her see the greed in his eyes, but Delia was in a playful mood and teased him.

'Was there something you were trying to tell me out there?' she asked him, nodding toward the door.

His face was still hidden from her and he was driven almost frantic by her evasiveness. He considered just having his way without asking her permission, and when he spoke again she could tell his torment was on the verge of anger.

The knowledge both scared and excited her at the same time.

'Don't tease me, Delia, not tonight—not now.' But she only smiled. She was being wanton and reckless, playing with fire; but it gave her a sense of power over him and she was curious to see where it would lead.

He began to fumble with the buttons of her blouse but his struggle only drove him wilder. She stilled his hands with her own and made him look at her.

'Sweet Daniel, never feel guilty for wanting me. Our joining created one of God's angels, and the seed of a second child lies within me. You and I are forever melded.' She brought his hands to her lips and kissed them. 'I am as hungry as yourself and my need is every bit as urgent as your own. We are blessed with a love that is deep and intense. I adore looking at you, my darling man, and I adore loving you.'

She looked at him with such love that he was overwhelmed. He kissed her, tenderly at first, and when she moaned he knew she was as impatient as he was. Still, he hesitated until Delia whispered softly in his ear. 'My precious Daniel, *all* that I have is yours. Please love me.'

Their eyes met in a new and deeper understanding and, seeing the unguarded adoration in his eyes, she lifted a breast to his lips, secure in the knowledge there would be no taboos, nothing they could not do together, while they shared such growing love.

Chapter 29

The flat above the Harkin shop on Marybone was in a busy congested area, and the indignant cries from a growing baby now joined the constant chorus of horses' hooves, the clink of harness chains and the shouts of the human traffic that seemed to choke the crowded pavements day and night.

At night the sounds were mostly from cheering spectators who gained perverse pleasure from circling the latest pair of brawling drunks. They watched from the window as the inebriated men threw wild punches into thin air and grappled each other, more in an effort to stay on their feet than to cause injury.

She wasn't surprised to find herself pregnant again when Joseph was barely two months old, given the frequency of their lovemaking.

There was some news from Keenagh Hall, in a rare letter delivered to the house in Stone Street, and she was delighted to recognize Catherine's childish scrawl on the envelope.

Dearest Delia,

I am writing this seated at the cook's table. I am in charge for a while because Mrs Cleary has gone to stay with her sister Agnes, who is ill and in need of care. Matty is here next to me and wants me to say that he is still heartbroken and surprised to have lived this long without his darling Delia.

Matty also tells us you are about to have a child. We all wish you well and send our fond wishes to your new husband. I wish Matty could write. He says you must name the child after him, but I don't think your husband would think too much of that.

Magdalen's horse was put down. He was hurt but I don't know how. Matty did all he could but in the end he had to put Earl out of his pain. We didn't give him to the knackers. His Lordship gave permission for him to be buried near the lake, so Matty can visit his grave.

God keep you safe and secure in the love of family and friends.

Yours, Catherine

Catherine's letter disturbed her, but she had precious little time to mope. She was totally preoccupied with the demands of baby Joseph and tired out from the effort of coping with a swelling belly and the shop. Business became brisker as word spread among the better classes of Crosby. A growing clientele now included several respectable customers from the better areas of Liverpool and its environs.

Katy was delighted at the increase in business and much preferred working in the comfort of a shop, but lately she had begun making trips to the fish market at dawn on Fridays; afterwards she would hawk her wares at the Pier Head.

Fish provided diversity and was more lucrative and since passengers poured off the ferries all day long she was always sold out well before lunch. Katy began to offer credit to her regulars, many of whom were paid fortnightly and who often found themselves short of coppers by the end of the first week.

She never took risks and steadfastly refused credit to those who walked off the ferries and into the pubs before they'd even opened their pay envelopes. She knew their weaknesses and they knew enough to accept her refusals. They'd seen her treatment of those who wouldn't pay. She was fearless and would follow them into the pub and belittle them in front of their workmates.

In spite of her illiteracy, Katy was a canny businesswoman who carefully memorized every order and knew exactly how much she was owed and precisely when payment was due.

Daniel kept to the routine of helping his mother whenever he could, as well as easing Delia's workload on his days off.

They established two regular delivery days for the most lucrative customers and had soon made enough profit to purchase a nag from O'Hagan's stables. The yard was situated a short distance from the shop in Marybone. Daniel used the old hand cart and made an agreement with O'Hagan, to have use of the horse whenever it wasn't needed by the family, in return, the Harkins would pay for the animal's feed and shelter.

Profit and workload increased steadily, and it was a full two months before Delia found sufficient time to answer Catherine's letter. She told her she was with child for the second time and gave her a full report of their new address and living quarters. She was concerned her letters might be dull, yet once she began she was surprised at the amount of news she had to relate.

Life, she wrote, seemed to be one constant round of food-related events, from selling it during the day to preparing it at night. Home laundering had long since been abandoned, now that baby Joseph was growing fast and demanding more of her time.

She paused to remove a piece of fluff from the nib of the pen and felt a trickle of breast milk from her bosom. She would need to feed the baby soon; she was lucky she always seemed to have sufficient milk, but lately she'd been supplementing young Joe's diet with mashed potato and butter in an effort to wean him before the new baby arrived. She had enough milk for both, but doubted she could afford the time to breastfeed two children.

He played quietly on the floor beside her and chewed at a string of large wooden beads Daniel had made to help him cut his first teeth. As she watched him, she thanked God for the umpteenth time for having given her a robust child.

He tired of trying to eat the beads and banged them on the floor as he attempted to say 'Dadda', but it came out sounding more like 'Dan-Dan'.

'That's my clever boy,' Delia said, as she tried to bend to plant a kiss on his head. He looked up at her and awarded her with a broad smile and then abruptly turned his attention back to the beads.

Later, when she told Daniel about his son's efforts, she teased him, pretending to be put out because nobody, not even his mother, had been allowed to shorten Daniel's name. It reminded her of her own poor Mamma, who'd always insisted her peers call her Margaret and who'd refused to acknowledge her own father if he addressed her as Peg or Maggie.

Memories of her mother always led to recollection of her life in the old country. *How sad it is*, she thought to herself, *that Mammy never knew such love as I have with Daniel.*

After a particularly busy Saturday she made her way wearily up the back stairs to their living quarters above the shop. Daniel and the baby were asleep in the chair beside the fire.

The baby lay across his chest with his head to one side, his little mouth half open and a tiny droplet of spittle poised on his bottom lip. He was still teething and Delia could see a dark patch on Daniel's shirt from the baby's saliva. The pair looked so contented, she couldn't bear to wake them, and, after she poured her tea, she sat and watched them.

'My God, but I'm a lucky woman,' she said quietly, 'to have two such handsome men.'

Daniel Harkin adored her and she knew it. Her mother would have given anything for just a taste of a decent man's love, but all she'd got from Barney Dreenan was something even worse than hatred; she'd suffered indifference and cruelty and, as much as Delia didn't believe in tempting fate, she knew with all certainty that Daniel would only ever touch her with loving hands.

As if on cue, he shifted in the chair and opened his eyes, catching the expression of pride on her face.

'What are you thinking behind those gorgeous eyes of yours?' he asked her. 'Do I see want in them? Are you lusting after me, even as I sleep, woman?'

'Indeed I am not!' she protested. 'I've scarcely energy enough to get out of this chair. It's the cock o' the North I've married, and, I'm thinking he's getting too big for his breeches.' She laughed. He laughed with her and tried to help her up, but she waved him away. 'Away with you Daniel Harkin! Put our son to bed and help me with the supper.'

She was at the table slicing bread when he came up behind her and cupped her breasts. She heard him approach and paused with a sigh as he pulled up her blouse and kneaded them non-too gently. As he fingered her nipples he sucked at the fleshy lobe of her ear, and when he flicked his tongue into the hollow shell he let out a groan and a cry that sounded like pain as her nipples began to ooze milk.

'Sweet Jesus, but they're lovely, perfectly lovely,' he murmured. His hands slid down to her belly as his tongue probed deeper into her ear. 'My God Delia, but you're big already. This child is going to be bonnier than Joe.'

His breath was hot and rapid in her ear and his caresses became more urgent. She heard him curse under his breath when he fumbled with his trouser belt and pulled at the buttons of his fly. She was dreamily resigned to having a delay in their meal, and beginning to enjoy his touch, when he grasped her shoulders and murmured with some urgency into her hair.

'Turn to me, my lovely.'

She put down the knife and made to face him, feeling the

heat of her own arousal, but before she fully turned he suddenly changed his mind and turned her back to the table, sweeping his hands across her shoulders and down her back to her buttocks.

The blouse was swept to the floor and he cursed afresh when the folds of her skirt hindered his efforts to free his manhood.

'Christ Almighty Delia, I'm going to spill my seed before I get the chance to plant it,' he said breathlessly.

One sharp pull removed her skirt and he gave a cry of release as the last obstacle fell away. He held her breasts again and pressed his loins hard against her buttocks. 'Can you feel that, Delia? I'll have a job holding him back tonight. Are you ready for some fun, my lovely?'

She felt his hardness against her and gave a small cry, wanting him inside her before he spilled his seed; knowing he was ready to please her. But he had lost his usual rhythm. He rubbed his member roughly across her buttocks and paused each time he slid closer to a part of her he had not formally explored. It confused her and robbed her of the role she liked to play in their lovemaking, and she was unsure of the reason for the knot of dread that began in her belly. She tried to turn, to see his face; needing the reassurance of the adoration in his eyes, but Daniel only restrained her and gripped her breasts more tightly. Then an old and dark familiar came to call and the heat of her passion was quickly doused by an icicle of cold fear in the pit of her stomach that melted her longing and replaced it with a mounting fear when he tried to bend her across the table.

The movement brought the source of her fear flooding to the surface and she screamed in terror. Her cries were alien, unnatural sounds that she repeated over and over again, until Daniel was beside himself, trying to quiet her, his shock mingled with concern. He tried to hold her but she wrenched free of his arms and screamed, over and over as she paced the room like a cornered animal.

'Hush, my darling.' What in God's name is the matter?'

Her noise had wakened the baby and little Joseph began to howl. Daniel was at a loss what to do next. He tried to hold her and calm her with tender words, but each time he touched her she shrugged him off, and as her cries subsided she crumpled to the floor and lay curled in a fetal pose sobbing hysterically.

It broke his heart to see her so distressed. He'd never seen Delia unhappy and the thought of being the cause of her hysteria frightened him.

'I'll go and see to the baby,' he told her, still not sure if he should stay with her. 'I'll only be a minute, my darling one.'

Joseph sucked on Daniel's little finger and was soothed and asleep again within minutes. When he stepped back into the room, she had put his dinner on the table and his tea was poured. He was silent as he tried to eat. He wanted to give her ample time to compose herself but every mouthful of food tasted like sawdust in his mouth and it took enormous effort for him to swallow.

After a few mouthfuls, he pushed the plate aside and watched her out of the corner of his eye as she went about her chores. He saw how she paused and hid her face in her apron, and each muffled sob was a fresh wound to him, until witnessing her grief became so unbearable he couldn't bear the torment a moment longer and he left to visit the privy. When he came in from the yard Delia was gone.

Chapter 30

Delia stumbled blindly along Marybone and turned toward the river, grateful for the cover of the dense shadows. When she reached the dock road it was almost pitch black. There were fewer street lamps and clumps of people still hung around the pubs, or stood in large circles playing penny toss in the pools of light from the alehouse windows.

It was too early for the serious drunks, but one man staggered leeringly toward her and when she side-stepped at the last minute to dodge him he shouted insults after her.

Somewhere in the far recesses of her mind she wondered where the tears were coming from, and if they would ever stop. She was so blinded by them, people came toward her in a complete blur, but she did nothing to stop the flow: it was impossible. The dam had finally burst and almost ten years of repressing the bestiality that scarred her memory was over. The monster was free to corrupt all the joy and happiness she'd found in her life.

She walked for miles, sometimes down the same streets twice, waiting for the weeping to abate. It scarcely mattered who saw her, nor did she care how she looked to others.

Her head was filled with wild thoughts and disjointed phrases, and long buried pictures flashed through her mind like lightning bolts. She had entered a waking nightmare of images and the menagerie was controlled by her murderous father. He had poisoned those she loved, and now he claimed the big prize.

His filth had seeped into her mind and she saw the people she loved transformed by the grossness of her father's imagination. Katy raised her skirts for Barney Dreenan and winked slyly as Joe looked on unfeelingly, and Kat and Suzy and her beautiful sister Niamh strutted through her mind dressed like tarts with their faces grotesquely painted.

The Devil had a long reach and his disciple required payment.

A fog rolled in from the river and crept up the grimy streets. The light from the gas lamps became hazy and faded, and she was weighed down by the smoke-tainted cloud, and the dank moisture that clung to the ends of her hair and permeated every layer of her clothes.

She ran a hand blindly along the brick walls of the building until she felt a break.

She reached a corner and looked up for a street name, and saw instead a swinging sign that told her she was outside The Grapes Hotel.

She stopped a moment too long and a voice called out from the interior. She backed into the fog and turned to flee, but Joe caught her by the arm.

'Delia lass, what are you doing out alone at this time o' night? You're soaked through, girl. Come—I'll walk you home.'

Joe would not have known it was Delia. He saw a vulnerable young woman alone and in danger and his intention was to caution the girl and accompany her to safety. Delia looked at him as if she didn't know him and it frightened him to see the madness in her eyes. He put his arm around her and she leaned into him without protest. He thanked God it was him that found her. She had surrendered to him without seeming to care who held her, and all the way home he talked to her, but she didn't seem to hear him.

The storm of her grief was replaced by a perfect calm and she was slipping into some form of hibernation; hiding her deepest self away. Not even the sight of Daniel, half-mad with worry and weeping with relief at sight of her, moved her.

She woke late next day with a throbbing headache. She judged from the level of noise in the street that it was well past noon. She had no recollection of being put to bed, but she was naked beneath the blanket and knew Daniel must have undressed her. The door opened and his head peered round.

'I'll have to bring Joseph to you, Delia. He's starving. I gave him some sugar and water and some leftover mash, but he's not happy at all.'

He brought the baby and left her dried clothes on the bed before leaving the room. Joseph was grouchy and wouldn't settle readily to the breast. She hugged him to her and whispered soothingly.

'Do you sense my misery, Joseph my angel?' she murmured. 'Am I turning the milk sour with unhappy thoughts?'

Nursing him was a comfort and Delia cradled him for a long while, kissing his face and dimpled hands before she placed him, full of mother's milk and drowsy with sleep, into his cot.

She dressed and was straightening the bedcover when Daniel returned with a cup of tea and a slice of toast. It felt awkward to be close to him and the intimacy made her uncomfortable. For the first time since she'd known him her husband felt like a stranger.

'I'll drink it by the fire, Daniel,' she said, moving away from him. 'I'm feeling cold.'

Once she was settled he took his jacket down from the back of the door and headed toward the bedroom.

'I thought I'd take Joseph to Stone Street for an hour,' he said quietly, 'to give you some peace.'

She looked at her beautiful, gentle, caring man and a wave of compassion brought more tears to her eyes.

'You don't have to do that,' she whispered. 'He's unsettled as it is and he didn't feed properly. I'm alright Daniel, for the time being at least. You have a right to an explanation and I *will* give you one, but not today. You must give me today without questions.'

His face betrayed no emotion and he answered her dispassionately.

'Well, in that case I'll join my father for a glass o' porter in the Grapes. I won't be more than an hour. Are you sure you'll be alright?'

She reassured him and watched from the window as he made his way down the busy street.

It pierced her heart to see him so dejected. His whole gait had changed. He walked with his head down and his shoulders hunched. 'Sweet Daniel,' she whispered. 'You're not the cock o' the walk today, are you?' He had lost his swagger and she suddenly felt a great surge of love for him, for her big strong man who looked so vulnerable. He had the posture of a beaten man and she shivered as she thought of what she must do, and wondered if he could take further punishment from her.

Kat and Suzy paid a surprise visit on their way back from church. They burst in like a blast of cold air and she 'd never been more glad to see them, if only because their chatter put a stop to her moping.

'There was a missionary preacher giving a special sermon in church tonight,' Kat explained. 'He has a rare gift of the gab—he told us he'd preached all over the world.'

Suzy headed for the bedroom so she would be first to pick up Joseph, calling to Delia as she disappeared.

'They're going to have more guest speakers at Holy Cross—one a month, we're told. You must come to the next one with us, Delia. Mammy will go mad when we tell her what she's missed. What's wrong with our Joe? He's not himself at all. I've never known him to be grumpy before.'

Suzy walked around the room with the baby in her arms, trying to quiet him while Kat hovered close by; waiting for the chance to take the baby from her sister.

'Give him to me, you useless lump. A child likes an ample bosom and you've no flesh on your tits.' She turned her attention to the baby, oblivious to the hurt on her sister's face. 'Here's your aunty Kat come to cuddle you, my precious one,' she cooed, holding him close to her more generous bosom and jogging him up and down as she sang to him.

Neither of them noticed any change in Delia; if they did, they made no comment, but she was glad they didn't stay long. Katy Harkin was under the weather and the girls were anxious to get home.

Daniel just missed them and she was still rinsing their cups when he came into the tiny kitchen.

'How are you feeling? Can I do anything for you?' he asked, keeping his distance. Normally he would kiss her as soon as he came in, but he was afraid to get too close until he knew the nature of her problems.

He had thought perhaps she was a little emotional from being with child so soon after Joseph and his father had agreed with him.

'Give her some space, Daniel and don't make too many demands on her; do you understand what I'm tellin' you, son?' he'd asked him.

Daniel *thought* he understood, but he didn't know how long he could keep his distance from her. He ached already and longed to comfort her in whatever way he could; yet he knew in his heart that a cuddle would turn into a romp; she drove him wild with her beauty and it pained him to think his advances were not welcome. She had shown herself to be every bit as wanton and bold as himself since they were married, which made her behavior so puzzling to him.

Delia kept an invisible wall between them for three weeks

and by the end of that time, Daniel thought he'd go insane with need of her.

He even considered finding a doxy for an hour, just for the physical relief. He'd already slipped out into the dark entry a couple of times, but he knew there could be no substitute for his Delia, and whenever he caught a glimpse of her flesh as she bathed or fed the baby, he left in a hurry and stood groaning in the privy, cursing his anatomy.

At night the agony was even worse as he held himself tightly coiled in the bed and tried not to brush against her.

Toward the end of the third week, he arrived home after having a drink with his father, to find the flat above the shop in darkness. Daniel was not a regular drinker, but the tension between him and Delia had stretched to the point where he was afraid to be in the same room with her. When his father had suggested a couple of pints after work he'd gladly accepted, feeling guilty because he was filled with relief at not having to face his wife and son so soon.

He hadn't stayed long though, and resisted Joe's offer of another pint. He'd exceeded his usual limit of two and was feeling slightly off center when he climbed the narrow stairs to the flat.

He had a little trouble keeping his balance and almost fell when he removed his trousers. The harder he tried to be quiet, the more noise he made; yet neither Delia nor the baby stirred, not even when he swore loudly when his braces snapped back against his bare chest.

He forgot about his usual habit of checking Joseph, and was about to climb into bed when Delia rolled onto her back, giving him a clear view of her body in the light that shafted across the bed and illuminated every curve of her hips.

Her movement pulled the tangled sheet tightly around her curves and accentuated the shape of her legs. He ached with the sadness of loss, even as his eyes devoured her. She was never as voluptuous as when she was ripe with child and he longed to hold the fullness of her.

She hadn't fastened her shift properly and below the long cascade of hair he had clear view of a bared breast, bathed in the same soft glow from the streetlight. Her generous nipple protruded from the pale flesh; the aureole dark and swollen with pregnancy and he stood rooted to the spot, afraid to move, and felt his resistance melt.

If he didn't move now, he would have to take advantage of her unwitting seduction. Drunk or sober, he could no longer trust himself in her presence; it was more temptation than a reasonable man could bear. He gripped his member tightly and picked up his trousers.

Tomorrow, he vowed, he would have to find comfort in a tramp off the streets. He gathered the rest of his clothes and tore his eyes away from her loveliness, and he left the room with a heavy heart, resigned to spend another long, uncomfortable night in the chair beside the fire.

Chapter 31

Delia woke with an immediate sense of dread and turned her face into Daniel's pillow. She hugged it close, to muffle the plaintiff mew that escaped her lips at remembrance of what she must do. His pillow held a slight tang of him; a manly scent of sea and tobacco. But it held none of his warmth; it was cold and had been for several nights. She burrowed deeper and clung to the lingering scent as if it were the last vestige of him left to her.

It was still dark outside and the street was quiet, save for the cries of cats in heat, their wailing calls sounding eerily like newborn babies.

She glanced across the room to Joseph's cot, comforted by the regular rhythm of his breathing that floated across the space between them. The rooms were silent. Daniel must have gone out while she was sleeping. *'My poor, poor man,'* she thought, *'how he must be suffering.'*

They hadn't lain together for weeks and she had tried hard not to make things worse for him, careful not to let him see her in a state of undress, and waiting until he'd left for work before she bathed. She'd even taken to feeding Joseph in the bedroom, discomfited to feel his eyes on her. She didn't want to be reminded of his mounting frustration, or to witness the need in him that became more palpable by the day, as her own yearning to be held and loved and caressed grew just as unbearable.

She was aware that men had ways to relieve themselves, but there was no way she could touch her private parts beyond the necessary. She had been indoctrinated since birth to believe her womanhood must be kept pure for her chosen life partner and no decent, God fearing Catholic girl would ever desecrate that most sacred and mysterious of places.

Just *thinking* about it was forbidden; still it stirred her, and she shifted, ashamed and uncomfortable as she felt the familiar ripples of pleasure.

She shook her head in dismissal and rose from the bed to begin her morning toilet, and was shocked when she entered the parlor to see Daniel gazing into the fire.

He looked up quickly and his expression betrayed his raw desire. His eyes never reached her face. They scanned her unfastened shift and lingered on that part of her which still felt uncomfortably tight. It was as though her covering was transparent and she felt a tiny trill of fear and had an urge to cover herself, to hide her body from his lascivious stare, knowing full well she tormented him.

If she could have seen her reflection, the image would have shocked her. The glow from the fire surrounded her in a halo of light and from Daniel's vantage point she might just as well have been naked. Every curve of her body was silhouetted so clearly he could make out the dark circles of her nipples and the shadow of dark hair below her swollen belly.

He shifted in his chair and coughed before speaking.

'Can I tell you how lovely you look, Delia, without causing you fresh discomfort?'

His kindness caught her unprepared and her face crumbled in pain. She didn't cry, but only put both hands over her eyes and answered without looking at him.

'I'm sorry, Daniel. I know an apology is not enough, not nearly enough, but I am truly sorry.' She stepped a little closer to his chair, still nervous of being within touching distance of him.

But Daniel suddenly shouted. 'Please, Delia—for the love of God—don't come any nearer!'

His agony immobilized her. 'I don't have to tell you what might happen if I'm persecuted much longer. My God, but I want you so badly—yet I won't distress you again. I know you don't want to speak of it, and maybe my intention was ill-timed and wrong in your eyes; for my part, I am truly sorry.'

There was another slight change in her demeanor and he fancied she was about to come to him, but he continued speaking, as much to stop her advancing any closer as to clarify his point.

'I'm thinking I was too hasty, borne away for the minute on my animal urges. It shames me when I think how willing you've always been, how you've never refused me. But if there is a part of me that repulses you I must know, so that you will never have reason to recoil from my touch again.'

Her whole being went out to him at that moment. Daniel was assuming blame when *she* was the sole cause of their mutual agony. The moment had come and she knew it. '*Thy will be done, not mine,*' she murmured, and felt an immediate calm descend, coupled with a fierce determination, and she almost believed she *could* withstand losing him, so long as he knew the truth.

'Can I sit down beside you, Daniel? And would you take hold of my hands and not release them, or indeed speak, until I have finished? Will you promise me that?'

He held out his hands to her and she came to him slowly. He thought he would explode with the intensity of his pain. She looked so frightened, and he felt her tremble as she kneeled on the mat before him. Despite her girth, she seemed frail and helpless and she shook like a scared doe. Daniel loved her more intensely than ever in her vulnerable state.

'What is it Delia? What can be so terrible that you can't share it with one who loves you so?'

His declaration and the firm grip of his hands suffused her

with strength. Her eyes locked into his and she never averted them until she'd finished speaking.

'I want you to know that you and Joseph and our unborn child are the most precious things to me. I love you with an intensity and joy I never thought possible after my family died. You've given me new life and the fruit of your seed. What further proof could I need of your ove?'

She spoke strongly at first, re-acquainting him with the place of her birth and the true names of her family. She was surprised at her ability to focus and the power in her voice as she re-lived the circumstances of her siblings' deaths. It wasn't until she was forced to recall Barney Dreenan that her courage began to fail and she had to stop and wait for the shivers of repulsion and fear to subside.

Daniel thought she was chilled because of her state of undress, and he had to release one of her hands to put coal into the dying embers of the fire, and he flinched to see she held her free hand, just as he had left it, until he clasped it again.

As she delved deeper her grip on him strengthened until her knuckles shone white. She clung to him, believing the touch of his hands would be the last touch of him she'd ever have, and tried not to dwell on the pleasure his hands had given her.

When she was calm enough to continue Daniel noticed a change in her voice; it had grown small and quiet; almost child-like.

'My father was cruel in the extreme, Daniel. While our family slid into the jaws of death, he wanted for nothing. He sold everything we had and would have sold me too, once my Mammy died. It was not for food for his children, but to fill his fat belly with ale and tobacco, and to pay his way to the mainland where he could rut with the worst kind of whores.'

She stopped and took a shuddering breath and Daniel was torn apart because he was not free to speak. He ached to comfort her, but he could do no more than bring her fingers to his lips and kiss them gently.

'It was autumn. I was gathering herbs and nettles from the fields when I heard Mammy's screams. It was nothing new; my father beat her regularly; but my mother was sturdy and she always recovered fairly quickly. But as the hunger weakened her she had no reserve, and after a beating, it took weeks for her to regain even part of her former strength. He was an ignorant coward, Daniel. He had more flesh on him than the lot of us put together, yet he used me and Mammy terribly. It made me sick to my stomach to have to listen to him violating her all hours of the day and night, and my mother no more than a walking corpse, having to take the weight of him, until he'd had his fill of her.

'If it was over quickly, I would lie next to him in terror in case he wanted more. I was certain he would rut with me once Mammy was gone. My father had no principles or morals: satisfying his bodily needs was paramount to him.'

Daniel began to understand her terror and he gripped her tighter as her trembles began anew. The tremors had grown strong enough to make her whole body jerk and her teeth to chatter.

Yet she felt warm and looked flushed from the heat of the fire and he, who had never harbored hatred in his life, was united with his wife in hatred of her father.

He tried to let go of her so he could fetch a shawl, but she held tightly and wouldn't let him go and he was filled with a sense of helplessness and for the second time, he cursed his male inadequacy.

'It's a horror that won't leave me Daniel. I live with a constant nightmare that has the power to paralyze me, even to this day. That last day he was—' she paused, hesitant to voice the final scene of grossness and perversion and rage she'd witnessed, and her voice lowered to barely a whisper, so that he had to bend low to hear the rest of her story.

He kissed her hair and rested his face on her head, which seemed to comfort her a little, and she squeezed his hand in response.

'I saw Mammy's clothes strewn across the floor and his...' She gave a sudden cry of pain and rocked back and forth, shaking him free when he tried to embrace her. 'Many a night I had spent listening to them, but I'd never actually *seen* until that moment. He was mating with Mammy in the same way a stallion mounts a mare, only it wasn't to make a child!'

She looked at him and prayed with all her heart that he would understand the vileness of her father's assault. But Daniel only shook his head and she mistook the meaning.

He wanted to tell her it was alright, that she didn't have to distress herself any further. Many of his workmates bragged about the added excitement of taking their wives from behind and he was led to believe the women never objected. He was told they preferred the position, especially when they were heavy with child because it meant they didn't have to bear the weight of their husbands on their bellies.

He looked at her in confusion and cringed to see she was still at a loss to find the right words.

'My father's member was not in that place where—'

She couldn't say it, but he suddenly knew what she was trying to tell him and she caught the recognition in his eyes and shuddered.

'As he rutted, he whipped Mammy about the head with his belt. There was blood everywhere and she was making gurgling sounds, as though she were screaming under water. I knew he'd finish her if I didn't do something, but I was weak from hunger and no match for him, so I hit him in the shoulder with the axe, seeking only to knock him out, but his flesh burst open and— Oh! Dear God—streams of blood sprayed from him. He fell and dragged my poor Mammy with him and—Oh! Daniel—I can't carry this pain inside me any longer! It's gnawing at my sanity. I'm going mad Daniel—my mind is poisoned by the memory of it all!'

Her voice had risen and he saw a glazed, remote look in her eyes, as though she wasn't in the room with him, but transported deep inside her nightmare.

She stopped and held her breath so long he felt she must surely pass out, and when she breathed again it came in short bursts of rising hysteria. Daniel *did* speak then but she didn't hear him.

He kneeled down beside her and clasped her tightly to him, rocking her back and forth in an effort to steady her, to slow the frantic pace of her breathing. He put his lips as close to her ear as he could and whispered.

'Shush now, my darling. There, my acushla, shush now. Calm yourself, my love. There's no need to be afraid any more. It's over now, Delia. Do you hear me? He's gone from you forever and he'll never come back. Please, don't take on. Think of our baby Delia. If he hears your distress he'll be afraid. I'm here with you, and I'll not leave you. I'll love and protect you always. You're safe now, so be calm my love.'

They sat in tight embrace and wept together for what seemed an eternity, and when the fire died to a pile of ash, and the lamplighter began his early morning rounds to snuff out the streetlamps, still neither of them moved, until the baby's hungry cries penetrated their thoughts and brought them back to the unavoidable business of life.

Chapter 32

Delia's relief was immeasurable. The heavy burden that had weighed her down for years was lifted, and she walked with a lighter step, now that she and Daniel had no secrets to distance them.

She was also grateful there was no discernable change in their relationship. After her confession, they coupled for the first time since that harrowing night she'd lost her wits and their lovemaking was prolonged by Delia's outbursts of weeping. She wept in gratitude for his forgiveness and for the immense sense of freedom she felt after unburdening her conscience.

He was patient and tender; qualities she attributed to a heightened sensitivity and awareness for her fragile state. But when he finally withdrew from her and they lay in each other's arms, she was given further proof of the depth of his adoration when she felt his warm tears trickle between her breasts, and she thanked God for leading her to such a caring and forgiving heart.

She turned to sooth him and they made love again, this time with more urgency as they were swept away on waves of diverse emotions, each wanting to bore deeper into the other, as if their melding would solder the wide chasm of hurt and isolation that had almost split them apart.

Summer was unusually hot and dry that year and the rooms above the shop were stifling. At night, they sought the breeze from the river and took Joseph for long walks.

Daniel took Joseph to the Corcorans for the first time, in order to give Delia a break. She was even bigger with this baby, and during the hottest part of the day, when the heat sucked all the moisture out of the air, it was an effort for her just to breathe. Kat and Suzy assumed some of her work so she could rest, and since Joe Harkin was almost completely retired from his job at the docks, he and Katy managed affairs in Stone Street.

That evening, Daniel and the baby arrived back in time to give Joseph his tea and a cool bath, before bed.

She and Daniel sat in front of the open window seeking relief from the heat and when Delia enquired after the Corcorans' welfare, Daniel surprised her with some news.

He took a generous swig of lemonade and wiped his mouth with the back of his sleeve.

'Everyone is in fine shape, Delia, and they all ask after you and send their warm regards. We've some grand customers alright. They pay on time and give us no grief in between. What more could we ask? Do you remember the first time we rode up to Crosby? We thought Lavinia Corcoran was a right old snot of a woman, didn't we?'

'Speak for yourself Daniel; I liked her from the start.' Delia blushed with shame when she remembered their first meeting at Katy's wheelbarrow. Mrs Corcoran had proved a true friend since then and had put lots of business their way. She made a mental note to send flowers with Daniel next time he visited.

'Well, I had a rare old blather with the mister.' Daniel told her.' He was in the front garden when I arrived and was quite taken with our Joseph. He told me of a house that's come up for rental in Marlborough Road, so I walked round to have a look.'

Delia stopped in mid-sip and stared at him in amazement.

'What for, Daniel Harkin? Are you gettin' too big for them moleskins of yours?'

He smiled slyly and bent toward her, sliding his hand beneath her skirt. 'Every time I look at you I grow bigger in my moleskins. My breeches are bursting as I speak. Can you not see it from where you're sitting?' His hands stroked her swollen belly and the unborn child obliged him with a series of movements.

'Oh Daniel, I can't even think of it, not tonight. It's much too hot.' It was only good-natured bantering on his part and she knew it, but she enjoyed their mutual titillations so much.

The baby lurched beneath his hands and Daniel sprang back quickly, as though he'd been scalded.

'Jaysus! The child can hear me. I think this baby is going to be even smarter than our Joe.'

'Our unborn son is merely protecting me as I protect him,' She told him, stroking her abdomen. Beneath her touch her belly hardened again, almost as if the child was sending her a signal of agreement.

'You're so sure we're going to have another boy aren't you? He said. 'How would son number two like it if I gave you a nice cool bath before bed?'

Delia purred with pleasure. She found it impossible to get in and out of the tin bath these days and had to be content with washing herself down. The thought of a bath was heavenly.

'Yes please, my darling. I would like that very much and so, I fancy, would our son.'

He stood and helped her to her feet. 'I'm glad he approves,' he said. As an afterthought, he shouted over his shoulder to the unborn baby as he left to fetch the bath. 'But I'm not making any promises, mind. The sight of your mother drives me wild with desire and I can't help myself.'

He bathed her slowly and gently, pouring cool water over her swollen body and making love to her in a more subtle way. He closed his eyes as he soaped her skin, and spread his slippery palms wide across her large breasts and over the high mound of her belly.

The bath was too small to allow much movement and there wasn't room for more than his caresses, but he admired her generous body and thought how lovely she was in these last weeks of childbearing. Her skin glowed and her hair seemed even thicker and more lustrous. It vaguely worried him that he wanted her so much, especially now; but their frequent lovemaking hadn't harmed their first child and Delia often sought him, despite the heat and her extra bulk.

She looked up at him with a half smile playing on her lips.

'What?' she asked him, pretending to be coy.

When he answered his voice had grown deeper. 'You know very well what, you vixen. Look at me woman, and then tell me you don't know what it is you're doing to me.'

She held up her hands to be helped out of the bath and when he rubbed the towel over her, he felt the itch of a temptation to move his hands to the most intimate part of her.

'Poor donkey,' he whispered, in a voice hoarse with passion. 'He's going through seven kinds of agony just looking at you.'

She slapped his hands away and roared with laughter, shattering his mood completely. His face flushed with indignation.

'Oh Daniel!' she cried at sight of him. 'Come here to me. I'm sorry for laughing; just when you were getting nicely warmed up too. But who, in God's name, is *donkey*?'

He couldn't trust himself to look at her, so he made a fuss of folding the towel and retrieving the washcloth from the bathwater.

'It's a name the lads gave me at the docks.' He mumbled so low she couldn't make out what he was saying, so she asked him to repeat it. He coughed and kept his back to her, although it killed him to do so because she was stark naked and he was depriving himself of the joy of looking at her.

'Remember I once told you how the lads on the docks give everybody nicknames?' he asked, finally summoning up the courage to explain. 'There's no escaping it. They used to say the only way to avoid being branded by your fellow workers was to keep your mouth shut and stay dumb, but one poor man tried staying dumb for weeks and it was worse for him in the end, because now they call him Dumb Balls and Chatterbox.'

She sidled up behind him and wrapped her arms round his waist and spoke into the damp fabric of his shirt.

'And what do they call *you*, Daniel Harkin? Are you going to tell me?'

There was a long pause. 'Donkey Dick.' He groaned without turning to look at her. 'They've christened me Donkey Dick.'

She let go of him and walked around to face him, needing to make sure she'd heard him correctly, *and* to see if he was still teasing her. But his face was serious and she stifled the urge to laugh again.

'Donkey Dick is it? Well! Aren't I a lucky woman? If this gets out among the whores in Paradise Street, I'll be robbed of a husband in *very* short order. How did it come about? You weren't parading your jewels along the dock road for all to see, were you?'

'No! I was not!' he shouted indignantly. 'I would never do such a thing. We were swimming in the canal during a lunch break and the water was like ice; when I got out to dry myself, the lads began to make comments. Jim Carney started them off. He said my tool was so long I could put a boot on the end of it and use it for an extra leg. Once the ball was rolling, Billy Murphy suggested I put a brush on the end and get a job as a street sweeper. Jesus! The jibes went on for a week and now all of them call me Donkey Dick. If I'm lucky, they shorten it to DD.'

Delia thought she'd burst if she didn't release the laughter bubbling inside her, but Daniel caught her and pleaded with her.

'It's not funny, Delia. I'm beginning to think I'm afflicted something terrible. I swear it's worse since I met you, for it stands to attention every time I think about you. I'm the laughing stock at the docks.'

She pulled open his trousers and examined 'Donkey' carefully, with the thorough scrutiny of a farmer buying a bull at the Puck Fair.

'I have to agree with them, Daniel,' she said, moving his appendage from one hand to the other, 'although I've no yardstick. Having said that,' she added, with a wicked smile, 'I don't think a yardstick would be long enough—'

He yanked it out of her grasp and, in doing so, spilled his seed.

'Now look what you've made me do, woman!' he said angrily. 'Is that not a terrible waste?'

'There's plenty more where that came from,' she spluttered, laughing helplessly. 'I'm telling *you* Daniel Harkin. I've seen a prize bull and a champion stallion in heat, but you could compete with any man or beast. My family have owned a few donkeys in the past, but that's the biggest one *I've* ever seen. Are you sure it wasn't grafted on at birth? It's too big to be natural.'

The more she laughed the harder it was for her to stop, but seeing the hurt and confusion on his face she took pity on him and with enormous effort, tried to be more sympathetic.

'You tell those mouthy dockers to send their women to me. I'll soon let them know the advantages of being married to Donkey. They'll leave here knowing they've been gypped in *that* department, so they will, and I'll be the envy of every woman in Liverpool. Except, I hope your reputation doesn't spread among the whores, else they'll be lining up outside the door to have you for a customer.'

They laughed together then and held hands as they headed for the bedroom, and after they had marveled again at the small miracle lying peacefully in the cot, and speculated, as they often did, about the child yet to come into their lives, they lay chatting well into the early hours of the morning, both of them content to leave 'Donkey' in his stall for the night.

Chapter 33

Margaret Harkin was born on the hottest September afternoon on record, leaving her mother wilting in a lather of sweat and with a portion of the afterbirth still within her womb that caused her two weeks of heavy bleeding, high fevers and near death.

It was the combined skills of the local midwife and the tender care from Kat, Suzy and Katy that brought Delia safely through. The baby was wet nursed for the first two weeks and, when Delia was finally able to put her daughter to the breast, she knew the milk was not as plentiful and perhaps not as rich as it had been with Joe.

It was another month before she felt restored enough to bask in the miracle of her new daughter and by that time Donkey was also braying; impatient after such a lengthy abstinence. It was after their joyous reunion one night that Daniel remembered a conversation he'd started with Delia before the baby's arrival.

'I want you to come and see the house on Marlborough Road with me, as soon as you feel strong enough to be jogged about on the cart for a couple of hours,' he told her, stroking her hair tenderly as they lay together with baby Margaret sucking away at her mother as they talked.

'I don't see it'll be any use, Daniel. We can't afford the rent on those posh houses.'

He took the baby from her while she wiped herself, and thrilled when baby Margaret grasped his little finger.

'I'm not thinking of renting, Delia. I mean to make an offer to buy. We've done well these last few years and I've enough put by. If it's out of our reach we can certainly rent for a year or so. It's high time our little ones had a decent roof over their heads.' He silenced any further objections with a firm kiss. 'I'll not accept opposition from you Delia, so you might as well save your breath.'

He was eager at the prospect of a new home away from the grime of the city and they visited the house one clear autumn day, when Marlborough Road was looking its best in a glorious autumnal carpet of gold and copper leaves. The quiet street curved in a wide crescent and there was a large tract of open parkland at one end. They were detached houses, mostly occupied by rich merchants and built with generous space between and the large numbers of mature trees afforded the owners total privacy.

Delia crossed her fingers as the cart rumbled past the imposing facades. She caught a glimpse of a uniformed servant girl cleaning the brassware on the front entrance of one of the homes and the sight reminded her of Keenagh Hall. One or two smartly-clad pedestrians paraded at a leisurely pace along the wide pavement toward the park.

It was so quiet after the constant noise of Marybone. The wind whispered through the foliage and freed showers of burnished leaves from the treetops.

She had never felt close to nature since her arrival in Liverpool and she gulped in deep, greedy breaths of fresh air.

'Oh Daniel,' she sighed. 'I feel revived already. It's a beautiful spot and a perfect place for our children.'

'Then start praying, Delia,' he told her. 'And don't stop until we find out—one way or the other.'

The house they sought was owned by Bartholomew Fallon,

a native of Roscommon, and his portly wife Catherine Quinn, formerly of Donegal County.

And Catherine Quinn's birthplace, Delia decided later, was their first stroke of good fortune. They were welcomed warmly into the house and the Fallons questioned them at length about all manner of things, from their origins to the current state of their finances. They were friendly, but blunt and businesslike when necessary.

Daniel liked them on sight. Bartholomew Fallon was a man who appreciated the extent of his own good luck. His humble background gave him a lack of pretension too often found among those who had bettered themselves since arriving from the old country.

He prospered in the business of horse and cattle trading and his skills at selecting the finest breeds had amassed him quite a fortune.

He told them he and his wife and daughters would soon be leaving for an extended tour of Europe and were expected to be gone for at least a year.

'I'm trying to persuade my good wife here to continue our journey to North America and, indeed, I still have high hopes she will consent, once we are abroad. I've a strong desire to visit Virginia and see some of the American studs for myself.' He opened an exquisitely carved box and removed a cigar, offering one to Daniel, who politely declined.

Fallon rolled it between his fingers and sniffed at it.

'Catherine and I also struggled for a while after our arrival in this country,' he told them. 'Although I concede, we didn't have the burden of hunger but came willingly to England, I being most anxious to try my skills at selecting the finest of the mainland breeds.'

When it came Daniel's turn to present his case, it was obvious from their expressions and the looks both Fallons exchanged that his offer fell short of their expectations.

Daniel was quick to notice and stopped before he made a complete fool of himself. He reached for Delia's hand and squeezed it as they turned to leave.

'I'm sorry for wasting your valuable time, Mr Fallon,' he said, touching his cap. 'I wish you a safe and pleasant journey. God protect all here.' Delia couldn't wait to get outside; she couldn't hide her disappointment and was angry at Daniel for raising her hopes.

But Bartholomew Fallon called them back when they were almost onto the street and made them a tempting, if unorthodox, proposition.

'How would it be if I were to lease the house and all its contents to you for the year? In return, and in addition to the rent of course, you and your wife would be responsible for the upkeep of our home, caretakers of sorts, and you'll be expected to pay for any damages or losses upon our return. How does that sit with you Mr Harkin?'

They were speechless and could only stare mutely at the Fallons. Fallon quoted an annual rent that would cripple their finances and suck up most of their joint savings, but Daniel knew it was an opportunity not to be missed and he was fiercely dtermined to get his wife and young family out of the filth and squalor of the city center.

'I don't know what to say, Mr Fallon.' He was dumbfounded by the man's offer. 'My wife will tell you I've never been stuck for words in my life, but my thanks are simply not enough. Your generosity is overwhelming.'

Delia tugged at his sleeve and, in spite of being extremely nervous, spoke out before the two men could shake hands on the deal.

'If I might make a suggestion,' she said, turning to Daniel, 'directed more to my husband than your good selves. We would like to pay the annual rent in full—and before we move in.' Daniel looked confused, until she added, 'I will be happier in my mind knowing I've already paid for the privilege of living here.'

The Fallons gave them a few days to talk it over, and it was agreed Daniel would visit Mr Fallon's office in the city with his answer.

A Harkin family conference was hastily scheduled and later that same week, when the children were settled for the night, Katy and Joe and the girls visited their rooms above the shop, bearing two large jugs of porter and a bottle of the finest whiskey.

'I want Delia to stay at home as much as possible,' Daniel explained to his parents. 'She had a rough time of it with Margaret and if we're to be blessed with more children, she'll need to be at home with them where she belongs.'

She loved Daniel's protective streak. It made her feel cherished and although she'd never had reason to doubt his ability to provide for her and the children, she had to wonder if he fully appreciated the enormity of the load they were about to assume, and she voiced her concerns as soon as the family left.

She still had money from her time at Keenagh Hall, but Daniel had never allowed her to use much of it, so she was as shocked as Katy and Joe when he finally agreed to let her contribute the money she'd put aside for New York. He wasn't comfortable relenting, but he couldn't deny his growing family the chance to escape the filth and stench of Marybone and in truth, Delia's money was needed if they were to make the move.

They were in good spirits during the discussion, knowing the change of circumstances would benefit them all. He and Delia had agreed his parents and sisters would share the house in Crosby as soon as they were settled.

'Hurray! Goodbye to rat-infested streets and nosey neighbours,' Suzy cried happily, when they bade them goodnight, to which Katy added, 'And no more trains rattling by, and we'll never have to put up with the racket from the warehouses—or hear their cursed whistles!'

Delia's heart went out to Katy and Joe as she watched them help each other down the dingy staircase to the street below. They weren't complainers, but she knew they both suffered increasingly from rheumatic pain.

'The Devil's screws,' Katy called them,on the rare occasions her tongue couldn't find an appropriate swear word.

They were forced to live in the flat above the shop for a while longer and didn't take possession of the Marlborough Road property until after Joe's third birthday.

The Fallons' departure was delayed almost a year by the untimely outbreak of a typhoid epidemic that swept most of Europe. The Harkin family was spared, but the Fallons housekeeper and scullery maid were not so lucky and Bartholomew Fallon waited until all possibility of contagion had passed. The wait was frustrating but it gave Daniel more time to put extra money aside for their move.

At last, they stood on the doorstep in Marlborough Road and performed the ritual invocation for health and happiness in the new home.

Bless us, Oh God; source of all calm,
Our refuge from danger, fear and harm.
You are the Light that pierces all dark.
The heart's eternal spark;
The door that's ever open wide;
Welcoming all to come inside.

One by one, they stepped over the threshold and gathered before the main fireplace, where the coals still glowed, kept purposely lit by the former residents; thereby holding the good luck within the walls. To let the fire die out was to invoke bad luck on the house.

'And God knows, we don't need any more bad luck than we've already had,' Katy said, when she added new coals to the fire and scattered ash fetched from the grate in Marybone around the new hearth. 'May we be blessed with warmth in our new home; love in all our hearts; peace in our souls, and joy in our lives,' she intoned slowly, as the grey ash drifted from her fingers to mingle with the new coals, and she was immediately joined by a hearty chorus of 'Amen'.

Custom having been fully observed, they made a toast and began the daunting task of making the house their own.

Chapter 34

Their lives absorbed the same tranquility that pervaded the quiet road outside their new home. The children were happy and placid, and Delia relished her new-found freedom from the shop to concentrate on those things nearest her heart: her husband and her children.

In June of the same year, Katy and Joe moved in, bringing precious few belongings. They didn't possess much of value and they walked away from Stone Street, leaving behind the bits of furniture they'd accumulated; taking little more than the clothes on their backs.

Joe now worked alongside Daniel, and the girls managed the Marybone shop between them. It was a convenient arrangement, since it meant the four could travel together each morning, and Kat and Suzy were more than grateful to be away from the drudgery of factory work and its unsociable shifts.

They rented the rooms above the shop to the Costellos, good neighbours from Stone Street, who were willing to assume the additional duty of resident caretakers, thereby making sure the shop was secure at night.

The house in Marlborough Road proved more than big enough for them to share comfortably and Daniel and Delia had the luxury of a new-found privacy—as much they needed.

The generosity of the leasing arrangement with the Fallons left Daniel with sufficient money to buy a small share in one of the coal yards at the north end of the dock road, on the outskirts of the adjoining town of Bootle.

Joe employed two young 'chippins', to fetch scraps and wood chips from the saw mills and the lads bundled them so Joe could sell them for fire starters, along with the coal. Sales from the firewood generated almost one hundred percent profit and the fast growing communities guaranteed increasing wood and coal sales for the foreseeable future.

There was only one cloud on the Crosby horizon—Daniel had some concerns about his father. The work was heavy in the coal yards and the air was thick with coal dust. The men came home at night as black as the coal they handled during the day. He worried increasingly about Joe, who'd developed a chronic cough, and as soon as he had a morning free, he took his protesting father along to the Northern Hospital and paid for a doctor to examine him.

Neither men were surprised to learn Joe had tuberculosis, but the doctor suggested it was more serious than they imagined, and it wasn't long before Daniel caught the flash of red whenever his father coughed into his handkerchief, and Delia had also seen unmistakable evidence of the disease's advance hidden among the laundry.

Katy was stoic, saying only that they had 'been blessed with a good innings,' and would be content to go, 'whenever God sees fit to call us'.

But it seemed that God was impatient and presumably short of angels again. He called both Joe and Katy within months of each other. Joe died of pneumonia during the damp winter months of 1860, when Delia was again heavy with child, having suffered a stillbirth the year before.

Katy slipped into a rapid decline after losing Joe, more from the magnitude of her loss than any physical weakness. She took to her bed, complaining her joints were too painful for any movement and the inactivity, combined with a deep melancholy, hastened her death. After Joe died, Christmas had been a quiet affair, and Katy passed away in her sleep in March the following year.

They were all heartbroken, but grieving was an indulgence none of them could afford. Kat and Suzy were kept busy at the shop and brought enough produce back to Crosby to make up the delivery orders, which still proved a lucrative part of the family business.

The girls were walking out with two brothers, the first boyfriends Delia had known them to have, and Daniel had approved of them after only one meeting.

'I know the family,' he told Delia one night, after the two couples had left in high spirits for a local musical evening. 'Their father worked at the docks with me and Da for a while. I didn't see as much of the man after I joined the ferries, but he seemed a decent sort. They're good people; regular church goers and passionate Catholics.'

There was always some demand on their time and on the rare occasions Delia and Daniel had the house to themselves, they followed a ritual both of them loved and as soon as the girls were out of the way and the children were asleep they acted like mischievous children.

They settled on the rug in front of the large fireplace with a bottle of best porter between them, and each would tell a childhood tale, or something hitherto unknown to the other.

It was a method of belated discovery for them both and they relished every opportunity just as much as they had loved discovering each others' physical attributes during the first year of their marriage.

Delia told him about her many trips to the job fairs with her Da, and was surprised to learn they'd both attended Rathmullen Fair.

'Good God! We could have passed each other a dozen times or more. Were you ever at the Donnybrook Fair?' Daniel asked her one night. Their bellies were warmed from the porter and the familiar longing stirred in their loins as they became gently intoxicated from a potent mix of spirits and increasing desire.

'No,' Delia answered in a distracted way. Her mind had preceded her up the stairs and into their bedroom. 'It was the only time my father ever showed any scruples. He always refused to take me to Donnybrook—*and* to the Puck Fairs, which he always called the 'fuck fairs', in reference to all the carrying on, I suppose.'

'Donnybrook was worse than any Puck Fair,' Daniel told her. 'A man was fortunate to get home in one piece from Donnybrook, and if you still had possession of your money you were a lucky man indeed. I never saw such debauchery and violence as I did at Donnybrook. After living all my life among animals I thought I knew every which way to copulate, but the demons who frequented Donnybrook taught me differently. They were less than human; lower than the beasts.'

'What were they doing that was so terrible?'

She had a feeling she shouldn't ask and knew she was treading on dangerous ground, but the ale had given her false courage and she was confident, being heavy with child, that Daniel wouldn't hurt her, however much she goaded him. It still amazed her that she could excite him with very little effort.

'I can't tell you. It's not fit for human ears,' he told her sternly. 'Let's just say they were a lot more adventurous than you and I, and leave it at that.'

'My father would have fitted right in, by the sound of it.'

She leaned toward him and took the glass from his hand and he caught a glimpse of her cleavage.

She was wearing a low pendant he'd bought her for Christmas, her only piece of jewelry, apart from her wedding ring. It nestled deep between her breasts and he envied the oval stone, just as he'd been envious of her babies when they had access to her bosom.

'Don't tell me then. Show me—if you dare,' she said boldly.

He held her at arms' length and studied her face in the firelight. Her eyes were unnaturally bright from the port and two rosy spots of bloom stained her cheeks.

But, by God, he thought, the minx had a defiant look about her. She was being much too bold for his liking and, in her present condition, he was afraid sometimes their rough lovemaking would hurt the child within her, especially after the stillbirth she'd suffered.

But it seemed his wife had no such fears.

'Wanton temptress,' he said to her, and it was clear from the look in her eyes that she didn't care what he said, or did, to her.

'You're asking for it, Delia. Don't push me beyond my limits of endurance. We've had the drink in us and I won't be answerable for my actions; nor can I guarantee any restraint once I'm roused, and by Christ, I'm roused alright.'

She saw at once that she'd gone too far and she regretted it when she witnessed the transformation in him. She wondered for a second if he would ever strike her, or punish her the way her Da had often punished her mother, but she dismissed the thought. What she and Daniel shared was totally different. Theirs was a mutual yearning, whereas her mother had been repeatedly raped.

They didn't get as far as the stairs, or even out of the room. He was trying desperately to be gentle with her because of her girth. She was much bigger with this baby and they had had great difficulty with their lovemaking from the fourth month.

They lay facing each other in front of the fire and Daniel grew serious for a moment. His voice was husky with passion and deeper in tone when he spoke: a sure sign of his arousal.

'Delia, do you remember the night you told me about your family and I thought I'd lost you to the river? The night you ran from our rooms in Marybone?'

Their faces almost touched and there was nowhere she could hide.

'Yes Daniel,' she whispered. 'I remember. How could I forget causing you so much pain?' she asked, tracing the outline of his lips with her finger.

He shook his head in denial. 'Well, you know the position you found your father in that terrible day? I've no wish to bring it back to you, but that's what they were doing at Donnybrook Fair, in full view of strangers—and they weren't trying to make babies either.'

Her eyes grew wide in shock and disbelief. 'You can't mean—women as well, Daniel?'

'Aye,' he scoffed. 'The women were more brazen than the men. But there *is* a similar position that's more acceptable to a married couple. Do you get my meaning?'

She shook her head in bewilderment and he had no choice but to be more specific. 'The women used animals one time and they allowed them entrance through the back door as well as the main entrance, if you follow my drift.'

She sat thinking for a moment until the truth of it dawned on her and she gasped and cried out again in horror.

'But Daniel—you can't mean it! Animals! What if a woman became pregnant?'

Daniel appeared much less concerned than she did and only shrugged his shoulders. 'I don't know why you're so shocked. After all, aren't you in the habit of cavorting with a donkey yourself, woman?'

By now he was laughing hard at her naivety and she gave him a playful shove. He held both her wrists and kept her at bay. 'Now I come to think of it Delia, a lot of the women had faces like horses. Perhaps the ugly ones gave birth to centaurs.'

Delia shoved at him again and but he only laughed more heartily at the at sight of her indignant. 'A lot of them were tinkers and tramps, love. Their lineage was doubtful to say the least.'

She became thoughtful again, digesting what he'd said. Then, with some hesitation, she revealed a secret she'd kept from him.

'Dr Kennedy told me as much during my last visit, when he asked if you and I still...' She paused, searching for the right words and her face tinged a deep scarlet from neck to forehead. 'He told me some ways to please you, to relieve you that is, until the baby comes.'

'Listen to me carefully, my darling one,' he told her gently. 'What your father did was very wrong and is against the law of man. Such behavior is illegal in this country and I daresay it's illegal in Ireland as well. He violated your mother in the *other* place, Delia. Decent, law abiding people know it as buggery and it is *not* part of our lovemaking and never will be.'

His eyes bored into hers, searching for the least flicker of fear or hesitation, but he saw none, and kissed her gently.

'Always remember this, my darling wife: you and I touch each other in the deepest, most spiritual love as man and woman, husband and wife. The shadows that have hung over you are no longer a threat. I am *not* your father and I am much more than your husband. I am your loyal friend and I will obey you in matters of intimacy, and I swear on our children's lives I will never touch you against your will.'

She returned his kiss lovingly and stroked his cheek before she rolled away from him, wriggling back of her own accord until the warm flesh of her buttocks was touching his belly, until she could feel his manhood against her.

He spooned into her and caressed her body for longer than he could reasonably withstand, before he convinced her in the only way he knew how.

They slept for a while after, and woke with a start when they heard the girls making their way noisily up the stairs. The lamps had burned out and the only light was a small glow from the fire.

He helped her to her feet and they crept like naughty children up to their room. Delia was ecstatic to be rid of another demon and found she enjoyed the new form of lovemaking, especially because it was infinitely more comfortable for her while she was so large.

Before sleep overtook them they clasped each other's wrists and locked hands in a sacred and private ritual they performed to reaffirm their loyalty and unity. 'D and D; you and me,' they rhymed together, 'joined in love for eternity.'

Chapter 35

The arrival of the twins were a precious blessing for both parents, who'd suffered agonies of tortuous guilt during the nine months of pregnancy. They had feared for the coming child and were only now accepting the sad truth about the baby they had lost. Their stillborn infant had been malformed and underdeveloped and not meant to live.

One evening, as she sat in the garden enjoying the warm summer weather, Daniel joined her and sat reading a copy of *The Derry Journal* he'd brought home from work. She was preoccupied with a particularly intricate piece of lacework that required more concentration than she could muster, when she heard Daniel utter a loud exclamation of alarm. When she looked up his face was set in angry lines and he stubbed out the cigar he was smoking with unusual force.

The shadows were unflattering and she could see fine lines beginning to show around his eyes and wisps of grey hair at his temples. Still, even in this light, she thought him more handsome than ever.

'Dear God, but this is too much!' he shouted, flinging the paper onto the grass. 'After all these years, will it never end?'

He bent over in his chair and put his head between his hands in dismay. She put down her work at once to retrieve his paper and leaned over his shoulder as he began to read the contents of the article that upset him. She heard the words perfectly clearly, but could not believe the content.

'*Among these isolated hills,*' read Daniel, '*subsist thousands upon thousands of human beings, although even the most astute would hardly recognize them as such. These are the forgotten children of God, every last one of them made into a likeness of ourselves. But these unfortunates are not like you or I, for they live as common sheep and cattle, combing the Irish hills in search of sustenance; without food or shelter and bereft of shoes, jackets and stockings.*'

He paused to light a fresh cigar and she took the opportunity to ask him who had written the account. He inhaled deeply and expelled the smoke slowly through pursed lips. It coiled lazily above his head and she caught a whiff of nutty tobacco.

'Whose account is it, Daniel?' she repeated, trying to distract him.

'Jim O'Hearn,' he told her. 'He's a well-respected journalist of long standing, and a Derry man at that. He's not given to exaggeration or untruths.'

She leaned over his back and planted a kiss on his head and began to massage his shoulders. Her touch must have comforted him, for when he resumed his voice was steadier.

'*They wander at the mercy of the elements, lesser even than animals, for they at least have tough hides and woolly coats to protect them from the howling winds and the killing cold of a Donegal winter.*'

He paused, this time to blow his nose, and made as if to stub out his cigar, but then seemed to think better of it, and instead, he rested it on the lip of a shallow bowl that stood on a nearby table. Delia topped up his water glass and brought it to him and he drank deeply and covered her hand briefly in silent thanks.

'*The animals are fortunate enough to find grass to live on, but the people cannot eat grass, and to the shame of every man and woman on this beleaguered island I tell you it's not for the want of trying. I've seen them with my own eyes, children and grown-ups alike, trying to chew the grass they walk upon, and I've watched heartbroken as they writhed in agony and regurgitated what little they managed to swallow.*'

Daniel banged his fist down hard on the arm of the chair.

'Christ, Delia! Isn't it about time someone was made accountable for this prolonged torture? Will they not cease their persecution until they purge every last man, woman and child from Ireland?'

Delia was crying by now and couldn't answer him, and he spun round to look at her, surprised and shocked by the depth of her distress. He re-folded the paper quickly but she pleaded with him to continue.

He did so with the greatest reluctance, sensing that worse was to come.

'*Some among us are indoctrinated to believe the people brought such circumstances upon themselves.*' He paused and looked across at her, his eyes ablaze with indignation. 'Who was it said recently that God gave us the blight, but the English gave us the Famine?'

He didn't wait for her to answer and the passion rose in his voice as the account revealed worse travesties.

'*I have listened to them pontificate around tables that groaned beneath the weight of fine food and expensive wines, and I've heard these puffed-up dandies expound on the perceived inevitability of what they dismissively call the "Irish situation." What do such people know of want? Have they any notion of the shame of having to beg for a crust of bread? Can they imagine the lengths a mother will go to keep her children from starving? These vain ignorant torturers are a direct cause of the situation. It is their collective greed and insatiable appetites that keep my people in want. But let there be no doubt; every last one of them bears the burden of guilt and yet they don't feel it. But they will, my people, they will, for if there's any justice left in this world, they'll all die screaming.*'

Delia crossed herself and broke a promise never to swear.

'It'll be a charity if they do, the thieving bastards. It's no more than they deserve. Read on Daniel. I must know it all.'

She was every bit as angry as he was. But there was more

horror to come and he wanted to spare her.

'The rest seems to be a list of statistics,' he lied. 'I'll read it later.'

His wife might be upset but she was no fool. She handed him the discarded paper again.

'You don't understand, Daniel. Any pain I suffer may lessen theirs. I made a pact with God a long time ago, when I was walking to Buncrana. I asked him to give *me* the pain and take it away from some poor soul who was about to go under. When I walked among them I asked the Lord to give *me* the suffering because I could bear it, if it meant some poor creature could die in peace, free of discomfort in their final moments. Now let me hear the rest, because you know, don't you, that unless you throw that paper into the fire I can always read it for myself.'

'You are one, incredible woman, Delia Harkin,' he told her, as he smoothed the pages and scanned the litany of shameful statistics.

'Jesus, this is unbelievable.' He shook his head as he read the report and Delia saw his face contort with pain. 'Are you sure you want to hear this, Delia? I'm destroyed myself from reading it, so I don't know what it must be doing to you.'

She nodded mutely and he reluctantly resumed.

'*There are eight hundred families subsisting on the spoils of the seashore on the west coast of Donegal. They are reduced to scraping lichen and moss off the rocks.*' Hearing this, Delia cried out and sank into her chair with her needlework clutched tightly to her chest.

'It's too close to home, Daniel!' She looked at the sky in supplication. 'God Almighty, won't you have some mercy on them!' she cried. He hesitated again, but she waved the swatch of needlework at him and indicated he was to continue to the end.

'*Seven hundred families are without a bed or a blanket, a further six hundred have no domestic animal and hundreds more adults and children are without shoes.'* He glanced up at her and his own heart was torn with pity for his countrymen and for his wife who, it seemed to him, would never be free of it and was being catapulted into the horror of it all yet again.

He brought the account to a close quickly, skipping over any further distressing sections of the report.

'He who is the father of us all said "Feed the hungry, clothe the poor; give succour to those who need it, even if it means selling all you have". Dear readers, the people of Donegal have given all they have and they are still paying every day with their lives. I appeal to my fellow Irish men and women to do all in their power to alleviate this ongoing tragedy.'

They sat in silence for a long time, listening to the blackbird, but even the beauty of its song couldn't lighten their mood and their hearts grew heavy under the burden of guilt they felt at being well-fed and safe in their English garden.

Delia shivered as the sun disappeared below the horizon and the shadows across the lawn deepened, bringing a chill to the air.

Daniel offered his arm and they made their way back to the house slowly.

'By God, Delia, if that account doesn't melt the public heart and open up the purse strings, I don't know what will.'

'They'll need to be opened awful wide, Daniel. We have to do something to help them. I'm going down to Holy Cross tomorrow to see if I can organize anything. I'll talk to the market folk too; they must have lots of clothes and bits and pieces they can't get rid of.'

Later that night, when she brought him a light supper of tea and toast, neither of them could swallow it.

'In all conscience we cannot waste it,' she told him with a heavy heart as they climbed the stairs.

Chapter 36

It didn't take long to rally strong support for the suffering in Donegal. Since their move from Stone Street, they were officially out of Holy Cross parish, but they had kept in touch with the regular congregation through the two businesses. They begged donations from the more humble immigrant population in the heart of the city as well as canvassing among the affluent residents of Crosby, Waterloo and Southport.

Kat and Suzy proved wonderfully efficient and before long, they had set up a system of steady relief shipments between Liverpool and their native county.

The girls touted every shop owner in the Marybone and Scotland road areas for donations. On pay day they positioned themselves outside the Baltic Fleet and other popular pubs on the dock road for donations from men who might be reluctant to donate going *into* the pub but, after a few jars of ale, were mellowed enough to be over-generous on their way out.

Paddy's Market, a rambling outdoor bazaar that had been started by the Irish Catholics in the area, was filled with merchants and dealers who swapped and sold everything, from second-hand clothing to skeins of silk, and the market vendors were renowned for their generosity. They kept them supplied with regular donations of much-needed items. Many of them had suffered through the worst of the Famine themselves and knew only too well the pain and struggle of trying to escape destitution.

Daniel's seafaring contacts provided free transport any time there was cargo space on the ships sailing between Liverpool and Belfast. And across the Irish Sea, men were appointed by Lord Keenagh himself to pick up the shipments for storage in one of the distribution centers that were set up and controlled by local churches in the ports of Londonderry and Belfast.

The charity work kept the family even busier and they treasured every moment of free time. Suzy and Kat flew into the house one night full of excitement with news that a certain Dr Petrie, a passionate and gifted preacher who'd recently returned from Africa, would be in the city giving several lectures and was scheduled to preach at Holy Cross.

'We're closing the shop early so we can get near the front of the church hall,' Kat told them, while the four sat in a circle on the parlor floor sorting bags of assorted socks for shipment to Donegal.

'Dr Petrie draws big crowds, and Father Riley told me even the largest venue in London proved insufficient for the numbers who showed up in the capital to hear him.'

'Jesus! You'd think it was the Pope himself paying a visit,' Daniel remarked, dismayed that tales of the preacher dominated yet another conversation.

Suzy was equally as excited as her sister and, on the appointed day the girls hopped from Benediction in the church just before the service ended, and they quickly took the shortcut across the graveyard to the church hall. They were among the first at the doors by four in the afternoon, a full two hours ahead of the famous Dr Petrie. Their efforts were rewarded when they claimed two coveted front row seats.

Daniel made it his business to be in the city that day, so he could pick the girls up and bring them home after the sermon. He took the opportunity to enjoy a quick drink with his former shipmates and was glad of the opportunity to thank them again for their contribution to the relief work.

Meanwhile, less than a half mile away, Dr John Petrie was taking the podium in a packed church hall, as people lined the walls and squeezed into every available space to hear him speak.

They filled the aisles, sitting three abreast on the cold stone floor and stared up at the man, enthralled before he even began his sermon.

The doors had to be bolted against dozens of disappointed parishioners, who had to be content to stand outside and wait for a second-hand account of the sermon. Inside, the air grew stifling hot and became seasoned with a strong miasma of unpleasant odors from the clothes of the laborers who had come straight from the stables, the tanneries, and the busy factories in the vicinity that manufactured dyes, glue, lye soap and tobacco products.

But the girls were far too absorbed by the imposing image of Dr Petrie to be bothered by smells. The missionary warmed up quickly and soon his resonant voice boomed to the back of the congregation and his accusing fingers jabbed in the direction of the assembled sinners, until even the most humble among them shrank beneath his pointed stares and God-fearing rhetoric.

Kat and Suzy were so enthralled they didn't hear the drunk's guttural cry of 'Fire!' Nor were they aware of the sudden unrest behind them as more and more people stood and tried to leave through the narrow doors that led onto the street, doors scarcely wide enough to permit two abreast.

By the time the emerging horror was reflected in the preacher's face, and those around them begun to turn in their seats, it was already too late.

The crush of bodies grew as the weaker were trampled underfoot in the panic to flee the stricken area. The wooden staircase collapsed with a loud, pistol shot crack that sent bodies crashing down on the clamor of people below. Candles were upturned in the melee and smaller fires started to supplement the hungry flames that already licked at the wooden structure, fed by stacks of prayer books, missals and other flammables stored in the basement.

The girls clung to each other and prayed in unison as the heat scorched their backs and singed their lungs, and their their lips moved in silent prayer, even as they dropped together in merciful oblivion before the flames reached them.

Daniel arrived to a scene of utter chaos. People lay in random order across the churchyard, while those who could walk spilled onto the street, dazed; shoeless and half naked, their clothes torn from them during the fight to escape the inferno.

The hall still blazed fiercely and showers of sparks erupted as the timbers crashed into the flames. A long bucket line of volunteers worked as fast as they could, but it was useless to even try. The wind fanned the fire and the building could not be saved.

Those killed in the crush lay in long rows along the pavement. They were unmarked and uncovered and in the bright glow of the blaze they could have been sleeping, but the numbers grew quickly and when the pavement became too congested more victims were piled on top and the rows of dead spilled into the graveyard. Daniel walked among them with his heart hammering. They were so fresh, he felt he could tap them and they'd wake and tell him where his dear sisters might be.

He finished his grisly inspection and didn't know if it was relief or a deep dread he felt after he satisfied himself the girls were not among the victims. Policemen and clergy were gently leading onlookers and anxious relatives outside the boundary of the church property as they tried to make space for more casualties.

He was led away, protesting loudly, and told to report to the Christian Street police station the next morning for news.

'I'm sorry sir,' the harassed constable told him. 'It doesn't look good for you, I know. But it is always possible your sisters had a change of heart and are at home waiting for you. I pray it is so.'

Unable to leave the area, Daniel walked the short distance through the crowded streets to the police station, where he joined dozens of anxious relatives waiting for news.

All night long, the air was filled with heart-wrenching cries, as men and women wept and keened at hearing the fate of their loved ones. He knew Delia would be beside herself with worry, but he couldn't tear himself away and his heart lifted with hope and was dashed again and again at sight of every young woman who approached the police station.

Some of the dead were already identified and a senior police constable read their names aloud. He was obliged to pause frequently, as his grisly litany was interrupted by screams of anguish.

When he finished, he addressed the crowd, and Daniel suddenly hated the man for his officious tone. It was as though he were mechanically reading out a list of parts. He knew it was irrational, but he wanted to wring the man's neck. How could the insensitive bastard remain so calm, while he, Daniel Harkin, wanted only to kill someone, *anyone*, in an effort to release the screaming rage that boiled in him?

He turned his face to the wall and punched at the bricks with his right fist until the skin hung from his knuckles and the force of his blows dislocated his index finger. Yet he felt no pain, and didn't feel any for days after. It wasn't until his wife noticed his crooked finger did he discover the fracture.

Delia fainted clean away at sight of him next afternoon. He showed up on the front step with his face and clothes blackened from soot.

His anguish was mirrored in his eyes and hadn't said a word to her, but only stood with drooped shoulders as tears streamed down his face, leaving pale runnels in the charcoal dust on his cheeks.

During the worst of their grief, Daniel and Delia were unable to comfort each other and on the day of the funeral they stood apart like strangers, as the girls were laid in the same grave as Joe and Katy.

Daniel had the additional agony of not knowing if it was his sisters being lowered into the ground. That was the worst of it. Two identical coffins were put into a grave that Daniel *hoped* contained their remains, but there was no way of telling for certain. He kept the hideous doubt from Delia, knowing it would send her toppling into madness.

As far as she knew the girls lay at peace, unbroken and unscarred beneath the nailed lids of their coffins.

His sisters were among the last victims to be recovered. Suzy and Kat's bones were found days later among the tangled debris of the fire.

They were hidden beneath fallen chimney bricks and charred beams, unearthed long after the blackened frame of the church hall had cooled. They were cremated in the flames to little more than a macabre collection of disjointed parts and grisly pieces of bone.

The total death count was seventy-four. Most of the victims died of suffocation or were trampled to death. Daniel found a small scrap of comfort knowing the girls, being found at the front of the hall, were not among those who endured the ordeal of being trapped beneath the feet of the hysterical mob.

He tried to further relieve the weight of his loss, believing perhaps they would not have known pain, but would likely have been rendered unconscious from the smoke before the scorching flames reached them.

He was grateful, too, that his parents were not alive to suffer the violent loss of their daughters. He knew he would never have been able to break the news to them—it had almost finished him having to tell Delia.

The undertaker had told him privately that among the

remains allotted to his family were two intertwined female ulnas they'd recovered near the location of the front pews.

'The phalanges, that is, the fingers, were still joined together when they were found,' he'd told him somberly. 'It seems very likely they were your sisters' remains.'

Daniel had to be content with the assumption and not drive himself into madness by mulling over futile uncertainties.

Delia kept busy in the weeks following the funeral. She had the added responsibility of informing their loyal customers about their decision to close the shop, at least for the time being, but Daniel was still anxious about her. His wife could appear tough, but he knew she wasn't the same; her spirit had somehow dimmed after the girls died.

He kept his grief close, and since the coal yard wasn't far away and he no longer had the responsibility of the shop, he found comfort in being home more often.

He drew his family tightly round him, but he worried himself sick about Delia. She grew listless and tired easily and it wasn't until the children began to notice and to ask questions that she made an effort to pull herself together.

It was a slow business, settling back into their lives, but with the softening balm of passing time they woke with a little less dread each day and were occupied enough to assuage the unexpected moments when grief threatened to overwhelm them.

After a while, the periods of sanity stretched into days, when they could be free of tearful reminders.

Young Joseph started at the local school and was gone for the best part of the day, and little Margaret quickly turned into a second mother to the twins and was now competent enough to alert Delia if either of the babies needed her. '*Poor little mite,*' Delia thought to herself, watching her daughter expertly pull Patrick up into a sitting position. '*She's forced into the role of mother already.*'

The park was a popular diversion and during the summer months they spent very few weekends in the house.

Crosby boasted a wide stretch of beach and they loved nothing better than to take family picnics, relaxing while the little ones played safely on the firm sands and ate almost as much as their parents after a day of fresh sea air and lively play.

'I think we may have to fashion a harness for her,' Delia said breathlessly one particularly hot Sunday, after she had chased her daughter for the third time across the sands.

She sat down and settled Margaret into the bowl of her skirts. In vain hope of keeping her still for a moment, she gave her a crust of bread spread thick with butter and in no time at all her daughter's face and chubby fingers were covered in grease.

Before she or Daniel could stop her, she stuck her hands in the sand, pulled them out and rubbed her eyes, screaming from the unexpected agony that followed.

'Shush Darling. Here, let Mamma wipe your eyes,' Delia pleaded with her. But she only arched her back and stiffened in Delia's arms and leaned so far back her mother almost dropped her.

Daniel took hold of her firmly. 'Let her cry, Delia. The tears will wash her eyes clean all the sooner.'

Later, after she calmed down and lay sniffling quietly in her father's arms, Delia bent over her and gently wiped away the last traces of sand and butter from her cheeks.

'She's starting to look like Suzy, don't you think?' she asked Daniel, who was relieved to hear mention of his sisters. 'I'm glad she doesn't take after me; I'd hate to think I was such a handful to my own mother.'

Daniel blew loud raspberries on his daughter's cheek and in minutes he had her squealing with laughter.

'Come on,' he said to her. 'Let's go and find the waves. I'll race you to the water.'

Delia watched their progress across the broad sands. '*Hardly an evenly matched race,'* she thought, noticing Daniel's long legs and their daughter's stumpy ones, but they receded into the distance quickly, their familiar shapes shrinking as they neared the waterline. The twins were sleeping and Joseph had found a friend close to his own age and was engrossed in the construction of a sand castle.

It was a rare moment of quiet and she was free to watch her son play. She enjoyed an unexpected sense of contentment; it was a welcome feeling after months of mourning.

She acknowledged her blessings. She had a husband who still loved her; four healthy children and a comfortable home. Life was good and so was business and she had to admit she had much to be thankful for. Yes, there were pangs of regret at times and bittersweet memories of her lost child still lingered, as well as the more recent loss of Daniel's family. But still, she acknowledged, she *was* incredibly lucky.

She took a deep breath of the clean sea air and exhaled slowly as she bent to gather the children's scattered belongings.

Later that evening, after they were safe in bed she and Daniel sat chatting amiably about their future plans.

'I wish you could find suitable coal yards closer to home. She told Daniel. 'Now that Bootle and Crosby are expanding, it makes no sense for you to travel back and forth such a distance.'

Daniel sipped at his nightcap and offered his wife a glass before answering.

'On the contrary, my love, Canada Dock is now completed, and you know, of course, it's been built specifically for the North American timber trade. With the explosion of new industries in the major cities, the demand for timber is growing at a tremendous rate and Canadian lumber is being unloaded in greater quantities every day. The canal barges need fuel, to transport the wood to the saw mills, and the iron foundries are hungry for fuel. All of this increases the need and our sales are increasing rapidly, and not just from the traders. I hear that every new dwelling in Liverpool will be built with coal-burning fireplaces from now on. We can't keep up with the demand and I was thinking I may have to expand even more if I can find suitable premises.'

She raised her glass to him and smiled. 'I concede defeat, Daniel Harkin. You have won the first round. I see I have married an astute businessman.'

He laughed at her and she thrilled to hear it. She loved him even more in that moment, seeing the smile that always began in his eyes and lit up his whole face. He hadn't laughed aloud for a long time and she thanked God for His healing powers.

'It's a contest you're after, is it?' He wanted to know.

Never one to shirk from a challenge, he turned and put his glass on the mantelpiece and leaned over her chair. His hands rested on the arms and he stared intently into her eyes. 'Have I not taught you to think twice before you challenge me, Delia? Do you think you can get the better of me now?'

'I *know* I can't,' she answered, without taking her eyes off him. He was hypnotized by the two bright green jewels that stared back at him with the bold defiance he'd loved since the day he met her.

'Jesus Christ,' he murmured, resting his gaze on the neckline of her dress. With one practiced sweep, he could have her breasts cupped in his hands. 'Where do you get your powers, woman? How many years is it that you've tormented me with your beauty and your beguiling ways?'

Delia still loved to play these games. They would tease each other with words and innuendos until one of them gave in to the desire to touch. Mostly it was Daniel who lost. She liked nothing more than to be openly wanton with him; knowing the longer she teased him the more he would please her.

He leaned closer, until she detected the pungency of the whisky on his breath and felt the heat of him. His passion was building and she recognized the signs that betrayed his battle for control.

His eyelids drooped and a dreamy look crossed his face, and when he spoke his voice was deep and hoarse, like his laugh. *'And every bit as compelling,'* she thought.

'You sound dry, my love,' she said, reaching for his glass. 'Are you in need of another whisky? Let me refill you.' She made as if to stand and he pushed her back into the chair.

'Not so fast Delia Harkin. You stay right there. I'm not dry and neither are you, if I know anything. Do you need proof, woman?'

'And how do you propose to give me *that?*' She tilted her face to one side and gave him a coquettish half smile that was so full of daring he wanted to show her right there and then how he proposed to prove it.

Instead, he stood and took her hands in his, pulling her from the chair.

'Come outside with me, to the arbor. I want to show you something.'

A light drizzle enveloped the garden in a soft mist and she was about to protest it would soak her muslin dress but before she could protest he drew her to him and placed his mouth over hers, silencing her with a long, deep kiss.

When they broke apart she looked into his eyes, curious to know what his game might be, and, like a trusting child, she allowed him to lead her to a far corner of the garden where he pulled her into the shadows of a wisteria. The blooms tumbled over the arbor in a thick blanket and the dense foliage protected them from the rain.

Daniel stopped her with another kiss, this one more urgent.

She felt her strength slip away and clung to him as she responded until, at the last second, before their lips parted, she flicked her tongue into his mouth and then stepped back just out of his reach.

'Now, Daniel my love. No more kisses for you, not until you show me why you brought me here. This dress is quite thin and I am getting very wet.'

His eyes feasted on every inch of her before coming to rest on her bosom.

'I can see that,' he murmured with a satisfied smile. 'It's a marvel that dress. You must let me know who made it so I can get you a whole wardrobe of them.'

His remark caught her off guard and she looked down, vaguely puzzled until she saw for herself. It was true: every curve of her body was visible to him and the thin fabric was plastered wetly to her skin. Tell-tale smudges and protrusions of ripe nipples betrayed any pretense of calm and showed him exactly where to place his hands for maximum effect.

He grasped her wrists and she gave a slight cry of alarm. 'You don't fool me, Delia darling,' he growled

He knew the force of her arousal and his hands moved tantalizingly slow; much too slow for Delia. She wanted to scream at him to hurry; was frantic to remove the layers of clothing between them; burning to feel his flesh on hers and his powerful fingers caressing every part of her. She was past caring who won, but Daniel hadn't finished his sweet torment.

He spread his palms wide and slid his fingers up her back, deliberately tracing every point of her spine. When he brought them to her breasts, she whimpered and sank, limp and languid in his arms.

He buried his face in her hair and murmured close to her ear. 'Do you concede yet?'

Her breasts tingled and every nerve in her belly screamed for him, for all of him, yet her body was without substance and she seemed to float within the circle of his arms. He smiled, victorious, and was about to release her breasts when she slipped her hands down and deftly untied his belt and Daniel let out a sudden curse.

'Jesus, Mercy! You're bewitched, you little hussy. There's no other explanation for your power over me.'

He raised his face to the sky and shuddered violently as she undid his buttons, and at the same moment, she undid him.

'God Almighty, there's no hope for me. I've had it, Delia. Do you hear me? I'm totally under your spell.' She stopped abruptly and left him quivering in an agony of want. 'You win Delia. Tell me what it is you want and it's yours.'

She took his face in her hands and smiled at him, outwardly calm, but if only he knew how she was seething with desire and heat and ripples of greedy lust. '*But not yet,*' she told herself. '*Not quite yet. This is one battle I'm determined to win.*'

She placed one of his palms to her moist breast. Her skin was slick with rain and his thumbs slid easily over the nubs of her nipples. They felt warm and hard beneath his fingers.

'Ah,' he murmured, as his eyes remained fixed on her face. 'My temptress is more ready than I imagined.'

He lifted the dress over her head and let it drop to the path. She was still outwardly calm but her eyes betrayed her. They were glazed with longing and her mouth was slightly parted and she had such a remote expression, he wondered if she could even see him.

The sight of her lips caused him to lose any remaining control. He asked her if she was ready, but she was incapable of answer and grabbed at him with eager hands to help remove the rest of his clothing.

When he lowered her to the ground he was smug with contentment. He had her exactly where he wanted her. He'd won the bet and he had to admit he'd never enjoyed a gamble more.

They lay in the damp grass and let the night air cool them. As darkness cloaked the flowerbeds the blackbird pierced the air with its evensong.

'A fitting finale, don't you think?' Daniel said drowsily,

unwilling to break the post-coital spell. She took his hand and squeezed it in reply. But Daniel was in a mood to talk and his head was already turning to practicalities as he gazed up at the house.

'I must look at that broken window sash in Margaret's room,' he said absent-mindedly.

She turned her head lazily and saw his face was still flushed from the exertion of passion.

'Now why would you think about the window at a time like this?' she asked him.

The window hadn't worked properly since they'd moved into the house. The sash rope was frayed and the window came down like a guillotine when you least expected it.

Delia had had several narrow escapes and knew enough to prop it open with a couple of heavy books.

'Because,' he answered deliberately, 'one day it will take somebody's fingers off and we can't have that now, can we?'

He took her fingers and kissed the tips, one by one, and this time it was Daniel's eyes that shone brazenly. 'Oh yes, my dearest, we have to protect these fingers at all cost.'

He lay back, grinning, and made a pillow of his hands, conqueror, and undisputed king of his own castle.

She cuddled closer to the heat of his body. She was cool and didn't relish the thought of putting on her wet dress to get back into the house. 'And who, may I ask, is *we*?'

He gave a little laugh and rose to help her to her feet. 'Why, me and donkey, of course.'

Chapter 37

Life settled into a comfortable pattern as the years sped by. The children grew faster than weeds and money shortage was no longer an issue. Joe had died intestate but he left a decent sum of money to Daniel that he'd managed to save in his last years of relative comfort.

Liverpool and its environs also continued to mushroom and Daniel became quite rich, though neither he nor Delia dwelt on their material assets and they never lost their keen sense of gratitude.

The Harkins were now proud owners of not one, but two houses. They purchased the Fallon home free and clear, but Daniel had lately bought a second house in the seaside town of Southport, which they named Sea View. He registered the deeds in Delia's name, and she found it almost too incredible to believe they had done so well, even though she was well aware they'd had years of healthy profits and had worked and struggled hard for their new prosperity.

She now assumed the additional role of landlady, collecting monthly rent from the new occupants of Marlborough Road, once she and Daniel moved into Sea View.

They fell in love with Sea View on first sight. There was an uninterrupted view of the river from the front windows and on clear days they could watch the steady procession of sailing ships as they slowly navigated the mouth of the Mersey, headed for the open sea. There was always an interesting vista and Delia spent many happy hours sitting in the large bay window. The sight of the children on the sands reminded her of when her own brood were little.

Joseph was now an admirable apprentice to his father in the coal yards and had given up formal schooling at fourteen, much to their dismay. But he was eager to learn and happy to follow his father around, deeply absorbed in every aspect of the family business.

He was the most introspective of her children and at times his willing and uncomplaining way was a painful reminder to Delia of her brother Vincent.

Margaret was much more spirited. She was a fiery redhead with a temper to match and both her parents agreed there was a lot of Katy Harkin in their daughter. Yet she was lovely and, as she edged closer to womanhood, she and Delia became better friends and shared closer intimacy as Margaret sought to make sense of her maturing body and irrational emotions.

Delia watched her blossom and hoped her daughter wouldn't have such a voracious appetite as she did for pleasures of the flesh; at least, not until she was safely married. She was nearing school-leaving age and had expressed a desire to nurse or to teach. She finally settled on the latter and applied to a teacher's training college in Wales.

The twins were alike in physical appearance only. James was something of a perfectionist and more like his father, while Patrick, the most rebellious, shared the strong build and coloring of Daniel. Both lads were equally good scholars. They were popular among their peers and had gathered a circle of reliable friends in the school they attended in nearby Waterloo.

The family seldom visited Liverpool these days. Daniel still had to make regular trips to the city for business purposes, but took care to avoid the roads that would lead him past the haunted wreck of Holy Cross Hall. Joseph was the only one of their children with sufficient sense to navigate the city and since he didn't brag about it, the rest of them showed no undue curiosity, being happy enough in their own surroundings.

One dismal day in late September, they accompanied their daughter on the first leg of her journey to Wales. A local train transported them to Liverpool and, although it was the first time the women had been on a train, none could derive much pleasure from the experience. Delia and Daniel were saying goodbye to their only daughter; both of them found it painful in the extreme.

Kat and Suzy's sudden deaths had proved a constant reminder to them over the years of the frailty and uncertainty of life and it was a thoughtful trio that made the journey into the city.

Liverpool's Lime Street station had recently been refurbished, and they stood in the vast concourse and stared in awe at the huge iron girders that spanned the roof high above them.

After they explored the station there was still plenty of time until Margaret's train left and they stood on the platform in awkward silence. Delia wracked her brain for something meaningful to say, but she was so upset it was all she could do to keep from crying.

She knew she had to let Margaret go, so she could discover for herself that being apart would have the singular benefit of teaching her how much she cherished her family; of how precious her parents and brothers were, and of how much she loved them. But, oh! How she longed to draw her back and take her home!

The train to Wrexham hissed and coughed out clouds of steam, and there was a sudden flurry of activity, and a loud chorus of bangs as the signalman made his way down the platform, thwacking the doors with one hand as he raised a whistle to his lips. And then Margaret was gone; she and the departing train were swallowed into the dark maw of the tunnel, and they were left, alone and bereft, on the deserted platform.

They made their way slowly out of the station into a grey drizzle that perfectly matched their moods and Daniel sought to find some diversion for them both.

'We have an hour before our train home. We can visit one of the yards if you like, or I can treat you to a variety show at the Big House.'

She looked at him, puzzled. 'But Daniel, the big house is miles from here. Do you mean to take me there once we get off the train?'

He smiled at her and explained. 'Not *our* big house, my love. The Big House I'm talking about is a pub just around the corner from here. Come on, we'll get a pie and a warming glass of sherry to cheer us both.'

The pub was packed to the walls with people sheltering from the rain. They were mostly working men, and a few rather dubious-looking women. '*Hardly ladies,*' Delia thought, taking in their low bodices and boldly-painted faces.

The atmosphere was smoky, noisy and smelt strongly of tobacco, hops and stale sweat. They couldn't find a seat and had to stand just inside the entrance, but Delia was glad to have at least some fresh air from the open door.

She could distinguish the Irish brogue above the general din and the old familiar musical cadence of the Gaelic tongue evoked long-hidden memories of Donegal. When one of the men began to sing her mother's favorite song, 'The Last Rose of Summer', she couldn't say if it was the pungency of the sherry, taken so early in the day, the pain of losing her daughter, or the acrid smoke that made her eyes water.

She was almost glad when a drunk pushed passed her and spilt a good portion of his beer down the front of her jacket.

He instinctively raised his hand to wipe at the stain, but

Daniel stood between his wife and the teetering drunk.

'That won't be necessary, mister. I can attend to my wife, if you don't mind.'

The man laughed in his face and turned to leave the pub and they could hear him trying to imitate Daniel's voice as he staggered along Lime Street.

'Friggin' snotty-nosed toff!' the drunk shouted to no one in particular. But to *everyone* that passed he suddenly broke into song. 'Did yer muther cum frum Ireland,' he wailed- and then he stopped singing long enough to answer himself with fresh curses. 'Indeed she didn't!' he cried angrily, turning to face the pub and shake his fist at Daniel. 'For if she did, she'd be ashamed of yer'. Yer nuthin but a bleedin' turncoat.'

Daniel took the glass from Delia's hand and led her away from the pub and back toward the safety of the station.

The train was preparing to leave and they barely had time to find their seats and shake the rain from their coats before there was a sudden jerk and a heavy metallic clink of couplings, followed by a rude 'Toot!' as bellows of steam spewed from some hidden place below the carriage windows and followed the moving train along the platform.

The iron monster stretched and groaned as it shunted slowly out of the station.

'Now you know why I don't encourage our children to visit the city,' Daniel said, settling into his seat. 'People do terrible things when they have the drink in them.'

'You've no need to tell me that, Daniel Harkin.' Delia stared out the window at the dismal industrial ugliness.

'I didn't have what you'd call a sheltered upbringing did I?'

He glanced across to where she sat, looking as uncertain and vulnerable as she had that first day he'd seen her on the quayside and his heart swelled with affection.

'I'm humbled, wife. I truly am. If it hadn't been to slake my own thirst and take your mind off Margaret leaving, I would never have suggested it.' He looked so crestfallen that she had to laugh.

'I thought the man was quite funny,' she replied. 'And you were right; the pub *did* take my mind off things, though I wouldn't like to make a habit of it. Thanks be to God, you and I don't need ale, or any other stimulant to enjoy ourselves, Daniel.'

'And well I know it, my darling,' he replied, bending forward to pat her knee as they settled into the plush velvet seats of the train to enjoy the journey home.

Chapter 38

Delia didn't have as much time to miss her daughter as she had first feared. The more independent her family became, the more she became involved in the church. The Harkins were highly respected members of their local parish of St Malachy and because of their obvious wealth, it was expected they should help those in need, especially the Irish poor.

The majority of the women on the church committee were snobs and she took care not to socialize with them. She knew instinctively those with similar humble beginnings as her own. As far as Delia was concerned, they were Catholic in name only and lacked a true Christian attitude. They barred from their circle anyone they deemed inferior and this was a dilemma for Delia. On the one hand she saw it as a duty to help the parish, yet on the other she didn't want to be in the company of such people and Daniel was quick to point out she herself was practicing a form of inverted snobbery by avoiding them.

In the end she compromised and attended the minimum of meetings, excusing herself from committee teas and private dinner parties, preferring instead to spend her evenings at home, sewing or knitting much-needed garments for the growing population of Liverpool urchins and workhouse inmates.

A local shop donated a large amount of wool, but it was delivered to Sea View in skeins, and she found it tiresome to have to hook each skein onto the back of a chair in order to wind it into balls.

She recalled how she and Katy would have had the tedious work done in no time at all. Whenever they balled wool together, Delia would stand with her arms wide and Katy would hook a skein over her splayed fingers and wind it expertly into a ball. Katy's gnarled and arthritic fingers could still work faster than anyone, and they had the added pleasure of being able to chat as they worked.

But Katy was gone and today Delia only had a chair for company which made the work tedious and boring. The more skeins she wound, the deeper were her daydreams. She missed Daniel's family so much, particularly Katy's dry wit.

She smiled, remembering the day Katy announced she would no longer visit them above the shop on weekends, even though Daniel pointed out the efficiency of the horse-drawn buses that now fairly galloped the length of the dock road.

'I'm not payin' tuppence to freeze my arse off in one of those death traps,' she told them.

She would never admit it was the pain in her swollen joints that prevented her from venturing outside the house.

Joseph entered the room so quietly she was unaware, until he crept up behind her and cried, 'Boo!' in her ear.

She dropped the ball of wool and it rolled across the room. While Joe retrieved it she thought how Katy would have chided her for dawdling.

Joe was apologetic. 'I'm sorry I scared you Ma, but you were miles away. What were you thinking about?'

'I was thinking about your grandma, and how she would have made light work of this wool. I don't think I'll ever get it finished.'

He unhooked the skein from the chair back and stood in front of her.

'Here Mamma, is this about right?'

She smiled and blew him an air kiss. 'Nanna Katy loved you very much and is it any wonder? I think you must have been her favourite, though she would never say.'

He nodded and became thoughtful, and for a while they enjoyed a companionable quiet, as they recalled memories of Katy and Joe.

Joseph broke the silence in the room.

'I know why your thoughts are turning to Nanna,' he told her. 'Today is the anniversary of her death.'

She looked up in surprise. 'Why Joseph, I believe you're right. It *is* today. How did you remember that?'

'Father and I pass Nanna Katy's old patch in Great Howard Street every night on our way home,' he told her. 'Today, someone had placed a small posy of flowers at the spot.'

'Oh, that's kind. I wonder who it could have been. Katy had the respect of a great many of the carters. Did you know she was one of the first to set up a wheelbarrow on Great Howard Street?'

They shared more treasured memories, and Delia was pleasantly surprised to find the skeins soon transformed into several colourful balls. '*Katy must have been watching over me,*' she thought.

One of the few consolations of growing old, she believed, was having your children spoil you once in a while. She found it hard to accept the fact of their maturity at times and missed the noise and bustle of small children in the house.

Margaret was already teaching in St Joseph's, a recently-opened Catholic school close to her father's coal yards, but she still walked along Christian Street and cut through to Marybone after work, so she could ride home with her father and Joseph.

The twins were not yet twenty, but were already responsible for the management of two, more recently acquired, shops in the area.

Patrick managed a general store on Scotland Road. His hours were irregular because he tended to stay open as long as the locals needed him and he was seldom home in time for meals. They had learnt not to rely on Patrick too much. He was the black sheep, the only one who caused his parents unrest but, as Daniel was fond of saying, 'Three out four isn't bad.'

James, his twin, had full responsibility for a food emporium and tea shop, and since both establishments were doing a good trade, and Daniel had a good crew of workers at the coal yards, his workload was considerably lighter than his sons and he was well pleased with his brood.

During preparations to celebrate their Silver Wedding, the happy event coincided with the arrival of an intriguing letter from a law firm in Donegal town.

It informed them a Nancy Harkin, native of Donegal, was seeking the whereabouts of Joseph James Harkin, late of Moville, also in the said county of Donegal.

A family meeting was called to discuss the lawyer's letter, and it was during the meeting that the children presented their parents with a surprise gift; a trip to the old country in celebration of their anniversary.

It came at the perfect time and they were delighted to accept and did so graciously. It had never occurred to either of them to make the journey back to Ireland, but it fitted in with a need to visit the law firm and any objections they may have had in accepting the generous gift seemed foolish under the circumstances.

It was also during this memorable meeting that Patrick chose to announce his intention to marry one Bridget Margaret Murphy. The shocking declaration was blurted out as they were about to disperse from the room and they stopped in unison and stared at Patrick in disbelief.

'You look like a tank full of fish,' he told them defiantly.

Daniel was first to recover his composure.

'I think we should all sit down again,' he said, 'unless, of course, Patrick needs to speak to me in private?'

'I have nothing to hide, father, and see no reason why the rest of the family shouldn't hear what I have to say.'

'Bridey', as he called her, was a regualr customer at the shop, he told them. But it was a lie.

He had admired her every time she passed the shop window on her way to work and he had followed her to her job at The Temple pub. Once he knew where to find her, he made it his business to frequent the place every night after work and the more he got to know her, the more infatuated he became. There was no question she was a beauty, but she was also very cunning and thought him a good catch, with his strangely cultured way of speaking and his smart manner of dress.

Bridey Murphy unknowingly caused the first rift in living memory among the Harkin family that night. They tried to talk sense into him; they pleaded with him to just wait a while. He had only known her a couple of months, they reasoned.

But, as much as his parents' distress upset him, he would not bend, or even consent to a short period of separation between him and his intended.

Margaret, his beloved sister, who was closer to his heart than any of them, tried hard, but even she could not sway him from his intention to marry Bridey as soon as possible. But it was to his sister he later confessed, in private, and on the point of tears, that Bridey was already with child and they must marry immediately.

Daniel tried to have the last word. He followed Patrick up to his room to voice his objections yet again and this time the argument could be heard from the parlor below.

In all the years she'd known her husband, Delia had seldom had to cope with his anger. Indeed, she hadn't seen him so distraught since his sisters had been taken from him.

He was white with suppressed rage when he returned to the parlour and the rest of the family very wisely left the room.

He sat down heavily and his fingers shook as he lit his cigar. Delia was at a total loss. She was filled with compassion for him and massaged his shoulders, feeling the hard knots of tension resist her skilled fingers. But when he spoke, it was with a terrible coldness.

'I think you should know,' he said, in a tone that made her shiver to hear it. 'I have told him that if he defies me by marrying the tramp, he can give me the keys to the shop. We will have nothing further to do with him or his intended wife.'

His unexpected orders angered her. She removed her hands and stood before him.

'Now just a minute, Daniel Harkin! What do you mean by *we*? How *dare* you make me party to your punishment! He is my son, flesh of my flesh. I cannot abandon him for a lack of judgment. How many of us can truthfully say we've never made an unwise decision in our lives? And who are you to decide it *is* unwise?' But Daniel would not look at her, and he stared into the fire with a grim expression on his face.

She crouched in front of him and tried to get him to look at her. 'Daniel, please. I beg you to reconsider. Give him a chance. Perhaps I can persuade him to bring the girl here; for all we know she may be good for him.'

He grabbed her wrists and shook her roughly. 'Aye, she's good for him alright, and we both know *how*, don't we?' He pushed her away and leaned toward the fire to light a taper.

'What do you mean by that remark? What are you trying to say? I don't understand what's happening to you, Daniel. Do you intend to take revenge for our son's mistake on the rest of your family? If that's your intention—how long are we to suffer, might I ask?'

Still he would not look at her, but only threw the taper into the fire and walked toward the window. When he answered, his voice filled her with trepidation and she felt a deep sadness, for the threatening rift between Daniel and herself, and for loss of her wayward son.

'He will not be welcome in this house as long as he insists on this madness. I wash my hands of him and so, my dear wife, shall *you*.'

'Yes Pontius Pilate!' she blurted before she ran from the room. He had never wounded her so deeply and after she was emptied of tears, she tossed and turned for hours, until she heard him making his way slowly up the stairs.

But for the first time since their wedding night, he didn't come to bed, but only sat in the armchair beside the window, still as the night, staring out into the void beyond. She watched him until her eyes burned from lack of sleep and prayed for some faint sign he would soften, would come to her. But when she woke next morning his pillow was undisturbed and his nightclothes were laid out as Sara had left them.

They didn't speak any more than was necessary for weeks, even as they began to pack for their trip to Ireland. Delia felt more bereft than she had when she'd lost her child. The estrangement caused a constant ache in her bosom and she was wounded afresh every time she looked at him for some sign he was softening; for some faint hope he might meet her gaze with kindness, but he had hardened his heart and was punishing her for her defiance.

Margaret had confided the news that Patrick was now married and living in one of the squalid courts off Gomer Street. Delia knew the area; she'd heard enough of its reputation during the time she worked with Katy.

'Nobody from the courts buys anything from me,' Katy used to say.

'I don't care how much money they offer, and if they ever *do* offer you coins, make sure they're not from your own pocket. The courts are full o' thieves and scoundrels. And mind you don't get too close to them—they're walking alive with lice and fleas, every jack man o' them.'

Katy's ranting caused Delia to blush. She remembered clearly, the state she'd been in when Lady Keenagh had found her, all those years ago. That was part of the reason she couldn't condemn Patrick's wife, not without knowing the girl's circumstances. She was stung by Daniel's lack of understanding and his short memory. Hadn't they both tasted poverty? Besides, who in God's name would *choose* to be poor?

She went through the pre-travel motions of sorting their clothes and deciding what to pack, but the tension between them was a crushing weight that nearly got the better of her.

At times, she pined for the solitude of her bed and it required such force of will to complete the simplest tasks.

It was a welcome surprise and a relief when Margaret announced she would accompany them. Delia didn't think she could suffer Daniel's coldness much longer and their daughter's company would perhaps lighten his mood.

Patrick had cut himself out of her life too, although in her more rational moments she knew he could not risk visiting the house. She fretted for both men, but deep in her heart, she blamed Daniel for the deep rift. His indifference was worse than bereavement because both he and her son were still very much alive and it made reconciliation impossible.

'Am I being punished again, Lord?' she asked, every time she prayed. 'Have I had too many years of happiness? Did I not pay enough when I lost my family and my own sweet child?'

If Delia perceived herself to be more upset than Daniel, she couldn't have been more wrong.

He was kept busy, which was always a blessing. With Patrick gone, he had to supervise the shop and find replacement staff, as well as ensuring business would run like clockwork at the coal yards during his absence.

'*Thank God for James and Joseph,*' he thought, in a rare,

introspective moment. *'We have two decent sons. I suppose there was bound to be one rotten apple among them.'*

He leaned too heavily on Joseph of late—and it worried him. He relied on the lad's quiet dependability. Unlike his brothers, Joseph hadn't had much chance for pleasure; like his father, he was married to his work.

Whenever he thought about Joe, he was overcome by sadness, yet the lad never complained, nor had he indicated any desire for change in his circumstances. He made a mental note to have a good talk with him once they returned from Ireland. One son was lost to him and that was more than enough. He understood a man's loyalty to his wife and deep in his heart, he couldn't condemn Patrick for his adoration when he himself still worshipped his wife. He winced in pain at the thought of Delia. God, how he missed her, in every way, but he must remain firm in his resolve. Patrick would see the error of his ways eventually and it would be an easy matter to pay the girl off, once she tired of playing with his son.

Daniel Harkin couldn't have been more wrong, and if his mother had been alive to counsel him, she'd have told him, in her own inimitable way, 'Daniel my boy—that arse of yours is out by a mile.'

Chapter 39

Their departure caused considerable embarrassment. James and Joseph were well aware of the discord between their usually affectionate parents, but Margaret's excitement infected her brothers and alleviated some of the awkwardness. When they parted on St George's landing stage, any lingering tension was forgotten in the flurry of last minute orders and best wishes.

Margaret had never travelled further than Wrexham and she was eager to see the birthplace of her parents. She'd heard them speak of it lovingly and felt she knew it intimately.

As soon as they boarded they were escorted to adjoining First Class cabins. *How different they are from the cubby hole I shared last time I was on a ship*, Delia thought, as she explored their quarters and put away her travel clothes. There was only a little unpacking to do; along with everything else, it would be taken care of by their cabin steward.

She was about to visit Margaret's cabin when their daughter joined them. Her enthusiasm filled the room and after listening to her chatter excitedly, Delia caught some of her exuberance and began to look forward to seeing the coast of Ireland again. She vowed to savor every moment of the trip, but she wondered if her and Daniel landing on Ireland's shore with a shadow of resentment between them might prove to be a bad omen.

Margaret left them before they'd finished dinner and they

strolled in silence back to the cabin. Delia couldn't bear the strained silence a moment longer and spoke.

'I never imagined I would ever see this day, Daniel,' she told him, as the ship rolled across the Irish Sea toward Belfast. 'It's hard to describe my feelings at the prospect of seeing home.'

'Do you still think of Ireland as home?' Daniel asked her, as he poured two glasses of champagne—a gift, from the captain, in acknowledgement of their Silver Wedding anniversary.

She was at the dressing table brushing her hair, and was just about to plait it when he held out the glass to her. She'd watched him through the mirror, expecting him to leave it on the table and she looked up in surprise. He stared at her for a long moment without speaking, until she turned away in some confusion, unable to comprehend his mood. She took a small sip and felt the bubbles tickle the back of her throat and, for some inexplicable reason, she wanted to cry.

'Leave it loose,' he said, so quietly, she had to turn and look at him again, to confirm he had spoken, or had she only imagined him making the first tentative overture of peace?

'Leave it,' he said again. 'How can you look so beautiful after a quarter of a century of being married to me?' He wanted to touch her so badly; to run his fingers through her hair; that would be sufficient to ease his unbearable pain.

Bathed in the muted light of the cabin, she had never looked lovelier and he admired the long waves of hair that cascaded about her bared shoulders.

Delia had been fastidious about not tempting him since their row. She still believed it unfair to taunt him and tonight, she had prepared herself for bed, with great difficulty, in the tiny bathroom.

Daniel knew it, and he loved her for her sensitivity. '*How she must have struggled in such a confined space,* he thought, yet she could be willful, and at times, she teased him without even knowing.

311

She turned back to the mirror and stared thoughtfully at his reflection.

'Something tells me I'm in trouble again,' she said, searching his face for a sign of encouragement. 'I wonder—should I call for help?'

There it was: a glimmer of a smile, and a slight shift in Daniel's mood; enough for her to attempt to close the chasm between them. She reached out for the service button beside the bed, but he grabbed her outstretched arm and swung her toward him. The initial touch of her took his breath away.

She was exquisitely lovely in the rose glow cast by the lampshades. Her skin belied her age. It was unblemished and virtually unlined and her eyes seemed darker. When he stared into them, he could see the reflection of the lamps flickering like beckoning fingers, tempting him closer. And her hair, God Almighty! That hair! He wrapped his fingers in it and bent to kiss her shoulders.

But it was the sight of it flowing in an untamed profusion around the pale flesh of her shoulders that finally crushed him. He surrendered to the driving urge to touch her and he lifted her from the stool and carried her to the bed.

'Forgive me, Delia, for being such a stubborn brute.'

He buried his face in her hair and murmured his apologies. The scent of her flooded his being and he was almost delirious from wanting her so badly.

Choked with the intensity of their emotions, they had no need of words and were already lost in a mutual desire to satisfy their physical hunger.

He thought he heard the ship's bell, far off, but he couldn't be sure and he didn't much care; his body melted into the bed as the tension poured out of him.

He was as bewitched as Patrick and he knew it. When he held her this close, he would willingly consent to anything she asked. No price was too high for the pleasure he felt having her in his arms, and he was impatient for her masterful touch.

His clothes felt restrictive and he couldn't wait to remove them—he had to have her now! She was trying to stifle her cries and he knew she suffered the same desperate impatience to have him inside her. They reached the pinnacle almost as soon as they fused and Daniel wasn't aware he'd cried out until Delia put a hand over his mouth.

'Shush now, my love,' she begged. 'Margaret is in the next room and these walls are thin.'

'Oh my darling wife,' he groaned, as he smothered every inch of her with kisses. 'I have missed you so much.'

They lay in close embrace and renewed their secret vows, while in the next cabin a young virgin lay alone on a similar bed, still ignorant of the heights to which passion and unselfish devotion can raise two deeply committed lovers.

But Margaret heard enough: she lay there, happy for them, and smiled in anticipation that one day, she would know the joy her parents found in each other.

Chapter 40

In spite of its relative spaciousness, the air in the cabin was stuffy. Daniel had tried to open the porthole earlier, with no success. It had been painted several times and the handle wouldn't budge. They'd made love a second time and slept for a while, but then woke together in a lather of sweat.

Daniel squirmed and fussed with his pillow and tried a change of position, before he suddenly stopped fidgeting and his voice penetrated the dark.

'Are you awake, Acushla?' he whispered. 'I thought I'd take a stroll on deck and get some fresh air.'

'I'm coming with you.' She replied. It didn't take long to prepare. She dispensed with undergarments and slipped on her long coat, not bothering to do any more than tie up her hair before they left. They crept softly past Margaret's cabin and along the passage where the air already felt cooler.

The upper deck was deserted and the ship was in such calm waters that its movement was no more than a gentle roll from side to side.They walked as though on land, strolling easily, arm in arm towards the stern, past moonlit hulks of shrouded tackle and a lone sailor partly concealed in the shadows, enjoying a furtive smoke on his watch.

Above them, the sails and rigging hung in the moon's silver light and only an occasional, disconsolate flap disturbed the unfurled sheets of canvas. The ship's bell rang from somewhere aft, to announce a change of watch, and they heard the low murmur of conversation and a soft 'Goodnight sir' as the men changed shifts.

They reached the stern and looked over the rail. Far below, the ship's wake churned phosphorous curls of white foam on the surface of the water yet they seemed not to be moving.

'This could be a long night,' Daniel whispered, eyeing the stars. 'We have no wind to speak of and will make slow progress. I don't think we'll see the Irish coast until well past daybreak.'

'I shall be glad,' Delia confessed. She was blissfully happy and not the least bit tired, despite their earlier romp. Yet the hypnotic combination of the still night air coupled with the gentle rocking of the ship lulled her into a familiar dreamy state.

Deeply at peace, she felt nothing could touch her soul. In the warm afterglow of their reconciliation, she was sheltered in a floating cloud of contentment. She reached for Daniel's hand and intertwined her fingers in his.

'When I left Ireland, it was with a very heavy heart and it seemed fitting that the night sky should hide everything from my view. I remember I couldn't even make out the buildings on the quayside, but I was glad of it, Daniel; glad I wasn't able to see my homeland fade into the distance. It eased the pain of leaving a little.'

'Oh, my own sweet Delia,' he said quietly. 'Didn't we both leave England with heavy hearts this very night? I should be horse whipped for what I've put you through.' He kissed the top of her head and squeezed her hand, releasing it only to pull her closer.

She felt her cloud disperse a little. As much as she was glad she and Daniel were on better terms, she knew it wasn't in his heart to forgive Patrick and the pain of it would be with her until he did. So she let the comment pass and allowed him to continue.

'When my family sailed for the mainland, I thought I'd go mad from the constant sound of weeping and the cries of the children that filled the ship's hold. I was torn between wanting to jump overboard and swim back, and finding the quickest escape from all the misery aboard ship. Do you know something? The only thing that held me together was my family. I took great comfort from knowing they were near. I had someone who'd stand by me, no matter what; who'd pick me up if I fell down from the hunger. That's what kept us all going. We stuck together and kept each other alive. Can you understand that Delia?'

She wondered if *he* understood his own words. He was as good as admitting his son had acted the way he himself would have, and his sentiments were in direct contrast to his behavior toward Patrick, whom he so determinedly cast aside.

She felt a little deflated when she answered him.

'I suppose I'm one of the few left who can tell you with my hand on my heart that I *do* understand.'

She knew he was trying to justify his behavior toward their son, and knowing threatened to negate all the warmth she felt at their reconciliation.

But she wouldn't have this night spoiled by anyone or anything. She leaned into him and stroked his chest with her free hand in a wordless gesture of comfort. Ireland would do a good job of sending their emotions into further turmoil during their visit; of that she had no doubt.

The past was too recent and much too painful to recall, and she was prepared to re-visit it, but not tonight. She'd waited almost two months for her husband's loving touch and kind words and she wouldn't have her memories of tonight ruined.

They fell silent for a while, both deep in thought. But the afterglow of their lovemaking was fading, and the longer Delia was left to her own thoughts, the more apprehensive she became. Up to now, there'd been no suggestion of them visiting her townland during their stay and she prayed it would not happen.

Neither of them had any idea how long the business portion of the trip would take. They were unanimous in their desire to visit Dublin and the solicitor's summons compelled them to stay in Donegal town for a period, and they were keen to make this trip memorable for Margaret's sake, but beyond that, they had a couple of weeks to tour the country at will.

Two conflicting voices in her head began to nag. She couldn't decide if she should give in to the urge of the first one, or to take notice of the second voice, the one that warned her to let sleeping dogs lie.

She shivered at the cruel irony of her last thought and Daniel mistook it for a chill and pulled her further into the shelter of his warm coat.

'You're shivering love. Let's go back inside?'

She buried her face in his shirt with a small burrowing movement, and tried to shake the memories of mad dogs out of her head.

'No darling, I'm alright. I'd like to stay here a little longer. It's so beautiful and God knows, we'll both need the peace between now and morning. Once that daughter of ours awakens there'll be no stopping her chatter.'

So they stayed a while longer and stared silently out to sea; both deep in thoughts they knew would not permit sleep for either of them.

Daniel was curious to meet his cousin Nancy. While he'd lived in Moville, the two branches of the family had very little contact; in fact, they hardly met, unless at a wedding or a chance meeting at one of the fairs. He couldn't imagine what business his cousin would want with him after all these years.

Delia's heart was torn in several pieces. She worried about the state of Donegal after the suffering and hardship of recent years, and it occurred to her they might be going back to places once familiar, but now inhabited by the English. One thing she was sure of; it would not be the same country she'd left. Whether it would be a better one was the key question.

Since the Hunger there'd been sporadic reports of violence erupting all over Ireland. The country was being ripped apart again by rival factions and hot-headed young rebels who'd banded together to bring about change and to loosen the stranglehold the British still held over her country—although why in God's name they should want it, now that they'd leeched all that was good from it, she was at a loss to understand.

She sighed deeply and glanced up at the sky. It was a long time since she'd seen the stars so clearly. There hadn't been a clear sky over Liverpool for months. The city's rapid industrial growth meant more frequent periods of smoke-filled fog, and even though Southport was a good distance from the industry, a clear evening such as this was a rarity.

'Doesn't it make you wish for wings?' she whispered to Daniel. 'So you could fly up to the stars and sit among them and feel the dazzling light of the moon on your face.'

'We'll be up there among them soon enough, when the Almighty sees fit to take us, so don't be too eager to sit among them. Speaking for myself, I can't bear the thought that one day we'll be separated forever.'

'Even to kings, Daniel,' she answered with a sigh of regret. 'Death comes, even to kings.' She looked directly into his face. 'Let's make another vow, Daniel. Let us swear on all that's holy never to allow anything to distance us again.'

He looked down at her and wished he could immortalize the moment. He wanted to hold forever the deep mutual bonding they shared. He shook his head to dismiss morbid thoughts of being without her and lifted her chin to kiss her.

'You have my solemn promise. But come my love, let's go and get some rest. I'm sure our daughter will have us awake before dawn.'

Chapter 41

He was right. Margaret was tapping impatiently at their door before the first prisms of daylight pierced the porthole.

They were among the first at the rails before breakfast and had a little more difficulty keeping their balance on deck. A swell had come up during the night and the coastline was barely visible through the pre-dawn grey and the soft hills were a muted black in the half light.

Ireland awoke from slumber slowly, but before long they could make out random pinpricks of light twinkling from various points along the coast and noisy flocks of gulls flew out to escort them into Belfast harbor. *'Irish gulls,'* thought Delia, as she linked arms with her excited daughter and listened to their rude cries. *'How many of you know my secret, I wonder?'* The closer they got to Ireland, the stronger the haunting images of the past became, and the more they filled her thoughts, waking and sleeping.

Margaret had her hopes fulfilled as it became very obvious her parents had made up their quarrel. She watched them nuzzle each other and was delighted to see the frequent looks of adoration between them, so much so, she was beginning to regret having accompanied them.

Her father complained he was famished and they went below for breakfast. All three downed generous portions of smoked haddock kedgeree, creamy porridge and several cups of fragrant coffee before they returned to the deck, just in time to hear the slip of the anchor.

Two smaller boats pulled alongside and the First Class passengers were transferred smartly and rowed to the pier, where capable hands helped them ashore.

Her parents laughed at Margaret's antics when her feet touched Irish soil. She flung up her arms to the sky and shouted theatrically, 'At last! Ireland—the land of my ancestors! Daniel saw the concerned look of an elderly passenger and led her away.

'She's prone to hysteria,' he told the startled woman.

Margaret turned her attention to one of the sailors. She thanked him for a smooth crossing, as though the man had manufactured the calm sea single handed.

Her parents gazed at the distant hills for a long time and inhaled deeply the sweet air of their beloved land. They seemed untouchable, yet she understood, and tried to subdue her own excitement, as she joined them in silent prayer.

The bustle of activity around them could not penetrate their little circle and they were oblivious to the sounds of the passengers, but the prayer circle swelled with a few others who were evidently returning after a long period of absence.

A man approached and asked Margaret for their family surname, but before she could answer her father was at her side.

'Cead Mile Failte,' said the man, and her father returned the greeting.

Margaret's Gaelic was limited and Delia saw her daughter's curious stares and explained.

'The gentleman extended a hundred thousand welcomes.'

Mr Flaherty had been sent by their hotel to convey them from the port, and he and Daniel retrieved the baggage as soon as it was unloaded and helped the women into a waiting coach.

Belfast looked very much like an Irish version of Liverpool, with its bustling quayside and dense crowds of people and the shores of Belfast Lough were filled with assorted steamships and barques.

Across the water, tall arms of heavy steel cranes rose above the highest masts. Belfast was rapidly surpassing Liverpool as a major shipbuilding town and there was talk her Majesty would soon confer the designation of 'city' to the growing town.

The carriage clipped through a maze of busy streets to the hotel and they were relieved to find the imposing neo-classical building was set back some distance from the noise and bustle of Belfast's main street.

Margaret wasn't in the least bit weary, unlike her parents, who wanted nothing more than to unpack and lie down for an hour or two. But allowing her to explore a strange city alone was out of the question and Daniel was forced to accompany her.

He soon benefited from his daughter's power to revive him. She was irrepressible, with her infectious enthusiasm and unquenchable curiosity, but he was hard pressed to find satisfactory answers to the constant stream of questions she bombarded him with.

Margaret was conscious of being the only one making any noise and she stopped and turned to look at him, seeing in his eyes something she'd never seen before.

'Are you alright, Da?' she asked. 'You must be tired after the long journey. I sometimes forget you and Mamma are getting old. Shall we walk back?'

He laughed at her insensitivity and elbowed her playfully.

'Hey! Enough of that now—I'm only fifty-six and your Ma is younger than me—and she's still as much a beauty as yourself, I might add.'

'You are *both* beautiful Da, inside and out. It must be the Irish blood in you.'

He loved it when she called him Da. Somehow, here in his

home country, it fitted him like a glove and sat more easily with him than the more formal 'father' or 'pappa'.

He sighed without being aware he'd done so, and she put her arms through his as they strolled back to the hotel.

'This place is churning up all kinds of memories for me,' he confessed. 'I'm a lucky man, Margaret, but it wasn't always so. You know your mother and I had a desperate time of it in this country, and there are going to be some difficult moments for both of us while we're here.'

He stopped for a moment and glanced down at her. She oozed energy and he knew if he blew a whistle this minute she'd be off like a hare. For a split second he envied her youth and vitality. It had been robbed of him and Delia. They had never known it; their youth had been spent fighting to stay alive.

'I'm very glad you're here to comfort us in our old age,' he teased. She smiled up at him and raised herself on tiptoes to kiss him.

'Thank you, my darling Da, for bringing me. Now, can we go and eat? I'm famished.'

Being a teacher didn't necessarily mean one was smart, but Margaret had deliberately cut her father off because she knew he was delving into painful territory. As much as she wanted, *needed*, to know their stories, now was not the time, not while they were so weary from the crossing.

She thought about the awful business with Patrick. She still hadn't told them Bridey was carrying Patrick's child. She would have to tell them soon. Damn her brother for leaving it to her!

Next to her father, Patrick was the most intellectual, but he was also an inverted snob and had always preferred the company of working class Liverpudlians to their more affluent friends in Southport.

He once told her he found the Liverpool natives infinitely more exciting than the Southport set. She thought he must have some perverse streak in his nature. Patrick frequented some very dubious clubs in the city and whenever they quarreled about his habits, he always pointedly reminded her of the fact that their own parents came from 'some pretty seedy alleys'.

'I'm aware of that Patrick,' she'd remind him. 'But they crawled their way out, and they did so with great difficulty and years of hard work.'

'What a waste of a good brain,' she suddenly said aloud.

'What—whose brain?' her father asked.

Margaret was startled. She hadn't meant to speak out loud.

'Sorry father, I was thinking about one of my pupils,' she lied.

She noticed the lines of fatigue in his face and her heart went out to him. *'Poor Da, as if he doesn't have enough to contend with.'*

But watching him mount the hotel stairs two at a time, she thought her sympathy a bit premature and knew full well the reason for his eagerness to reach his room.

After all, the last thing he'd said before leaving her had been, 'By God but you're the spit of your mother.'

Daniel and his wife were locked in an embrace before Margaret even reached the top of the stairs, but Delia was being a little reluctant tonight for some reason.

'Not here, Daniel, there are too many priests around.' He laughed at her and caught the glimmer of a smile.

'For a minute there I thought you were serious,' he said, thinking she alluded to the convocation of priests they'd spotted earlier in the hotel dining room. 'But just in case, let me look under the bed and in the wardrobe. Priests are adept at hiding. They have a rich history of it.'

She had rested for an hour and her tiredness was no longer evident.

'Let's wait until after dinner, Daniel. I have a feeling in my bones: tonight is going to be different somehow; more special.'

'Every time I look at you it's special,' he told her. 'And every time I touch you is a joy to my heart. I'm puffed up with pride to have two beautiful women in my life. I, Daniel Harkin, am the envy of the mainland, and I'll be the envy of all Ireland, once people get a look at you and Margaret.'

He gave her a quick peck on the cheek and headed for the door. 'I'm going down to order a bottle of champagne for later,' he told her, 'as befitting the upcoming occasion you might say. I hope you're well rested, Delia Harkin, 'cause if I've got anything to do with it, you're going to be awake half the night.'

They were on the road early next morning, taking the first ferry across Lough Neagh. Daniel hired a sturdy brougham in Dungannon and by noon they were heading west for Donegal. The road was well-used and in poor condition and in spite of the tight springs on the carriage, they were bumped about and all three were sore and bruised, by the time they stopped for the night on the outskirts of Omagh.

There hadn't been much of interest to see on the early leg of the journey. The weather was fair and dry most of the way but their route was very rural and Margaret was beginning to tire of the passing miles of fields and hills.

They lunched on a hefty farmhouse meal and accepted a delicious loaf of soda bread the farmer's wife insisted they take, 'to ward off the pangs of hunger', yet they were more than ready for dinner when they finally pulled in at a whitewashed inn just off the main road.

'What do you think of Ireland so far?' her father asked her as they ate.

'It's too early to say Da, but it's not unlike Wales, with the low mountains and the endless vista of green.'

'Not at all,' Daniel protested, spooning a large helping of rice pudding into his mouth. 'For a start, Ireland is much greener than Wales. The air is softer, and the food is magnificent,' he added loudly, seeing the waitress approach.

She and Delia both laughed at him and he stopped spooning

the pudding into his mouth and looked at them.

'*Now* what have I said? Am I having to watch my every movement and guard my every word while we're here?'

The women laughed again and Delia, feeling sorry for him, tried to explain.

'Oh Daniel love, listen to yourself. You're sounding just like one of the natives.'

'What do you mean, woman?' he asked, beginning to feel a little put upon.

'It's your accent, Da,' Margaret piped, in her best Irish accent. 'Sure, haven't you slipped right into your auld way of talkin', but speakin' for meself, I'm likin' it well enough, so I am.'

Her imitation caused fresh spasms of laughter between the women until, in the end they were laughing so hard they were forced to make a quick exit from the dining room.

They walked along the narrow lane leading from the inn to the main road, glad of the chance to stretch their aching muscles.

Daniel complained as they walked. 'My rear end is so sore, I'm sure it'll be black and blue by morning.' The women agreed, and Margaret commented that, from the rear, they must present a strange sight, with all three of them rubbing their sore bottoms.

'There's pishogue about I'm sure,' she said in her newly acquired Irish lilt. She was surprised when her mother reprimanded her.

'Don't mock them, Margaret. We've enough to face without incurring the wrath of the fairleeuh.'

'Fairleeuh mother—what's that?' She was beginning to discover just how ignorant she was about her parents' pasts, and of how little she knew of Ireland's customs.

'Fairleeuh are bad spirits or fairies,' Delia explained, and Margaret made a derisive sound that Delia chose to ignore. 'You have to remember,' she cautioned, 'before the Famine our people put great store on the spirit world; indeed, the spirits were as important to them as the God they worshipped. You must never mock them, daughter.'

'I am well rebuked, Mamma, and I apologize to you and Da, *and* to the fairleeuh,' replied Margaret, trying to restore the good humor.

Daniel could see his wife was becoming agitated and he changed the subject quickly by suggesting they make their way back but he determined to have a good long talk with his daughter as soon as the opportunity presented itself.

The remainder of the journey to Donegal was without incident, though Margaret was more guarded and they were all deep in thought as they neared the town. Delia wondered about Nancy Harkin and her reasons for seeking them out.

She had never been to Donegal town, but Daniel remembered the layout well enough and had them settled into a small hotel off the Diamond before nightfall. Margaret was excused after dinner and her parents walked a little before retiring for the night.

'Has it changed much, Daniel?' Delia asked as they navigated the unfamiliar streets.

'Not that much. I remember most of these houses were here, and the Diamond looks the same, save for a change in the shop owners.'

She couldn't engage him in any lengthy conversation and was glad in a way; they both had much to think about and tomorrow would be filled with challenges enough for Daniel.

'Come, my darling,' she murmured, suddenly feeling fatigued. 'Let's get to bed. I'm as shagged as a prize mare.'

'Not quite,' he said to her jokingly, 'but you could well be by morning.'

Chapter 42

The solicitor's office was located in one of the more imposing buildings in the town and Nancy Harkin was already waiting for them when they arrived next morning.

They were ushered into a large, oak-paneled room and Arthur Lynch, the solicitor, introduced Daniel to his cousin and he found himself face to face with her for the first time since his early childhood.

He was shocked by their physical similarities and Nancy Harkin mirrored his surprise as she clasped his outstretched hand in both of hers.

'I'm so glad to meet you after such a long time cousin,' she said warmly. Without waiting for him to reply, she embraced Delia and their daughter and then stood back, boldly staring at all three of them.

'Glory be! The resemblance is so *strong!*' she gasped, and put a hand to her mouth and looked in amazement from Margaret to Daniel and back to Margaret again. 'You've both the exact coloring of my father.'

She then turned to her lawyer, 'I've no doubts, Arthur. It's not just the physical similarities—he has the build and voice of my Daddy. This man is unquestionably my cousin Daniel.'

Arthur Lynch had to agree and they dispensed with formalities and sat round his enormous desk and got down to business.

While Lynch assembled various papers Delia had a chance to study Daniel's new-found relative. Nancy Harkin was of generous build and ruddy-faced in the extreme.

'Cheeks like a farmer's arse on a frosty morning,' is how Katy would have described Nancy's florid cheeks and wind-burned hands. But Delia only saw that the woman was robust and looked the very picture of good health.

Nancy's sharp eyes caught her staring at her hands and she sat on them, apologizing for their rough appearance.

'Please Nancy, don't,' began Delia in embarrassment. 'We know too well how hard it is to work the land. Never apologize for having such a worthy profession.'

Nancy looked in surprise at Daniel's wife and gave a hearty chuckle. 'Well, I've never heard land work described quite so delicately before, but your sentiments are certainly accurate.'

Arthur Lynch coughed impatiently and they turned their undivided attention toward him as he prepared to read.

'On behalf of Nancy here, I would like to thank you for being so obliging and for traveling such a long way, Mr Harkin,' he intoned in a slightly bored manner, as though he had been through the procedure a thousand times before.

Daniel interrupted to explain to Lynch and Nancy the circumstances of their visit. It was not merely to keep this appointment, he told them, but it was primarily a celebration.

'I have had the extraordinary good fortune to have been married to this beauty for a quarter of a century,' he said, proudly beaming at Delia.

'Well now, isn't that grand?' replied Lynch. 'We must celebrate. Allow me to offer you a sherry.' He made his way to a table and poured two glasses, giving one to Daniel and, to the consternation of the women, he held up the second glass to propose a toast, but Nancy put up her hand and glared at him.

'Arthur Lynch! Was there ever a man so mean? Why, you're tighter than a virgin's quim—no wonder you're so bloody rich!'

Arthur Lynch squirmed in embarrassment, Daniel choked on his sherry and Margaret and her mother gaped at her, but Nancy was unfazed as she continued to belittle Arthur Lynch.

'Blow the cobwebs off the cork and give us all a decent measure of that cheap sherry you're hoardin', or you'll get no more business from the Harkin family, you gnarly-faced auld miser.'

Lynch filled three more glasses without a word, grateful for the chance to hide behind the official tone of the documents he read out to them.

'I am instructed to inform you of the death of your uncle, John B Harkin, who passed from this life on the 23rd of June in the year of Our Lord eighteen hundred and seventy nine.' Lynch made the sign of the cross and Nancy farted—bang on cue and very loudly. He wrinkled his nose in disgust and continued.

'Miss Nancy Harkin...' Her name was uttered as though it were a dreaded disease, '...being sole surviving issue of the said John Harkin's brother, Matthew Harkin...' Lynch paused again and looked up long enough to say 'God rest his soul,' before continuing, '...is charged with the management of John Harkin's estate in the absence of any living relatives and until such time as they can be traced. Should there be no claimant after a period of two years, and upon proof of sufficient effort on Miss Harkin's part, she shall be deemed inheritor of John Harkin's estate in its entirety.'

At this point, Arthur Lynch paused and shuffled through another pile of papers, giving them a chance to question him. They all began to fire questions at the flustered lawyer who put up a hand to stop them. Nancy, very wisely, kept quiet.

'I appreciate the circumstances are a little strange,' explained Lynch, 'but this is a complicated situation. Mr John's solicitor tells me his client was well aware of the possibility of relatives being scattered across Ireland and was unsure if any had survived the famine. During the last years of his life he felt honor bound to make some effort to find out. Sadly, the poor man died before he could fulfill his mission. Nancy is doing her part and has expended a great deal of time and money to carry out his wishes. John Harkin had a large number of siblings, mostly males. Matthew Harkin, Nancy's late father, was the only brother to settle close to John's estate, but neither of them knew the fate of the rest of the family after the Great Hunger of '48 and, to be blunt, they were too busy tending their own families and building up their shattered lives to make too much effort to find them.'

Daniel had been thinking hard and trying to fit Matthew and John into the few stories his father had told him of his childhood.

'My father, the late Joseph Harkin, told me few tales of his brothers. According to him, they left home at an early age and settled within the county, although he could never say exactly where. To my shame I never knew them, and my father wasn't forthcoming, most likely because he didn't know them for very long himself and felt no great affinity for his siblings.'

Nancy made a great issue of draining her sherry glass, but Lynch failed to take the hint. She stood to leave and placed the glass on the desk as hard as she could without smashing it.

'I can fill them in from here, Arthur, so don't worry about your sherry supply dwindling any further. I can see your panic rising in case we ask for a refill. We'll retire to The Clover Inn and resolve any remaining problems ourselves. I'll be in touch.'

Over a bowl of stew and a glass of stout they discovered more about the new branch of Daniel's family.

'My Da was always fascinated by horses and he studied animal husbandry all his life,' Nancy told them. 'I didn't see too much of him myself—when he wasn't out looking for four-legged mares he was away shagging the two-legged ones.'

Margaret almost choked on a chunk of bread and Daniel had to thump her on her back to dislodge it.

Nancy was oblivious to their discomfort and went on filling in the details for Daniel, the picture becoming clearer as the information she gave fitted the fractured segments in his own mind.

'My father settled in Moville,' he told Nancy. 'He also had a great love of horses and was renowned for his skill at spotting good, solid animals. Unfortunately, he wasn't so skilled when it came to choosing landlords. We were threatened with eviction like so many others, and when we were reduced to selling the pig we fled to England.'

'I suppose you know our struggles didn't end with the Famine,' Nancy declared. 'Now we're left with a worse legacy. Not only do we have greater poverty than before, but there's fighting breaking out all over. Brothers are killing each other for a patch of land. A civil war would suit the English pariahs just fine, for they see our people culling the population further. If these people could only see that as we kill each other off we're helping the English with the clearances.'

Delia found herself warming to Nancy Harkin. She was a little crude perhaps, but she'd been raised on a farm and possessed a strength of character and a no-nonsense attitude that Delia admired.

Daniel explained their current circumstances and thanked her for her efforts in tracing them, but, he assured her, his branch of the family had no need of his late uncle's legacy.

'That may well be,' she told him firmly. 'But you can't speak for your children. Who knows what may be round the corner for us? My rope is getting shorter by the day and I'm anxious to pass this albatross on. It's hunkered on my back for long enough. It seems to me we are both well placed cousin, so why don't we wait another year, in case any other Harkin clan should come forward? At the end of that time, we can meet again and legalize the disposal of Uncle John's legacy.'

Daniel agreed and they shook hands. There was a moment of awkwardness, when neither of them knew quite what to say. In the end, Nancy gave him a firm hug and, after squeezing the breath from the women in like manner and issuing an open invitation for them to visit the farm, she left, exchanging a few words with the innkeeper before disappearing through the door of the tavern.

It was as though a tornado had blown through. They finished their drinks in silence, each of them deep in thought until Margaret disturbed the quiet with a sudden giggle.

'Did you see the look she gave Arthur Lynch? If looks could kill, he'd be hunched over his desk by now. I really like my new aunt.' She laughed as she rose to leave and looked down at her parents. 'Well, we can sit here and wait for dark, or we can explore the town. What's it to be, Father?'

Daniel was thoughtful for the rest of the day, happy to let the women walk a little ahead of him. Nancy Harkin was an only child, which in itself was something of a miracle in Ireland. She'd been raised in a prominently male environment, which surely accounted for a little coarseness in her manner.

'I am the only child,' she'd told them. 'At least I *think* I am. But here's the rub. My father owned our farm, free and clear. He was never one for renting and I'm sure you can understand why. When he married my mother, her dowry included sixty acres of Culdaff farmland. Now, it's not prime land, mind you, precious little of it has ever been fit for crops. Most of the land in this county isn't even fit for grazing goats. We've always had a hard time making a living from it.'

She further explained that her father had concentrated on pig farming, whilst maintaining his skill with the horses.

'I've managed well enough since his passing, but I have a need to tidy things up in case God should surprise me before I'm ready. The farm is rightfully yours cousin, since it looks as though you and me are the only ones left, and *that's* why I needed to find you. Thank God you weren't victims of the Hunger, for I had no way of knowing. But Arthur Lynch, in a rare moment of lucidity and intelligence, suggested I enquire on the mainland, as well as America, and after almost two years we managed to track you down. So if you want to leave the farm to the local church, or to one of your favorite charities, that's fine by me.'

She pulled out a man sized handkerchief and made a great show of blowing her nose. 'Uncle John's legacy is less complicated. His estate was converted into money years ago and I have no need of it. If you have strong desires to keep our uncle's legacy you'd do better than to leave it in my keeping, dear cousin. I have a hard enough time organizing my own affairs these days.'

She scrutinized him closely. 'I'm glad we aren't shilly-shallyers, Daniel. I like to speak plainly and I see it's a trait we both inherited. Life's too short to be playing dodge.'

Daniel had proposed finding a good manager for the farm, so that Nancy could spend the rest of her years with a little more freedom. Running the place had likely robbed her of the chance to find a husband and he thought she'd paid price enough.

He'd need to find himself a good solicitor in Ireland and resolved to contact Nancy at a later date for some advice. He was sure Arthur Lynch would *not* be recommended, though the poor man had done a decent enough job with Nancy's family, if the healthy state of her current fortunes was any indication, and he had been successful in tracking down his own branch of the family.

He caught up with the women and made a firm promise not to dwell upon business for the rest of the day. The three linked arms and explored the town together until it was quite dark; until a chorus of rumbling stomachs sent strong signals it was time to eat.

Chapter 43

They stayed in the town for two extra days, partly because Arthur Lynch couldn't fit them in for some paper signing, but also because they wanted to see Nancy again. Delia found her mannerisms a strong reminder of dear Joe, and the likeness brought Daniel's father closer to her somehow.

Margaret adored her new aunt for being so forthright. You knew where you stood with Nancy Harkin. She spoke plainly and she spoke her mind. She was a strong, no-nonsense woman; exactly the sort of woman Margaret aspired to be.

They took leave of her reluctantly, but she promised she would give some thought to visiting England one day.

'Not quite yet though,' she told them. 'I'm not as forgiving as you, Daniel, and I'd likely get myself into some very hot water and end up in an English goal. Just make me one promise: don't ever sell my farm to an English man. By Jesus, I'll haunt you day and night if you do.'

As soon as business was concluded they turned west and drove through the foothills of the Blue Stack Mountains, heading for an overnight stop in Glenties. The air cooled considerably as they neared the mountains, as did Delia's mood. There was a widening pool of fear in the pit of her belly, coupled with a reluctance to see the place changed, as she knew it must surely be.

Daniel's proposed route after Glenties included Letterkenny, Buncrana, and his own townland of Moville. After that, they planned to cross Lough Foyle and turn south for Dublin. If the plans changed, they would be on a good route to return to Belfast.

Keenagh Hall *had* to be included in the itinerary, and Delia comforted herself with the happy prospect of seeing at least some of the staff. She looked forward to showing her daughter and Daniel the beautiful house and extensive grounds.

They made excellent time and didn't have to stop as often to relieve saddle soreness.

'We've likely got segs as tough as walnut shells on our arses by now,' Daniel joked. But he was right; their backsides were tougher and they *had* got used to the rough roads and the constant buffeting in the carriages.

By the end of the first week they reached Buncrana and entered the town from the south. It did not dawn on Delia she was in the town until she saw the familiar church and the inn where she and Matty had parted so tearfully all those years before.

She quietly withdrew from her family and retraced the old familiar steps. Here was the spot at the kerb where she had almost succumbed, until little Magdalen was thrown at her feet; and there was the old inn, looking exactly the same. She strolled on, past the Meeting Hall, and stood near the spot where the soup line had formed.

A cry rang out from a nearby street. 'Whoa boy—hold! Hold!' And then the sound of a whip crack sliced the air and she jumped, startled by the noises as a host of disturbing memories tumbled in quick succession into her brain.

She remembered how Matty cursed the horses when he tried to get the carriage through the throngs of people. She caught the strong whiff of fried onions and mindlessly, began to follow the scent. At the top of the main street another veil was lifted to reveal sight of the beggar man whose cries of desperation had scalded her heart. 'Please missus,' she heard him cry. 'Give me a lick 'o the ladle.'

336

She was unaware she'd begun to whimper and beat at her breast, and stared wild-eyed as the paralyzing scenes invaded her mind. Daniel caught her on the point of hysteria and spun her to face him.

'Delia! My love, what's wrong with you? Come Delia—don't take on so. I'm here with you, and so is Margaret. You're safe now.'

She thought she heard a woman's voice far off, calling her, but she couldn't respond. She was powerless to erase the shocking images that spun in an endless stream through her head. She recoiled from touch and shook off helping hands as though they were contagious.

The faces trapped her. There were so many: curious faces; strangers; lots of them. She closed her eyes tight shut and pushed away blindly, until someone caught her wrists in a vice like grip and spoke to her roughly and still she fought, with every ounce of strength, to break the hold on her, until a black veil descended and she slipped gratefully beneath it folds.

She came to in Daniel's arms and tried to sit up, filled with relief to see both Daniel and Margaret sitting either side of her.

'My God, but it was all a dream!' She reached out for Margaret, who fell upon her at once. 'What happened to me?' she asked them.

'You fainted, Mamma.' There was such fear in Margaret's eyes it filled Delia with remorse and she hastened to comfort her.

'I'm sorry, my darling. Did I frighten you? I think it must be all the traveling. I'm very tired.'

Daniel gave his daughter the nod and she left the room.

'Delia.' His tone was a familiar one and there was a hint of urgency when he spoke. 'It's high time that girl knew the truth—part of it, anyway.' He put his hand up when she shook her head, trying to silence him. 'No Delia, listen to me now. She has to know, and for many reasons. On her shoulders sits the responsibility of teaching the next generation of Irish. You and

I will never forget, dear wife, but we have a duty to our country to make sure the rest of the world never forgets either.'

She was still shaking her head in protest, but Daniel knew this was the time and he was determined not to put it off any longer.

'My love, look at me now.' He cupped her cheeks and made her look into his face. 'We will tell her together. She won't thank us for keeping it from her, and well you know it.'

Delia began to sob. 'Oh, Daniel, it will upset her so much. I can't be the one who casts a shadow over the rest of her life. What right do I have to pass my torment on to our children?'

'Because that's what loving families do, Delia. They pass on the threads that bind us, even the painful ones. Remember what I said when Patrick left the fold and threatened to split the fabric of our family? I told you then—the only thing that held the Harkins together when we were forced to flee Ireland was family. Secrets will destroy us, Delia; as surely as the rot destroys the potato crops, it will seep into our pores and be the ruination of us. She *will* be told, my darling, I have only to ask: do we tell her together—or would you prefer I told her?'

He wiped her eyes tenderly and offered her his kerchief and she blew into it wetly.

'I will be there, Daniel. If she must find out, then she hears it from both of us.'

He took her in his arms and hugged her. 'That's my brave Delia,' he said, and when he held her tightly he felt her warm tears soak through his shirt. Her mouth trembled and he kissed her again and again and reassured her of his love and protection.

'I will make you a promise,' he said, finally releasing her. 'You will feel a ton lighter after you tell her. She's a strong girl and well able to handle anything we throw at her.'

When Daniel had gone, she got up wearily and rinsed her face before making her way downstairs.

On the bottom step, she paused and looked into the large dining room where they sat. Margaret was staring through the window, looking very serious, and Delia saw a likeness to herself in her profile. *'Perhaps she's more like me than I'll admit,'* she thought. If that was the case, Daniel was right in his assumption that she possessed strength enough to know the awful truth.

Still, she was crushed by a terrible sad fact. Her daughter would be forever changed once she knew. Her air of innocence and carefree nature would be lost forever and Delia was filled with a wave of uncertainty again and for a second, considered leaving the hotel before they spotted her.

The battles with her conscience stirred up hatred of her father again. *'You'll never stop hounding me, will you? You filthy old bastard! When will you have your pound of flesh and be done with me, Barney Dreenan? Now, my children are to be tainted with your poisonous legacy. Are you happy now? Or will you never cease to plague me? You couldn't take my body while you lived, but you're determined to take my soul. Am I to be haunted the rest of my days by your foul memory?'*

Even as she raged she knew the answer. With time, the memory might fade, but it would never leave her and she must accept the awful truth. Her murderous father had surely won the final victory.

Chapter 44

The rain fell in torrents when they turned into the small square and pulled up outside McGlory's pub in Culdaff. The women couldn't afford to stand and look around, but ran out of the downpour into the grateful warmth of the cozy bar.

The landlord greeted them warily and hadn't quite finished wiping the puddles of water they'd trailed in with them, when Daniel burst in out of the deluge with his greatcoat dripping over the newly-wiped floorboards.

He exchanged a few words of greeting with the landlord and placed his order.

It was quiet, except for a couple of hunched figures at the bar and a farmer sitting in a far croner engrossed in his newspaper.

'I've tethered the horse and carriage beneath the shelter of a large tree just inside the graveyard,' he told the women. 'I hope the priest doesn't see it before we've dried off and had something to eat,'

He groped through his pockets for something to dry his hands and Delia and Margaret both offered a napkin. He accepted them and rubbed fiercely at the raindrops that hung from his fringe and blew hard through pursed lips to dislodge a stubborn drop that dripped from the end of his nose.

'Does it always rain this earnestly?' Margaret asked them. 'It's coming down in rods out there.'

They settled down to a bowl of thick stew of mostly potatoes and large chunks of carrot and the women gave their bread to Daniel. It was spread too thickly for Margaret's liking, but it brought back memories for her parents, who remembered times when their diet consisted of little else, especially during the long winters.

Sharing the recollection with their daughter brought them neatly to an opportunity. At the mention of childhood memories, they shared a knowing look, each waiting for the other to begin, but they let the moment pass, reluctant to spoil the meal.

'This is a blind stew if ever I saw one,' said Daniel, pushing his spoon through the pile of vegetables in search of a piece of meat.

He caught Margaret's questioning look and explained. 'It's known as blind stew because a man could go blind from searching for a scrap of meat in it.' Her laughter eased the tension a little and they ate the rest of the stew in easy silence.

As they prepared to leave, the door burst open, letting in a gust of cool air. Daniel was at the bar paying the bill and turned at the sudden flurry.

A gypsy woman entered and looked around at the meager collection of patrons. She caught sight of the only two women in the place and made a beeline for their table.

Margaret was in the act of putting on her hat when the woman grasped one of her hands and turned it over, palm up.

'Bejaysus! You're a strange one,' she murmured, studying the palm carefully. She met Margaret's gaze and Margaret found herself staring into strange, tiger-like eyes, set deep in a face grown brown and leathery from years of exposure to the elements. The hands that gripped her were darkened with grime and the hag's long nails were filthy.

'Would you care to know more?' the stranger asked, but Margaret was already withdrawing her hand, when her mother restrained her and nodded for the gypsy to continue. Delia groped in her pocket for a coin and placed a shilling in the gypsy's outstretched hand.

'Come, beauty,' said the woman. 'Sit beside me here and let me see what's in the stars for such a bonnie one.'

The owner emerged from behind the bar and approached as the gypsy bent over Margaret's hand.

'Now Ruby, leave these people alone and don't be invitin' any pishogue on my house, or you'll be out on yer arse before ya can say hubble bubble.'

Ruby scowled at him and went back to her business. Delia assured the landlord they weren't being bothered and Daniel, who had watched the proceedings with only a mild curiosity, left to fetch the horse and carriage.

The gypsy didn't speak for a long time, but only made the odd incoherent sound every so often. Now and then she'd lift her head and look over at the bar, licking her lips as though parched.In the end, the owner relented and brought her a small glass of ale.

'I wouldn't say no to a thimble of whisky, for to warm me poor auld bones,' she said to him, but he ignored her request and shouted over his shoulder.

'Get that down ya, woman and then get out of here sharpish, before I show yer the darker side of *my* nature.' She made a face at him and whispered something in Romany.

She took a deep swig of her ale and studied Margaret's face. Then she turned to her mother and spoke directly to Delia in a strange rhyme.

'*This daughter is precious, her beauty is rare, and she's spent many a year without scarcely a care. But mind, there is one who means to be paid. One day, he will damage this beautiful maid. She will bear a scar for all to see—*' She stopped and peered at Margaret's palm again and then looked directly into her eyes. '*Beware lass, of bitter gall and give it no part; remember—he may take all; but not your pure heart.*'

Then she was up, away, and out the doors before they could stop her. Margaret stared after her with a dazed expression and Delia sat her down and had Daniel fetch a drink.

'Why in God's name did you encourage her?' he wanted to know, but Delia glared at him.

'Because,' she said slowly, 'you know as well as I do how unlucky it is to refuse a gypsy, especially in these parts.'

She turned to her daughter and spoke with authority. 'Margaret! You are not to dwell on her words. If she'd stayed long enough she'd have told you that your fate is in your own hands and nobody else's. Nothing she foretold need happen, so you're not to fret. She's most likely an imposter and not true Romany. In our day we put great store on magic and superstition, but your generation is more enlightened and, while I believe it is bad luck to turn a gypsy away, I doubt they have any real powers as seers.'

She was lying and she knew it. There *were* men evil enough to steal a girl's heart. Wasn't she proof of the fact? The gypsy's predictions applied more accurately to her own experience than to Margaret's and, truth be told, Delia was far more disturbed than her daughter. The pit of fear had grown with a vengeance. It gnawed at her for the rest of the day and as they drew closer to Keenagh, she felt any resolve she'd gathered to face her demons slip away from her, until the growing dread made her feel physically sick.

She clung to Daniel with a tenacity that increased with every mile. He thought he understood, and now and again would pat her arm reassuringly. Margaret sat behind them in the phaeton they'd hired, and Delia couldn't tell if she was absorbed in the scenery or her own thoughts. She only knew she was uncommonly quiet.

There was something not right and it wasn't just the gypsy's words unsettling her. Delia felt the approach of something unknown, a mounting terror, as they neared their destination. Something sinister was at odds with the peaceful surroundings. *'He's here, in this place,'* she told herself. *'I can feel his evil presence.'* She glanced at Daniel, comforted by his solidness, and pulled her coat across her as yet another icy shiver passed through her.

They'd been riding for almost two hours and saw few signs of habitation, apart from the odd farm buildings in the distant hills, and one or two humpback bridges that once separated the remaining shells of long-abandoned homes. It was the silence. It was eerily quiet, with no bird song, but only the whistle of the wind in her ears as they drew ever closer to the sea.

Margaret had sensed the tension building in her mother, she had noted the stiffness of her posture and the way her father sought to comfort, and she wondered if it was because her mother was disturbed over the gypsy's prophecy.

She tapped her on the shoulder and Delia spun as if she'd heard a gunshot, her face contorted with fear. Margaret was shocked by the response and stumbled over her words.

'Sorry mother. I didn't mean to scare you.'

Delia tried to answer but her hair flapped madly about her face and she was forced to let loose her hold on Daniel as she tried to tuck it beneath her bonnet. She had to shout against the wind to be heard.

'Almost there. About another ten minutes.'

Margaret saw how her mother locked her arm in her father's, and how tightly she gripped him and it unnerved her. She was unaccustomed to being fanciful and scolded herself. *'She's holding on tightly for practical reasons,* she reasoned. *So she won't fall off this contraption.'*

They passed the outfields that led to Delia's old dwelling and took the narrow seaweed track down to the beach.

She and Daniel had decided on this location earlier, agreeing the shore would prove less distressing than the cottage. But when they rounded the last bend and swept downhill to the sands, Delia felt the gore rise in her stomach and as soon as they alighted from the carriage, she fled behind a large boulder and brought up her stew.

Even after her belly was emptied she continued to retch, and the spasms were so strong she could hardly take a breath in between, but only clutched at her abdomen and prayed they couldn't hear.

When she recovered Daniel and Margaret were some way off, having strolled away to give her some privacy. She looked around her and identified the familiar crags in the rising cliff and the unique formations of the giant boulders that were staggered across the sand to the water's edge.

Above her, the air was filled with gulls, and the white clouds scudded quickly across the sky in constantly changing shapes, trying to block out the sun, while the Atlantic foamed with familiar fury.

She loved to interpret the shapes of clouds and thought wistfully how right Katy had been when she chided her for being a cloud watcher. She could spend a whole day watching them float by and had gone missing so many times as a child, hidden behind the shelter of a boulder, out of the wind, lying flat on the sand, staring at the sky, until one of her brothers would yell from the road that she was to stop daydreaming and get back to the house.

But today her head was not in the clouds. It was firmly fixed on the confusion of emotions that churned her insides so much she thought she'd be sick again. Yet her practical side told her she couldn't leave this beach until the deed was done; there was no putting it off any longer. To delay was to prolong the agony, so she began to walk, reluctantly, toward them.

She thought of the nine months she'd carried the twins. She'd been filled with a similar sense of foreboding even as the twins kicked within her; terrified she would lose them, and she now had a clear vision of her stillborn, her darling

Lucy, who'd looked like a porcelain doll at the foot of the bed where the midwife had placed her. Delia had been too weak to sit up after her birth and must have slept, because when she opened her eyes the baby had been wrapped like an Egyptian mummy and placed on the table ready for burial, and Delia was left to wonder afterwards if the brief image of the child she'd never held had been a mere trick of light or the onset of milk fever.

Daniel had been a great comfort during her subsequent pregnancy; but he was a practical man and wasted no time in pointing out to her the futility of spending the whole nine months in a state of wasted agony. *'It's far better to put off your worrying, until the first pangs of labor,'* he'd told her. She'd seen the wisdom in his words and they were a help to her, though she worried just the same.

Yet God had been generous and had given them two children to replace Lucy and, at sight of Margaret's approach, she had a brief moment of gratitude for her surviving children and offered up a silent prayer of thanks.

'Dear God,' she prayed, as they drew closer. *'Forgive my lack of faith. Give me strength enough for what I have to do. Send me some sign of approval, for as I speak, I doubt the wisdom of my actions. I have no right to ask, for I cannot yet forgive my evil father. Look beyond my weaknesses, Lord, and my cold heart, and give a poor coward some measure of peace this day.'*

The three sat on the sand and leaned back against a dune. Daniel was careful to sit Delia between him and his daughter, and it was Daniel who provided the opening, after giving Delia a look that said *'It's alright, I'm here. Be strong.'*

She took Margaret's hand in hers and swept the horizon with her free hand.

'It's beautiful, isn't it?' she began. 'Did you ever see water that colour before? They used to say it was the emeralds lost from the shipwrecks and ground to powder by the waves that turned the sea so green.'

Margaret interrupted her. 'Shipwrecks—did you ever see any, Mamma?'

'Oh Lord yes,' Delia answered. 'As a child, I spent most of my days on this beach. When I wasn't helping to bring in the seaweed, my brothers and I would be scavenging for loot from the ships that foundered on those rocks out there. The children in this area kept the whole clachan supplied with dishes and tools—and the odd coin besides, and there was little need of a distillery in these parts; the men were always finding barrels of rum and other spirits washed up on the shore.'

Margaret smiled to hear how pronounced her mother's accent had become as she recounted her childhood escapades, while Daniel stared out to sea and listened with all his senses finely tuned. He knew Delia was preparing the ground, before she dug it up to expose the rot beneath.

'Mamma, what a life you led! Why haven't you told us these things before? It's the stuff of fairytales. My pupils would love to hear you.' She turned to wag an accusing finger at her father. 'And you too, Dadda,' she admonished. 'I must hear your story while we're here. I bet it's every bit as fascinating as Mamma's.'

Her face glowed from the bracing sea air and Delia thought their daughter had never looked more radiant, even with her skirts hitched above her knees and her long tresses blowing freely in the wind.

She looked excitedly from one to the other as she spoke, and Daniel began to worry that Margaret might be finding the whole thing too entertaining and he shushed her when she began to prattle.

'Shush now, my darling girl. Your Mamma has something very important to tell you, and I want you to know it's the most difficult thing she's ever had to do in her life, and that includes giving birth to you and your brothers. So please promise

Dadda you'll be quiet and hear your mother without further interruption.'

Her demeanor changed in an instant and she turned to face Delia, who gave her a fierce hug before she continued.

'Life here was far from idyllic Margaret, and I am sorry if I gave you that impression. The sea is lovely now, but it's rare to see it like this; more often than not it can turn on a penny and become very cruel. The fierce currents and the gale force winds caused many a tragic accident on this beach, and men perished in the fragile fishing vessels offshore. Storms were frequent and destructive and they can last for days. Have you noticed how inhospitable the land is in these parts? Fishermen risk their lives every day. There aren't many who can make a living from this land, no matter how expert they are, or how long they labor. We always had to turn to the sea to supplement a constant lack of food and money.

'The famine plagued us, year after year, and conditions worsened as we became more destitute. I lost my sister and two brothers to the hunger, and by the time Mammy and I were on the very edge of starvation and almost out of our minds from a lack of sustenance, my father came back from the mainland. I can see him now, crossing the fields back there with a jig in his step; looking as fat as a prize porker with his belly full of food and drink.'

She paused, deep in thought and fixed her eyes on the ocean. 'He had a fixed routine and the first thing he did when he got back was to chase us kids out of the cottage with orders not to return before dark. We'd only a single room and we all slept on the one pallet.

We had no need of clothes and were always naked, so it didn't take much imagination to know what he was doing to my dear Mammy.'

She glanced at Margaret and thought she saw a flash of compassion in her eyes. 'I love you,' she mouthed, and fortified by the love of them both, she cleared her throat and continued.

'After Mammy lost her children she deteriorated quickly. I know she lost the will to live. She taught me all she knew, and her skills were many, and I think she knew I'd be alright after her passing. *She* was finished with life, but my Da wasn't finished with *her*, and he abused her night and day until she was no more than a shadow and he a great heaving bully who almost killed her every time he lay with her. Many a night I ran far from our place, so I didn't have to lie there and listen to her weak cries of protest and his ugly grunts of carnal pleasure. He always brought her to heel with his threats to kill her and there wasn't a day went by when he didn't smack her around, especially on the occasions she didn't please him. Sometimes, when he'd done with Mammy, he would fumble around with his filthy fat hands, seeking me in the dark. I knew what lay in store for me once Mammy was gone.

'Then one day, when things were at their worst and we'd nothing left to barter for food or a drop of milk, I heard her screaming while I was gathering herbs in the fields back there, and something inside of me snapped.' She stopped and covered her face with her hands, to spare Margaret the fear and loathing in her eyes and to ease the pain of her Mamma's dying moments.

'I saw him through the door. He was beating my dear Mammy over the head with his belt and rutting with her at the same time. I wanted to help Mammy, so I hit him…' She paused again and an anguished sob escaped her. Daniel saw the terror in her eyes and he longed to gather her into his arms and comfort her, but he dared not. As tortuous as it was, she had to finish it, once and for all. He squeezed her hand and nodded encouragement.

'The devil claimed me for his own that day. I meant only to stun him, Margaret, to give Mammy time to get away from him, but the axe—' Margaret gave a strangled cry and joined her hands as though in prayer, bringing them to her lips.

'Oh Mammy, an *axe!*' she cried, and Daniel restrained her when she jumped up to leave.

'Remember your promise Margaret,' he told her firmly. He squeezed her arm tight, and there was enough warning in his voice to stop her. She sank back to the sand with her head bowed and twisted her hands in her lap. Delia gave him a look of pleading, but his lips mouthed two words: 'Go on.'

'Try to understand, Margaret,' she continued. 'It was the only thing we owned—there was nothing in the dwelling, nothing at all but the old kettle and the axe. I aimed for his shoulder. As God and all the angels in Heaven are my witnesses, I swear to you, I aimed for his shoulder. I only wanted to knock him out, but it was awful heavy and my swing was unpracticed and—and the blade hit him in the neck.'

Margaret kept silent. She didn't look up but her hands stilled as she tried to absorb the shock of her mother's confession, and the three of them sat for an age in the heavy silence.

Delia was first to rise and she looked down at their bowed heads. 'I don't know what I can say to ease your pain. My heart is too full of my own agony. Would that I could turn back the clock and change the events of that hellish day.' She gave a deep sigh and turned away. 'I'm going for a walk up the road. I'll meet you both at the carriage.' Neither of them attempted to stop her.

She climbed the seaweed road and saw the crumbling remains of the dwelling silhouetted against the sky. The roof had long since gone and so, too, had most of the walls; no doubt the stone had been carried off long since by a neighboring farmer. There were no doors and she hadn't expected to see any; in fact, she was surprised so much of it was still intact.

She approached cautiously from the gable end, and ignored the ruins of the house until she located the spot where her family lay buried.

It was overgrown and well hidden, and when she parted the

long tufts of grass, she found the sunken rocks beneath, and fancied she could make out a rusted band of metal from the old barrel she'd used for a marker.

She kneeled in prayer and felt the cold seep through her dress. She was impervious to her old foe, the wind. It carried her words away as soon as she uttered them.

But this was a wind she almost welcomed. It was strong and cold, but refreshing. It rushed through her hair and clothes and right through her body and raised her until she was almost on tip toe. She felt it whistle down the neck of her blouse and she turned and faced it head on as she unbuttoned her jacket.

For a moment she and her old foe were intimates; locked in a secret ritual of cleansing. She closed her eyes and felt the goose flesh rise on her arms. The cold air blew relentlessly, through every orifice in her body. It whistled up her nostrils, into her mouth, through her ears, and through her skull until the air made hee weightless. She knew if she spread her arms like wings she would be lifted off the ground. It was a glorious feeling of release and she opened her eyes and smiled in acknowledgement as the wind dropped to a low moan.

'Glory to God,' she cried, 'and peace to our people. I have seen his glory and feel the lightness of his being.' She kneeled beside the grave to say a final prayer.

'Goodbye, my darling ones. I love you, Niamh: you too, Dec and Vin. Rest easy Mammy and please God, when my time is up, let me see them again.'

When she looked around, the shadows were long and the air had grown cold. Daniel and Margaret stood off to one side, waiting patiently, and she beckoned them forward.

'This is your grandmother's burial place Margaret,' she told her. 'My darling brothers and sister are also resting here.' She told them in a cold and business-like voice, and it frightened them but they knelt with her and made the sign of the cross, and chanted a quick prayer for the dead before leaving the place for the last time: *'Eternal rest give unto them Oh Lord, and let perpetual light shine upon them. May they rest in peace. Amen.'*

Margaret added an unexpected prayer of her own. She prayed for the living, asking the Almighty to bring them peace and ending with words that soothed Delia's heart and allowed a little hope to penetrate the dead weight in her soul.

'My mother has suffered more than any reasonable God would demand of her. Please Lord, free her of torment and give her some real peace.'

The women wept together and hugged long and hard, and both blew air kisses at the grave before joining Daniel who stood patiently beside the carriage. Nobody spoke until they were about to pull away. Delia put a restraining hand on the reins and looked across to the grave site.

'One day soon, we must have a stone erected for my family. Here, or in the local churchyard. A lot of my ancestors are buried in St Mary's at Lagg,' she told them, 'in a beautiful spot, close to the sea.'

She looked so lost Daniel felt again the strong urge to crush her to him but she seemed fragile and remote and in another world. He had to accept she was out of his reach, and he could do no more than assure her the memorial would be arranged, before he flicked the reins and set the horses into an easy trot. He'd never seen the accursed place before today, but he had a strong urge to get as far away from it as he could.

Delia remained twisted in her seat, even when there was nothing to be seen of the dwelling; long after the outfield had receded into the distance. It wasn't until they reached a bend in the road that she turned and felt the wind blow away the last lingering wisps of unease.

They had plenty to reflect upon, but Daniel thought they were in need of some diversion. There was something unresolved about today's events and it disturbed him, but he wasn't yet able to pinpoint the reason for his unease.

Margaret wasn't the same exuberant girl she'd been on the journey either. She sat silent and brooding, like her mother, and when they arrived at their lodgings she excused herself, giving her parents a cursory peck on the cheek before hurrying upstairs to bed.

They picked at their meal and the wine was left untouched. Later, as they lay in the strange bed with the width of a pillow between them, Daniel really feared losing her for the first time and cursed himself for his insistence on taking them to the haunted spot.

He resigned himself to getting no sleep and tarried with the idea of getting up and taking a walk. He had risen and was fastening the last button of his shirt when there was a soft tap at the door. Margaret stood there in a thin white shift with her face streaked with tears and her hair so disheveled she looked like a wild woman.

At sight of her distress he brought her into their room and led her to the bed and in a second, Delia had her wrapped in her arms. The gesture did both of them in, and he left them sobbing together; feeling his own heart lightened by the possibility of reconciliation and healing between the two most precious women in his life.

Chapter 45

When Daniel returned, his daughter had left and Delia was sitting propped against the pillows waiting for him. Impatiently, it seemed; she abandoned the warmth of the bed to help him undress.

He had left them crying and laughing intermittently, and he was grateful not to have to face Margaret a second time. He was weary and didn't think he could bear to witness any more pain. He poured them both a nightcap as she filled him in on some of the details.

'I'm so proud of her, Daniel,' she told him, and seeing her face, still blotched and bloated from crying, he wondered briefly what state his daughter had been in by the time she left.

'Far from her usual pretty self, I can tell you that much,' Delia told him when he asked. Her voice sounded nasally and the tip of her nose looked raw.

'She just needed time to assimilate, and to recover from the shock. But she *understands*, Daniel. Our daughter doesn't hate me or see me as some kind of monster. She told me her heart bled listening to my confession. Oh! God is good. I know that now: I have two people who love me enough not to turn away from me, in spite of my wrongdoings. I have come to see there is no 'him', there is only 'me'. He is inside me; not hovering close by waiting for me to fall prey to evil. And I don't need to wait for him. When I accept him as an integral part of who I am, then it follows I can never be separated from him.

'My earthly father can never destroy me as he did my mother, and if I believe in punishment and damnation for those who practice evil then I must accept he is being made to pay by one who is more qualified than I.

'I have done God a great disservice Daniel. I've allowed my fears to taint the good in my life and the good have suffered because of my lack of faith. It grieves me to think how much time I have wasted, but as long as I walk God's earth I will trust in his wisdom and his protection.'

'Didn't I tell you it would be alright, Delia love?' They were sipping their drinks in bed and he gently took the glass from her. He dipped a finger into the sherry and skimmed it lightly across her lips. She licked them and he repeated the action, feeling the first stirring of arousal at touch of her tongue. He had no intention of taking her tonight, but she was full of that vulnerability that he found so utterly irresistible. It made him proud of his maleness. He was her protector and her strong man and he found the thought wildly evocative.

'You seem to be recovering nicely,' he murmured. He kissed her tenderly and licked away the sweetness of the drink from her lips.

Before he could draw back she forced his mouth open with her tongue and plunged it deep into his mouth, causing fingers of heat to shoot through his body.

They clung to each other and kissed with a savage intensity borne of their distress. Whenever they were upset their love-making took on an almost brutal intensity. It was as if they needed to deaden the pain of loss and to satiate a mutual thirst for comfort. As if by boring deeper into each other, to the edge of physical pain, the emotional hurt would recede. It was no occasion for leisurely foreplay. They would nip and bruise and leave love scars; and they would drown in each other's passion until they exhausted every limb and every sinew, enough to bring instant sleep.

But their recent sorrow was diluted with relief, and it was early, and she teased him with kisses until the essence of the sherry was quite gone.

'Are you playing games with me, Delia Harkin? Knowing your daughter sleeps only yards away and could very likely knock on the door again before the night is out?'

'If she does, she'll find us awake and in the state of undress expected of two married people who have retired for the night.'

A slow smile spread across his face and he shifted in the bed. He felt more relaxed than he had in months, due in no small part to the news of Margaret's favorable reaction to his wife's confession.

'And tell me, if you dare—how would you explain *this* monstrosity to your daughter?' He nodded to where the sheet rose in a sharp tent just below his waist.

She laughed and put down her glass and Daniel was never more glad to hear her laugh and to see her happy again.

'Do you have any notion how precious you are to me Delia?' he sighed.

She sidled closer and stretched a leg across him and he caught a whiff of lavender and thought of the garden at home and the special times they had shared in a particular corner beneath the arbor.

He kissed her belly and ran his tongue around her navel, breathing in her essence deeply, content to lie this close, but he couldn't resist the urge to kiss her again and he looked deep into her eyes, helpless with love for her.

'I have no words for the depth of feeling I have for you Delia. The most celebrated of poets would fall short in their praise. I am overcome with love for you.'

They were serious for a moment, locked in the mutual flood of a mysterious communion; a sacred intimacy that transcended any physical pleasure.

'Dearest Daniel. My precious man. With you beside me I am ready to face anything.'

'No more secrets?' he asked her, as he lay back and she nestled her head in the crook of his arm.

'No more secrets, my precious man,' she answered truthfully. 'Today, I buried many ghosts on that beach. They are banished from me forever. I felt my mother's forgiveness Daniel, and my heart is lighter, and I fancy I felt a lifting; perhaps some understanding of my father.

'It's the seed of a beginning; nothing more. I can't say I love him, but he will no longer haunt me, not while I have the love and support of you and Margaret. And I'll find the strength to tell our sons if I know you are both beside me. Take me, my darling man. Take me with the sure knowledge that nothing can ever separate our bodies, our minds, or our souls, ever again. We are one, you and I, fused by an impenetrable bond. We two are complete.'

They lay and kissed for a while and whispered endearments, and they never tired of reaffirming the great love they shared, secure in the knowledge that there wasn't a thing on God's earth could touch them, now that the shadows of Donegal had been blown away forever.

ABOUT THE AUTHOR

Elizabeth was born and educated in England. She moved to Canada in 1979 and lives with her family near Toronto. She is a keen genealogist, paints canvases for charity auctions, and records audio books for the visually impaired. *The Strangling Angel* is her first novel and she is currently hard at work on a sequel.

ACKNOWLEDGEMENTS

There are so many friends and family members on both sides of the Atlantic who encouraged me to keep going.

I am grateful to Michelle Lovi, who rescued me from drowning in the techno pool and who designed the cover so beautifully.

A special thanks to my family, and to my husband Bob, who supplied me with endless cups of tea.

Made in the USA
Charleston, SC
26 December 2010